LEXI MONARCH
BOOK TWO OF THE WINGED

T.K. PERRY

Scarlet Note Publishing, LLC
308 E 4th Street
The Dalles, Oregon 97058
scarletnotepublishing@gmail.com

Cover art by: Angela Bruggeman
https://www.facebook.com/annysart3
https://www.instagram.com/annys_art

To the hardworking people who helped make this book possible:
Kara, Melody, Angela, James, Mom, Laura, Sandy H., Heather, Susie,
Sandy B., and Dave. Thank you so much!

Contents

Preface

Dr. Mason King set down the fairy figurine with a sigh and straightened the pink bedspread. She wasn't coming back, but he couldn't bear to change anything she had touched. The best he could do was spend a little less time in her room every day. Yesterday it was only twenty-eight minutes; today it would be... he glanced at his wristwatch and frowned: thirty-one minutes. Pushing his thick glasses back up his short nose, he stood, and the wicker chair creaked its relief. He padded down to his lab, his slippered feet making a quiet *shush shush* in his empty house. It had been six months, but he still ached with her loss. He replayed their tea parties in his head, both of them wearing fancy feathered hats and gloves—hers white polyester, his blue latex. His ginger mustache twitched at one end with a hint of a smile as he remembered.

"Okay, one more cup of tea, then Daddy has to work."

"Okay, Daddy, here you go." She handed him an empty pink plastic tea cup, then giggled with delight when he made slurping noises.

"Delicious! Now go help Maria make dinner while Daddy makes things in his lab."

"I don't want to help Maria with dinner," she pouted. "I want to help *you*."

He thought of the delicate embryonic gene editing experiments he was monitoring. "Not today, sweetheart," he said, removing her feathered hat to kiss her golden curls.

Her pout deepened as her brown eyes filled with tears.

"But someday you will, and we will make marvelous things together," he promised.

"Can we make a fairy?"

He couldn't help but laugh until he saw her disappointment. "Sure," he said quelling his amusement. "We'll make a fairy."

She clapped her hands together in perfect delight, her fancy gloves muffling the sound.

i

He flipped a switch, and the memory faded under the bright lights of his lab. He took a deep breath of disinfectant-scented air. Maybe that was a promise he *could* keep.

For the next twenty years, he chased that goal. By the time he succeeded, the world around him was in turmoil. Natural disasters steadily increased in frequency and severity, taking a heavy toll on the world's population just as he was building a new one. He made his human/butterfly hybrids resistant to the diseases plaguing humanity. When the ice caps melted and record-setting storms flooded the Earth, most of the surviving humans eventually starved or died from illness, including Dr. King. But his hybrids lived on to reproduce with the remaining humans. Centuries later, this is their world.

Chapter One

The door from the servants' quarters creaked open, and wary turquoise eyes with thick black lashes peered around it. Spying an empty courtyard, a tall girl darted toward the stables. She was dressed in men's clothing, her long dark hair knotted up into a rough cap. Several horses whinnied at her approach, but she headed straight for the sturdy midnight mare with the glossy coat.

"Raven," she whispered, drawing an apple from her borrowed coat with a perfectly manicured hand. Raven gathered up the apple in her dry lips while the girl ran her fingers through the animal's coarse mane. When the horse swallowed, the girl led her out of the stall and leaped onto her back.

"What do you think you are doing?!" Someone yelled from behind her. "Get off that horse *now*, boy!"

The girl wrapped her legs tightly around the dark mare and clutched her mane as Raven accelerated to a gallop without being told. The giddy laughter of the girl only spurred the horse onward and they disappeared into the trees. As Raven leapt over a brook, an ecstatic shriek escaped the girl and she clung tighter.

"Stop!" the voice called from alarmingly close behind her as the trail opened into a meadow. The girl took one hand off Raven's mane to tug her cap lower and hold it there.

"You will stop now or I will pull you off that horse!"

The girl peered around her hand at the furious young man flying beside her with large brown and orange wings. His blue eyes flashed while his mouth tightened into an angry line. He was dressed in the elegant clothing of a noble, and his haughty expression left no doubt as to his class. She turned abruptly into the trees to escape him, but he caught her arm and wrenched her off Raven's back. He struggled for a moment to hold her aloft, then tossed her to the muddy ground.

"How dare you ride one of the King's horses!" he raged, landing in front of her with his fists clenched. "What are you, peasant? A stable boy? I will see you lose your apprenticeship for this!" Impatiently he watched her reposition her cap, then struggle to

1

stand. With an angry huff, he again grabbed her arm, this time to drag her to her feet.

The girl kept her chin tucked to her chest, letting the brim of her cap hide her face.

"I am Lord Admiral's son and you will answer me," he growled, knocking the cap from her head. For a moment he stared in confusion at the knot of long hair now visible, then he reached forward and lifted her chin. His tanned skin paled beneath his light dusting of freckles and a quiet oath escaped his shocked mouth. He immediately dropped to his knees with a muddy splash. "I am profoundly sorry, Your Highness. I did not recognize you," he managed in a tremulous voice, his light brown hair falling over his eyes as he bowed his head. "Have I injured you, Princess?" he asked, daring to look no higher than her small, dimpled chin.

Lexi, she corrected silently. She hated it when he called her Princess; no one else did.

Raven trotted back to stand next to her, nuzzling her with a quiet whinny. Lexi patted Raven's nose reassuringly, her eyes never leaving the young man's repentant face.

"Get up, Talan," she answered finally, watching the mud seep into the rich fabric of his pants. "Have you just arrived?"

Talan flew to his feet. "Yes, Princess. My wing birth was yesterday."

"Has your father arranged your marriage yet?" she asked, retrieving her cap from the ground and brushing it off before she replaced it on her head.

"No. What are my choices?"

"Just two. Delpha and Juno," she announced, her eyes suddenly alight in anticipation of his reaction.

He groaned and covered his eyes.

Lexi turned into Raven's mane to hide her grin. "There's always the Mating Mountain."

Talan looked up irritably. "I will *not* marry a commoner."

She frowned. "Yes. Everyone knows how you feel about *peasants*. Clearly they all need a good thrashing," she chided, rubbing the bruised flesh above her elbow.

Talan grimaced and rubbed the lower half of his face. "Could we keep that between us?"

A mischievous smile slid over the Princess' lips. "You don't think my father would be pleased to hear how you defend his horses from presumptuous stable boys?"

Talan swallowed, his adam's apple bobbing. "You could ruin me."

Lexi's amusement faded at his panic and she shook her head. "I would rather no one else knew about my rides." She turned to leap up onto Raven's back, but her body ached and protested as she moved. With a slight frown, she turned back to face him. "Will you help me mount?"

"I hurt you," he moaned, his blue eyes haunted as he moved to help her.

"Wasn't that your intent?" she asked, turning her back to him as his hands encircled her waist, lifting her high enough to swing a leg over Raven's back.

He frowned unhappily. "I wouldn't have done that to a noble."

"And yet you did," the Princess replied, a slight laugh in her voice as she cantered away.

Chapter Two

"Lexi, what are these bruises on your arm?" the Queen demanded, her dark eyes flashing as she pushed aside the lacy sleeve of her daughter's gown.

The Princess fought the little wave of panic that sloshed in her stomach with a studied air. She moved to the mirror to examine her injury while she fabricated a plausible lie. "I did trip on my dress this morning and nearly fell down the steps. A servant caught my arm just there. I suppose that's how it happened."

The Queen's eyes narrowed shrewdly and her mouth assumed a grim pucker. "*Which* servant?"

"I hardly keep track, mother; there are so many." Lexi shrugged.

The Queen's penetrating gaze remained on her daughter's face while she impatiently clicked her fingernails together. "You cannot wear that gown now. You will have to change."

The girl suppressed a sigh.

The Queen pointed to a red, off-shoulder, elbow-sleeve gown lying over a chair. "You will wear that instead."

"It's not finished yet. It's only here for my fitting."

Sweeping across the room in a dark gown that offset the scarlet of her wings, the Queen flipped the dress over to expose the unfinished back. "Have Cercy sew you into it, then."

"Mother," Lexi complained.

The Queen whirled around without a single strand of her dark hair falling out of place. "Lexi," she began, enunciating each word succinctly, "a lady does not complain." She stared sternly into her daughter's face until Lexi swallowed uncomfortably. Pivoting on an elegant high-heeled slipper, the Queen issued commands over her shoulder as she exited the room. "You will be in the reception room in twenty minutes. You have guests to greet."

Lexi sighed as her lady's maid sullenly helped her remove her dress. After several moments of silent dressing, Lexi let out a noise of exasperation.

"Why are you looking at me like that, Cercy?"

"'I hardly keep track, mother; there are so many,'" she imitated.

"You know I didn't mean it. I know all the servants' names," Lexi said, pulling on the sleeves of the red gown.

"You shouldn't lie to your mother," Cercy chided.

"Fine. Next time I'll tell her you gave me your son's old pupa clothes so I could sneak out and ride my horse whenever I want," Lexi declared with a smirk.

Cercy yanked the dress closed in the back and pinned it, pricking Lexi's skin.

"Ow!"

"'Lexi, a lady does not complain,'" Cercy imitated, and Lexi grinned. "But you may want to; you've grown again and this isn't going to fit. When I sew you in, you'll hardly be able to breathe."

Lexi groaned. "Just do it. It's one night. I can bear it."

The dress was suffocating.

Lexi gracefully slid a hand over the tight bodice that clenched her rib cage like a vise and smiled graciously.

"Lord Admiral," she greeted in a lilting trill as he pressed her hand.

"Your Highness," he greeted with a charming bow. His gorgeous underwings were a kaleidoscope of browns and blues with a heavy streak of red smeared across each forewing at the height of his head. His unfortunately matching hair color created the impression that long strands of hair were exploding out horizontally from his ears. It had taken Lexi years to school herself to look at him without giggling. Instead, she focused on his bright blue eyes and bulbous red nose.

"My son tells me you have become quite the accomplished rider," the Admiral announced, his bushy red eyebrows rising in his forehead to punctuate his compliment.

Lexi swallowed her alarm while forcing her face to relax into a gentle smile. "I thank him for his praise," she answered with a small nod.

"I will be certain to tell him." The Admiral smiled, then drifted away while Lexi glanced surreptitiously at her mother to ensure she had missed the exchange. Her mother stood at her father's side, tenaciously assuring the treasury minister that the King felt very strongly on some particular point. Her father yawned and caught Lexi's gaze with a patient smile.

Lexi returned his smile with a warm grin until her mother's disapproving glare checked her. The Queen stood taller, and pulled back her shoulders while elongating her neck. Lexi sighed, then imitated her, pasting a decorous half-smile on her face. Her mother nodded approvingly and returned her attention to the recalcitrant minister.

Lexi surveyed her guests and then moved to calm an escalating argument between two newly-winged females who had joined the court the day before.

"He's not interested in you! If your father manages to arrange a marriage, it will only be because Lord Admiral needs money," hissed a willowy girl with long blonde hair.

The face of her portly victim reddened, her mouth pulling down into a sulky frown. "Well, he *can't* want you; you're just too mean!" she retorted, fanning her white-striped brown wings in agitation and twisting her orange gown in her chubby fists.

Lexi laid a comforting hand on the plump girl's arm. "Delpha, you look lovely in orange. Your dressmaker has matched your wing tips exactly."

Delpha cast a triumphant look at the blonde, who twitched irritably. "Thank you, Your Highness," she beamed, bobbing a curtsy.

7

"And Juno," Lexi said fluidly, "your hair looks beautiful."

Juno pulled her thin lips into a tight smile. "Thank you, Your Highness," she replied and bowed gracefully.

Delpha let out a loud gasp. "He's here!" she chortled, bouncing up on her toes. "Oh, he looks so handsome!"

Lexi followed Delpha's gaze to where Lord Admiral's son, Talan, stood. Lexi's anger blazed up at the sight of him, but a slight flaring of her nostrils was all that betrayed it. He approached them with a rapid gait and bowed.

"Princess, ladies," he greeted.

"Hullo, Talan!" Delpha giggled a trifle hysterically, followed by a little snort and profuse blushing.

"Have our fathers come to an agreement yet?" Juno asked him, a malicious smile marring her beauty.

Delpha made a choking noise and abruptly excused herself.

Talan let out a startled laugh. "I don't believe so, no. Perhaps you should go negotiate with them directly. They're arguing in the corner."

Juno's golden cheeks colored briefly as she turned to observe her father gesturing irritably to the Admiral. "Perhaps I will," she said evenly as she moved away.

"You told your father you saw me riding this morning," Lexi said, her tone frigid while her expression stayed soft and pleasant.

Talan's mouth slipped into an arrogant grin. "I didn't tell him the circumstances, Princess, if that is what concerns you."

Lexi's eyes flashed with anger, but a rigid smile held her face. "It has been a while since you last visited court, Talan. Perhaps you don't know that my mother only lets me ride once a week, and then only around the courtyard, led by a groom."

Talan's arrogant grin disappeared. "Oh. When did that change?"

"Two months ago when my sisters both failed to produce a male heir to the throne."

"And you became the last hope."

Lexi gave him a grim nod.

"Was today at least your riding day?"

"No, it was not."

"It seems I owe you another apology," Talan said, biting his lip.

Lexi waited a moment for his apology, watching his teeth work his bottom lip. It was strangely distracting watching his mouth, and she suddenly drew back in alarm when she realized she had leaned closer to him.

He inhaled with a bemused expression on his face. "You smell like apple blossoms."

"There's an apple tree in the courtyard."

Talan inhaled again. "No, it's coming from you."

Lexi turned her head and sniffed her sleeve. "I can't smell it."

Talan glanced around them and then spoke in an undertone. "Come to the garden with me."

"It's nearly time to go into dinner," Lexi protested, eyeing a clock and then her mother.

"It will only take a moment," he replied, walking away without her.

Lexi hesitated a moment and then followed him. When she caught up, he was standing among the blooming azaleas with a hopeful expression. The delicious scent of the blossoms interlaced with hickory and cloves reached her nose. Lexi inhaled deeply, a soft smile on her face.

"You like the scent," Talan said, an imperious grin lighting his face.

Lexi stared at him a moment, her bemused expression slipping into understanding. "The hickory and clove is your pheromone scent? You signaled me?"

Talan nodded.

"Why? I'm not in season."

"Are you sure about that?" Talan asked, stepping closer.

"Yes!" She pointed emphatically over her shoulder. "No wings."

Talan looked thoughtful. "I've noticed you don't usually like me to stand close to you or touch you."

A slight blush crept into Lexi's cheeks.

Talan grinned. "I know you don't like me. Our little misadventure this morning didn't help, either," he added, taking another step towards her until only a few inches separated them. "But I'm very close to you now." He tipped his head slightly as he watched her lips part to draw a ragged breath. "And you're not moving away," he noted, meeting her eyes. "Can you explain that?"

His hot breath on her face seemed to make her skin tingle and she marveled at the sensation, forgetting his question. Talan watched her a moment, a triumphant smile stealing across his face.

"Now," he said, stepping back from her, "I must ask you to excuse me. I need to speak with my father immediately." He ran off in a happy trot that reminded Lexi of Raven coming home after a long ride.

Lexi drifted back to the now empty reception room, playing with one of her artfully cascading ringlets until it lost its curl. She winced when she realized what she had done, and tucked the strand behind her ear. *Maybe Mother won't notice*, she thought. Then the clock chimed the hour.

"Oh, no," Lexi murmured, a little crease of panic appearing between her brows. Lifting her long skirts, she ran unsteadily in her dainty red heels.

The grand dining room was heavily accented in polished copper, giving everything within it a bronze gleam. Even the palest face wore a healthy glow here. Lexi slowed to a graceful walk as she entered, grateful that only a few of their sixteen guests were aware of her mother's mania for timeliness. Those few tensed at Lexi's entrance, quickly turning to the far end of the long, rectangular table to observe the Queen's response. Nostrils flared, her expression bore the promise of a most unpleasant conversation when no one was watching. Lexi took her assigned seat mid-table at Talan's side, grinning to herself when she realized if she leaned back a bit his large wings completely blocked her mother's view of her.

The Queen smiled broadly, if not warmly, at her gathered guests and nodded to her husband.

"Let's begin," her father responded on cue, motioning the servants poised in the corridor to bring out the food. The King glanced quickly to ensure his wife's attention was elsewhere, then bowed his head for a short moment, his lips moving.

"Your mother does not look pleased," Talan whispered, the corner of his mouth drawn up in amusement. Lexi watched its inviting curl until he turned to look at her.

"I should not have followed you," Lexi murmured, then turned her head to smile warmly at Juno and Delpha across the table. Delpha's face still bore signs of tears and her answering smile was half-hearted. Juno ignored Lexi's smile and stared at Talan with poorly-concealed fury.

"Why is Juno so angry?" Lexi whispered.

Talan's full lips stretched into a merry grin. "She was eavesdropping when I had my father call off the marriage negotiations."

Lexi turned her head abruptly to stare at him, her mouth open. Talan chuckled at her sudden lapse of composure. Lexi sat up straighter on her stool and schooling her face to polite interest, turned to engage one of the treasury minister's twin daughters in conversation. When the fourteen-year-old had finally exhausted her store of anecdotes about her new pony, Lexi turned back to Talan.

"Are you going to marry Delpha, then?" Lexi whispered.

"Delpha smells like peas."

"Peas are pleasant."

Talan cast her a quizzical expression before turning to answer his father, who was seated to the right of the Queen.

Some time during the meal, Delpha had been apprised of the canceled marriage negotiations, and her countenance was now beaming.

"What a delicious meal!" Delpha praised no one in particular, adding a twisting flourish as she brought her fork to her mouth.

"Perhaps if you didn't eat so much of it, your wings might be more than ornamental," Juno spat, tossing her long, blonde hair so that it cascaded over her beige forewing.

Delpha stopped chewing as if she had been stung, then swallowed laboriously. "Well," she finally said, turning to Juno and speaking softly. "I would be fairly upset if I had lost him, too."

"I have *not* lost him," Juno hissed, then blushed as Talan looked at her.

A smile tugged at the corner of Talan's mouth. He leaned slightly so that his wing grazed Lexi's bare shoulder and made it tingle. With her breath coming a little too fast, Lexi turned to the treasury minister's daughter and asked her to retell one of her pony stories. When the meal finally ended, her mother took sharp hold of her arm before Lexi had even stood, and swept her from the room before she could speak. Dragging her into the King's council chambers, the Queen briskly shut the door.

"Lord Admiral is under the impression that your season has begun. Is he correct?"

Lexi shifted uncomfortably, and the Queen relaxed her grasp. "I don't know," she answered honestly.

"No back pain?"

Lexi shook her head.

"Words, Lexi. Use them, please."

"No, Mother, my back does not hurt," Lexi said succinctly.

"Careful of your tone," the Queen warned, then clicked her nails together. "You will tell me the moment you sense any pain."

"Yes, Mother."

The Queen met her eyes for a moment. "You look very pretty in red."

Lexi's face softened at the compliment, and a little lump formed in her throat. "Thank you."

"And don't be late to dinner again," the Queen said brusquely, exiting the chambers as rapidly as her formal gown would allow.

"Could have been worse," Lexi sighed, smoothing the ruined ringlet behind her ear before hurrying after the Queen.

In the smaller of the two concert halls, musicians were warming up their instruments as the guests meandered to their seats. Delpha and Juno clustered around Talan; Juno speaking in strident tones. Lexi's Mother caught her eye and nodded to the group with a single raised eyebrow that said, "Fix it." Lexi nodded and stepped forward.

"If Talan wants me to go away, I will," Delpha said sulkily, gazing up at Talan with subdued hope.

"Of course not," Talan said easily.

"But Talan," Juno purred, slipping an arm through his. "We need to talk."

Talan extricated his arm from hers with a pinched smile.

"The concert is about to begin," Lexi announced, "and the Queen would like everyone to take their seats. Juno, Delpha, I would be pleased if you both would sit next to me." Lexi ushered the protesting girls to a cluster of three seats near the front.

Talan grinned after her and claimed a seat near the door.

The Queen had chosen the works of a new composer for the evening's entertainment. Though unique, the music was slightly discordant and agitating. Mixed with the heat of the room and her overly-tight bodice, Lexi was soon writhing in her seat. She alternately clenched and relaxed the muscles of her legs in a vain effort to remain outwardly still. Her handkerchief had become increasingly damp as she blotted her perspiring face and neck. Finally, she could endure it no longer.

Turning to her companions with a pleasant expression, Lexi spoke in an undertone. "Please excuse me."

She could well imagine the wrath she would see on her mother's face, so Lexi kept her gaze focused on the open door and slipped out quickly. The unpleasant music spilled out into the corridor and drove her away. She jogged unsteadily in her impractical shoes until there were no servants or guards in sight. Finally alone, she clutched at the tight bodice of her dress in a vain attempt to loosen it, her gait increasing until she ran headlong into the garden. Taking gasps of the cool night air, she sat heavily on a dimly lit bench and lifted her skirt to cool her legs. Kicking off her heels, Lexi's bare feet beat a staccato rhythm against the flagstones.

"Feeling a little warm?" Talan asked, laughing as he approached her.

Lexi let out a little shriek, flipped her skirt down, and leapt to her feet.

"Don't cover up on my account," he said, grinning wryly. "You and I are practically engaged anyway."

"What?" Lexi demanded, her mind reeling.

"Your mother has agreed." He took her hand and she immediately withdrew it. "We are only waiting for your wing birth to make it official."

Fury and a sense of futility warred within her, producing a most aggravating result: tears. Lexi quickly dropped her gaze, turning aside to examine a rhododendron blossom.

Startled out of his smugness, Talan lifted a hand to gently wipe her tears. "Don't cry, Princess. I will be very good to you. You may not like me now, but in time, we'll learn to love each other. Until then," he lifted her chin with a soft caress, "focus on this." His lips were soft upon hers and hesitant, waiting for a response. When she continued to cry, he kissed her cheeks in the moist paths where her tears fell. Her crying slowly quieted at his touch, his hickory and clove scent heavy upon the air.

"What about the display laws?" Lexi murmured, her voice still full of tears. "We're violating them."

Talan grinned and kissed her mouth again, pleased to feel her lips move with his. "Actually, until your wing birth, the laws don't apply."

Lexi contemplated that as she returned his kisses, enjoying his arms wrapped tightly around her back. Everywhere he touched her seemed to be on fire, radiating a pulsing heat that shut off her mind and all the objections it was shouting. Reluctantly, she broke away from his mouth to gasp for air, her lungs aching in their bodice-vise while a searing pain wrenched her back. With a suppressed shriek, Lexi collapsed into his arms.

Talan dragged her to the bench, lying her prone across his lap as he tore at her dress. Cercy's careful stitches held, so he ripped the sleeves from their seams and tore her bodice open from under her arms, exposing her bare back. At first it appeared terribly bruised, and a panicked thought flashed through Talan's mind that he had done this. He ran his hands lightly over the darkened skin, feeling her skin pulse under his fingertips. Another swallowed shriek and Lexi's back split open over her left shoulder blade, clear fluid running across her back, spilling onto his pants and the remainder of her dress. A heavy clump of dark tissue protruded from the opening, steadily growing as it split and lengthened.

A laugh of wonder escaped Talan's mouth and he patted Lexi's head. "You have your left wing set," he announced, watching as black and orange panels extended out, wet and wrinkled. Lexi only groaned in response, the sound rising into a soft cry of pain as another eight-inch slit burst open over her right shoulder blade and a second clump of dark tissue emerged.

"I need to move you," Talan said, carefully sliding her knees to the ground, her head still on his lap as her right wings began to expand. "The worst is over," he assured her, brushing away damp tendrils of hair that had escaped their elaborate coiffure.

Lexi panted heavily, trying to lift her head from his lap, but lacking the strength. She could feel the front panel of her bodice askew on her chest, the soft fabric of his trousers meeting her skin. Trembling, she drew one weak arm up to clutch at the remains of her dress.

"Now we can be married tomorrow," Talan said, smiling happily as he watched her large wings slowly expand. "And in nine months, you'll be mother to a king."

Lexi moaned softly, feeling the tears once again prick her eyes.

"Is it still painful?" he asked, softly caressing her face. "Stretch them out a bit and the cramping should go away."

Dutifully, Lexi opened and closed her wings, feeling the strange new muscles in her back, and the pull and drag across the air of her lovely new appendages. Shifting her head in Talan's lap, she turned to look at them. Beautiful orange panels, veined and rimmed in black with a white spotted border met her eyes.

"I have my father's wings." Her voice was soft, almost reverential as she reached out to touch her dewy forewing.

Talan chuckled warmly. "Yes you do, but they look rather feminine on you."

Lexi smiled and lifted herself weakly off his lap with her free arm, her detached sleeve bunched around her wrist.

Gently, Talan touched the exposed heavy bruises just above her elbow. "I'm so sorry I did that to you."

"You thought I was Tiger this morning, didn't you?" Lexi asked, shakily teetering to her feet.

A look of confusion crossed Talan's face.

"The stable boy? Remember you broke his nose two years ago?"

"You mean the one who always followed you around?" Talan asked, a look of irritation flickering across his face.

Lexi let out an angry breath. "He was my best friend; he wasn't following me."

"You shouldn't be making friends with servants, Lexi. I won't have that in my household." Talan shook his head as he removed his jacket and helped her put it on. "Tell the stable boy to keep a respectful distance from now on."

"Is the Mating Mountain far enough?" she asked wryly, jamming her shoes back onto her feet with enough force to send one skittering across the paving stones.

"That will do," Talan conceded with a returning smile. He recovered her shoe and placed it before her with a bow. "Now, my dear Princess, how do I get you back to your room without parading you by your mother's guests?"

Glaring at him, Lexi slipped on her shoe, noting the way her leg still trembled as she did so. She would be wise to accept his help. "This way," Lexi conceded, pointing. Out of necessity, she allowed him to take her arm as they passed through the blossoming garden. "You *did* think I was Tiger. It was him you meant to hurt."

Talan shrugged. "Not him necessarily. Just a stable boy with no business riding the King's horses, especially bareback, and at a gallop," he said, patting her arm. "That was dangerous, you know. You should have obeyed your mother."

Lexi clenched her fists, feeling her manicured nails press into her skin. "But riding makes me happy." A deep sorrow settled over her as she realized she had taken her last ride.

"You'll find new things to make you happy. I would miss riding, myself, if flying weren't so exhilarating."

Lexi stopped in the abandoned hallway to work her drying wings, then tried to lift off the floor.

Talan laughed. "You won't be able to fly yet." He watched her a moment, concern flickering across his face. "I'd prefer if you didn't fly at all."

Caught completely by surprise, an unladylike snort escaped her. "You're joking." Her wings stilled as she tried to read his face.

"You're the last hope for a male heir, Lexi. You have to be careful."

Lexi's mouth fell open as she stared at him.

"But I could compromise. We could fly together, holding hands," he suggested, taking her hand in his.

Lexi pulled her hand away. "I'll only get to fly maybe a week of my whole life, and you would take that from me?" she asked, already sensing the answer.

He turned to her, caressing her face as he spoke. "You're a *princess*; your life is not your own."

Reaching up, she took the hand he had laid alongside her face and removed it. "I don't want to be a Princess, Talan." She gave him a long look. "Thank you for your assistance; I can return to my room alone." A traitorous tremble vibrated through her legs, but she ignored it, and stalked away from him.

Chapter Three

"Cercy!" Lexi called as she stumbled weakly into her room, for once seeing the wisdom of the square doorway as her wings easily cleared it. The long walk unassisted had drained her strength. Staggering, she made her way to her bed perversely pleased that she had dismissed Talan, even if she *had* needed him. She collapsed onto her bed only to feel her wings bend against the soft cushions. Panicked, she stood back up and checked each wing for damage.

"You hollered, Your Highness?" Cercy drawled as she walked in, then clapped a hand over her mouth. "Oh! You've gotten your wings! You're all grown up now, and only eighteen!" Cercy embraced her, then pulled back to point at the jacket. "This looks like quite a story."

"It is," Lexi assured her, fumbling with the buttons under her wings to remove it. Cercy moved to assist her, then gasped at her tattered dress.

"Did the owner of the jacket do that?"

Lexi nodded, letting the story spill out as Cercy helped her remove what was left of the dress and wash. Cercy's frown grew with the telling until her face had settled into a deep scowl. Lexi flinched at the expression, then replayed her wing birth in her head, trying to see it from Cercy's perspective.

"I know you don't like Talan because he hit Tiger," Lexi finally ventured.

"It's not that he hit my boy, it's that you don't like him either. You never have. Just this morning he treated you brutally, and now you're ready to marry him?!" Cercy finished helping her into a backless nightgown from her wedding trousseau, then carried off the torn dress, muttering to herself.

"What else can I do? He's the only available mate, and the Queen has already arranged the marriage!"

Cercy spun back around, yelling from across the room. "Appeal to your father, that's what! Tell him what happened this morning and beg him to let you wait for another nobleman to come into season!"

Lexi sat down glumly on an elegant little stool and caught her face in her hands. "I hate creating strife between them," she moaned. "She makes life so miserable for him when he disagrees with her."

"Fine. Then marry a man you don't like and have children who turn out just like their daddy," Cercy retorted and left the room.

Lexi scowled at the image Cercy had created in her mind and began pulling pins from her hair, flinging them irritably on the floor.

"I hope you enjoy picking those up as much as you're enjoying flinging them," Cercy said, returning to the room.

"Some maid you are," Lexi complained with a feeble grin as she bent and retrieved them.

"Quit moping and climb into bed. I'll wake you up when your father is free," Cercy commanded, turning down the lights.

"My mother is going to come marching in here any moment," Lexi argued as she lay down on her stomach, cradling her pillow under her head.

"I imagine Talan has already informed her of your wing birth, and she'll wait until her guests have gone to their rooms for the night to come assure herself that you know your duty."

"I *know* my duty. I always know my duty."

Cercy smiled to herself as she pulled the adjoining door shut. "Good night, Your Highness," she whispered.

An hour later the door banged open and all the lights came on. "I thought we agreed you would tell me as soon as you had back pain," the Queen declared, sweeping into the room.

Lexi blinked sleepily at the bright lights. "Talan didn't tell you?"

"Not until *after* the concert," the Queen said irritably, waving a beautifully-manicured hand. "It certainly would have helped to have known why you were fidgeting around so badly during the concert or why you felt you had to rush out in the middle of it and never return."

"I didn't have pain then," Lexi mumbled as she pulled up on all fours, opening and closing her new wings as she yawned. "I didn't feel any until right before they burst out."

The Queen's perfectly-shaped eyebrows drew together. "Talan said you were weak with the pain and that he had to help you to your room. I assume Cercy helped you with the birth?"

A little late, Lexi perceived the service Talan had done her with his lies. "Oh, yes," she said vaguely. "It was so intense, I suppose I forgot."

The Queen sniffed. "Well, I'm pleased you managed not to make a spectacle of yourself."

Lexi could feel the blood flooding to her face, and quickly stood with her back to her mother for an exaggerated stretch.

"Now get dressed. I've arranged for a brief meeting with Talan." The Queen colored slightly, and paused as Lexi turned to look at her. "I do not condone public displays of any kind or even private displays where the parties are not married, but compatible pheromone scents are a good indicator of fertility." The Queen turned away with a sigh as Lexi suppressed a giggle. "I have asked him to signal you. If the scent is pleasant to you, we will schedule your wedding for tomorrow."

What an excellent liar Talan must be, Lexi thought as she watched her mother rummage through her wedding trousseau.

"This will be suitable," her mother said, laying out a teal-green dress with heavy flared skirts extending to the floor.

"That is a winged dress?" Lexi asked, turning it over to see the open back. "It looks too heavy and cumbersome for flying."

The Queen nodded sagely. "Talan and I discussed that. It is better that you don't fly. It's a risk you ought not to be taking."

Lexi felt as if she had just fallen off Raven, and all the air had been knocked from her lungs. When she finally spoke, it was little more than a squeak. "You're not going to let me fly?"

A momentary spark of sympathy lit the Queen's eyes, then went out. "It just isn't prudent. Meet us in the library in fifteen minutes," she commanded, then turned and left the room as Cercy entered.

One look into her maid's eyes made Lexi's fill with tears. "She isn't going to let me fly."

Cercy shrugged. "She tried to stop you from riding, too. You'll find a way around her."

Lexi walked to the closet and rummaged through the trousseau. "They're all so heavy and impractical...except for the nightgowns. Did she ever plan to let me fly?"

Cercy shook her head. "I don't know. But I can tell you it will be no trouble at all to alter your riding clothes for your wings."

Lexi smiled and swallowed back the tears. "Thanks, Cercy," she said, hugging her.

"Let's get you dressed," Cercy replied gruffly, picking up the teal dress.

"Did you hear how Talan lied for me?" Lexi asked, removing her nightgown.

"Mm-hm...did that awfully well, didn't he? Makes you wonder how much practice he's had," Cercy remarked as she helped Lexi into her dress.

Lexi frowned. "He was protecting me."

"The truth would have exposed him far more than it would have you. He was protecting himself."

Lexi drew her dark brows together. "Maybe he lied badly."

Cercy shook her head. "The Queen is far too shrewd a woman for that. It's taken you most of your life to learn to fool her."

"Do you think I could be happy with him, Cercy?"

"Only you can decide that, Your Highness. Shall I put your hair back up?"

Lexi shook her head and sat down as Cercy brushed her hair, then attached a jeweled clip.

"You've five minutes to get to the library," Cercy said, patting her shoulders.

Lexi leaped up. "Then I'd better hurry."

Chapter Four

The library was a towering room with shelves from floor to ceiling and sliding ladders to access the plethora of books that filled the room with their musty scent. Heavily curtained windows stood guard over the precious occupants, protecting them from destructive sunlight. Soft divans were clustered about the room like grazing sheep. The Queen stood in front of the glass double doors that led into the room, one hand on the door handle, the other smoothing the delicate lines of her aging face.

"You are late," the Queen announced, immediately dropping her hand as she saw her daughter approach.

"I am sorry, Mother."

The Queen briefly examined her daughter, then nodded, her hand still on the closed door. "He is inside. Spend a few moments with him, and be certain the scent is pleasing," she admonished, opening the door and ushering her daughter through.

Talan stood up with a grin as the door shut quietly behind her.

"What a lovely farce you've arranged," Lexi said, noting that Talan was wearing new pants and a matching jacket.

"As you are not honest with your mother, I saw no reason why I should be," Talan said, signaling.

Lexi inhaled the hickory and clove scent with an involuntary little smile. "Since we're already being dishonest, maybe I'll tell her your pheromones are unappealing.

A slight shock of alarm crossed Talan's face before he replaced it with his usual smug grin. "Then I would have to tell her the truth about this evening's events in the garden."

It was Lexi's turn to feel a little flash of panic. Smoothing her face, she smiled blandly. "Go ahead. I am her daughter. She would forgive me."

"I doubt that," Talan replied, looking amused. "But since you don't seem to want to marry me, let's consider your other options."

Talan rubbed his chin thoughtfully a moment. "Oh yes, you haven't any."

Lexi controlled her expression with great effort; only her eyes burned with fury.

Talan's expression sobered, and he began to count off his points on his stubby fingers. "I have always treated you well, and I will continue to do so. We are a pheromone match, which should guarantee us children, as well as make our lives much more pleasant. And finally, our parents have already agreed; going against them now would be exceedingly difficult, if not impossible. I want this marriage. I want you to be my wife. If you run away from me, who will you be running to? What if Chip is the next to come in season? Or Quin?"

Lexi stifled a shudder as her mother opened the door.

"Shall I plan the wedding?" the Queen asked, a slight blush staining her cheeks.

Lexi swallowed, a hollow emptiness spreading out from her chest. Giving her mother a short nod, she brushed past her and hurried away.

She was sobbing by the time she reached her father's door. She knocked softly, then held her breath, listening for movement inside. A small, expressionless man opened the door, his dark brown wings seeming more like a misshapen shadow.

"Ambly," Lexi choked out. "Is he in his rooms?"

Ambly stood aside without answering, and Lexi moved past him. Her father sat at a little table with cards scattered across the top of it, looking expectantly towards the door.

"What's the matter?" he asked, jumping off his stool and dropping more cards on the table. His forehead wrinkled up in concern and he held out his arms as Lexi ran to him. Her sobs redoubled at the kindness, and Ambly quietly withdrew to another room as they embraced. The King let her cry without answering his question.

"You got my wings," he said happily, waving his own.

Lexi nodded into his shirt and then reluctantly pulled away to face him. "Father, I don't want to marry Talan."

"Why not?" the King asked, assuming a business-like tone as he sat her down on Ambly's abandoned stool at the card table.

"I don't like him."

"Why not? List his crimes." Her father's turquoise eyes twinkling with humor as he took his seat and folded his hands together.

A tiny smile crossed Lexi's tear-stained face and disappeared. "When he was eight, he kicked my dog because she wouldn't play fetch with him."

Her father grinned at the pettiness of the "crime," and Lexi's own mouth curved into a smile.

"And when he was twelve, he killed a whole family of robins with a rock before you made him stop."

The King scowled. "I remember that."

"When he was sixteen, he picked a fight with Tiger and broke his nose. And this morning," Lexi hesitated just a moment before she rushed forward with the truth. "This morning, I was riding Raven wearing Tiger's old clothes, and Talan pulled me off her back and threw me on the ground."

The King sucked in his breath sharply, a dark look of fury clouding his face.

"He didn't recognize me," she added quickly.

"That's no excuse! Did he hurt you?"

Lexi slid up her sleeve and showed him the bruises, then lifted her skirt to display the matching set on her knees. "He keeps apologizing, but he would have been perfectly happy about it if it had been Tiger or another servant. And he says he won't have me making friends with the servants when I'm his wife. And he and Mother don't even want me to fly," Lexi finished, her voice quavering as fresh tears threatened to fall. She put her hands to her eyes as if to plug her tear ducts. "Oh, and he's been lying to Mother and she can't seem to tell."

27

"About what?"

"He signaled me even before my wing birth, and he told Mother he hadn't. She even set up a meeting in the library just now, so he could signal me and make sure we were compatible." One corner of Lexi's mouth turned up. "Mother was embarrassed."

The King cleared his throat and ducked his head, but his shaking wings gave away his laughter.

"And he lied about my wing birth, too," Lexi said, not able to stop the truth that kept spouting from her mouth, despite her embarrassment. "He was with me when it happened," she confessed, her eyes on her hands.

"Why would he lie about that?"

Lexi grimaced and hid her face.

"Something else I won't like," he guessed, and Lexi nodded miserably without uncovering her face.

"Mother is already planning the wedding," she continued, speaking into her hands. "Even if I told her all this, I think she would still insist I marry him."

"That doesn't make sense. Why would she do that?"

Lexi let her hands drop. "Remember the 'something else' that I didn't want to tell you? Talan will tell. He already threatened to tell her."

The King took a deep breath and blew it out slowly. "So if you don't marry him, it's going to come out?"

Lexi nodded, her face stricken.

"You're not going to marry him, Lexi, so it's best you tell me now."

Lexi let out a sigh. "We...could you not look at me?" Lexi paused while the King dropped his head and lifted a hand to block his view. "We were kissing when my wing birth started," she said in a strangled whisper. "He had to tear my dress apart; Mother had Cercy sew me into it."

"Oh." They were silent for a time, neither one looking at the other. "I think you are right; she will insist."

Lexi put her forehead down on the table. "Am I being unreasonable? I am attracted to him. It would be easier to just marry him. And if Mother won't let me wait for another noble to come into season, what choice do I have?"

The King sat up straighter on his stool. "Lexi, do you want to be a Princess?"

Lexi looked up at her father. "I want to be your daughter."

The King patted her hand. "You'll always be my daughter. But do you want to be a Princess?"

Lexi was quiet for a moment. "No."

A new excitement lit her father's face. "I didn't want to be a prince."

Lexi blinked rapidly. "What?"

"When my wing birth came, I left my father a note abdicating my throne, and flew off to the Mating Mountain to start my new life."

Lexi let out a shocked laugh.

"I met your mother there. She's a farmer's daughter. After she agreed to marry me, I told her who I was, and she insisted we come back here. She talked my father out of disowning me, got him to reinstate me as his heir, and now I'm king."

Lexi's mouth hung open, all humor gone.

"We made up a story about her being a noble from a distant land, and me traveling to her father's estate after our parents had arranged the marriage by letter. She's such a good queen that no one ever doubts it."

Bewildered, Lexi got up and began to wander aimlessly around the large room.

"You asked what choice you have...you can make the same choice as your parents. You can go to the Mating Mountain and marry someone you love. If you want to come back here, *I* will always welcome you."

Lexi stopped abruptly. "But what about a male heir to your throne?"

The King shrugged. "Your cousin can be the next king."

"But Mother said…"

"It's natural for her to want one of her descendants to sit on the throne. But as I will be dead, I doubt it will matter to me. Your cousin is capable; as long as he marries well, he'll be a good leader. And with some luck, I'll live longer than most, and you won't have to determine my heir for another twenty years," he finished, looking at his daughter with a grin.

Lexi bounded to her father and hugged him, then grew thoughtful. "If Cercy helps me, can you keep Mother from firing her?"

The King grimaced. "What help do you need?"

"Something I can fly in, and everything I'll need for the trip."

Chuckling to himself, the King jumped up from his stool and fairly skipped to his dressing room. Lexi followed him, watching him push hanging clothing aside and remove the wall panel behind. Old hinges creaked loudly as her father drew a bag out of the chest hidden there, then spun around to show her.

"I kept it," he said, grinning.

"Was this yours?"

The King shook his head. "No. It was your mother's. Open it."

With a look of wonder, Lexi took the faded leather bag from her father and unbuckled the straps. Inside was a metal canteen covered in spotted cowhide, and several articles of red clothing. Lexi pulled out a ruffled shirt and held it up.

"She sewed all of her clothes herself." He fingered the ruffles with a nostalgic smile. "She asked me to burn it all, but I couldn't do it. You're taller than your mother, but hopefully they'll still fit." He crossed the room to rummage through a gilded bureau before drawing out a large wad of money. "You can buy whatever else you need," he said, stuffing it into a side pocket of the bag.

Lexi put the shirt back into the bag with an absent air.

"So I'll just show up at the mountain and say: 'Hi, I'm the youngest of the triplet princesses. Would any of you like to sire a king?'"

The King chuckled and put a hand on her shoulder. "Lexi, you can be anyone you want to be. I only ask that you keep your mother's secret. If it had not been so tied up in my own secret, I would not have told you."

Lexi nodded, then grinned. "So I'm a farmer's granddaughter, but I can't tell anyone?"

"It could be your new identity," he suggested. "You could be Lexi Viceroy, the farmer's granddaughter."

"A viceroy? That would still make me a noble."

Her father reached up to run a hand along her left forewing. "The problem is these big, beautiful monarch wings. They're very distinctive. You could claim to be a fritillary, but only a fool would believe you."

"Who did you tell them you were?"

"Chip Viceroy, the illegitimate grandson of the last governor."

The volume of Lexi's laughter surprised her, and she quickly clapped a hand over her mouth.

"*Before* that unpleasant young man of the same name was born, of course."

"But didn't the governor mind?" Lexi asked, still giggling.

The King shook his head. "It was his idea. It gave him an excuse to keep a close eye on me."

Lexi grew thoughtful. "Well, I obviously can't be Limen's illegitimate granddaughter, since we're nearly the same age."

"But he is your brother-in-law, so he should feel obligated to help you."

"I should ask Mona if she wants me to carry a letter to him."

"No! The fewer people you involve the better. Your mother will be very angry when she realizes you're gone. I want the blame to fall on only one person: me."

Lexi looked down at the bag in her hands with a frown. "I don't want to cause strife between you. Maybe you should put it back," she said, holding the bag out to him.

"So that you can marry the elitist fool who threw you off a horse, blackmailed you, broke your best friend's nose, won't let you fly, and would never condone the relationship you have with Cercy?"

Lexi hugged the bag to her chest as her eyes filled with tears. "I love you."

"I love you, too. Now put on some of your mom's old clothes so you can try out your wings," he encouraged, stepping out of his dressing room and shutting her in.

Lexi lifted the ruffled shirt back out of the bag and smelled it. Musty. She pulled out each item and sniffed with the same result. With a slight grimace, she slipped out of her dress and tried some red pants that were uncomfortably small, a top that rubbed her wings, a blouse that pulled so tight it was difficult to move her arms, and a pair of pants she couldn't get over her hips. Unfortunately, the ruffled top fit, but made her feel ridiculous. She was desperate when she drew out the last item of red clothing: a soft stretchy dress with long sleeves, a high banded neck, open back, and shorts sewn into the skirt. It fell above her knees, exposing the bruises, but it felt weightless. With an approving nod, she opened the door to see Ambly waiting for her.

"The Queen requested an audience with your father, and he suggested a stroll in the garden. He recommended you return to your room, and dismiss Cercy for the night. As the bag is too conspicuous to wear or carry back to your room, he'll bring it to you in one hour."

"Thanks Ambly," she said, then shut the door and removed the dress. She put all the red clothing that hadn't fit into the wall chest, and left the bag, packed with the canteen, the dress, and the ruffled shirt, in the middle of the floor. She dragged her own heavy dress back on and opened the door. Though the room appeared empty, she knew he would hear her.

"Goodbye Ambly," she called.

"Good luck, Your Highness," came the deferential voice from the other room.

Lexi smiled as she left. Then she began to practice her yawns. Lolling her head back until her hair tickled her wings, she let out great, jaw-popping yawns as she walked through the palace. At her door, she stopped abruptly, then grinned when the natural urge to yawn came on irresistibly. She fought it a moment, then entered her room.

"Cercy," she called, letting the yawn interrupt and distort the name.

"There you are. Your mother came by to make sure I got your wedding clothes right. You and Talan are to be sealed just before breakfast in the morning."

All pretense of sleepiness fled. Lexi blinked wide-eyed at her elaborate wedding gown laid out on the divan, then dragged her eyes back to Cercy's face with a heavy swallow.

"Did you talk to the King?"

Lexi nodded dumbly.

"Good. Because that's where I said you were."

Lexi returned to her ruse with a yawn. "Could you help me get this off?" she asked, fumbling with her neck buttons as if her fingers were too weary for dexterity.

"Well? Is your father going to rescue you?" Cercy demanded as she moved to assist her.

Lexi gave her an artful shrug. "He's talking to her now."

"I doubt that will be sufficient," Cercy muttered as she took the dress away and then returned with a nightgown. "A wedding mania has seized her. Just look at your dressing table. She's laid out every single pin I'm to use in your hair, and she insisted I demonstrate on her own head so she was certain I understood the style." Cercy snorted. "Six years! Six years of being your lady's maid and she still treats me like an apprentice." Cercy shook her head as she pressed Lexi onto the dressing table stool.

Lexi forced herself to yawn again as Cercy removed the jeweled clip from her hair and brushed Lexi's waist-length tresses vigorously before twisting them into their nightly bun. Cercy was too agitated to be gentle, but rather than wince, Lexi couldn't help the secretive smile that stole across her face.

"And why are you smiling?" Cercy demanded from Lexi's mirror image, continuing her rant. "If your father doesn't succeed, you will spend tomorrow traveling to your new home with Lord Admiral and your new lady's maid."

Lexi spun around, forcing Cercy to leap out of the way of her wings. "You're not coming with me?"

"Your mother said Lord Admiral's household will not require my services."

"But," Lexi insisted, her eyes filling with tears, "I know my father would continue to pay your salary, so you could stay with me."

Cercy shook her head. "Talan told your mother that he finds your relationships with the servants here *inappropriate* and wishes for you to have a *fresh start*."

Lexi rose slowly from her stool, fury igniting her blood until she shook with the heat of it. Lips twitching, her voice remained deceptively steady. "Cercy, there will be no wedding in the morning— even if I have to save myself."

Cercy squeezed Lexi's shoulders proudly. "Good girl. Now how can I help?"

"Take the night off."

Concern puckered Cercy's forehead. "If I happen not to see you for a time, I want you to know that I love you like my own child," she said, her voice breaking as she gathered Lexi in a fierce hug.

"I love you, too, Cercy." Lexi pulled away from the hug with a serious smile. "Now, take the night off," she said slowly, emphasizing each word.

Cercy gave her a proud nod and wiped at her cheek as she hurried into the other room. Moments later, she reemerged holding a tan shirt. "I didn't have time to do the finish work yet, but your riding shirt has become a flying shirt. I'll just hide it away with the rest of your riding gear," she said, disappearing into the dressing room.

Lexi swallowed at the persistent lump in her throat, her eyes burning. "Thank you," she called, climbing into bed.

Cercy reappeared and dimmed the lights.

"See you in the morning, Cercy."

"Mm-hmm. Don't forget your prayers."

"I won't."

"Goodnight, Your Highness."

"Goodnight."

The moment the door closed behind her, Lexi was out of bed. She ran about the room, clutching various toiletries to her chest, then dumping them in a back corner of her dressing room. Next, she dug out her riding clothes, smiling as she fingered the neat little wing panel Cercy had sewn into Tiger's old shirt. Adding them to her pile, she attacked her wedding trousseau next, selecting a blue nightgown to join her growing pile. Thinking of her mother's red dress, she selected some matching slippers and flung them onto the pile. Looking around the large room with its myriad of fancy dress clothes on display, she marveled at the sheer impracticality of almost everything she owned. She glanced down at her little pile. She would just have to shop. Lexi grinned at the thought. Since she and her sisters had been babies, her mother had designed and commissioned all of their clothing from the royal tailor. Never once had she been allowed to buy clothing from a store. Caught in her reverie, the soft knock at her door panicked her. Yanking down several heavy ball gowns, Lexi flung them across her pile on the floor, then hurried out to the door, realizing halfway that she was flying. She stumbled awkwardly back to her feet, then took a deep breath.

"Who is it?" she called in a sleepy voice.

"Talan."

Lexi jumped as she realized the voice came from behind her. Turning slowly, she looked out at her balcony to see him watching her from the other side of the glass doors. Heart sinking, she wiped the fear and panic from her face, and walked hesitantly towards him.

"I can't let you in."

"I'll be your husband in nine hours. What's the difference?"

Lexi watched him steadily. His movements as he shifted his weight were irritable and impatient. He ran a hand over his jaw, then tried the door handle.

"Open the door, Lexi."

With a trembling hand, Lexi unlocked the door. Talan pulled it open, biting at his bottom lip as if waiting for her to speak first. Lexi crossed her arms and stepped forward to block the doorway.

"You were flying," he accused.

"And you were peeping through my bedroom windows," she said evenly.

Talan bit his lip again. "You were also packing."

Lexi shrugged easily. "I'm moving tomorrow."

"Your maid should be doing that, and you gave her the night off."

Lexi swallowed. *How long had he been listening?* "I wanted to give her the chance to say goodbye to her friends."

Guilty knowledge and surprise flashed across Talan's face. "You haven't spoken with the Queen yet?"

"Not since we met in the library. Is there something I should know?" Lexi asked innocently.

Talan shrugged and shook his head. "Nothing that can't wait until tomorrow." He signaled, then lifted a hand to caress her cheek, using his thumb to play with her bottom lip. "Remember your focus," he whispered, leaning in to run his lips across hers.

Lexi took in a jagged breath, the euphoric scent of him momentarily overcoming her anger and fear. He swept her lips again, and she mentally berated herself with his list of crimes and the near certain knowledge that he would tell her mother about this in the morning.

"Let me in," he pled softly, toying with the long ribbon that ran down the front of her nightgown.

"No," she whispered.

"But your maid is gone for the night."

Lexi placed her hands on his chest and pushed him away from her firmly. "I'm still expecting visits from both my parents tonight, and you are not my husband." *Nor will you ever be,* she thought, her head clearing from the haze.

"One more kiss," he bargained, leaning in to take it.

Lexi turned her head abruptly, and his lips caught her ear instead, sending a little ricochet of tingles down her neck and arm.

"Go," she commanded, shivering involuntarily as she reached forward to grab the door handle and pull it closed.

"Goodnight, Princess," he called as he jumped out of the way of the shutting door.

Lexi merely frowned and locked the door. He grinned impishly, then leapt off her balcony. His dark brown wings blended into the night; only the spots of white and streaks of orange seemed to suspend him in the air. Lexi let out a breath through her teeth, drew the filmy curtains that offered no real privacy, then shut off every light in her adjoining rooms. Bathed in protective darkness, she peeked around the curtain to ensure he had not returned.

She let out a tiny scream when she heard the knock. It took her a moment to realize the sound was from the hallway door this time.

"Lexi?" her father called.

With a sigh of relief, she flew across the room, stumbled a landing, and opened the door.

"Were you sleeping?" he asked.

Lexi shook her head as she switched on a light. "Talan was watching me. He saw me pack, and he knows I sent Cercy away for the night," she told him, pulling him quickly into the room and shutting the door. "He wanted to come in. I'm worried he'll come back."

The King's affable mouth pulled into a grim line. "I really don't like that young man."

"Maybe you could convince Mother not to be so fond of him."

The King shook his head. "Because he is the only nobleman available and a pheromone match, she is disposed to think well of him. I told her he was violent with the servants, and far too free with you."

Lexi looked up at her father anxiously. "Oh, no."

The King winced. "It wasn't a wise thing to say. She wheedled out of me that he's kissed you, that he saw your wing birth and tore your dress. I'm sorry. I didn't mean to tell her."

"Oh, Dad," Lexi laughed sadly as she patted his arm, "I know you didn't mean to."

"She was only mildly irritated at his dishonesty, I'm afraid."

"And more than ever determined that I marry him?" Lexi asked with a grimace.

The King nodded. "She planned to bear down on you with a furious lecture, and force me to perform the ceremony tonight, but I pointed out that the decorations and food were not ready yet, and that her parting conversation with her last unmarried daughter ought not to be an angry one."

Lexi rubbed her forehead with both hands, covering her face. "It's hard to believe I might actually escape."

"The sooner you leave, the better. Can you fly yet?"

"Yes, but my landings aren't good."

The King gave a heavy sigh. "I hate to send you alone, but anyone I ask will have to bear your mother's wrath." He frowned unhappily. "I don't think they would simply lose their position...it's more likely she would imprison whomever helped you, perhaps for a long time."

Lexi nodded grimly. "I can do it," she said in a small voice.

Her father smiled sadly. "I know that you can." Glancing quickly out at the balcony, the King switched off the light and led her into her dressing room, shutting the door before he turned on the light there.

Lexi lifted the heavy dresses that concealed her little pile, and her father held out her mother's bag. Looking inside, Lexi grinned.

"You stopped by the kitchen."

Her father nodded. "The canteen is full, too, though it's rather heavy."

Lexi knelt beside her pile, quickly concealing the shirt Cercy had altered into the mouth of her riding boot. She knew her mother would extract every detail from her father in the morning, and she did not want Cercy to be a casualty of his confession.

"Now I just have to change," she said, standing.

Her father hugged her warmly. "Oh daughter, I will miss you so much. Please be careful, and when your mother has calmed down some, come visit me with your husband."

Lexi giggled. "How long do you suppose that will take?"

Her father chuckled. "Maybe you should send me a letter first. Now," the King said, releasing his daughter, "it's time I had 'the talk' with my future son-in-law."

He laughed at Lexi's startled bemusement.

"It will keep him occupied for the next hour, so I'll know he's not following you," he explained. "Now, strap on the bag under that billowy nightgown, and walk down to the stables. If anyone catches you, you can claim you had to say goodbye to your horse. You can change in the tack room."

Lexi smiled. "I love you. Thank you for helping me do this."

"I just want you to be happy. Choose your mate carefully, Lexi. And when you've chosen, don't forget to ask God if He approves."

Lexi nodded soberly.

"Pray with me?"

"Of course," Lexi said, kneeling.

The King knelt beside her. "God in Heaven, I entrust my daughter to Thee. Please watch over her. Amen," he finished in a choked voice.

Lexi patted her father's arm with a teary grin. "Have fun lecturing Talan."

The King chuckled. "That I will," he admitted, getting to his feet. He leaned forward and kissed her forehead. "Love you, daughter," he whispered, then turned and left the room.

Lexi pulled Tiger's shirt out of her boot and packed it into her mother's bag, then strapped the bag beneath her nightgown and slipped into her riding boots. She laughed at her appearance in the mirror. Taking a deep breath, she turned out the lights, and stepped out into her dark room. It was odd knowing she might never come back.

"Perhaps I've had my last day as a princess," Lexi said aloud, grinning at the thought. "On to my next life," she whispered, opening the door.

All the palace lights had been dimmed for the evening, and Lexi slipped through the shadows, calming the nervous flutter in her stomach by pretending she was only going for an early morning ride. When she reached Raven's stall without being seen, she was giddy with success.

"Raven," she whispered, drawing out an apple from her bag. "I'm running away in the night like a naughty child; what do you think of that?"

Raven happily crunched her apple, then sniffed at the bag through Lexi's nightgown for more.

Lexi grinned. "One more," she said, drawing up her nightgown, "but only because I'll miss you so much." She produced a second apple, and stroked Raven's neck as she ate it. As she swallowed, the horse pulled up to sniff at Lexi's wings.

"Gentle, girl, I need those," she said, kissing her horse's nose as she turned into the tack room to change. She was tempted to put on Tiger's clothes and cap to disguise herself, but if she were caught, she didn't want to be wearing something that would get Cercy in trouble. Instead, she chose her black riding pants and her mother's frilly red top. She groaned as she looked down at the ruffles, but it was better than wearing the dress. Stuffing her nightgown back into her bag, she strapped it on and peeked out the tack room door.

Moss, the stable apprentice, was checking on the horses, and Lexi shut the door quickly. The tack room had a row of high windows, but they were impossibly small to get through with wings. Crouching behind a row of saddles, she held her breath. The door opened and Moss came through, the heavy tread of the seventeen-year-old stopping just short of her hiding place while he straightened the hanging bridles. He brushed his hands heavily against his pants, sending little clouds of dust into the air that made Lexi want to sneeze. Then he went out again, leaving the tack room door open. Peeking around the saddles, Lexi watched his lanky form walk the long row of horse stalls, smacking his lips and receiving responding nickers from his favorites. Just before he reached the end of the row, Lexi darted out of the tack room and flew from the stables, praying that Moss would not turn around. She listened, breathless, for shouts behind her, but heard nothing but her soft wing beats as she climbed into the moonlit sky.

She flew over the tops of the forest trees that surrounded her father's expansive lands, part terrified and part thrilled at the height and speed. Accustomed as she was to horseback riding, it was alarming to move so fast with nothing to cling to. Her arms and legs hung superfluously as her wings worked, and she wondered if she looked as ridiculous as she felt. She tried flying with her hands clenched together on an imaginary bridle, then fisted apart as if gripping Raven's reins, but both felt equally silly without the powerful horse beneath her. Eventually, she gave up and just let them hang. "I must look like a mosquito," she said with a soft laugh.

As the sprawling Royal City began to peter out beneath her, Lexi panicked. The Mating Mountain was too far off to be visible, even if it weren't dark, and Lexi wasn't sufficiently familiar with the landscape to know what direction she was flying once outside the city. She was tempted to stop for the night or at least purchase a compass, but she knew she would be easily recognized, and that her mother would likely punish anyone who helped her. Slowing down and gradually approaching the ground, Lexi executed another ungraceful landing, tripping several steps before she caught her balance in the empty field next to a road sign. Peering up at it, she read "Shady Cove," and nodded. Shady Cove was straight north of the Royal City, wasn't it? She couldn't remember, but hoped it was close enough. Leaping back into the air, she marveled that her wings weren't tiring, that the muscles of her back still felt invigorated. *I'm made for this*, she thought with a pleased smile, then fell to experimenting with arm positions again as she kept the moonlit scratch of road in sight beneath her.

Three hours later, she guzzled the last of her water and panted so loudly that she could no longer hear the night sounds of the forest beneath her. She had expected to see the next city an hour ago, but still the pale road meandered beneath her, and no welcoming lights lit up over the next hill. Massaging her shoulders, she forced herself to fly higher to see more of the landscape ahead. There were lights over the next hill, but not the right size to be a city, maybe a large country estate. *At least they will have water*, she thought. Driving herself onward, she focused on the lights, flying away from the road to meet them. As she flew closer, she could see a vast property encased in stone and wood fences with heavily-manicured gardens to set it apart from the surrounding forest. A draconian iron gate blocked its entrance from the road with two guards leaning sleepily against it. Lexi quickly rejected this mode of entry and scanned for the stables, resolved to fill her canteen from a trough if necessary. The house with its rambling out buildings reminded her of a miniature palace, and Lexi was struck with the uncomfortable certainty that she was looking at a noble's home; someone who would likely recognize her. Finding the stables, she landed well away from the horses, then waited for her breathing to return to normal as she listened for anything unusual. Cautiously, she began to approach, murmuring soothing streams of nonsense that she hoped were too quiet to arouse a sleeping stable boy. Several of the horses whinnied at she approached a water pump over an open trough. She set a hand against the cold metal, her canteen in the other, praying that it wouldn't make a noise. It screeched, splashing out enough water to fill her canteen if she hadn't jumped at the sound and missed most of it. Setting her teeth, Lexi grimaced and pumped it again, neatly filling her canteen.

"This is private property!" a young voice announced with a slight tremor, just as she capped her canteen.

"I'm sorry," she answered, turning her face away from the boy. "I just needed some water. I'll be on my way now," she said, sliding her canteen back into her bag.

"Uh...wait," the boy said, walking into the lantern light. He was small, perhaps twelve, with a shock of blond hair sticking out from a cap too large for him. Bits of straw clung to his rumpled clothes. "Are you going to the Mating Mountain?"

Lexi looked at him curiously, keeping her face in shadow. "Yes."

"We have some letters; would you take them? We could pay you a bit or trade food or shelter."

Lexi considered that a moment as her muscles screamed for a rest. "I would like to help you," she said hesitantly, visualizing the royal flying guardsmen catching up to her and turning the letters over to her mother. "But it's best if no one knows I was here," she finished apologetically.

The boy examined her closely, stepping nearer. "Why?"

Lexi mentally berated herself for not having answers prepared in advance. Sighing, she told the truth. "My mother didn't want me to go. She'll be angry at anyone who helps me."

"Are you a noble lady, then?" the boy asked, taking a few more steps forward as Lexi receded into the shadows.

"I have to go." Lexi jumped into the air, then gasped and stumbled back to the ground, her back muscles cramping severely.

"Shelter in exchange for the letters?" the boy offered, a smile in his voice.

Lexi turned to face him. "You could lose your place for helping me."

He shrugged. "Don't care much for the master anyway."

"Who is your master?"

"Lord Admiral."

Lexi's heart began to pound, her breath coming in shallow little gasps as she tried to calm her face. "I can't stay here."

The boy's light eyebrows drew together like a long, fuzzy caterpillar. "He's not home right now. And none of his family ever comes into the servants' quarters, anyway. They'll never know you were here."

"How close is Shady Cove?"

"Walking?" he asked, waiting for Lexi's nod. "An hour."

Lexi nodded again and turned north, steeling herself against the long walk ahead of her.

"If you won't take the letters, will you pass a message?" the boy asked, walking alongside her in a jogging gait to keep up with her long strides.

"I suppose so."

"My aunt's a life servant on the mountain. Her name is Marina Blue. My mom wanted her to know that their father died, and that my grandmother lives with us now."

Lexi stopped walking and looked at the boy's shadowed face. "I'm sorry."

The boy merely shrugged as he stared at the ground. "That's all," he said quietly, glancing up at her. "The property is only fenced along the road. You can walk out through the forest." The boy took off at an uneven lope back to the stables and disappeared into one of the stalls.

"Thank you," she called softly after him.

Urging her exhausted body forward, Lexi began to walk.

Chapter Five

Lexi snuggled deeper into the luxurious bedding, her wings shielding her pale face from the afternoon sunlight streaming in from a high window. Her boots and clothing were strung across the floor in a path from the door to the bed, with her bag splayed open near a foot that had escaped the confines of her covers. With a noise of contentment, she unwound an arm from beneath her head and stretched, then let out a little yawn.

"Good morning, Princess."

Lexi's eyes jolted open, and she flew out of the covers to land on the far side of the bed, her wrinkled nightgown slowly untangling from her legs. "Talan!" she gasped, eyeing the door.

Talan sat casually with one foot up on his knee, twirling a smooth, white stone around his fingers. "How did you sleep, my love?"

"How did you get in my room?" she demanded, inching forward to grab her bag.

"After I visited your balcony last night, your mother thought it prudent that we be married right away. Your father married us late last night, and we left on our honeymoon journey together, reaching my estate in the early hours of this morning. Unfortunately, we had a bit of a quarrel over your maid. Sulking, you took yourself to the nicest inn in town, where I found you this morning. Now, we shall make up and return to my estate," Talan announced, sliding a folded paper from his jacket pocket, and slowly unfolding it.

"You know that didn't happen," Lexi said in a choked voice, irrational tears pricking at her eyes.

"It's not what I know, it's what the rest of the world *thinks*. Now, if you are finished behaving like a peasant maid, sign this, and we can get on with our lives," Talan said, holding out the paper he had just unfolded.

Without touching it, Lexi leaned forward to read it. "Solemn Marriage Sealing" was written in fancy letters across the top with her father's signature at the bottom. Backing away, Lexi clutched at her bag, white-knuckled.

"That's not binding," she whispered.

With a slight frown, Talan laid the certificate on the table and placed the rock on top of it with a forceful thunk. "Your father will make it more official when we visit next week. Until then, we will live at my estate like reasonably happy newlyweds and do our best to give your father an heir."

"No!" Lexi exclaimed, the word coming out like a cry.

An unpleasant smile flitted across Talan's face. "But that's the part you enjoy, my love; have you forgotten?" Talan asked, making the air heavy with his scent as he stood and moved towards her.

"Stay away from me," she ordered, swallowing to still the tremor in her voice. "I am still a princess, and I command you to leave this room."

Talan's skin pulled tight across his jaw. "Very well, *Princess*, I will wait outside. But understand that wherever you go, I go. I have been *commanded*," he spat the word out bitterly, "to follow you, and nothing but delivering you back to the Queen or your marriage to another man will set me free." He stared at her, his face a furious red, fists clenched at his sides.

"Get out, Talan," she commanded, each word clipped.

Talan spun on his heel, his wings grazing her face as he turned, and stalked from the room. The walls reverberated with the slamming door.

Lexi let her breath out slowly, cursing herself for sleeping so late. She yanked her bag up from the floor, then dropped it again when her gaze fell on the incomplete wedding certificate. She pitied her father the argument that must have preceded his signature. She slid the paper out from under Talan's rock and tore it in half, careful not to tear her father's name. She ripped carefully around it, then slipped it into her bag with the roll of money. The rest of the certificate she tore into tiny shreds, scooped up the pieces, and walked to the door. Opening it, she tossed the pieces into the hallway and shut the door again before they could flutter to the floor. Smiling, she washed carefully, put on her mother's red dress, and let her hair down. Her riding boots wouldn't fit inside her bag, so she wore them once again. With satisfaction, Lexi noted that the dark boots helped distract from her bruised knees. Nodding at her appearance in the mirror, she picked up her bag and opened the door.

"Your Highness," a uniformed flying guardsman said, bowing stiffly, his companion doing the same while the scent of mustard filled the air.

"Oh," Lexi said, glancing up and down the hallway. "Is he gone, then?" she asked, noting that the shredded bits of wedding certificate had disappeared as well.

The first guard elbowed the second as he shook his head. "Your husband is in the dining room."

Lexi shook her head vigorously. "He is *not* my husband. I am going to the Mating Mountain, and he is trying to stop me." Lexi watched as the guards exchanged an uncomfortable expression. "What are your orders?"

The first guard cleared his throat. "We are your escort, Your Highness. The King commanded us to see you and uh...Lord Admiral's son safely to your destination."

"The King?" Lexi's voice was suddenly soft. "Is the Queen aware of your orders?"

"Yes, Your Highness."

Lexi let out a breath, her shoulders relaxing. "Good. What are your names?"

The first guard's heavy brown eyebrows arched into his forehead as his yellow wings twitched. "Uh, I'm Vaden. This is Celus," he added, pointing to the smaller guard with the broad brown wings.

"Are you hungry?"

Vaden shifted his weight and exchanged a glance with Celus. "Yes, Your Highness."

"Let's eat, then." Lexi marched down to the dining room with the two perplexed guards in her wake.

Talan stood as they entered, and walked up to usher Lexi to his table.

"No, thank you," she said, choosing a larger table on the other side of the room. "Sit down," she commanded the guards, indicating the chairs on either side of her.

Fighting a scowl, Talan requested the waitress move his meal to their table, then walked reluctantly over to sit down between the two guards.

Watching their mutual discomfort, a giggle bubbled up Lexi's throat before she could choke it.

"Does something amuse you, Princess?" Talan asked, his handsome face twitching with irritation.

Lexi smiled pleasantly. "Yes, something does amuse me. Talan, have you been properly introduced to Vaden and Celus?"

Talan's visage turned a mottled red, his mouth a tight line and his nostrils flared. Both guards kept their heads down.

Lexi fought the amusement that insisted on turning up the corners of her mouth during their silent meal. Talan looked horrified when she attempted conversation with the guards, and only slightly relieved at their monosyllabic answers.

"May I speak with you privately, Princess?" Talan asked as she stood at the end of the meal.

Lexi frowned, but followed Talan into a small room crowded with a large table. Talan reached around her to shut the door, and she quickly moved away from him.

"What is left to say, Talan?"

"You are humiliating me!" Talan blurted, a vein in his temple bulging.

Lexi stifled another giggle with a cough. "Then you are easily humiliated."

"I live near here! I am the local nobility! I do not eat with guards or get snubbed by my wife!"

48

"I am not your wife, and if you have let anyone think so, you have only yourself to blame," Lexi retorted heatedly.

"That's not true! Your mother ordered me to follow you. The story of our marriage was *her* fabrication." Talan paced back and forth in the tiny space, his wings rubbing against the wall. "I *did* want you very much." He stopped pacing near her and lifted a hand to her face, which she quickly slapped away. Grinding his teeth, he sucked in a heavy breath. "I would *still* take you if you would stop making everything so difficult!"

With effort, Lexi controlled her temper. "I am sorry for my mother's orders. I would remand them if I had the power. If you return to my father alone, I am certain he will do so."

"The King hates me! You told him I kissed you and came to your balcony. He lectured me for two hours! He would rather strip me of my land and title than help me!"

In spite of Talan's angst, Lexi laughed. The thought of her father lecturing him while she escaped was too amusing to hold in.

"And now you laugh at me?!"

"I'm sorry," Lexi apologized, forcing her mouth into a dour line.

"Why didn't you just tell me you would never marry me from the beginning? You could have spared me all this!"

His words sobered her mirth instantly. "I meant to be obedient. I didn't see the choice I had until I spoke to my father."

"And you couldn't have told me?" Talan asked with exasperation.

Lexi shook her head. "You would have stopped me."

Talan blew out a long breath. "What now?"

"I'm still going to the Mating Mountain. If you feel you must follow me, I'll try not to humiliate you."

"Are you going to tell the peasants there who you are?"

"I had not meant to, but I am afraid my escort will give me away," Lexi said, rubbing her earlobe thoughtfully.

"Princess, every male there will pretend to be in love with you for the sake of your wealth and power," Talan warned.

Lexi frowned at him, but didn't disagree.

Talan stepped closer to her, his scent wafting around her. "Please Lexi, just marry me. It will be so much easier for both of us."

Lexi shook her head. "It's not *easy* that I want. Wouldn't you like to try falling in love, Talan?"

"With you? Yes."

Lexi gave him a light laugh. "Talan, my lady's maid is like a mother to me. My best friend is a stable boy. I'm more comfortable sneaking around in servants' clothes than I've ever been in a formal gown receiving guests. If I weren't a Princess, you would never consider me as a mate."

Talan frowned. "I would still be attracted to you."

"But you would get over it quickly when you had been sufficiently repelled by my behavior." Lexi sighed as she looked at him. "Now, I need to do some shopping. Will it embarrass you if I do it in this town? I can wait for the next one."

Talan's gaze had fallen to her bruised knees and his voice was pained when he spoke. "I would appreciate it if you waited."

Lexi nodded her head. "Done. I'm going to leave now. Are you flying with us?"

Talan bit at his lip, distracting her. Looking up he caught her watching his mouth and grinned. "I'll fly with you."

Lexi tore her gaze away, and nodded absently as she opened the door. "Let's go," she announced to her waiting guards.

It was odd flying in a group, clustered together like an uncoordinated flock. Talan had tried to insist that Lexi hold his hand, but one frigid look from her had been sufficient to foil his plans. Now the two guards were flanking her while Talan flew above the three of them. Having him stare down at her was disconcerting, but when she complained, he only offered his hand as an alternative.

Once again catching Talan staring at her, Lexi scowled, then launched into conversation with the guards. "Vaden, is the Royal City your home?" Lexi grinned as she heard a murmur of exasperation from above her.

Vaden looked startled at her question, again exchanging a glance with Celus before speaking. "No, Your Highness. My family is in Rogue River."

"Were you an apprentice guard before your wing birth?" Lexi continued, glancing up at Talan and enjoying his frown.

"No, Your Highness. We have a bakery."

"How did you come to be one of the King's flying guard?"

Vaden blushed. "The pay is very good, Your Highness. If my season lasts a couple more weeks, it will be enough to build a new oven for the bakery."

"And then you'll return to your family?"

Vaden nodded happily. "My wife is expecting any day," he added, his smile growing wistful.

"Congratulations," Lexi said warmly. "What did you think of the Mating Mountain?"

"Food stinks," Celus blurted, then blushed deeply and mumbled, "Your Highness."

Lexi laughed. "Then perhaps I should bring some with me."

"I am certain Your Highness will be well fed," Vaden insisted, giving Celus a disapproving glance. "The Governor is your brother-in-law, after all."

Lexi looked between the two guards with confusion. "Is the food very different for the Governor, then?"

"*Everything* is different for the Governor," Celus muttered, then blushed again as he glanced at Vaden.

"As it should be," Talan murmured, nodding his approval.

Lexi ignored him and turned to Celus. "For instance?"

Vaden shook his head slightly, but Celus was already speaking, his blush bleeding down his neck. "The Governor and the life servants get all the good food, the cleaner washing pool, and warmer bedrooms. The in-seasons get treated like dirt, and are driven away as quickly as possible."

Lexi turned a questioning glance to Vaden, but he only sighed and looked away.

"Did either of you report this to my father? I am certain he does not know about this." She frowned as both guards shook their heads. "Well, I will certainly tell him."

An uncomfortable silence fell over the four of them as they flew on, stopping in two small villages for food and water to break up their long journey. As the sky began to darken, Vaden pointed at the faint glow behind the northern hills.

"We've made good time. That's Oakridge. We can stop there for the night if that is acceptable, Your Highness," Vaden suggested.

"Yes Vaden," Lexi panted. "I am ready to stop."

With a burst of speed, Talan darted ahead of the group. In a few minutes, his brown and orange wings were nothing more than a smudgy blur on the horizon.

Odd, Lexi thought.

Celus muttered something under his breath, then snorted at his own joke while Vaden gave him a warning glance.

They watched Talan until he disappeared over the hill, the natural urge to increase their speed squelched by exhaustion. Lexi pulled out her canteen and drank the last of it, slowing as she did so. The guards slowed to match her speed and Vaden held out his canteen.

"No, thank you, Vaden," Lexi assured him. "I will be fine."

Just as they reached the outskirts of the city, Talan reappeared.

"The finest accommodations are this way," he insisted, leading the group out of the city, to the west.

After a few moments of following him, Lexi frowned. "That looks like a private estate. I'd prefer a public inn."

Talan turned around with a grin. "But Anna West is already expecting us. Surely you don't want to be rude."

Lexi clenched her teeth, but kept her face impassive. "Of course not."

As they neared the courtyard, a beautiful blonde with wide blue eyes walked out to meet them with a gaggle of servants scurrying around her.

"Your Highness! Talan!" the blonde greeted them with a delighted grin, and took their hands as they landed next to her. "Father is away, and I've been so bored! You must stay with me and keep me company," she insisted, pressing their hands warmly.

"Of course. Thank you for your invitation," Lexi replied, her smile frozen in place as she caught Talan and Anna exchanging a conspiratorial glance.

"And now that you're here, I won't even try to keep our great secret. Van's wing birth was a month ago, but he wickedly ran off to the Mating Mountain instead of going to the palace. Father is perfectly frantic that my foolish twin will get stuck there or come home married to a nobody. He hasn't let me tell a soul! He just keeps hoping that Van will come home repentant, and he'll still be able to arrange a marriage with a noblewoman," Anna paused, glancing back and forth between the two of them.

"So this must be your honeymoon journey! Whatever brings you so far north?" she asked, looking at Lexi expectantly.

Slipping her hand out of Anna's, Lexi held a tight smile. "We're not married, Anna. I've decided to go to the Mating Mountain, and Talan is...escorting me."

Anna's eyes widened in feigned surprise. "But surely your parents arranged a marriage for you?"

Lexi stood taller, feeling miserably conspicuous in the sweaty red dress next to Anna's elegant blue gown. "Perhaps Talan will tell you about that while I prepare for dinner."

"Oh, of course! How rude of me. Let me show you to your room, Your Highness," Anna insisted. "Talan, you can have your usual room, of course," she added, giving Talan an easy smile. "Dinner will be served in half an hour. You do remember where the dining room is?" Anna teased.

Talan grinned back at her without answering.

Anna offered her arm to Lexi and steered her into the palatial estate. "You may not have been aware that Talan and Van are the best of friends. Talan always spends at least a month every summer with us. I am certain Van will be delighted to see him on the mountain, and then perhaps Talan can talk some sense into him."

Lexi hid a sigh, knowing Anna neither expected nor desired any verbal response.

"You must let me lend you a dinner gown from my wedding trousseau," Anna insisted, giving Lexi's dress a disapproving glance.

Lexi repressed a laugh as she looked down at the girl, a full head shorter than she. "I don't think it is likely to fit."

"Of course it will!" Anna assured her, patting her hand. "You have a tiny waist, and shorter hems and sleeves are very popular this season."

Lexi laughed out loud this time, partly from the image of appearing at dinner in Tiger's clothes.

Anna smiled patiently at her laughter. "We'll find something that works. Here's your room. I'll send my maid with some dinner gowns shortly. Is there anything you need, Your Highness?"

Lexi glanced around the large room where every piece of furniture or decoration was a shade of lavender. "No, this will be perfect. Thank you, Anna."

"No thank *you*, Your Highness. It is has been a long time since we have had a royal guest." Anna smiled and pulled the door shut behind her.

Lexi sucked in a huge breath and blew it out slowly. The room smelled like her mother's, and she had to fight the claustrophobic feeling that she was imprisoned. Taking another big breath, she ventured into the adjoining lavender bathroom and began to wash. A soft knock sounded at the door just as she was finishing. Lexi started to wrap a towel around her and caught her wings. Cringing, she tried to drape it up underneath her wings and high over her chest, but it tickled her wings unpleasantly. Finally, she just clutched the towel to her chest and opened the door a crack.

A short, brown-haired pupa girl stood outside her door, her face bowed respectfully into a pile of brightly colored finery that she toted in her arms. "Your dresses, Your Highness," she said, her voice muffled by her load.

Lexi let the girl through, and quickly shut the door behind her. The maid laid her load lovingly across a divan, then faced Lexi, her eyes on the floor. "Shall I help you, Your Highness?"

Lexi glanced at the stack of elaborate finery, then put a hand up to her wet hair. "Yes, please."

The maid helped her try on all five of the dresses before she settled on a bright pink gown replete with a riot of bows. Lexi hated it, but it fit much better than the others and mercifully covered her bruises. Then the maid drew her hair up in an elaborate coiffure with hanging tendrils and matching pink ribbons. Finally, Lexi slipped on her jeweled red slippers, hoping the color difference would not be obvious in the dimmer evening light. The maid led her to the dining room, then backed away shyly.

"Thank you. I really appreciate your help," Lexi whispered sincerely.

The short maid blushed, bowed, and mumbled something before hurrying away.

"Princess," Talan called, his face alight as he came out to usher her in.

Lexi reluctantly took his proffered arm, noting the subtle scent of hickory and cloves emanating from him.

"You look lovely," he said, guiding her to the seat next to him.

"Who's this?" an elderly lady demanded from the end of the table.

"Remember, Grandmother, this is Her Royal Highness, Princess Lexi," Anna reminded her patiently, patting her heavily jeweled hand.

"What's she doing here?"

Anna blushed. "Lady Nessa isn't well," she whispered apologetically.

"I can hear you!" Lady Nessa fairly shouted.

Lexi gave her a polite smile and extended her hand. "Lady Nessa, it is a pleasure..."

"You are in season, too? What are you doing here?" Lady Nessa interrupted.

"She's going to the Mating Mountain, like Van," Anna explained.

"She's going after Van?" Lady Nessa demanded.

Lexi blinked. Anna's mouth opened, but no words came.

"Well, good! Best news I've heard in a month! If a princess can't bring him home, no one can." Lady Nessa looked around the table in grim satisfaction. "Where is my dinner?!"

Servants rushed around serving her while she made various critical comments. Talan frequently covered his mouth with his napkin or hand, his wings shaking with silent laughter while Anna kicked him under the table. Lexi held a pleasant smile as she ate, pretending to be elsewhere.

"This tastes terrible!" Lady Nessa announced, flinging her dessert spoon. "I want to have my walk in the garden now," she demanded, her faded black-tipped orange wings twitching. Two servants quickly helped her up and supported her as she hobbled towards the door. She pointed a gnarled, thick-nailed finger at Lexi as she passed. "You tell my grandson to marry you quick or I'll leave all my money to his sister here."

A slight blush crept up Lexi's cheeks. "Goodnight, Lady Nessa."

Talan and Anna echoed her sentiments. As soon as Lady Nessa was out of hearing, Talan turned to Anna.

"She won't really disinherit him?" he asked.

Anna shrugged. "Grandmother has become unpredictable," she explained, standing. "She also gets irritable when I don't join her on her walks, so if you'll excuse me." Anna left the room, her elaborate underskirts rustling as blonde ringlets bounced down her back.

Talan looked at Lexi with a grin, his scent suddenly much stronger. "Will you tell Van?"

Lexi's eyes widened. "Of course not."

Talan laughed. "I will."

Lexi shifted uncomfortably on her stool and pushed the last bite of pie around her plate.

"It will be much harder for you to find your beloved peasant with two nobles vying for your hand," Talan predicted happily.

Lexi scowled at him. "Is that your plan? To drive away all the other men?"

Talan considered seriously for a moment. "Not Van."

Lexi let out an irritated breath. "What's he doing on the mountain anyway?"

Talan folded his lips tight, then shrugged.

"You weren't surprised that he had gone."

"Why do you say that?" Talan asked, staring down at Van's jacket as he removed invisible lint.

"When Anna told us, you didn't respond."

Talan shrugged. "I had spoken to her earlier." Talan stood and held out his hand to her. "Would you like to see Van's stables? I know it's not as much fun since we can't ride them anymore, but he does have some beautiful stallions."

Lexi considered for a moment, then looked down at her dress. "I think I had best return this dress to Anna and get some sleep."

"You slept half the day," Talan complained. "You can't be tired yet."

"Goodnight, Talan." Lexi stood in an attempt to terminate the conversation.

"Wait," he said, taking her wrist and moving close to her.

"Don't, Talan," Lexi warned, trying to ignore the little thrill that ran up her arm at his touch.

"Why not?" he asked, releasing her wrist to run his fingers up her arm in an exhilarating crescendo.

Lexi caught his hand and pushed it away.

"What if I let you keep your lady's maid?" he blurted.

"Then you would only lecture me more often about the way I treated the servants," Lexi said wearily.

"Lexi," he pled softly, artfully biting his lip.

Lexi frowned as she watched, then turned away quickly when he leaned in to kiss her. "Goodnight, Talan," she repeated, moving swiftly from the room. In the hallway, she pressed a hand to her pounding heart as she took deep breaths of the unscented air.

"Your Highness!"

Lexi turned to see Vaden hurrying down the hall towards her, an irritated steward on his heels.

"Her Highness is not to be bothered," the steward announced haughtily.

"It's not a bother," Lexi assured him. "Vaden, did you need something?"

The steward retreated with a comically juxtaposed sullen glare for Vaden and an obsequious bow for Lexi.

"Your Highness," Vaden said, taking a moment to catch his breath. "I'm leaving now, returning to the Royal City."

"You're abandoning your duty?" Talan demanded from the dining room doorway.

Gritting her teeth, Lexi ignored Talan, shrugging him away as he tried to take her arm.

"No, My Lord," Vaden bowed, then turned to Lexi with a slight blush in his cheeks. "My season ended, Your Highness. When one of the royal flying guard loses their ability to fly, we are to report back to the King immediately."

"Oh. Do you need money for transportation?" Lexi asked.

"No, the mail coaches have to take us for free," Vaden assured her.

Lexi smiled. "Hurry, then. Maybe you can make it home before your children are born."

An answering smile flitted across Vaden's square jaw, then disappeared as he faced Talan's scowl. "My Lord, might I have a word with you?"

"Perhaps later," Talan said irritably, trying to lead Lexi away.

"But he's leaving now," Lexi argued, removing Talan's hand from her arm.

"Fine. Speak," Talan growled.

Vaden looked uncomfortably at Lexi, then back at Talan. "It regards Her Highness' safety."

"Surely she is entitled to hear about that?"

Vaden's face flamed red, and he stared at the floor. "It's about Celus. He's...very attracted to Her Highness; he has even presumed to signal her on occasion. He should not be left alone with her."

The tendons in Talan's neck stood out as he clenched his fists. "Excuse me," he said with a brusque bow, then flew away with rapid strokes.

"Thank you for the warning," Lexi said when she found her voice. She *had* noticed a mustard scent when Celus was around, but had assumed it was merely food on or about his person.

Vaden bowed, then hurried away.

Lexi stood in the hallway a moment, watching him go, before she finally returned to her room. Despite sleeping past noon, the long hours of flying had drained her, and she was asleep soon after she crawled into bed.

Chapter Six

Lexi awoke before dawn and was eager to be gone. Finding a servant out in the hallway, she requested breakfast in her room, then surveyed her clothing. Tiger's cast-offs were all that remained clean, and she cursed herself for not asking the lady's maid to do some laundry for her. Sighing, she pulled on Tiger's clothes, hoping neither Anna nor Lady Nessa would catch her wearing them.

"Breakfast," a female voice called, followed by a rapid knock.

Lexi opened the door and took the tray from another pupa girl whose constant bobbing curtsies were upsetting the contents.

"Thank you," Lexi said, moving to close the door again. The girl's imploring eyes grew wide as the door moved, her eager pink lips open to speak. Noticing her expression, Lexi paused. "Was there something else?"

The girl curtsied again. "Forgive me, Your Highness," she mumbled, then peeked up at Lexi through her lashes. Her mouth opened again, then snapped shut, punctuated by a running curtsy as she disappeared down the hall.

Lexi pressed her lips against an amused smile and shut the door. The breakfast was elaborate: delicious pastries, creamy beverages, and eggs prepared every conceivable way. Lexi ate until her stomach hurt, sampling a little of everything and grinning with delight when she discovered something especially good. She entertained the thought of stealing away Lady Nessa's cook to the palace, until she remembered it was no longer her home.

With a slight frown, she strapped on her bag, then spent several minutes fiddling with the window latches until they unfastened. Fully opened, the windows were expansive—just large enough to leap through with wings spread and her legs tucked up beneath her. She sailed out, an excited giggle bubbling out of her throat as she glided over the twilight courtyard. She flew east into town, hoping she could find an open store and make her purchases before Talan woke up in a fury that she had left him. She intended to return, dressed in her purchases for a polite departure from Lady Nessa and Anna, but the thought of leaving Talan and Celus behind was particularly pleasing. She smiled as the orange and pink of the sunrise suffused the sky's rich night blue.

Oakridge was a middling-size town, with several clothing stores. Lexi flew down to the first she saw with light in its windows, then knocked politely at its locked door.

"We're not open yet," a voice called from behind it.

"When do you open?" Lexi called through the door, feeling foolish in the empty street.

"When I finish my breakfast!" The voice was distinctly cross, and Lexi was eyeing another clothing store when a scowling face appeared at the window, evaluated her clothing, the previous night's elaborate coiffure, and her dramatic orange and black wings. The scowl faded into surprise, and the face abruptly disappeared with a series of clicks and sliding locks that accompanied the opening of the door.

"Who are you?" demanded a pug-nosed woman with shrewd eyes.

Lexi fought down the color rising to her cheeks. "Your customer," she replied evenly.

The woman snorted, a smirk twisting up one side of her pursed lips. "Come on, then." She opened the door wide and shuffled out of the way. Lexi glanced down at her, taking in the plain woolen dress, practical shoes, and oddly-shaped brown wings that reminded her of puzzle pieces.

"Are you headed to the Mating Mountain?" the shopkeeper asked, flicking on lights.

"Yes," Lexi answered, glancing around at the dizzying variety of clothing in a multitude of colors.

"And what do you need?"

"Everything."

The woman gave her another little snort. "What size of everything?"

Lexi blushed. "I didn't bring my measurements."

"You don't know what size you are? You *are* a noble, then. Had a personal tailor all your life, I imagine."

Lexi met her gaze, unanswering.

"Ran away in stolen servants' clothes, I expect."

"They're not stolen."

"Well, my *lady*," the shopkeeper said with an exaggerated bow, "how long before your angry parents descend upon me?"

Lexi flinched. "Sorry to have troubled you," she said, turning to leave.

"Wait!" the shopkeeper commanded imperiously. "I rather like your pluck." Moving back to the front door, she drew the locks, then switched off the lights. "Come into the back room." She guided Lexi by the elbow through the maze of displays in the darkened store. Lexi followed with a vague sense of unease. She was contemplating flying back to the front door when the shopkeeper opened a hidden door and pulled her inside, then flipped on the lights. The chilly room was rimmed with boxes, a cluttered desk at its center.

"I'll make you a deal," the shopkeeper offered, crossing her bony arms tightly across her chest. "Tell me who you are and I'll help you—and promptly forget you were ever here."

Lexi considered, smiling faintly at the woman who reminded her so much of Cercy. "Deal. I am the Princess Lexi Monarch."

"Ha! I knew it! Welcome to my shop, Your Highness. I'm Faun." The shopkeeper grinned and bobbed a curtsy. "Who were they forcing you to marry?" she asked pleasantly as she began sifting through boxes and removing clothing. "I'll forget him, too, if you like," Faun offered when Lexi didn't answer.

"Talan Admiral."

Faun scrunched up her face in distaste. "Isn't he the young snob that spends summers with Lady Nessa's grandson?"

Lexi smiled at the description, and nodded when Faun turned to look at her.

"Can't blame you a bit, then," she said, handing Lexi a pile of clothes. "I guessed on your size. I don't carry a lot of fancy things, but I don't imagine that's quite Your Highness' style anyway."

"You are perceptive," Lexi replied, her smile widening.

Faun shrugged. "Any lady who looks as comfortable as you do in men's clothing isn't much of a girly girl. Now, you try those on while I finish my breakfast."

"Thank you, Faun."

"Yep," Faun said, shutting the door behind her.

With a happy grin, Lexi sorted through the clothes, delighted at the prospect of choosing clothing her mother had not designed for her. She quickly discarded all of the reds, choosing instead the dark, subdued hues that her mother never let her wear. She found a full-length mirror behind a stack of boxes and admired herself in the lightweight, comfortable clothing.

"Goodbye, Princess," she said to herself, eagerly removing the plethora of pins that held her hair. When she set down the last pin on one of Faun's empty boxes, she shook her head wildly. Her long, ebony hair was now a riot of temporary curls and crimps. Lexi grinned at her reflection, then started as a brief knock was followed by the door opening.

Faun nodded approvingly, and held out two pairs of water shoes and several bathing suits. "You'll need these, too. The bathing pools are jagged with volcanic rock, and thanks to the new governor, you'll be washing in front of the men." Faun made a clicking sound of disapproval and shut the door behind her.

Lexi held up the bathing suit and blushed. She and Tiger used to swim in a small lake on the south side of the royal grounds, but always in their clothing. Officially, she wasn't allowed to swim at all, as the Queen considered swimming attire "unseemly." Lexi found a high-necked black suit with an attached skirt in the pile. It was ridiculously short, and Lexi's ears burned scarlet when she turned around to see how much of her nether region was exposed by the suit. When Faun knocked, Lexi spun around, pulling awkwardly at the little skirt.

Faun laughed heartily when she saw her. "Not used to bathing suits, are you? You can always bathe in your clothes, it's just not as effective. But seeing as how you're a princess, I'm sure the Governor will arrange a private bath for you."

Lexi shook her head and slowly stood. "I don't want special treatment. I plan to keep my identity a secret."

"Does anybody up there know you?" Faun asked.

"Yes."

"Can you trust them?"

Lexi thought of Van and Limen with an anxious frown. "I don't know."

"If they can't be trusted, then your secret won't last long, especially not with those wings. Who will you claim to be?"

"The Governor's illegitimate sister," Lexi asserted, watching Faun's face carefully for her reaction.

Faun's dark brows drew high into her forehead. "That might actually work. It'll attract a great deal of attention, of course. Is that what you want?"Lexi frowned. "I can't think how to avoid it."

Faun scowled thoughtfully a moment. "Neither can I," she conceded. "Holler when you're finished."

When the door closed behind Faun, Lexi changed into a pair of soft brown pants with a simple navy shirt. Then braided her hair, grateful that Cercy had taught her. She strapped on her bag, gathered up the pile of clothing she had made, and kicked her chosen water shoes across the floor. She fiddled with the handle a moment before Faun drew it open from the other side.

"You're quick," she praised, picking up the shoes Lexi was kicking. "Stay in there while I add this up," she advised, glancing quickly out her front windows where the morning light was streaming in.

Lexi drew out the wad of cash her father had given her, carefully tucking the paper fragment with his name back inside. With a little smile, she hid some cash in a pile of bookkeeping on the desk. Faun appeared at the door a moment later with her purchases wrapped tightly in a fabric bag.

"Here. You can use the bag to keep your clean clothing separated from your dirty," she advised as she handed the receipt to Lexi and set the bag on an box.

Lexi paid her, then drew Tiger's clothes out of her mother's bag to place with her new things.

"You want to keep the servants' clothes?" Faun asked with surprise.

"Yes," Lexi said, hugging them to her chest.

A knowing smile slid across Faun's face. "Perhaps you're going to the mountain to find the owner of the clothes?"

Lexi fought the blush with a quick swallow and soft smile. "He's my best friend," she said simply. "I miss him." Lexi turned away from Faun's perceptive eyes to pack her new purchases into her mother's old bag. It was a tight fit, but it still buckled down.

"Well, I hope it works out for you," Faun huffed as she heaved several large boxes in the back of the room to reveal a door. "This lets out into the alley."

"Thank you, Faun," Lexi said, smiling as she opened the door. "And..."

"I know. I never saw you," Faun said, waving away her concerns.

Lexi grinned back at her, then flew out of the alley. She thought of Tiger, trying to see him through in-season eyes and gauge his attractiveness, but it seemed impossible without smelling him, so she quickly abandoned the effort. She flew east towards Lady Nessa's estate with misgiving. Why was she going back for Talan and untrustworthy Celus? Just to be a polite guest to people who would probably never speak to her again after she married someone they didn't consider to be her social equal? Ridiculous.

"Sorry, Lady Nessa, Anna," she said, as she turned north. "Thank you for your hospitality." She thought of Lady Nessa's message for Van and felt a momentary pang. This would be rather a bad start with his family if she did marry him. She tried the same futile exercise with Van that she tried with Tiger moments before. Van was nice-looking and always spoke pleasantly. However, his close friendship with Talan didn't speak well for him. If only she had left a note! Groaning, Lexi flew back towards the estate, resolved to scribble a quick thank-you note, and disappear again. She flew by her windows, frowning when she saw them closed. Someone knew she had left. She flew over the sprawling house to the stables and landed in the yard. A groomsman was saddling a chestnut mare with an ornate lady's saddle.

"Pardon me," Lexi said, startling him. "Is Anna coming out to ride?"

"Y-yes Your Highness," the groomsman stuttered, knocking his head lightly against the saddle as he bowed.

"Soon?"

"Now, in fact," Anna said, coming around the horse with an amused smile. "Good morning, Your Highness." She took the reins from the groomsman and sent him away with a little toss of her head. "Talan's in a rage. He thinks you have gone off and left him again."

Lexi gave her a polite smile. "I wanted to thank you again for your hospitality, and to say goodbye to you. Is Lady Nessa up yet this morning?"

"Grandmother doesn't sleep well anymore. I believe she's been up for several hours. Shall I take you to her?"

"I wouldn't want to interrupt your ride," Lexi protested.

"Not at all," Anna assured her. "Tinus!" she called, holding out the mare's reins to the groomsman, who trotted over to grab them. Anna took Lexi's arm companionably as they returned to the house. "Talan will be so relieved you haven't left yet. He should be ready to leave now. He promised to find me out riding and say goodbye before he left. Perhaps we should go by his room and relieve his mind?"

Groaning inwardly, Lexi managed another polite smile and a nod.

Anna smiled to herself as she launched into her monologue. "Poor Talan is quite devoted to you, and determined to protect you.

He has already fallen in love with you, I think. I have never seen him so passionate. Imagine, attacking one of the King's flying guard to defend your honor. He has nearly lost his reason over you." Anna laughed confidentially behind her riding glove.

Lexi blinked rapidly. "Did Talan fight with my escort?"

"You didn't know?" Anna asked innocently. "But surely you overheard your departing guardsman explain his companion's lascivious intentions? Naturally, Talan felt it was his duty to handle the matter immediately."

Lexi frowned, irritated that she had not anticipated Talan's reaction nor the way he would interpret Vaden's warning. "Was he injured?"

"Only his lip. That horrid guard actually dared to hit Talan in the mouth! After being assigned to protect him, no less!"

Lexi's frown deepened. "I meant the guardsman."

"Oh." Anna managed to infuse the word with confusion and disapproval. "Well, naturally Talan responded to the insult of being struck, and the guard's wing was broken in the resulting scuffle. I think the guard left town with the other one."

Lexi smoothed her brow, trying to wipe away the anxiety beneath her fingers as Anna knocked at Talan's door.

"What now?" he demanded irritably without opening it.

"Don't be grumpy," Anna chided. "I've brought you a surprise."

Talan yanked the door open, the storm lifting from his brow the moment he saw Lexi. "You didn't leave me," he said.

Anna rolled her eyes. "Come say goodbye to us in Grandmother's sitting room," she called over her shoulder as she walked away.

Talan's soft tone and accompanying scent of hickory and cloves sent a little thrill through Lexi, and she shook it off irritably. His bottom lip was swollen and divided with an open cut down the middle. A little well of pity sprung up in her before she remembered she was angry.

Talan tossed the hair off his forehead without taking his eyes from Lexi's face. He lifted a bulging new bag from the floor and began fastening it. "I sent the steward to do some shopping for me; is that where you went this morning?"

"What happened with Celus?" she demanded abruptly, trying to refocus on her anger.

Talan's brow furrowed, and he looked down at his bag as he fastened the last strap. "You don't need to worry about him. He won't be coming with us."

"Surely that wasn't necessary."

Talan looked up at her, his beautiful eyes darkening with fury. "Trust me, it was."

Lexi stifled a little shiver, unsure if it was the vague threat of Celus or Talan's wrath that had caused it. She trailed slightly behind him as they made their way to Lady Nessa's sitting room. Several times he stopped and offered his hand, but each time she refused it.

"You're still here?!" Lady Nessa demanded when she saw Lexi. "You're wasting time, the both of you. Go marry my grandson, and get him down off that cursed mountain. Go!" she shouted, waving her bejeweled hands emphatically.

"Goodbye, Lady Nessa," Lexi said, furious with herself for thinking a goodbye and thank-you had been necessary. She smiled grimly as Talan piloted her from the room with a hand at her elbow.

Anna jumped up to follow them, her golden tresses buoyant on her shoulders. She took Talan's hand to stop him, then handed him two letters. "Take those to Van, please," she said with a grin. "Grandmother and I were busy this morning."

"I am sure he'll enjoy your tender lectures," Talan teased her.

Anna lightly smacked his arm. "*Mine* is pleasant. I told him to stay there as long as he pleases."

"Of course you did; you want his inheritance," he chided her.

Anna turned up her little nose and smacked him again. "You want his bride," she accused.

"*My* bride," Talan assured her, taking Lexi's hand tightly and walking away.

"Goodbye, Anna," Lexi called back as she tried to release her hand. "Thank you for your hospitality."

"Anytime, Your Highness. It was an honor to have you here."

"What about me?" Talan demanded with mock hurt.

"Goodbye, beast," Anna called with a teasing smile.

Talan growled playfully, and held Lexi's hand tighter.

"Talan," Lexi said quietly as they turned a corner where Anna could no longer see them. "You're hurting my hand."

He released it at once. "I'm sorry, Princess."

Lexi sighed as they stepped out into the garden. "Talan, please go back to the palace."

"No," he said cheerfully, and jumped into the air. "I am your escort, Princess. And I will not shirk this rather pleasant duty," he announced, grinning as he flew around her.

Lexi gave him a martyr's smile as she flew by him. She set a punishing pace to avoid conversation, then scowled with panting annoyance when he endured it far better than she. In three hours, she emptied her canteen and looked down at the dry, empty road beneath them.

"How far is the next city?" she gasped.

"I think," he panted, "there's nothing but Scio between us and the Mating Mountain."

"How much further is Scio?"

He shook his head, freeing little droplets of sweat as his wing beats became uneven and he began to lose altitude.

"Talan? What's the matter?" When he didn't reply, Lexi swooped down and took his hand. "Are you all right?"

Talan's eyes were wide with fear, his mouth still open with labored breathing as he shook his head again.

70

Lexi took his hand in both of hers, struggling to slow his descent as his wings continued their ineffectual, jerky movements. He landed a little too hard, and Lexi had to release his hand quickly to avoid a wing collision. Talan stumbled forward onto his hands and knees next to the road. She landed next to him, breathing heavily.

"Are you okay?" When he didn't answer, Lexi walked around to face him, leaning down to lift his chin when he didn't look up. "What happened? Can you talk?"

Talan wheezed and began to fumble with the buckles of his bag with one hand. Lexi helped him to his knees, then opened his bag herself, and drew out his canteen. She handed it to him, and he drank greedily.

"My wings," he panted, when he finished drinking. "They don't feel right."

Lexi turned away as panic flooded her face, and she struggled to clear her thoughts. Composing herself, she turned back around.

"It's only been four days since your wing birth, so it can't be the end of your season yet. Even the shortest season lasts at least a week. So it must just be physical strain. We'll rest for a while," she assured him.

Talan nodded, struggling to get to his feet, and Lexi quickly helped him.

"How much water do you have?" she asked.

He shook his head. "Not much, but there's a stream that runs near this road." He cocked his head to one side, listening. "I think it's this way," he said, pointing east.

Lexi took her dirty clothing out of her bag, and reached for Talan's canteen.

Talan pulled away, one hand on his canteen. "You're going to leave me?"

"It's faster than walking, and I'm completely out of water."

Talan held out the canteen reluctantly, tightening his grip, instead of releasing it to her. "How do I know you'll come back?"

71

Lexi ground her teeth together. "You think I would leave you here, flightless and without water?"

Talan dropped his head with a look of shame. "No," he mumbled. "But couldn't we walk together?"

Lexi looked into the thick trees that fringed the road. "I don't see a path. We'll tear up our wings trying to get through there." She pulled the canteen away from him, and slipped it into her bag.

"Wait," Talan said, putting a hand on her arm, then looking foolish. "Could you check something for me?"

Lexi waited patiently as Talan struggled with his evident embarrassment.

"Could you tell me…I mean…are my pheromones still working?"

Lexi inhaled, then leaned closer. "Are you signaling?" she asked, her brows drawn together.

Alarm ran across Talan's face. "You can't smell me?"

Lexi stepped close to him, her nose nearly touching the skin of his neck that was still wet with perspiration. She stepped back and looked into his face with such pity that he flinched.

"I am so sorry, Talan," she whispered, her voice catching. "I feel as if I've robbed you."

Talan blinked in disbelief. "This can't be happening. I know my family has a history of short seasons, but surely I can't be setting the new record." Talan clutched at his forehead and began to walk around in a grief-ridden circle. "I'm the first-born son. I'm supposed to inherit, and then my son after me. My son…" Talan stopped walking, and swallowed loudly. "I'm not going to have children," he whispered, "or get married." He laughed bitterly. "At least I got to kiss you."

Lexi walked to him with her arms outstretched, her face stricken. She held him, feeling him tremble in her arms, and hoped desperately that he was not crying. "I'm so sorry," she murmured in his ear. "But maybe it's not what you think. Maybe it's not too late."

"But you still can't smell me?"

Lexi inhaled the salty ripe smell of sweat, but nothing more. "No," she said, holding him a little tighter to cushion the blow.

"And...and you aren't attracted anymore?" he asked tremulously.

Lexi tried to put aside her crushing sense of guilt, and concentrate on his arms wrapped low under her wings, his head close to hers. *Still pleasant*, she thought as he pulled back to look at her, then leaned in to kiss her gently.

"Anything?" he asked, his face a mask of anxiety.

Lexi hesitated a moment. *Not like before*, she thought, but didn't want to tell him.

"Let me try again," he pleaded desperately. He kissed her harder this time, wincing at the pressure on his injured lip, then pulling back in dejection.

She was grateful he was looking down; she couldn't meet his eyes.

"No, no, no," he repeated in quiet anguish. He took one hand from around her waist and held it up against her cheek. This kiss was different. It was long, searching, and strangely insistent. One hand wrapped around the end of her long braid, pulling at it until she tipped her head back, and he kissed her neck. The hand holding her cheek slid down to her collar, tugging at the buttons, and Lexi's eyes flew open. Talan's wings had begun to thrum the air fluidly, and an unmistakable scent filled the air.

She broke away from him, hastily redoing the top two buttons. "You're still in season," she assured him, her body on fire and her mind riddled with suspicion.

"Then I can still have children," he said with relief. "But if I can't fly, this has to be the end of my season." He hesitated, staring steadily at the ground. "Would you reconsider me as a mate?" he asked, barely above a whisper.

The air was thick with his scent now, and it was difficult for Lexi to think straight.

"You said you felt like you had robbed me…that doesn't have to be true," he said, biting at his split lip as he walked towards her.

Lexi watched him, her breath coming at panic speed. Why was saying yes to him always the easy choice? Once again, the thought of Talan as her husband brought the cold, hollow feeling to her chest. She watched apprehensively as his hand reached for her like a tide of confusion about to break over her head. Jumping away from him, she flew.

"I'll be back with the water," she shouted, fleeing from the temptation.

Lexi found the stream quickly and stood on its broad bank, puzzling over the filter she had found attached to Talan's canteen. She scooped it into the water, hoping she was using it correctly. The filter was tiny, and it took a while to fill both canteens. As she worked, she alternated between planning the walk back to Oakridge, and suspecting Talan of deceiving her about his symptoms. On the way back, she flew low over the stream a ways before returning to the road in the hopes that he wouldn't see her coming.

As she approached, she could hear him singing tunelessly to himself as he ran back and forth along a fallen tree trunk, doing flying flips off the ends. Lexi hid behind a tree to watch him. After a minute, he flew straight up, peering stealthily over the tops of the trees in the direction she had flown, then back down to continue his acrobatics.

Trembling with fury and relief, she leaned against the tree and considered her options. She looked longingly at her little pile of dirty laundry, and tapped irritably at his canteen. Talan flew up to peek over the treetops again, his song faltering as he flew back down. He stood on the fallen log and looked uncomfortably into the trees. A little smile played over Lexi's lips.

"Princess?" Talan yelled into the trees. He meandered up and down the log, then yelled again. He walked over to the tree line, peering through the dense undergrowth for a reasonable path. "Lexi?

Are you okay?" Hands on his hips, he paced, muttering to himself. After some creative cursing and rock kicking, Talan gathered up her dirty clothes and stuffed them into his bag. Lexi's smile abruptly vanished. Talan flew up to tree level, scanning for her, then flew towards the stream.

Lexi darted out from her tree, flying low to the ground. She dumped his canteen next to the fallen log, and then hurried up the winding road. She kept low to the zigzagging road for the next hour, flying fast, and munching heavily on the snacks her father had packed for her. Talan would expect her to stop in Scio, but there were other towns around the base of the mountain. Visualizing the map in her mind, she turned east, away from the road, and hoped she had the strength to reach Pine Hollow—the last stop before the mountain on the eastern route—by nightfall. She calculated it would add at least three hours to her trip, but she would be temporarily free of Talan. She grinned at the thought, and wiped the sweat from her eyes. Six hours later, as she skirted the base of the mountain, she realized she had badly miscalculated. Hungry, lost, and exhausted, she landed next to a stream as the light began to fade, the sun well-hidden behind the perpetually snow-capped Mating Mountain. Lexi listened to the soothing rush of the stream and stared down at the white water curving around a jagged rock. The movement in her peripheral vision startled her, and she had already begun to fly when she realized what she was seeing.

Across the stream, a girl lay sprawled out on a bed of bright green grass. Her vivid red hair was wildly tangled and her dark leggings generously powdered with dirt. Pretty blue wings rose and fell with each sleeping breath.

Lexi flew across the stream towards her, landing a comfortable distance away with a purposeful thump. The girl did not stir.

Lexi cleared her throat and took another step towards the sleeping form. "Excuse me," she said, watching with relief as the girl closed her wings and turned her pretty face towards her. "I apologize for waking you," Lexi continued, "but I've lost my way."

"Oh," the girl mumbled sleepily. "Are you going to the Old Castle?"

"Eventually," she answered without hesitation. "Am I close to Pine Hollow?"

The girl rose to her knees and hastily began to brush grass and dirt from her clothes. "No, it's three hours away."

Lexi swallowed. She would have to sleep in the forest.

Looking around, the girl pointed uncertainly to the left of downstream. "I think it's that way. Sorry, I'm not very good with directions," she apologized, her pouty lips pulling down into a frown.

Lexi smiled. "Neither am I. Are you going to the Castle?"

The girl shook her head, and looked at the sky, her forehead wrinkling up in a way that reminded Lexi of a child about to cry. "Just came from there," she murmured absently.

Nearly everyone left the mountain in pairs. A lone female was most likely pregnant and abandoned. "Are you all right?" Lexi asked her gently.

The girl seemed surprised by the question, and tried to pull a dirty hand through her riot of curls. "I don't look it, do I?" she asked, laughing.

Lexi smiled with relief and shook her head. "No."

"I'm okay. I'm just waiting for my husband," the girl assured her, blushing. "I should probably get cleaned up before he gets back," she added, lifting a bedraggled bag from beside her as she stood.

Lexi smiled and turned to go, then hesitated. "Might he know the way?"

"I'm certain he does," the girl replied, her forehead wrinkling up again in that distressed expression, "but I don't know how long you'll have to wait for him."

Had he abandoned her, then? Lexi asked her next question with the same gentle tone she used with her baby nieces. "Where is he?"

"Upstream. He...he can't fly anymore, so my friend is trying to help him down the waterfalls." The girl's eyes filled with tears, but she blinked them back.

Why did she leave him?

The girl must have seen the question in Lexi's face. "I can't really fly anymore either," she admitted.

"I'm sorry. I'll look for them," Lexi promised, her stomach growling loudly as she turned away. Lexi sighed, then turned slowly back around. "I apologize for asking, but do you have any extra food?"

The girl laughed merrily. "No, but you could ask my friend, Cam. Maybe you could even fly with him."

Someone with food who wasn't lost? Lexi smiled. "Is he the friend that's helping your husband?"

The girl nodded cheerfully.

"I'll find them," Lexi reiterated her promise, praying she had enough energy left to fulfill it. "Maybe I can even help," she called back as she flew, knowing there was no better way to thank this girl than to help her husband.

"Thank you," the girl called, the words sounding choked with emotion. "Good luck to you!"

Lexi found the men twenty minutes upstream, walking slowly. One of them leaned heavily on a makeshift walking stick, his rusty, white-streaked wings shuddering behind him at his uneven gait. The other had golden patchwork-patterned wings, and curly dark auburn hair. The latter was telling a story while the former threw back his head with a particularly infectious laugh. Lexi smiled and landed in front of them.

"I was told you gentlemen could use some help," she announced, wishing fervently that she knew the pretty redheaded girl's name.

Both men looked startled, but golden-wings recovered first, his cheeks folding into delightful dimples as his grin spread. "And just who is coming to our rescue?" he asked, the slightest of lisps peppering his speech.

"Raven," Lexi blurted, then nearly laughed out loud.

"Did my wife send you?" the man with the walking stick asked.

Lexi smiled. "Little redhead with blue wings?"

He nodded enthusiastically. "Is she all right?"

"Yes."

"I'm Cam."

Golden-wings stepped forward, and Lexi caught a scent that reminded her of raiding the palace pantry for cookies. She held his hand for a moment, inhaling, and enjoying the memory it invoked. The man with the walking stick cleared his throat as their greeting lingered.

"Oh, right," Cam said, releasing Lexi's hand. "This is Mit. His wings don't work anymore...or his foot," he added with a wry grin. "You want to help me fly him?" Cam asked, openly admiring Lexi's expansive wings.

"I'll try." The ache in Lexi's back was so acute that she found it difficult to concentrate on words. She desperately wanted to lie down, but instead she smiled apologetically. "I'm afraid I need to rest first."

"Of course," Cam said, taking her hand again and glancing quickly around him at the rocky bank rimmed with trees.

"There's a small meadow a few minutes downstream," Lexi suggested, moving her fingers lightly over the callus-roughened palm of his hand.

Cam looked down at Mit's foot. "Might take us a while to get there."

Lexi clenched her jaw against the pain, and smiled reassuringly. "I think I can help fly him that far before I rest." Lexi laughed inwardly at her own assertion; she had no idea if she could fly him at all.

Cam released her hand and looked at Mit. "Running start? Hopping start? Come on, old man, give me something to work with."

Mit laughed good-naturedly. "I'm younger than you are."

Cam's dark eyebrows rose is disbelief. "Really? Does Elissa know that?"

Mit grinned, but didn't answer. "I'll run and jump," he said, hobbling upstream.

"I'd like to see that, grandpa," Cam teased.

"You will," Mit assured him.

"What happened to his foot?" Lexi asked softly.

"He shut an animal trap on it." Cam suppressed a smile, but his dimples only deepened. "He was trying to set it to catch a turkey."

"That sounds painful."

"I'm sure it is," Cam nodded. "He won't let me look at it, though. I think he's afraid I'll tell his wife."

"And would you?"

A self-conscious grin spread across Cam's face. "Probably. Okay, he's turning around. Stand over there," he directed, motioning her back. "When he leaps, fly up, and we'll each grab an arm. It's a real heavy pull at first, but it gets better."

Lexi moved back obediently, imitating Cam's position just as Mit tossed his walking stick and began to run, beating his wings with irregular, futile movements. As he leaped, Lexi flew up and clutched his arm, gasping as she felt the drag of Mit's weight. She spared a quick glance for Cam, whose face was ruddy with exertion. *Just a few minutes*, she assured her aching body as they flew low over the rocky streambed. She was panting heavily as they set Mit down in the little meadow, and she turned away from them, rapidly wiping the new perspiration from her face as she fought to control her breathing.

Cam let out a jubilant whoop, and Mit laughed. "No offense Mit, but that was *way* easier than flying you with Elissa."

Lexi turned around with a pleasant smile. "I'm glad I could help."

Cam yanked a green tarp from his bag and laid it over a patch of tiny blue and white flowers. "Your bed, my lady," he offered with a bow and flourish.

Mit snorted, "The flowers look more comfortable to me." He flung his bag and sprawled across the soft vegetation.

Cam lifted the corner of the tarp and examined the flowers. "Maybe," he conceded. "What do you think, Raven?"

Lexi removed her bag and crawled down onto the tarp with a grateful smile. Cam grinned, and knelt next to her as he fished around in his bag.

"I have some raisins left, if you're hungry," he offered, holding out a little bag.

"Thank you." Lexi forced herself to hold out her hand rather than snatch them out of his.

"You can eat them all," Cam assured her as he unstrapped his bag and knelt beside her.

Lexi fantasized dumping the entire bag into her mouth as she ate the raisins one at a time.

"So, where are you from?" Cam asked.

Lexi swallowed carefully as she thought about her answer. "A little farm in the middle of nowhere."

Cam laughed lightly. "I never would have guessed."

Lexi smiled. "What would you have guessed?"

Cam gave her a dimpled grin. "Princess in a castle."

Lexi choked on a raisin, and began to cough, her wings fluttering.

"Are you all right?" Cam asked, pulling the canteen from his bag and handing it to her.

Lexi took a drink, then coughed some more. "I'm okay." She wiped her watering eyes, then handed the half-eaten bag of raisins back to him, along with his canteen. "I think I'll rest now." Lexi laid her head down on her arms and shut her eyes, hoping to effectively end the conversation. She held still, listening to Cam shuffle around on his grassy bed, the scent of stolen cookies dancing on the air.

"Raven," Cam whispered softly. "Raven, we need to go. It's dark and Mit is worried about Elissa. Can you fly yet?"

Lexi lifted her head groggily, her eyes focusing on thick, dark brows framing even darker eyes. Sighing, she pulled herself up, suppressing a groan. Her muscles had stiffened while she slept and were more painful now, protesting every movement.

"I think so," she answered belatedly.

Mit was up and standing expectantly on one foot, while Cam knelt beside her, offering his hand to help her up. Gratefully, she took it and forced herself to stand.

"Drink a bunch of water," Cam advised, "that always wakes me up."

Sleepily, Lexi obeyed, the cold water chilling her all the way down to her stomach. She shivered.

"You'll warm up as soon as we start flying," Cam encouraged her, lightly touching her arm.

Lexi stowed her canteen and strapped on her bag, peering at the dark woods that surrounded her. "How long did I sleep?"

"Only an hour," Mit said apologetically. "I'm sorry it wasn't longer. My wife hasn't eaten in a while."

"I'll be fine," Lexi assured him, wishing she hadn't asked Elissa for food. "Let's go."

Mit limped to the far side of the meadow while Cam and Lexi lined up at the stream.

"Run like the wind, old man!" Cam hollered with an infectious grin.

It was too dark to see Mit's expression as he hurtled across the meadow and leapt into the air. Lexi's entire back cramped as she beat her wings, but she bit down on her lip and fought through it, catching Mit's arm and fighting to keep him airborne. Lexi and Cam huffed and panted through the strain while Mit concentrated on moving his wings.

"How far downstream is she?" Mit asked.

"Twenty minutes from where I found you," Lexi gasped.

"How much slower are we flying?"

"Don't ask her to do math, Mit! We're trying to tow an anchor here," Cam protested.

Mit laughed shortly. "Sorry." He was silent for several more minutes, straining to see the ground beneath him. "Elissa!" He began to yell at regular intervals, pausing to listen carefully for a response.

Lexi flew on, marveling that her wings were still moving, and promising her body days of sleep in exchange for a little more functioning. She could hear the roar of the big waterfall as they approached it, grateful the ground would fall away soon, and her flying could become nothing more than a gradual fall.

"Elissa!" Mit called again as they went over the falls.

"Mit!" a high-pitched voice called back.

As they drew closer, Lexi could see Elissa splashing around in the stream in complete jubilation.

"You found him!" Elissa shouted, her voice choked with joyful tears. "Thank you! Thank you!"

Lexi watched apprehensively as Elissa leaped up and grabbed Mit, hastily bringing their landing to a clumsy end. She released his arm as Elissa and Mit stumbled, their arms wrapped tightly around each other. Chuckling, Cam reached out and steadied Lexi as they landed on the bank.

"I was so afraid I wouldn't see you again! Does your foot hurt? Come sit down! I made an almost fire," Elissa warbled happily, not pausing long enough for answers.

Cam's chuckle transformed to a booming guffaw as he walked over to light the fire. Lexi turned away from the happy reunion with a smile and joined Cam. Lexi admired the neat little fire pit and makeshift stools that Elissa had arranged during her absence, then sat down. Happy conversation and kissing noises carried up from the water, and Lexi was grateful for the darkness to hide her blush.

"Enthusiastic, isn't she?" Cam commented, smiling.

"We're going hunting," Mit announced loudly. "Might be awhile."

Something in his tone made Lexi's blush deepen as she watched them trip into the woods, laughing as they clung to each other.

"That's okay," Cam called after them, blowing on the now softly glowing fire. "We have snacks." Cam looked away from the fire to give Lexi a dimpled grin as he patted his bag.

"More raisins?" Lexi asked hopefully.

Cam produced the little half-eaten bag with a flourish. "They're yours. And, I have thistle roots," he said, waving long white roots at her. "They look weird, but they taste like potatoes. Mit showed me how to dig them up. Apparently the food is lousy on the mountain, and I need to learn to forage to impress the ladies."

Lexi gave him a tired smile, and gratefully took the food he offered.

"And, since I suspect you are thoroughly exhausted," Cam began, pulling the tarp from his bag and laying it out a short distance from the fire, "your bed."

"Then where will you sleep?" she asked, biting into the strange root.

"There's a lovely little patch of grass right there," Cam replied, pointing to the spot where Elissa had been sleeping earlier.

"I can sleep on the ground."

Cam's mouth twisted up in half a smile, sinking a single dimple into his left cheek. "Have you ever done it before?"

"No," Lexi answered honestly.

"Then it's not happening on my watch."

Lexi smiled, leaning towards the fire as she ate, even though she hadn't stopped sweating from the flight. Her hair and clothing were damp with it, making her feel ripe with the unpleasant smell. She shifted away from Cam, hoping to hide the scent.

"You smell wonderful," Cam said, ducking his head in embarrassment at his own words. "Just in case you were wondering."

"So do you," Lexi said, her voice barely audible as she blushed crimson. She ate the rest of his offerings without speaking as he silently stoked the fire.

"Aren't you going to eat anything?" Lexi asked as she finished.

Cam shrugged. "Mit will catch a rabbit or something."

"Did I eat all your food?" she asked, the sudden realization turning her stomach.

Cam smiled. "I had a big lunch."

"Cam, I'm sorry. I can pay you for it," she offered, opening her bag.

He waved it away. "Farm girls from nowhere should hold onto their cash."

Lexi bit her lip and looked away.

"Don't feel bad about it," he said gently. "That was exactly what I planned to do with the rest of my food."

"Give it to a hungry stranger?"

"No," he said with a droll grin. "Use it to beguile a pretty girl. Did it work?"

Lexi smiled tightly, and looked around them. "Are we far enough up the mountain that the display laws don't apply?"

Cam let out a surprised laugh. "I don't know. What do you have in mind?"

Lexi blushed so deeply she felt compelled to hide her face. "I just meant camping together."

"Well, we have married chaperones," Cam pointed out.

"Who are not here."

"Are you uncomfortable with me? I can camp somewhere else."

"No." Lexi put a hand on his arm to assure him, then let it rest there. "You stay here with your friends. I just need a rest, and then if you could point the way to Pine Hollow, I'll go."

Cam frowned. "That's not a short flight, and I doubt it's easy to find in the dark. Why do you want to go back there?"

"I'm out of food, and I would love to get cleaned up and sleep in a bed tonight." Her hand felt hot where she was touching his arm, and she slid it back self-consciously until he caught it and held it.

"Then I'll come with you."

A swell of warmth and comfort washed through her. "Okay."

Cam grinned. "Then it's settled. We'll sleep until they come back. Then we'll have dinner with them, and afterwards, we'll go."

Lexi stood up, and he held her hand a moment longer, letting her arm brush across his face before he let go. Lexi smoothed down the corner of the tarp that had flipped in the breeze, then laid down with a soft smile on her face and his pleasant scent in her nose. She was asleep in moments.

It was the snoring that woke her up. Closing her wings, she rolled to her side to see Cam asleep on the grass, his mouth wide open and emitting a cacophony of sound. A tanned arm was flung across his forehead, nearly obscuring the dark eyelashes that brushed his cheeks. She shut her eyes again, and folded one arm up over her head to cover her ear.

"I don't think she likes your snoring, Cam," Elissa giggled.

"Maybe the singing frogs were bothering her or the crickets...both terribly annoying sounds," Cam suggested.

"Oh yes, very," Elissa giggled.

"They're the real reason no one camps anymore," Cam asserted sagely.

Mit snorted. "She's awake, you know. Nobody could sleep through your chatter."

Elissa shoved Mit playfully and he teetered on the tree stump.

"No, she's not...is she? Raven? Are you awake?" Cam called quietly.

"Shh, Cam, let her sleep." Elissa gave him a mischievous smile. "The rabbit's not burned yet."

"I'm not burning it," Mit said, tickling her.

Elissa giggled. "You *always* burn it. Charred and flavorless is how I like it, remember?"

"Cam, could you hold this a minute?" Mit asked, passing a roasting stick to him as Elissa shrieked and ran, giggling wildly.

Cam chuckled at Mit's lopsided, hopping gait as he ran after her. "I expect they'll be gone a while. Go back to sleep, Raven."

Lexi's eyes had been open the tiniest of slits, the effort to do so feeling tremendous. At Cam's words, she relaxed again, and sleep overcame her.

When she awoke, there was sunlight on her face. Lexi startled up to her elbows, groaning involuntarily at the pain in her back as she did so. She glanced around her, disoriented.

"Good morning," Elissa greeted her pleasantly as she added more wood to the small fire.

Lexi gingerly pulled up to her knees. "Where's Cam?"

An uncomfortable expression flickered over Elissa's face. "He should be back soon."

"Where did he go?" Lexi asked, wincing as she slowly stood.

Elissa grimaced. "I know you two were going to go together, but you were so tired that you didn't even stir when he left. He figured you'd been flying hard all day, and he'd only flown a few hours, so it just made sense..." Elissa trailed off with an apologetic wince.

"He went to Pine Hollow?"

Elissa nodded, her face stricken. "But he's going to bring you back food, and he would still like to fly with you. Don't be mad at him; he was just playing the hero again. Mit started running a fever last night; his foot is infected. Cam went to Pine Hollow to get him some medication."

"Oh," Lexi said, the irritation draining out of her. "Is Mit okay?"

Elissa shrugged with a small frown. "He says he is, but I think it must hurt a lot. He's wading downstream." She smiled wistfully. "He thinks he's going to catch a fish without a pole or a net. So I'm building up the cooking fire."

The girls exchanged smiles, then Elissa looked down, the lines of worry etched across her forehead.

"I'm sure the medicine will take care of the infection," Lexi said.

Elissa nodded absently and stoked the fire. "Oh, if you want to bathe, there's a good spot just upstream, and I'll keep Mit away. You'll just have to watch for flyovers."

Lexi glanced at the empty, cloudless sky, then upstream.

"A lot of the newly winged follow this stream up the mountain," Elissa explained.

"Thank you for the warning," Lexi said, lifting her bag.

"He really should be back very soon. He left just after midnight."

Lexi nodded and walked upstream. She found the spot where the stream pooled without difficulty, and quickly removed her clothing. She considered slipping on the bathing suit, but the morning chill and icy water guaranteed a washing too short to be worth the change. She rinsed herself speedily, then dressed in warm blue pants and a long-sleeved green shirt. She thought of Cercy as she struggled with the buttons beneath her wings, and again as she washed and braided her hair. A little lump rose in her throat as she realized how completely she had cut off her old life. It was difficult to imagine a scenario in which her mother would ever welcome her home again. Frowning, Lexi returned to the campsite.

Mit and Elissa were giggling over the campfire, their arms entwined around each other.

"He caught one!" Elissa announced triumphantly as Lexi joined them.

"Smashed one," Mit corrected.

"Would you like fish for breakfast?" Elissa asked with a grin.

"Ewww...don't offer her that! Nobody likes fish for breakfast," Cam said, landing next to them with two bags strapped ridiculously to the front of him. "How about a delicious fruit pastry? Or some cinnamon bread?" he asked, pulling them out with a flourish.

Elissa let out a little squeal of delight, and snatched the pastry from his hand. "Were you able to get the medicine?" she asked around her first bite.

"Would I dare come back without it?" Cam asked, drawing out two bottles and a little package from the other bag. "This stuff kills the infection, this one helps the wound heal, and these, obviously, are bandages," he explained as he handed it all to Mit.

"Thank you," Mit said. "Really."

Elissa nodded, swallowing a large mouthful of pastry. "You saved us, Cam."

"Does this mean I get to name your kids or something?" Cam joked.

"They'll all be Cams and Camis," Elissa said, grinning.

Cam held out the loaf of cinnamon bread to Lexi. "Are you mad at me?" he asked in an undertone.

"How could I be? You're the hero," Lexi replied, breaking off a small piece of the bread.

"You still want to fly with me?"

Lexi studied the dark circles under his eyes. "You should rest."

"Are you leaving now? I'm not tired," Cam insisted, removing the second bag and handing it to Elissa, who squealed when she saw what was inside.

"You got me a pie! I've been craving pie," she exclaimed happily, breaking off a piece of the crust and nibbling it.

"I'll be ready to go in just a minute," Cam assured Lexi, hurriedly scooping a pile of clothing into his bag and removing more food. "Can you carry this?" he asked, handing her the loaf of cinnamon bread.

Lexi took the loaf hesitantly.

"Are you two going now?" Elissa asked, her face sad.

"Thank you for sharing your campfire with me," Lexi said. "It was nice to meet you both."

"Thank you so much for helping us, Raven. And Cam, Mit says you and your family can have free dental work for life," Elissa announced with a grin.

"Let's hope I won't need to take you up on that," Cam said, rubbing his hand across his jaw. "You two going to be okay without me?"

Elissa glanced at Mit, who was already applying the medication to his foot. "I think so," she said, smiling. "Mit thinks we can make it to Oak Springs in three or four days, and since I'm an *expert* camper now," she added, her grin widening as Cam snorted, "I can take care of us."

"I still think you two ought to settle in Wallowa," Cam complained.

Elissa hesitated for a moment, then hugged Cam briefly. "Come see us," she said, her eyes filling with tears.

Cam nodded, swallowing as he looked at the ground.

"Thanks again," Mit said, "both of you."

Lexi smiled and leapt into the air. "Goodbye," she called over her shoulder, the sound muffled by her wing beats.

89

Cam caught up to her holding two apples. "Do you have room for these, too? I'd eat them, but then I'd have to vomit."Lexi let out a surprised laugh as she took the apples.

"I figured I should eat as much as I could, so I could give away all the food I carried."

"Planning to beguile more ladies?" Lexi asked, smiling as she tucked the apples into her bag.

"Nah, still working on the first one. But she's resisting me."

"Why do you say that?"

"Well, for one thing, she's not holding my hand," Cam said, holding his out to her.

Lexi glanced at his hand, then shook her head. "Display laws," she explained.

"But they don't apply on the mountain, and since we just flew over the last big waterfall, I think it's official," he argued, his hand still held out to her.

She knew it was irrational, but Lexi didn't want anyone to hold her hand while flying, *ever*. It smacked too much of the restrictions Talan had intended to put on her as his wife and the heavy, winged gowns her mother had given her to ensure she didn't fly at all.

Lexi shook her head again. "No," she said without looking at him.

"Ouch! She really is resisting me. Now what do I do? Cinnamon bread and apples failed...wait! I've got it!" Cam rummaged around in his bag, finally producing a small package. Raisins," he announced in mock triumph as he held them out to her.

Lexi took them with a smile for his antics. "If I eat them, will you expect me to hold your hand?"

Cam nodded. "Of course."

Lexi's smile dissolved as she handed them back.

"What? Your affection can't be bought by shriveled grapes? You really are difficult to beguile."

Lexi laughed.

"Okay," Cam said, poking around in his bag again. "How about nuts? Pastry? Cheese?"

Lexi laughed again, and waved away his offerings.

Cam frowned. "Raven, I know you're hungry. Why won't you eat anything?"

"I had some bread," Lexi answered, hoping he didn't hear her stomach growling.

"A tiny piece. I'm not flying any further until you eat."

"See you at the castle, then," Lexi replied, increasing her speed as he slackened his.

"Are you trying to get away from me?" Cam asked as he caught up to her, his face full of concern.

"No," Lexi said, trying to keep the irritation out of her voice as she stared straight ahead at the slope of the mountain. She reminded herself that she had already forgiven him for going to Pine Hollow without her, so her rising resentment really was unfair. Yet it wouldn't go away.

Cam flew in front of her, catching her eyes and holding them. "Would you rather fly without me?"

"No," she said, trying to fly around him, but he caught her arm. She was irritably yanking it away when his voice stopped her.

"Please," Cam said. "Please tell me what's wrong so I can fix it."

There was such kindness in his tone, it reminded Lexi of her father and filled her eyes with tears. She let him lead her gently to the ground beside the stream, her head turned away as she fought to banish the tears. When she turned to look at him, they were gone.

"Why don't you want to eat any of my food?" he asked in the same gentle tone. "I want to share it with you."

"This food is to attract a mate. You give it with...expectations."

"And you don't wish to raise mine?" he asked, his voice losing its softness.

Lexi could still smell the stolen cookies, and the scent made her sad. "Not...yet."

Cam stared at her thoughtfully, a little muscle in his jaw jumping. "What if I sell some food to you? Would that be better? Or I could take you back to Pine Hollow and you could buy your own."

Lexi opened her bag, and carefully slipped some cash from the outside of the large wad and held it out to him wordlessly as a scrap of paper fluttered to the ground. Cam glanced at the money in her hand, then bent to pick up the fallen paper.

"This is the *King's* signature," he said, looking up at her with confusion. "How did a farm girl from the middle of nowhere get this?"

Lexi snatched it away from him and pressed the cash into his hand. "That's for the bread and apples." She hastily tucked the signature back into her bag as she searched fruitlessly for a plausible explanation. When she looked back up, Cam was staring at her wings in wonder.

"You really are a princess in a castle, aren't you?"

Lexi sighed. "This is a long story and I'm in a hurry. Fly while I tell you," she commanded, jumping into the air.

Cam followed and Lexi spent the next three hours laying out her life and answering his questions, with very few omissions. She blushed deeply as she told him about Talan, feeling guilty all over again.

"I can't believe he pretended his season was ending to try to get you to mate with him! What a cretin!"

Lexi smiled, enjoying his anger, then chastising herself for her enjoyment. "So now you understand why I need to get to the castle first. If he talks to the Governor, who is also my brother-in-law, before I do, he could make things very unpleasant for me."

"What is it you're afraid he'll say?"

Lexi frowned. "I think he might try to convince Limen—the Governor—that we are already married, and I have run away from him."

Cam groaned. "That would be bad. Let's fly faster."

Lexi laughed. "You already look exhausted. Why not stop and rest? We can meet up at the castle for dinner."

"No way," Cam said, shaking his head with dogged determination. "I just met my very first princess, *and* she confided in me. Now I must rescue her from her evil ex-fiancé."

Lexi smiled. "No rescuing necessary; I can rescue myself." Lexi's smile grew thoughtful as the truth of her own words sunk in. She *had* rescued herself from Talan...twice. "But could you please call him something else? I don't like to be reminded how close I came to marrying him."

"Fine," Cam nodded, "evil lying cretin it is."

Lexi laughed. "It's a little long."

"Hmm...it makes a lousy acronym, too. I'll work on it." Cam looked at her curiously a moment until she felt his gaze and turned. "What do I call you?"

"Lexi will be fine."

"Aren't I supposed to address you by your title? Her Masterful Worshipfulness or something?"

Lexi laughed humorlessly. "I don't like titles."

"Why not? You could make everybody call you She Whose Jokes Are Always Funny or Princess of the Perfect Lips," he suggested, then blushed and looked away.

"Titles are barriers; they make people feel separated from you and inferior."

Cam scratched his chin thoughtfully. "So when you get to the castle, you'll tell everyone you're Raven the farm girl?"

"I don't know yet. I need to talk to Limen first."

A look of determination crossed Cam's weary face and he doubled his speed. Lexi caught up to him, panting.

"We're going to get there before the Cretin," he announced, his breath coming fast. "Can you keep this pace?"

"Can *you*?" Lexi panted.

Cam grinned, the dimples sinking deep into his cheeks. "Maybe."

They flew hard for two and a half hours before Cam landed in a little meadow. "Mit said there's a trail somewhere around here that we can follow in, but I don't see it yet," he managed between ragged breaths. Sweat ran down his face as he spoke, and he pulled up his shirt to mop it. "Ready to fly again?" he asked when he had caught his breath.

Lexi shook her head, panting. "We shouldn't arrive together."

"I think we'll get there before the Cretin."

Lexi took a long drink from her mother's cowhide canteen before answering. "I don't want it getting back to my mother that someone helped me get here."

"What if the Cretin is waiting for you?"

"Then I will face him and undo any damage he's done with Limen as best I can." Noting Cam's thoughtful frown, she surprised him by taking his hand. "You can't help me now, but I appreciate that you want to."

Cam stared down at their joined hands for a moment. "Stay with me until we find the trail," he compromised.

"Do you promise you will let me go alone once we find the trail?"

Cam nodded, running a calloused thumb across the back of her petal-soft hand.

"The trail is right there," Lexi said, pointing behind him. She gently pulled her hand free as he turned to look. "Goodbye, Cam, and thank you."

"You already knew where it was!? That's not fair!"

Lexi let out a small laugh as she flew towards the trail. "I am certain we will see each other again."

"Wait!"

Lexi turned and frowned. "You promised."

Cam grimaced. "I know, but..."

"Bye, Cam!" Lexi called over her shoulder, and flew hard for the trail as the overcast sky began to drizzle. By the time the trail finally opened up into the castle courtyard, the drizzle had become a deluge and Lexi was forced to walk, her wings heavy and dripping. The courtyard was deserted, with puddles flooding the gray flagstones while the heavy raindrops plinked off fifty metal tables and stools. Lexi sloshed towards the enormous front doors, the impressive five-story facade little more than a gray blob in the obscuring downpour. She put a hand to one of the ridiculously oversized handles and pushed. A resistant scraping and two inches of give rewarded her efforts. Lexi sighed, folded her sodden wings, then shoved an aching shoulder into the door. The door reluctantly opened with an eery creak and she slid inside. The interior architecture was much like the palace, but the stench coming from the stained tapestries ruined the illusion. Home always smelled of flowers or spices, depending on the season. A couple having a rather intense conversation in the corner looked over irritably as she approached, scowling when they recognized she was about to speak with them.

"I'm sorry to interrupt your conversation. Would you please tell me where I might find the Governor?" Lexi's polite smile faltered when she realized they were both whites. Their heavily-streaked wings had appeared green and gold from across the room, but the background color was clearly white. Lexi took an involuntary step backwards. She had been warned about whites. The hormonal changes associated with wing birth and being in season brought on temporary mental illness in whites: they were perpetually angry and frequently aggressive until their season ended.

The man flicked his lime-streaked wings and fixed steely gray eyes on her. "One floor up, first door on the right." He jerked his platinum head towards the balcony above them as the scent of pine trees caught her nose.

The woman rolled her eyes and tucked her matching platinum hair behind her ears. "*New arrivals* have to check in with the *clerk*," she informed Lexi coldly as she nodded across the room to the first of two doors, both of which stood open.

Lexi gave them both a bland smile and a pleasant "thank you" as she moved to the dark hallway beyond them to hunt for the staircase.

"You can chase her later; we're having a conversation now!" the white-winged girl snapped as she yanked on the man's arm to stop him from following Lexi.

"Fine," he conceded, knocking her hand away.

The remainder of their strident conversation faded into a bristled murmur as Lexi turned into the stairwell. Her riding boots made a soggy slurping noise with each step while her clothing continued to rain down on them. Lexi rung out her braid and wished for a place to change before she met with Limen. Wistfully, she peeked at the mostly dry clothing inside her bag. Frowning, she removed a clinging, wet fragment of cinnamon bread and stuffed it in her mouth just as she reached the top of the stairs. The double doors before her were nearly as grand as the Old Castle's entrance, and reminded her of her father's throne room where he performed wedding sealings. Running her tongue quickly over her teeth, Lexi knocked.

"Check in with the officiant," a gruff voice said through the door.

"No," Lexi answered, then waited as bolts slid, and the door opened an inch.

"All business must be cleared through the officiant."

"This isn't business," Lexi said, drawing herself up to her full height. "Tell Limen I need to see him *now*."

The guard raised bushy eyebrows at her casual use of the Governor's first name, then shut the door and locked it.

Lexi swallowed her rising irritation and listened. Two minutes later, the bolts slid back again and an mischievous face met hers, his eyes lit up with anticipation.

"The *Governor* will see you now," he announced, grinning as he folded his white wings to let her by. He eyed her curiously as he pulled back a curtain that led into the throne room.

The two-story room was decorated in brightly-colored tapestries, giving it a lush feel that combined pleasantly with the scent of fresh orange rind. The Governor sat on a red velvet stool with the heavy ornate framing of a throne behind him. His cranky expression fell away as Lexi approached, and his face paled as his mouth hung open.

"Mona," he gasped, leaping to his feet and taking a few hesitant steps towards her. "How?"

The mistake was easy to understand. Lexi and her sister Mona were nearly identical. Lexi shook her head quickly, liberating more rain from her drenched head.

"No, Limen. Mona is at home with your twin daughters," Lexi said, smiling a little as she thought of her baby nieces. "I'm Lexi," she added, pushing the dripping tendrils back from her face.

Limen let out a huge breath, stealing a guilty glance at a curtain to the right of him. "I apologize, Your Highness. I should have recognized you."

Lexi shook her head. "You could not have expected me, and we hardly know each other well."

Limen nodded his agreement. "Why are you here?"

Lexi stood taller, and steeled her shoulders. "To find a mate."

Limen snorted out a surprised laugh, then his face grew somber. "Weren't there any noblemen in season?"

Sensing the battle before her, Lexi took a deep breath before answering. "Only Talan Admiral."

"And he was not a pheromone match," Limen guessed, nodding sagely. "Fortunately, Lady Nessa's grandson Van is here. Perhaps we can solve this dilemma quickly. Erynnis!"

The curtain to the right of the Governor quickly parted, and a small man with somber brown wings scurried out.

"Get Van," the Governor commanded. "And I know I don't have to remind you that this is *strictly* confidential."

Erynnis dipped low in a menial bow aimed at Lexi, then quickly disappeared behind the curtain.

"Beck, Charis," the Governor called, then waited as the two guards came around the curtained doorway. "That goes for the two of you as well—especially you, Beck," the Governor warned.

The guard, who had let Lexi in, made a face and rolled his eyes, but nodded as he shuffled back behind the curtain.

"May I assume you arrived with little fanfare?" Limen asked, returning his attention to Lexi.

"Yes, but I should warn you that Talan is following me," Lexi said, wondering how much she ought to tell him.

"You were the only in-season noblewoman?" Limen asked, his dark eyebrows arching in surprise.

"No. The Queen commanded him to follow me."

"The only available nobleman, and she made him your escort?" Limen asked, unspoken questions troubling his brow as he stepped closer to her. "What am I missing, Your Highness?"

"The Queen intended us to marry; the king helped me escape."

Laughter danced in the Governor's hazel eyes for a moment before it began to play about his mouth. "You ran away to escape Talan?" he asked, struggling to suppress his amusement.

A small smile crept across Lexi's face.

The Governor cleared his throat several times with a wide smile. "Wait. How did you know the Queen commanded him to follow you?"

Lexi's face sobered. "He caught up to me in Shady Cove."

"And you managed to escape him?" Limen asked, open admiration in his face.

"Not until yesterday," she conceded.

Limen frowned, running a hand over his jaw. "Have you been flying alone with him, then?"

"Only yesterday morning. Before that, we had two of the royal flying guardsmen with us."

Limen's dark eyebrows climbed high into his forehead again. "What happened to them?"

"One's season ended. Talan broke the wing of the other."

Limen frowned. "Your Highness, I apologize that I must ask this, but has Talan…" he hesitated, searching for the right words, "…compromised your honor?"

Lexi's jaw set tightly; she knew how her mother would answer that question. "I have not mated with him."

Limen raised a placating hand. "Of course you haven't." His mouth opened, then he shut it again with a quick shake of his head.

Lexi jumped slightly as a heavy knock sounded at the outer door followed by muffled conversation and angry demands.

She sighed. "Talan is here."

Beck's irate face appeared around the curtain, but Limen interrupted before he could speak. "Just let him in."

The command did not improve Beck's sullen expression, nor did the angry shove Talan gave him on his way in. Talan marched angrily around the curtain, then stopped dead when he saw Lexi. The mottled look of anger on his wet face dissolved into concern as he hurried to her, trying to take her hands in his. Lexi backed away from him warily.

"What happened to you? I worried that you had drowned or gotten lost. I spent most of yesterday looking for you. Are you all right?"

"I am fine," she answered stiffly, trying to ignore the haze of hickory and cloves that tainted the air. She sidestepped the arm Talan tried to slip through hers and retreated behind her brother-in-law.

Talan glared at the Governor, then sniffed. "Limey, you're still in season," he accused, glancing suspiciously between them.

The Governor scowled. "Don't call me that, Talan. I outrank you here."

"Yes," Talan smiled condescendingly. "You're king of the peasant mountain."

"Perhaps you would like to experience the peasant dungeon?" Limen threatened through clenched teeth.

Talan stared him down a moment before his face relaxed into an easy laugh. "You always were a hot-tempered kid, Limey," Talan said, clapping Limen's arm.

Limen knocked his hand away. "Guards," he called. Beck and Charis surged forward, then stood hesitantly behind Talan.

Talan gave them both looks of disdain before he turned back to the Governor. "Come on, Limen, you're not still angry about the deer carcass, are you?"

Limen's jaw worked, a purple hue suffusing his face.

Talan laughed. "You are! It was just a joke, Limen, and it's been three years; let it go."

"I *have*," Limen growled.

"Good. Then why don't you write us out a new marriage certificate, as the last one was...damaged." Talan gave Lexi a chastising smile. "Then we'll be on our way."

"Limen," Lexi said, laying a hand on his arm and turning her back to Talan. "I haven't married him, and I *will not*."

The Governor glanced down at where her hand lay, his muscle tensing beneath it. "Talan," he began.

"She *ought* to marry me, Limen. It's gone that far," Talan asserted, stepping up between her wings and placing a possessive hand on the back of her neck.

Lexi struggled to remove Talan's hand as he brushed up against her wings. Limen's eyes darkened in fury, and he nodded to his guards who quickly separated the two.

"Dungeon," Limen decreed, pulling Lexi to him protectively.

"Don't think I don't know why you're doing this," Talan spat out venomously. "It's just like having Mona back, isn't it? I'll bet she even smells the same!" Talan shouted as the guards dragged him from the room.

Limen released her as soon as the door shut. "It's not...I mean, you don't..."

"It's okay, Limen. Talan would say anything to get what he wants," Lexi assured him, brushing at the wet spots she had left on his white shirt. She glanced surreptitiously at his handsome face, wondering if the orange scent she had caught before was his. She remembered Mona sobbing as she inhaled the scent of Limen's pillow after he left. Her sister had been very attracted to him. Was she? Lexi abruptly abandoned the wet spots on Limen's shirt and stepped back, uncomfortably aware that they were alone.

The awkward silence was broken by a discreet knock from the side door. Limen turned to it, his face a tangle of emotions.

"Yes, Erynnis," he called.

The door opened, and the brown-winged officiant emerged with a polite bow. "Van West, grandson of Lady Nessa," he announced as Van moved around him with a charming smile. He flew towards them, his underwings an intricately-patterned beige camouflage. Halfway across the room, his face registered shock and he landed abruptly, his mouth hanging open.

"Limen, is that...?" he faltered.

The Governor nodded at his officiant, chuckling. "Thank you for your discretion, Erynnis." The officiant simpered at Lexi and disappeared behind the curtained door. "Yes, Van. This is Her Highness, Princess Lexi."

She smoothed her braid self-consciously, uncomfortably aware of her soaked clothing and the puddle beneath her boots. "Hello again, Van." In the three years since she had last seen him, Van had grown much taller, and his long, slightly crooked nose seemed to better fit his face. His blonde hair still clung to his head in ethereal wisps, and Lexi had the sudden desire to touch it.

"Your Highness," Van effused, moving smoothly across the floor to take her hand and kiss it, "you grace the mountain with your presence."

Lexi inhaled the scent emanating from him; it was sweet and familiar. She breathed deeply, trying to recall the memory it stirred. She could see herself hiding in the vegetable garden from Tiger, giggling behind a big, green...ah, yes, cabbage. He smelled like cabbage. Lexi swallowed down her disappointment with a polite smile. *Cabbage is...pleasant*, she thought, then laughed inwardly as she recalled saying the same thing to Talan over Delpha's pea scent.

"Allow me to escort you down to the hot spring pool so you can get out of that wet clothing," Van urged her, a soft smile curving his full lips. Lexi shivered; the thought of a warm bath made her realize how cold she was.

Limen raised a hand to stop them. "Wait! You can't parade the King's daughter around in public. Take her to my private bath, and you will need a guard. Beck!" Limen called, then frowned when he received no answer. "Charis!"

"Both your guards are gone?" Van asked, incredulous.

A smug smile lit Limen's face. "I forgot; I sent them to escort an old friend of yours to the dungeon."

"An old friend of mine? Who?"

"Talan," Limen replied, enjoying Van's reaction.

"Talan's *here*? And you put him in the *dungeon*?" he demanded peevishly.

"He deserved it," Limen assured him.

Van shook his head, sending his wispy hair aflight. "Limen, he's not accustomed to answering to you. To him, you're still the little kid that followed us everywhere."

"Let us hope he adjusts quickly." Limen scowled as he turned to face the officiant's door. "Erynnis! The Princess needs a guard and a lady's maid. Recommendations?" The brown-winged functionary appeared promptly from around the curtain, and opened his mouth to speak.

"Limen," Lexi interrupted. "That's not necessary. I was hoping to blend in here."

Limen lifted one dark eyebrow. "I don't see how that's possible."

Lexi cleared her throat uncomfortably. "I could say I was an illegitimate relative of yours."

Limen and Van were silent for a moment as they exchanged a glance, and Erynnis faded quietly back behind the curtain.

Limen cleared his throat. "We can discuss it after you've had a bath and a warm meal. Are you tired?"

"Limen," she said, placing a hand on his arm again, then pulling it away self-consciously. "I want to decide this now. Van, I would like to speak with Limen alone for a moment."

Van's eyes flicked between them, his brows raised. "Of course," he agreed, "I have a friend to visit anyway. Goodbye, Your Highness," he said, with a short bow and charismatic smile.

Lexi sucked in her breath as he spun around, displaying the beautiful orange and black backside of his wings. As he flew from the room, Lexi's stomach fluttered with him. When she turned back to Limen, he was wearing a knowing smile.

"Shall I arrange the marriage contract with Van while you bathe and rest? Or would you rather wait, and have the Queen handle it?"

Lexi turned quickly to hide her blush. "I would rather...arrange it for myself."

"Are you certain?" Limen asked, his dark eyebrows arching into his forehead. "At least allow me to make your intent clear with him."

"No!" Lexi blushed at her own vehemence, then smiled apologetically at Limen. "I'm sorry. I know you are trying to help, but I want to get to know him first."

"You're not still considering Talan?"

"No, but there are more than two men here, Limen."

Two spots of color brightened Limen's pale cheeks. "Only two potential husbands."

Lexi shook her head decidedly. "He need not be a noble."

Limen's eyes went wide. "Your son will be king; you need a noble husband."

Lexi's smile drew tight. "Perhaps it won't be an issue. In the meantime, I need a name. It doesn't seem wise to use my own."

Limen sighed heavily. "I agree, but I still want you guarded, and you ought to have a lady's maid."

Lexi trilled a little laugh. "Limen, you will give me away with your worrying."

Limen smiled sadly. "There are dangers here, Your Highness, and you have led a very sheltered life."

"Then I'll share a room with someone who hasn't, and she can instruct me."

Limen frowned. "And who will you tell her you are?"

"A farm girl from the middle of nowhere."

Limen laughed.

Lexi waited patiently for him to finish, a fixed smile on her face.

"I'm sorry, Your Highness. What name would you like to use?" Limen asked, laughter still in his voice.

"Raven Viceroy...if you don't mind claiming me as an illegitimate relative."

Limen sobered and turned to finger the intricate woodwork behind his throne. "Your Highness, I already have illegitimate relatives, both siblings and cousins. Two half-brothers and a half-cousin are here on the mountain. They will know you are not related to them as soon as they detect your scent, and they will expose you."

Lexi blinked, wondering if Mona knew about all her illegitimate relatives, then forced her mind back to their conversation. "I don't smell like a Viceroy?"

Limen smiled sadly. "If you were related to us, we wouldn't be able to smell you at all."

"Could we trust them?"

"No," Limen averred, turning away again.

"Then I'll say I'm a Fritillary."

"You will excite suspicion," he predicted, studying the pattern of her wings, so similar to his own.

"Is there a better option?" Lexi asked, hiding her exasperation.

"Yes. Let me negotiate your marriage to Van, and send you home in the morning."

They exchanged a long look, each measuring the tenacity of the other. "A room, please," Lexi said finally.

Limen blew out a long breath. "Erynnis!"

"Yes, Your Excellency?" the officiant asked, stepping out from behind the burgundy curtain.

"Get Eros."

Erynnis dipped another deep bow and disappeared.

"Do you mind if I tell my clerk who you are?" Limen asked her.

"I assume you trust him?"

Limen nodded. "It would be useful to have his advice on a suitable roommate."

Lexi studied the Governor's furrowed forehead, and the discontented set to his mouth as they waited. "Are you happy here, Limen?" she asked, after a long silence.

Limen met her eyes, his expression hardening. "Of course not."

Lexi dropped her eyes. "I'm sorry."

"Why are you sorry, Your Highness? The governorship is the responsibility and curse of my family. When my grandfather died, I was the only one in season. It was fate. No one's fault." Limen turned away, controlling his bitterness with a grimace.

"I meant I was sorry for asking," Lexi said, wanting to touch his arm again and comfort him.

Limen acknowledged her words with a nod as the main doors opened and shut. A gray-haired man with blue wings strode purposefully out from the curtain, Erynnis tagging sulkily at his heels.

"Eros Bl-" Erynnis began.

Eros turned to glare at the officiant until he scurried back to his office door.

Limen smirked. "Eros, this is my sister-in-law, Her Highness, Princess Lexi."

Eros' jaw went slack a moment, then he bowed. "Your Highness," he greeted respectfully.

"The Princess has the novel desire to blend in among the rabble up here. She doesn't wish to have a guard or a maid, so she needs a roommate that can unveil the base natures of the men here, and offer her some protection from them."

"Limen," Lexi reproached softly.

"Your Highness, I am only fulfilling your wishes. Eros, whom do you recommend?"

The corner of Eros' mouth twisted up in an enigmatic smile. "Perhaps two roommates would be more effective than one?"

"That would be acceptable," Lexi assured him.

"Then I recommend the queen's suite," Eros said, his mouth sliding into an ironic slant.

"With your daughter?" Limen asked with some surprise.

"Psyche knows everyone, and the new roommate I assigned her this morning would make a good protector for the Princess."

Limen shrugged thoughtfully and looked at Lexi for approval.

Lexi nodded silently.

"What name shall I put down on the records?" Eros asked.

"Raven Fritillary," Lexi answered confidently.

Eros raised a single eyebrow, but didn't comment.

"I'll be back with a map," Eros promised with a quick bow, leaving just as the guards returned.

"Beck, you are reassigned to guard *Miss Fritillary*," Limen commanded easily, then nodded towards Lexi when Beck looked confused.

Lexi shook her head. "That would be conspicuous."

"Be inconspicuous," Limen directed Beck.

"Limen," Lexi reproached again.

"Your Highness, do not ask me to leave you unprotected here. I will accede to your wishes as much as possible, but having you wander about alone makes me feel ill."

Beck slipped off the faded black shirt that identified him as a guard, removed the club and holster from his waist, then looked up at the Governor for approval.

"Do you have your whistle?" Limen asked.

Beck slipped it from his pants pocket and held it aloft.

"Good. I'll send one of the other guards to relieve you at the dinner hour."

"I can countermand your orders, Limen," Lexi said very softly, so only he would hear.

"And I am asking you not to," he replied in an undertone.

Lexi sighed, watching him.

"Please," he added.

Lexi tore her gaze away from him as Eros returned. He gave the naked-chested Beck a look of contempt, then handed Lexi a crudely drawn map.

"Thank you," she said, turning it to try to orient herself.

Eros nodded in an abbreviated bow, then turned and left.

"Will you join me for dinner?" Limen asked. "I will invite Van."

Lexi smiled as she shook her head. "I have dinner plans."

"With whom?"

"Goodbye, Limen," Lexi finished, leaving the room with a smile. She could hear Beck following behind her, and in the hallway she turned to wait for him.

"I think it will look less odd if we appear to be friends," she suggested, eyeing a group of in-seasons just down the hall.

"And even less odd if we actually are," Beck grinned. "Where to?"

"Queen's suite."

Beck gave a surprised chortle of laughter. "This way," he nodded, still laughing.

Lexi smiled back at him. "Where are you from?"

"Tiny town out east called Sumpter."

"Is anyone else from Sumpter on the mountain?"

"No, Your...er...no," Beck stumbled, flashing an embarrassed grin.

"Are there farms nearby?"

"A few ranches. Too many trees for farming."

Lexi nodded. "Then I'm from a horse ranch just outside of Sumpter."

Beck's grin widened. "Right, the old Fritillary place; and I've known you since you were a child when you used to come into my family's store for candy."

Lexi's smile widened as she looked at the stocky, muscled guard. He was several inches shorter than she, and the shiny bald spot atop his closely-cropped copper head was distracting.

"How many years has it been since we last saw each other?" Lexi asked, fleshing out their story.

"Five. If you didn't look so much like your mother, I might not have recognized you," he lied happily.

"Remind me how you became a guard up here? I know I should recall from the letters you send your mother; she shows them to everyone," Lexi said as a big male with green wings stopped in the hallway to stare at her.

"Tragedy of the whites," Beck quipped. "I got all nasty tempered as soon as I got my wings, and wasn't back to my charming self until my season ended one month later. I picked so many fights during that one month that I got to know the guards pretty well. So when I woke up one morning and couldn't fly anymore, I volunteered to be a guard. Beats kitchen duty," he added with a grin.

"And your siblings?"

"My twin talked a girl into marrying him the first week he was here," Beck said, his voice laced with jealousy and exasperation. "He couldn't keep his temper either, but she didn't seem to mind. He followed her home to Elgin to help run her family's pottery business. Now there's nobody to take over our family store, so my parents will probably just sell it when one of them dies." Beck looked down at the stone floor with a frown.

"I'm sorry, Beck."

"Yeah, that's life. And this is your room. Give me five minutes to go get a shirt, and then I'll be back to show you around," he offered, already moving down the hall.

"Thanks, Beck," Lexi called. "Good to see you again."

Lexi knocked, waited a moment, then opened the door. A petite blonde with blue gray wings jerked around to stare at her, her face lined with sleep.

"Who are you?" she demanded, squinting at Lexi over her wings.

"Your new roommate," Lexi replied, shutting the door behind her and surveying the room. A single solar lantern hung from the high ceiling casting feeble amber light. At the far end of the suite, large double doors were closed to invading daylight with rugs stuffed untidily beneath them. The stench of mildew wafted up from them, freshly damp from the rain. A wrought iron table with three matching stools stood near the hallway door, and five beds were evenly spaced across the long room. Steady snoring was coming from the bed nearest the balcony doors, a large blonde with creamy black-striped wings the obvious source.

"Fabulous. Another giantess," the blue-winged girl quipped, and dropped her head back onto her pillow.

Lexi eyed the three empty beds between the sleeping girls, and selected the one in the center. Unbuckling her bag, she dropped it onto the floor and stripped off her wet clothing. The room felt chilly, and she shivered as she changed into her bathing suit. She briefly considered pulling her wet clothes back on over it, but they felt so cold when she lifted them from the floor that she quickly changed her mind. Frowning, she pulled on her last clean shirt and walked to a full-length mirror near the double doors. One look at her long, exposed legs and she returned to her bag to slip on her dirty brown pants.

A snort of disgust sounded from the petite blonde. "You can't wear those filthy things in the water. So unless you're trying to allure all the men by undressing in public, just go in your suit."

Lexi fought down the flush that rose to her cheeks, and stepped back out of her pants. She started to unbutton her blue top, then moved back to the mirror uncertainly.

"If you don't have any clean pants, what are you going to wear after your bath?" the blue-winged girl asked, rising up onto her elbow.

Lexi frowned. "That's a good question. Will someone launder my clothes while I bathe?"

The blue-winged girl laughed. "You can drop them off at the laundry, but they probably won't wash them until tomorrow, and they won't be dry until tomorrow night. Guess you'd better get comfortable with wearing that bathing suit."

Lexi's cheeks flamed and she turned away to hide them. Was it too late to ask Limen for a lady's maid? Frowning, she unbuttoned her shirt and hung it up on one of the hooks next to her bed, then hung her canteen from another. Returning to her bag, she removed the now empty sack that had held her new clothes and stuffed it with dirty laundry. With her last handful of clothing, she sent a chunk of cinnamon bread tumbling across the flagstones. Groaning inwardly, she retrieved it, then held it up to the weak light while debating if it was still worth eating.

The blue-winged blonde was up on her knees in a moment. "Are you sharing?" she asked, eyeing the bread.

"It fell on the floor."

"I don't care," the blonde said, her hand outstretched.

Lexi's eyebrows rose as she gave her the bread. *Perhaps Celus hadn't been exaggerating about the lack of good food.* "Are you Psyche?"

"My dad been singing my virtues again?"

"I'm Raven," Lexi announced, ignoring the question.

"Nice to meet you," Psyche mumbled insincerely around a mouthful of bread.

"Likewise." Lexi kept her face carefully blank as she returned her dirty laundry to her mother's bag and headed for the door.

"How'd you get the big bruise on your arm?"

Lexi covered it with her hand self-consciously and turned back around. "Just a little riding accident."

Psyche's eyes narrowed shrewdly. "Wear the shirt."

Lexi looked down at the bruise that circled her upper left arm in the shape of a hand. The edges had turned a sickly yellow while the center still bloomed dramatic purples and blues. The bruises on her knees could almost be mistaken for shadow beneath knobby kneecaps, but her arm was startling.

"Or come up with a much better story," Psyche directed as she returned to her pillow, her wings again hiding her face.

With a small frown, Lexi walked back to the head of her bed and slipped the blue shirt off the hook. Buttoning it quickly, she opened the door and slipped out into the hallway.

Beck gave her a friendly grin. "To the hot spring pool?"

Lexi returned his smile. "Yes."

Beck nodded and began to walk down the dimly-lit stone hall as Lexi kept pace with him. "Did you meet Psyche?"

"Yes," Lexi answered with a carefully neutral voice as she examined the odd lanterns that lined the walls.

"She's a fiery little thing. Did you know she's attacked her dad twice? Got dungeon time for it."

"Are they reconciled now?" Lexi asked.

"Well, she hasn't attacked him for quite a while, but I'm pretty certain she still hates him. Most of Eros' kids do. Most every time one of his sons shows up on the mountain, Eros is blowing his whistle for the guards to come rescue him from his angry offspring." Beck stopped his narrative to chortle to himself. "But Psyche's the only time he ever blew it over a daughter."

"How many children does Eros have?"

"Thirty-seven. The old devil seduced *fifteen* women in his day. Everybody knows because he holds the record," Beck explained, his voice frankly disapproving. "He might have seduced more if Psyche's mom hadn't broken his wing." Beck laughed to himself. "Like mother like daughter."

Lexi pressed her lips together and changed the subject. "Is there a way to get my clothes laundered quickly?"

Beck raised his ruddy eyebrows. "How quickly?"

"By the end of my bath?" Lexi asked, anticipating his response with a slight frown.

Beck laughed heartily. "Maybe if I told them who you are, but they'd still have to drip dry...no fancy equipment up here. Are you out of clean clothes?"

Lexi nodded.

Beck looked over at her with a thoughtful frown. "I may be able to borrow some for you. Did you want to stop at the laundry now?" He paused in front of a propped-open door where women bustled around steaming vats, hauling sopping clothes at the end of flat sticks.

Lexi opened her pack and retrieved her shopping bag, now filled with dirty laundry.

"Let me," Beck said, taking the bag from her. "You wait here." Beck's white wings bounced happily behind him as he disappeared into the overheated room.

One of the laundresses gave Lexi a sour look. "Like to stand around and watch the unfortunate, do you?"

Averting her gaze, Lexi walked a short distance away until the laundress snorted and returned to her task.

Beck reemerged with his hands hidden behind his back. "The laundry mistress likes me. She said she'd get to it sometime today. They'll be dry in the morning. And she let me take something from the unclaimed pile for today." Beck held up a faded, long, yellow dress with a shabby lace collar and short sleeves.

"Thank you." Lexi hid her distaste behind a grateful smile as she tucked it into her pack.

"It reminded me of the kind your mom always wears," he added, winking, "and it will cover those knees." He nodded at her bruises.

Lexi shifted her bag to hang in front of them as she gave Beck a polite smile. She let him prattle their way to the pool, enjoying the monologue. Beck hesitated outside the door.

"Haven't been in there in eight months."

"Will it attract attention if you go in there now?" Lexi asked.

Beck made a face. "It won't be *inconspicuous*. I can take you to the Governor's bath instead, but we'd need to get the key from his steward."

"I'll take her in," Van offered, landing beside Lexi and letting his long fingers brush her arm.

Beck considered for a moment before he nodded, then extracted the whistle from his pocket and held it out to Lexi. "Want my whistle?"

113

Van shook his head. "We won't need it." His caressing fingers found her hand and lightly grasped it as he opened the door.

Lexi's hand tingled at his touch, the cabbage scent seeming more pleasant than before. The room was surprisingly warm and stank of sulphur. A large pool with bright green water dominated the space, with little trails ringing its rocky edges. Protrusions from the floor that looked like broken stalagmites were cluttered with clothing and bags. Their owners crowded the pool with lively conversation, and the occasional shout bounced off the water in strange echoes. Van walked her the length of the room, leading her to a small empty space of water. He released her hand to remove his shirt, then slid off his pants. Lexi looked away in startled discomfort, realizing for the first time that some of the bathers were naked. She could hear Van stepping into the water, and her face flushed with embarrassment as she carefully averted her gaze. Letting out a ragged breath, Lexi steeled her expression and set her bag on one of the strange blunted stalagmites. Removing shampoo and soap, she turned back to Van, grateful that the semi-opaque water hid him from the mid-chest down.

"You're going to wet your shirt?" Van asked as she took a first step into the pool.

Lexi hesitated, then decided it was better to expose her bruise for a few minutes now than to expose it all night in the yellow dress. Handing Van her soap and shampoo, she turned away and unbuttoned her shirt quickly, remembering Psyche's words about the allure of undressing in public. Sliding it off, she tucked it quickly back into her bag, then hurried into the water. She winced as the water bent her wings and forced her to slow down.

"That's a bad bruise," Van commented, gently touching Lexi's arm beneath the surface of the water.

"Talan didn't tell you?" Lexi asked, moving her arm out of his reach.

"*Talan* did that?" Van's face was incredulous.

Lexi swallowed uncomfortably before meeting his eyes. "He thought I was a servant. He pulled me off my horse."

114

Van let out a low whistle. "No wonder you won't have him."

Ignoring his comment, Lexi unwound her braid. "What *did* he tell you?"

Van ran his fingers through her long hair as it floated on the surface of the water. "That my grandmother approves of you," he replied, his large mouth twisting up into a v-shaped grin.

Lexi suppressed a groan and dipped her head under the water, keeping her eyes tightly shut. When she opened them, Van had moved up close to her, tentatively sliding a hand around her waist.

"Shampoo?" Lexi asked, her voice sounding deceptively calm as tingles ran up and down her spine from his gentle caress on her lower back.

Van retrieved the shampoo without releasing her, and her hands trembled as she poured the shampoo into her hand.

"You are making me uncomfortable," Lexi reproved him.

Van flashed her a charming grin and leaned in to whisper in her ear. "This is how I negotiate my own marriage contract."

Lexi groaned inwardly, deploring Limen's lack of discretion. She was still searching for an appropriate reply when something splashed into the water beside them, quickly followed by another splash. Van's clothes were slowly sinking into the emerald water.

"Dina," Van chided, quickly exiting the water to lead a furious brunette away.

Lexi stared after the brunette's beautiful pink and blue wings, at the same time relieved to see that Van was still wearing underwear. They stopped near the door, Dina yanking her elbow from Van's grasp and casting a venomous glance back at Lexi. Dina gestured angrily, her pink lips moved rapidly, but Lexi couldn't make out her words. Turning away, Lexi lifted Van's clothes from the water and laid them near the path. She returned to washing her hair, resisting the temptation to watch the argument. As others began to notice the altercation, a hush fell over the room which made Dina's invective audible.

"Fine! Then go tell her I'm your mate! Walk over with me right now and tell her!" Dina yelled, then let out a noise of disgust at Van's soothing reply. "That's what I thought, you..." Dina muttered a string of obscenities, then spun on her pink slipper and stalked from the room. The conversations in the pool abruptly resumed with an amused tone, everyone commenting at once.

Lexi folded her lips tightly as her vision of bringing Van home and pleasing her mother evaporated. Shaking her head slightly, she submerged to rinse her hair. When she came up, cabbage scent met her nose, and Lexi was tempted to keep her eyes shut. Soft fingers pushed a tendril of hair back from her face, and Lexi leapt backwards, bumping the wings of a man behind her.

"Hey, watch it!" the man growled without taking his eyes off the girl in front of him.

Lexi murmured an apology, and dragged her eyes to Van.

Van gave her a once-charming smile. "Sorry about that. We had a little misunderstanding."

"Oh?" Lexi was no longer interested in the lies she knew he would tell.

"She has feelings for me I can't return. I try to be kind to her, but she's become so demanding...even delusional." He shook his head sadly. "I wish I knew a way to truly help her. I'm afraid my kindness has given her the wrong impression."

Lexi washed herself carefully, letting her eyes travel around the room. It was unpleasant to listen to Van's genuine tone as he lied, but more so to watch the face she had thought so charming sully itself with false expressions. She groaned inwardly that Limen had obviously told him of her interest, and hoped he would be easier to repel than Talan.

"What will you do?" Lexi asked as she stepped out of the water.

Van followed her out, touching her back lightly. "Tell her I'm marrying you," he grinned.

Lexi suppressed her rising irritation with slow, deliberate movements as she repacked her bag before turning to face him. "Van..." she began.

Van's grin faded quickly. "I'm sorry. That was presumptuous," he interrupted. "Forgive me."

His repentant expression seemed so sincere and sorrowful that Lexi doubted for a moment, caught up in his beautiful green eyes.

"I would like to spend more time with you. May I escort you to your room?" Van asked, taking her hand between his, his long bony fingers pressing hers gently.

Lexi exhaled slowly as she removed her hand from his grasp. "There's a guard waiting for me outside. Two escorts will look odd."

"I can send him away," Van suggested.

"So can I, but I'm not going to." Lexi summoned an artificial smile before she turned and walked away. "Goodbye, Van."

Near the door, Cam intercepted her path, dripping heavily in his bathing shorts, his eyebrows arched high in question. Lexi grinned.

"Hello, Cam."

Cam nodded behind her where Van stood watching them. "Is that the Cretin?"

Lexi squelched a soft laugh. "No, that's his best friend."

"Is he any better?" Cam asked, the heavy shadows beneath his dark lashes looking pitiable.

Lexi shook her head slightly. "Probably not."

Cam's features settled into a soft scowl. "He's coming."

Lexi sighed and edged around him.

"You want me to stop him?" Cam asked as she passed him.

A curious smile stole over Lexi's face. "No," she decided, reaching back to take Cam's hand and pull him along with her.

"I could make him leave you alone," Cam insisted, eyeing Van's tall, lanky frame.

Lexi glanced back at Cam, eyeing the tightly-defined muscles of his chest and stomach as she pulled him through the door. "Yes, you *could*, but you're not going to."

Beck jerked out of his awkward strolling as he saw them, alarm rising in his face upon seeing Cam, but cooling again as his gaze settled on their entwined hands.

"Didn't you go in with somebody else?" Beck teased as they approached him.

"Beck, take Cam back to his room, and make sure he stays there. He needs to rest," Lexi ordered, shaking her head pleasantly when both men protested.

"What? I'm guarding *him* now? I mean..." Beck faltered, recognizing his error.

Lexi smiled. "He knows who I am."

"Yes, and *he* doesn't want to rest," Cam asserted.

Lexi gave him a patient smile. "You're exhausted," she told Cam, giving his hand a squeeze. "I want you to sleep." Releasing his hand, she pushed him along to Beck, who regarded her with a sulky expression. "I'll make sure Limen knows you were following my orders," she assured Beck.

Smelling cabbage, Lexi spun around. "Van, go put your clothes on. I'll talk to you later," she said dismissively, heading down the hallway in the direction she hoped her room lay.

Van stood dripping in the hallway, a startled yet obedient expression on his face. "Meet me for dinner?" he called after her.

"I have plans," Lexi answered without turning. A look of satisfaction flitted across her face as she heard the pool door shut behind her.

Chapter Seven

Psyche groaned when Lexi opened the door, flipping one wing closed to glare at Lexi. "Are you going to do this all afternoon?" she demanded. "I'm trying to sleep."

Lexi took a long breath before answering, her face carefully blank. "I haven't decided my schedule as yet," she quipped, hesitant to change while Psyche stared at her.

"Lovely. You're making a puddle on the floor," Psyche groused, dropping her wing to cover her face.

Lexi took another long breath as she began to change. *Perhaps roommates had been a bad idea.* She cast a glance at the slumbering form on the other side of the room. Peaceful snores kept time with the slow rise and fall of the creamy, black-barred wings. The heavy patter of rainfall hit the balcony just beyond and seeped into the pungent, mildewed rugs beneath the doors. Lexi breathed through her mouth as she pulled on the yellow dress, hating it even before she stepped in front of the mirror.

Psyche snorted, lifting her wing just high enough to get a good look at the dress. "Unclaimed laundry?"

"Yes," Lexi answered, frowning as she buttoned the blue shirt over the top of the dress, futilely attempting to make the lace collar and puffed sleeves sit flat beneath it.

Psyche erupted in a dry laugh, her blue wings shaking with mirth. "The laundry mistress only gives away the most hideous clothing. That thing is only fit for rags."

"I agree with you, but I haven't anything else to wear."

"Rip off the sleeves and collar, then put the shirt back over it unbuttoned and tie it in front," Psyche directed, flopping her head into her pillow and muffling the last couple of words.

Lexi removed her shirt and stared at the dress for a moment before ripping off a sleeve. A slow grin spread across her face at the satisfying sound. She reached for the other sleeve and tore it away.

Her other roommate lurched up, mid-snore, to stare at her. "What are you doing to your dress?" she asked in sleep-dampened horror.

"I'm sorry to wake you," Lexi said smoothly as she yanked at the lace collar.

"Don't!" the girl interceded, leaping from her bed, her perfectly-tanned skin paling.

Lexi paused as the girl approached her. "I don't like the lace," she explained.

"I do! Can I have it?" the girl asked, her soft blue eyes never leaving Lexi's collar.

"The lace? Yes. I just need to get it off."

"I'll do it," the girl offered, retrieving a tiny pair of scissors from her bag that looked dwarfed in her calloused hands. At Lexi's nod of permission, she snipped at the thread that attached the lace, then unraveled the seam. Holding her breath, she gently detached the lace undamaged and let out a great sigh.

"My mom would love this," she said reverently, folding the lace and stowing it in her bag with her scissors. "I'm Clodi," the girl announced, her pretty face bright with enthusiasm. "What's your name?"

"Raven," Lexi answered, tying the shirt over the modified dress and nodding at her appearance.

"You're as tall as I am!" Clodi chirped happily. "Maybe we can share clothes."

Lexi glanced quickly at Clodi's solidly-built figure. "Maybe," she said, politely.

"Could I wear that sometime?" she asked, nodding at Lexi's clothing as she quietly collected the discarded sleeves from the floor and tucked them into her bag.

Lexi's eyes traveled over the men's clothing that Clodi wore, the fabric and buttons straining at her curves.

"Brother's hand-me-downs," Clodi explained, her already rosy cheeks warming to a deeper blush. "He's a minute younger than me, but he's always been bigger, and we didn't have a lot of money for clothes."

"After today, the dress is yours," Lexi assured her.

Clodi hugged her with a delighted giggle. "We're going to be just like sisters!"

Psyche covered her ears with a noise of exasperation.

"Sorry, Psyche!" Clodi shouted to be heard past Psyche's futile hand barriers. "She's just a little grumpy because she's tired," Clodi explained in a loud whisper. "But you can be our sister, too!" she shouted again, beaming at Psyche's twitching wings.

Hiding her amusement, Lexi gave Clodi a warm smile as she moved out of reach. "Thank you for making me feel so welcome, Clodi."

Clodi waved her calloused hand dismissively. "Of course! We're sisters now!" she declared grinning.

Lexi nodded uncomfortably as she looked down at her bag, then picked it up. "I need to go now, Clodi, but it was nice meeting you."

"I could go with you," Clodi suggested. "I'm wide awake now. We should explore, have some fun. They give tours here, you know. Want to take one?"

"Perhaps later; I have something I need to do," Lexi explained, backing towards the door.

"But you'll be back before dinner?"

"I think so," Lexi replied, opening the door.

"Can we go on a tour then?" Clodi asked, stepping towards her.

"If I'm back." Lexi felt a pang of guilt as some of the light went out of Clodi's pretty face. "But I should be," she added hastily, gratified by the bright smile that returned. "See you then," she said, hurrying out the door and shutting it quickly.

Lexi had flown halfway down the corridor before she heard the door open behind her.

"You promise?" Clodi leaned out to ask.

Lexi winced slightly. "If I'm back," she called without turning. *Roommates had been a bad idea.* Frowning slightly, she increased her speed, deftly dodging a few solitary men and two nervous, tittering girls as she flew through the stone-lined halls. Landing, she glanced quickly both directions before she stepped into the officiant's small office.

Erynnis sat behind his desk, frowning at the page in front of him while his wings twitched.

"Erynnis," Lexi said, "May I go in?"

"Of course!" Erynnis exclaimed, jumping up with an obsequious flourish that knocked over his stool. He stumbled across it as he moved to open the door that adjoined his office with the Governor's. A blush rose to his pale cheeks as she passed him.

Limen was irritably pacing around the room when she entered, and Lexi softly cleared her throat to attract his attention. She watched his eyes flick over the length of her then travel back to her face with an expression that made her uncomfortable.

She quickly drew the wad of cash and her father's signature from the outer pocket of her bag. "Could you store this some place safe? My father gave me too much, and I don't want to risk my roommates finding it."

Limen crossed to her, touching her fingers as he took the bundle from her hand. "Of course. How much is it?"

Lexi gave him an embarrassed smile. "I haven't counted it."

Limen unwound it to count the money, then held up the slip of paper she had tucked inside. "The King's signature?"

Unable to stop the color rising from her cheeks, Lexi met his eyes. "Could you store that, too?"

Limen flipped it over, examining the grain of the paper. "From a marriage certificate?"

Lexi swallowed her panic as she watched the warring emotions on his face. "I didn't sign it, Limen. There was no ceremony. Talan brought it when he followed me."

"But your father signed it," he said stiffly, still holding it out.

"Limen, my father is the one who helped me escape. He got me this bag and he distracted Talan so I could leave." Lexi let out her breath unevenly. "Even Talan admitted we weren't married."

"Why would he help you get away from Talan, and then sign your marriage certificate?"

Lexi's eyes were pleading as she tried to take the signature from his fingers. "You've met my mother, Limen. Do you really need to ask?"

Limen slowly relaxed his fingers, and let her take the scrap of paper from him. "Will she accept your marriage to Van?"

Lexi stared down at the signature in her hand. "I doubt I'll be marrying Van."

"Why not? He wants to marry you."

"I think Van already has a mate," Lexi replied without meeting his gaze.

"I'm sure that's just a rumor," Limen soothed.

"No, I saw her. Her name is Dina."

Limen stared down at the money in his hand, thumbing through it as he counted. "Did Van say she was his mate?"

Lexi's mouth tightened. "No," she admitted.

"Then don't believe it," he said easily, and pointed to the scrap of paper in her hand. "Do you still want me to store that?"

Lexi held it for a moment longer, then placed it in his outstretched hand with a nod.

"Erynnis!" Limen yelled, winding the money tightly around the little scrap of paper before handing it over to his officiant. "Put that in the safe," he directed. "And tell Beck to come in here."

"You wish me to locate Beck?" Erynnis asked politely.

"He isn't in there," Lexi explained quickly. "I sent him on an errand."

Erynnis disappeared as Limen frowned deeply. "He is your protection here. You need to keep him with you."

Lexi gave him a tight smile. "Thank you for you concern, Limen, and for storing that for me. I need to go now."

"Take Charis with you until Beck comes back."

Lexi sighed. "No, but thank you."

"Then I will escort you myself," he declared, following her towards Erynnis' office.

Lexi turned abruptly and stopped him with a hand to his chest. "I'll never be able to explain that. Raven Fritillary does not know the Governor."

"Then let me get Van."

"Stop," she ordered, authority in her tone.

"I'm the Governor," he began petulantly.

Lexi raised a single eyebrow and waited for him to realize his mistake. Limen took a big breath, then closed his mouth, a sheepish expression softening his features.

"Sorry. Habit," he explained. "I'm just trying to keep you safe." He looked down at her hand on his chest and covered it with his own.

"I know that, Limen." She slid her hand out and walked away. "But let my anonymity protect me. When I need help, I'll ask."

Limen's sigh was heavy behind her. "It won't be enough. There are men here that will prey on you, regardless of who you are."

Lexi turned back around at the curtain that hid Erynnis' door. "Tell me who they are, and I'll avoid them."

Limen's hands tightened into fists at his sides. "I don't even *know* all of them! A new one arrives every day. Can't you just marry Van and go home?"

"No," Lexi answered, slipping behind the curtain and through the officiant's door. Erynnis sat uneasily at his desk, quickly dropping his expectant gaze as she walked through the room. "Thank you, Erynnis," she murmured, shutting the door behind her before he could reply. She gazed sourly at the stone wall a moment before hurrying down to the clerk's office near the entrance.

Eros didn't look up when she entered, his voice a mindless droning. "Name?"

"Could you tell me where Tiger Swallowtail's room is?" Lexi asked, annoyed that her heart was suddenly pounding.

Eros glanced up sharply and gave her a deferential nod. "One moment, Miss Fritillary," he responded, rifling through his records. "He has the room just above yours: 415."

"Thank you." Lexi hurried away to the swift staccato of her heartbeats. She passed her bag from hand to hand as she flew up the stairs, swinging it into the face of a man walking down. He clutched the bag reflexively to stop it from careening into his wings and she landed awkwardly beside him.

"I'm so sorry! Are you hurt?"

He slowly lowered her bag to reveal dusky brown hair slung carelessly across his forehead and intense brown eyes that gave her careful evaluation. A sharp nutty scent punctuated the air, both repellent and alluring in its intensity. Wordlessly, he held out her bag to her, his mouth an unreadable line.

Lexi reached out to take it, fighting the slow blush that crept up her neck, but he did not release the bag to her. He flicked his wings, drawing attention to the wide, sky-blue swathes that ran the length of his black wings, then slid one hand off the bag to cover hers. His hand was soft and uncalloused with long, agile fingers that gently caressed her wrist.

"I'm Nireus," he announced, his bottom lip seeming to roll into a pout when he spoke.

"Raven," she said evenly, wondering why she wasn't yanking her hand away or moving at all.

"I'll carry it for you," he offered, taking the bag from her, and turning to face up the stairs. "Where are we going?" he asked, taking her hand.

Despite her efforts, the blush spread across her cheeks. "To visit a friend."

"Are you sure?" he asked, caressing the back of her hand with his thumb. It was odd how natural it felt for him to touch her, like returning to a pleasant habit. "We could go dancing."

If she weren't so eager to see Tiger, she would have succumbed. "Later, perhaps?"

Annoyance flickered through his dark eyes as his mouth pulled into a pleasant smile, and he began to climb the steps. "And who is your friend?"

Lexi swallowed as she tried to fabricate a plausible explanation for Raven Fritillary being friends with Tiger, and failed.

"Van West," she substituted, marking the sudden rise of long, arched brows at the name.

"And how do you know him?"

"We met today at the pool," she lied fluidly.

Nireus stopped at the top of the stairs and turned to face her, drawing her closer by pulling the hand he held behind him. "Then I'm in time to save you."

Lexi turned up her face to his with a bemused expression. "Save me?"

Nireus nodded, his large eyes steady on hers. "Van already has a mate, and she's not even his first."

Lexi swallowed, a long icicle of humiliation and fury sinking to her belly. "How do you know?"

Nireus gave a tight little shrug, his shoulders remaining tense. "Common knowledge. I doubt Dina will be his last."

Lexi looked down, taking a moment to compose her face. Nireus set her bag against the wall, and ran a hand along her jaw to lift her chin. "Dance with me now?"

Lexi nodded. "Just let me drop my bag. My room is down that hall," she said, pointing back down the stairs. He released her chin and lifted her bag again, letting her guide him. At the door, she took her bag from him with a smile, and slipped her hand out of his to open the door.

"You came back!" Clodi crowed happily, as Psyche groaned and covered her ears. "Are you ready for our tour?"

"Not just yet," Lexi said, stowing her bag and sliding back out the door.

"Where are you going now?" Clodi asked, following her out into the corridor.

Nireus smiled with only one side of his mouth as he took Lexi's hand. "We're going dancing."

"Can I come, too?" Clodi asked, her wide blue eyes mournful in their pleading.

"Sure," he drawled, nodding tolerantly while he narrowed his eyes at the wall.

Clodi gave a low squeal and shut the door behind her. Lexi glanced at Nireus' face, but he stared straight ahead, his expression blank as they walked.

"They have a dance every year back home, and my dad always dances with me, and sometimes my brother, but I guess it's different if you can fly," Clodi babbled as she closed her wings to walk alongside them.

An insincere smile curved Nireus' mouth. "Yes," he said without turning his head.

"I'm Clodi, by the way. What's your name?"

Nireus leaned forward with an expression of vague amusement so he could see Clodi, while Lexi answered her question.

"This is Nireus," Lexi said.

"So you two know each other from home?" Clodi asked.

Lexi took a long breath to soothe away her irritation. "No, we just met."

Clodi raised her contrastingly dark eyebrows. "And you're already together? That was fast! Hope that happens to me!" Clodi wrinkled her perfect little nose and peered around to stare into their faces. "How did it happen? Did he just walk up and take your hand?"

Lexi concentrated on her blank expression, willing away the blushes that begged to bloom on her cheeks.

Nireus gave them both a smug smile. "She hit me, actually. It was quite a novel approach."

Clodi chortled. "Really?"

"It was an accident," Lexi clarified, trying to pull her hand from his, but he only held it tighter.

"She apologized, and then I took her hand," Nireus supplied, his upturned nose and smirk giving him an impish mien.

Clodi laughed. "I think I'll try that."

Nireus said something under his breath that Lexi couldn't quite catch.

Ahead of them, couples mingled outside large double doors that were propped open, a cacophony of conversation and music spilling out. Nireus led them inside, deftly steering around knots of dancers, some of which spiraled up to the three-story ceiling in a dizzying fashion. A haphazard band of creative instruments dominated a corner, the musicians' expressions ranging from politely bored to martyrdom. The scents were intense and varied, some blending horrifically together, and Lexi found herself pressing her nose into Nireus' shoulder, their wings tightly closed as they moved through the crowd. Nireus curled her body into him when they found an empty space.

"Have you done this before?" he asked, leaning into her ear to be heard and letting his lips brush against her lobe.

A little electrical current seemed to be running a circuit through Lexi's body, and it was a moment before she remembered to shake her head. He slid a hand around her waist and made a few circles on the floor in time to the music.

"Will you dance with me next?" Clodi shouted.

Nireus spun Lexi up into the air without answering, pulling her closer against him when she had trouble keeping the same height.

"You're doing well for your first time," he complimented her, speaking loudly into her ear, and again letting his lips graze her lobe.

Lexi slid her arms around his neck, clinging to him in dizziness as they continued to spin. "I feel like I'm going to crash."

"I'll keep you safe," he assured her, sliding his other hand around her waist.

Her drying hair spun out behind her, tangling and tickling her wings until she clutched at it irritably. "I should have put my hair up," she apologized, trying to tuck her tresses between the two of them. When Lexi looked up again, the other dancers had become a confused blur of color and motion. "Could we land?" she asked weakly.

"Sure," he said, his tone laced with suppressed irritation.

Her knees buckled as they touched the ground, and she clung to him helplessly, waiting for the room to stop spinning. "I'm sorry, I can't let go," she apologized, embarrassed at her own weakness.

The corner of his mouth twitched in the suggestion of a smile, and he leaned in to kiss her.

"That was wonderful!" Clodi enthused, pushing past another couple to get to them. "You moved clear across the room spinning! I almost lost you!"

Nireus' pulled back from the almost-kiss, his mouth stretched into a tight smile. Lexi fought the desire to laugh.

"Is it my turn now?" Clodi asked.

After a moment's hesitation, Lexi slowly disengaged herself from Nireus' arms. "Yes," she answered, shakily standing her ground while Nireus reached out a hand to steady her. "I'm all right now," she assured him with a wan smile.

Clodi clapped her hands together and seized Nireus. They were the same height, but Clodi seemed to dwarf his slender build as they spun a small circle around the floor, then jerkily leapt into the air. Lexi couldn't watch them or any of the dancers; their spinning only increased her dizziness. Instead, she moved carefully through the crowd until she found a wall and leaned her forehead against its cool, stone surface, her eyes shut. A tantalizing scent of floral musk weaved into the tangle of smells around her, and her eyes flew open to identify its source. The man who had signaled her tipped his chin up in an arrogant greeting, his dark eyes never leaving hers. Tall as she was, he seemed to tower over her, displaying his muscled build and enormous yellow and black wings with perfect awareness of their effect. Lexi pulled away from the wall with a self-conscious smile, swaying slightly as she did so. He caught her wrist quickly in his rough hand, steadying her.

"You okay?" he asked, his low voice a pleasant rumble.

"Just dizzy," she said weakly, admiring the perfect curve of his lips that seemed to melt into his tanned face with hardly a color change.

"Maybe your partner was doing it wrong," he suggested, stepping closer, and placing a hand on her shoulder as if to dance.

Lexi looked up into his face, his long, dark lashes heavy on his cheeks as he looked down at her without dropping his chin. Her stomach fluttered and her skin overheated beneath his hands, his thumb moving softly across her collar bone. Pulling her away from the wall, he beat his huge wings, the black cascading through the yellow like spilled ink.

"Wait," she gasped as he lifted her off the ground, belatedly beating her wings to keep up with him.

"No spinning," he assured her, sweeping her up by the waist and pulling her to him. She pressed her hands against his chest, making a little more space between them as they rose to the ceiling.

"Does it count as dancing if we don't spin?" she asked with a forced smile, uncomfortable beneath his subtly moving hands.

"Does it matter?" he asked rhetorically, guiding her between couples as they moved across the top of the room. The song she had been dancing with Nireus ended, and they hesitated above the doors before the next one began.

"Do you want to sit down?" he asked, deftly moving her through the doorway before she answered.

"I came with friends," she said, trying to pull away from him. "They'll be worried."

He shook his head dismissively. "We'll only be gone a little while."

"Where are we going?" she asked, stilling her wings and slowing their flight.

"Just a quiet place to sit down," he assured her, narrowly avoiding someone descending the stairs.

Lexi found it unnerving that he could still fly and support her weight. Sweat had broken out on his forehead and upper lip at the exertion, and somehow it only made him smell better. A little pulse of fear was throbbing through her stomach, and she pushed against his chest again, only to have his grip on her waist tighten.

"I want to go back to the dance hall," she told him, a slight tremor breaking her voice.

"We will," he told her, landing beside a door. He slid a hand up her back between her wings, holding her securely while he opened the door. Peering in, he swore and shut the door again, setting his free hand on her shoulder. He rolled his bottom lip into his mouth, chewing on it thoughtfully as he gazed down at her. "You want to go back now?"

Lexi nodded, releasing the anxious breath she had held.

He barked a little mirthless laugh. "I don't even know your name."

Lexi hesitated a moment, her mind hazy from the twin distractions of his scent and her fear. "Raven," she finally answered.

"Wes," he announced, letting his fingers play about her neck as he swept back her hair. He ran a finger along her neckline, and Lexi began to tense again.

"I'm leaving now," she declared, starting to wriggle away from him.

"Without me?" he asked, loosening his grip, but managing to keep her in his arms. He signaled again, and she stopped struggling as the scent washed over her, soothing her fear. With a smirk, he bent towards her mouth, then pulled back when the door behind her opened.

"Got a new victim, Wes?" a familiar voice asked.

Lexi tried to turn and look, but Wes held her against him possessively. "None of your business," Wes warned. "Why don't you go find your little moth-brained girlfriend, and let us have the room?"

"Does she *want* to be alone with you?"

"Tiger?" Lexi asked, closing her wings to see over her shoulder.

"Lex?" Tiger's mouth hung open in shock, then shut abruptly, his square jaw clenched. "Let go of her."

Wes released her, and held his hands out wide. "I'm not making her do anything she doesn't want to."

"Right," Tiger muttered. Before Wes could reclaim his prize, Tiger grabbed Lexi's wrist, yanked her into the room, then slammed the door.

The door was open again before the slam had finished shaking the frame. "Hey, this is my room, too," Wes growled, "and I did not bring her up here so *you* could have her."

"Wes, you moron, do you know who she is?" Tiger demanded, shoving a cowlick-ridden lock of honey blonde hair out of his eyes.

"Don't," Lexi warned, her eyes pleading with him.

"Yeah, her name is Raven," Wes said defensively. "She's new here, and she doesn't like to spin. How do you know her?"

Tiger's brown eyes danced with humor as he looked at Lexi, who shook her head almost imperceptibly. "Raven," Tiger said, holding back a snicker, "why don't you tell my cousin how we know each other?"

Lexi swallowed, her mind racing. "You and the royal stable master visited my family's ranch and bought some horses six months ago."

Tiger hid a smirk and turned back to his cousin. "Right. She's a business partner. So, I can't let you victimize her."

"I'm not victimizing her. I'm just getting to know her." Wes stepped closer to Lexi and ran two fingers up her sleeve. "Leave us alone."

Tiger knocked his hand away and stood in between them. "Not a chance. Not this one."

A little muscle pulsed in Wes' jaw as he glared at Tiger. "She likes me. You're just jealous."

"L—Raven, Wes here would like you to join his harem of mates, and bear him some more illegitimate children; would you like that?" Tiger asked without turning to look at her.

Wes swore under his breath and took a threatening step towards Tiger. "You'll pay for that."

Tiger's frame was rigid as he glared at his cousin. "As long as she doesn't."

Wes snorted, then leaned around Tiger's forewing to look at Lexi. "Don't believe him."

Tiger stepped forward menacingly, effectively hiding Lexi from view.

"Now who's building a harem?" Wes mocked as he slowly backed out of the room. At the doorway he stopped. "Hey Raven," he called, then waited until she peered around Tiger's wing. "I'll find you later," he promised.

"No, you won't," Tiger snarled.

Wes grinned. "You can't stop me," he taunted, walking out without shutting the door. His cheerful whistle echoed down the corridor until Tiger slammed the door.

He stood there, tapping his fist to his forehead with a pained expression for a full minute before he turned to her. "You want to tell me why you're here?"

Lexi took a deep breath, hoping to clear Wes' heady scent from her mind, but the room was saturated with his floral musk. Feeling a little dizzy again, she sat down heavily on the only stool in the room. "Talan was the only one in season. Mother arranged the marriage, but Father helped me escape the night before the wedding."

Tiger's unruly dark brows were lifted high into his tan forehead, but he said nothing.

"Mother commanded Talan to follow me, even made Father sign a marriage certificate. Talan caught up to me in Shady Cove, and I didn't escape him until yesterday. The Governor shut Talan up in the dungeon when he got here, and he wants me to marry Van West; do you remember him?"

"Yeah," Tiger said, his voice incredulous.

"But he already has a mate, so…" Lexi trailed off shrugging.

"So you figured you'd let my cousin sire the next king?"

Lexi met his troubled eyes with a little grimace. "He just picked me up, and brought me here. I didn't even say I would dance with him."

"And you didn't scream or kick him?"

Lexi stared at her hands and shook her head.

"What if I hadn't been here?" Tiger demanded, his tone increasingly angry. "Do you even realize…" he trailed off with a muttered oath. "Lex, he's gotten three girls pregnant, and he thinks it's funny. He lets them fly home sobbing and alone, then he laughs about how stupid they were to mate with him. You want to be one of them?"

Lexi shook her head again without looking up.

"What's the matter with you?" Tiger demanded, walking over to lift her up by the arms. He shook her gently until she looked at him. "Your eyes are dilated," he noted, his anger quickly fading to concern. He swore again. "I heard about this, but I didn't think it was real." He set her back down gently. "How do you feel?" He walked over and pried open the balcony doors, the rugs dragging along the floor beneath them. Frigid air and blowing rain burst into the room, pelting Lexi's wings.

Jumping up, Lexi fled the splattering rain. "Why did you do that?"

Tiger gave her a small grin and grabbed her hand. "That sounds more like the Lex I know," he nodded, dragging her out onto the balcony.

"I just got dry! And I don't have anything else to wear!" Lexi complained, fighting him.

Tiger's grin widened. "So?"

"Let go of me, and shut these doors *now*!"

Tiger chuckled cheerfully. "Not yet. You're pheromone drunk. You need some more air."

"I'm what?" Lexi demanded, yanking her hand free.

"Wes' pheromones mess with your head. A minute ago you were completely docile—not at all like yourself." Tiger grinned as she scowled at him. "Here, I'll show you." Tiger shut the doors again and kicked the rugs into place, then walked to the nearest bed and lifted the pillow. "Inhale that," he commanded.

Lexi stared at him irritably a moment, wiping the rain from her face and clothing. Then she took the pillow and put it near her nose, inhaling Wes' distinctive scent. "It's Wes'," she said, tossing it back onto his bed.

"Do you still feel feisty?" Tiger asked.

Lexi shrugged, and wiped the rain off the stool before sitting down.

135

Tiger chuckled, then frowned. "That's really bad, Lex."

"This whole room smells like him," Lexi commented, a faint smile tickling her lips.

Tiger inhaled, his frown deepening. "Let's get you out of here, then. Where's your room?"

"Beneath this one." Lexi replied, letting him pull her off the stool and out the door.

"Somebody is going to have to guard you all the time," Tiger decided as he towed her along by the arm.

Halfway down the hall she pulled away from him. "That hurts. I have a big bruise there from when Talan pulled me off of Raven."

Tiger stopped walking to stare at her. "He did what?!"

"I was galloping bareback in your old clothes and he thought I was a servant, so he flew after me and pulled me off."

Tiger chuckled without amusement. "I'm going to kill him."

"No, you're not. He'll just break your nose again," Lexi argued, her eyes drawn to the crooked bridge of Tiger's nose.

"I was a lot smaller two years ago, and his brother was holding my arms," he reminded her, stopping when he realized she was staring at him. "What?"

Lexi shook her head with a little frown.

"It's a little late to start keeping secrets from each other, Lex. Out with it."

Lexi pursed her lips for a moment, then began walking again. "You have the same eyes and wings," she murmured. "Even your mouths are very similar."

Tiger grimaced as he followed her down the stairs. "Our fathers were identical twins."

"Why did he turn out like...that?" she asked, waiting at the bottom of the stairs until he joined her.

Tiger shrugged. "I don't know. My other cousin is a nice guy."

"Is he here, too?" Lexi asked, walking alongside him down the hallway.

Tiger shook his head. "He got married a week after I got here."

"Are you..." Lexi hesitated, a blush creeping up her neck and seeping into her cheeks, "...getting married soon? Wes said you had a girlfriend."

Tiger laughed. "Since when do you blush?"

Lexi stopped in front of the door to her room and wiped her cheeks with her hands as if to rub away her embarrassment. "That's not an answer."

"You're right, it's not," Tiger grinned, then chuckled warmly as he slipped a hand under her chin and lifted it. "Missed you, Lex."

Lexi met his eyes for a moment, then pulled away as a heavy blush suffused her face and her heart began to pound. She turned quickly and opened the door.

Psyche growled, one wing folded back to glare at them.

"Sorry," Lexi apologized, and immediately shut the door. "Now where?"

"Does the Governor know you're here? He needs to assign you a guard."

Lexi frowned.

"Lex, Wes is going to find you. I'm not sure he cares if you say no."

Lexi's frown deepened and a little pucker appeared between her brows. "I already have a guard. But...I sent him to watch someone else."

Tiger laughed. "And who else needed guarding?"

"A friend who wanted to beat up Van and follow me around."

Tiger instantly sobered. "You gave away your guard to a *man*?"

"He wouldn't go to sleep! And I didn't want him fighting."

"Is he four years old?" Tiger asked, his eyes wide in mocking incredulity.

"No," Lexi said frowning. "He's our age."

"So why are you treating him like a child? And why is he letting you? Does he know who you are?"

"Yes, he knows," Lexi said wearily. "And I don't know the answers to your other two questions."

"Well, *Your Majesty*, let me know when you figure it out."

Lexi gave him a light shove. "You promised not to call me names like that. You know I hate it."

"Lex, you're acting like your mother."

"I am *not*!" Lexi yelled at him, her eyes flashing fury. "Don't you *ever* say that to me!"

"Is that an order?"

"As if you would obey one of my orders," Lexi retorted.

"What? I've been a faithful servant—mostly," he conceded with a grin.

Lexi shook her head, the faintest smile playing about her lips. "Not to me."

"Apologies, Your Highness," Tiger gave her another mocking bow, breaking into laughter when she yanked one of his coarse sandy locks hanging over his ear. "Now you must pay," he threatened with an enormous grin.

Lexi shrieked and flew backwards, but he caught her around the waist and shook his rain-wet hair in her face. Laughing, Lexi shoved his head away, and kicked lightly at his legs.

"You put her down!" Clodi thundered as she swooped towards them. Tiger turned to look behind him, his arms closing protectively around Lexi. "I know all about you! You can just go seduce somebody else! That's my roommate!" Clodi landed next to them with a thud, and reached for Tiger's nearest wing.

"Clodi, don't!" Lexi wriggled out of Tiger's grasp and stood between them.

"Nireus says he's a..." Clodi lowered her voice to an indiscreet whisper, "a seducer! Get away from him, Raven! His intentions aren't honorable!"

Lexi laid a hand on Clodi's arm and carefully suppressed the giggles that rose in her throat like hiccups. "It was his cousin that you saw me dancing with. Remember he had dark hair? This is a good friend of mine: Tiger."

Clodi's suspicious scowl relaxed minutely. "Oh." Motioning Lexi closer, she whispered, "Are you sure he isn't like the other one?"

Lexi allowed herself a slight smile as she glanced back at Tiger. "I'm sure."

Clodi let out a great sigh as her shoulders sagged. "Thank goodness! Nireus was so angry when he saw you dancing with...the other one. He said you were as good as lost when he saw you flying out the doors, and he wouldn't help me find you." Clodi's tone of distress changed to embarrassment as her rosy cheeks turned a deeper shade of pink. "I got lost looking; I'm sorry."

Lexi patted Clodi's arm. "It was very thoughtful of you; thank you for warning me."

"Did he," Clodi grudgingly motioned to Tiger, "save you?"

A look of discomfort twitched across Lexi's face before she replaced it with a tight smile. "Yes, he did."

"Then thank you," Clodi told Tiger earnestly. "I'm sorry I almost broke your wing."

"It's all right." Tiger nodded with a smile. "It's about time somebody thanked me."

Lexi's nose wrinkled slightly with the urge to smack him, but instead she turned to him with a gracious smile. "Thank you." She wanted to mean it, but was piqued by the mocking amusement in his eyes.

"You're so wet," Clodi commented, eyeing their spattered clothing and damp hair. "Did you have to fly outside to get away from him?"

"Perhaps I can tell you the story later," Lexi suggested. "Would you mind if I finished catching up with Tiger?"

Clodi's unconscious pout made it clear that she did mind, very much. "Oh sure, that's okay," she answered vaguely.

"I will come back for our tour," Lexi promised with a guilty pang.

Clodi gave a despondent nod and opened the bedroom door. "See you later," she sighed, then shut the door behind her.

Tiger shook his head in mock disapproval. "Heartless."

Lexi glared at him, then began walking away.

"And so fake. Am I the only one who really knows what you're like?" Tiger asked, laughing as he followed her.

Lexi answered him with a scowl over her shoulder.

"You don't have to go all princess up here. You can be yourself. After all, you're a horse now," Tiger said, his laughter redoubling as she spun to smack his chest.

"Will you stop it? I'm not being fake! I'm just being controlled and considerate," she explained, choosing her words carefully.

"And fake," Tiger added, grinning. He caught her wrists easily at she came at him again, and laughed as she struggled.

"Where's the muck pile when I need it?" Lexi threatened.

"As if you could still toss me in it," he taunted. "Your last victory was seven years ago."

Lexi gave up with a growl and resumed walking. "Curse your brute strength," she muttered.

"Speaking of brutes, who is this Nireus guy who abandoned you to Wes?"

Lexi shrugged uneasily. "Some guy I met on the stairs."

"Wandering *alone*?"

"I was on my way to find you," Lexi said defensively. "I got your room number from the clerk."

"Is that why you were letting Wes take you inside?"

Lexi shook her head. "I didn't even know where we were. He flew me backwards, and I was already dizzy. I didn't even notice the door number."

"He *flew* you? You weren't flying with him?"

Lexi shook her head. "I stopped flying when he left the dance hall. I didn't want to leave."

Tiger frowned. "You need that guard *now*...maybe two."

Lexi put a hand on Tiger's chest to stop him just outside the clerk's office. "I'm working on it. Stay here."

Tiger snorted and followed her, receiving her glare with a grin.

"Eros, could you tell me which room Cam is in? I'm sorry, I don't know his last name, but he did arrive today."

Eros gave them a piercing glance, then consulting the pages before him. "Cam *Crescent* is in Room 217, Miss Fritillary. Do you need directions?"

"Nope," Tiger answered for her. "Come, *Miss Fritillary*." Laughter danced in Tiger's eyes as he offered her his arm. "Allow me to escort you."

Lexi turned to face him and stuck out her tongue before taking his arm. "Thank you," she said, her tone sounding gracious while her expression was sour. Tiger led her out of the clerk's office before his chuckles burst through.

"Fritillary? You don't look like a Fritillary! Who's going to be dumb enough to believe that?"

"Shhh!" Lexi hushed him irritably as she glanced around the empty entry. "There wasn't another choice."

"You should have said you were a Viceroy," he said, looking at her wings. "That's believable."

"I couldn't. Limen has," she paused uncomfortably, then continued quietly, "illegitimate male relatives here. They would know I was lying when they could smell me."

"Oh. Guess the Governor is carrying on a family tradition, then."

"What do you mean?"

Tiger's shoulders shifted uncomfortably. "He cheats on Mona, Lex...a lot, if the rumors are true."

Lexi stopped walking, her eyes filling up with tears. "Are you sure?" she asked without looking at him.

"Pretty sure. I've heard some of the girls complain about him coming on to them." Tiger patted her arm. "Sorry Lex. Have you been to see him already?"

Lexi nodded, and dropped her head as a tear ran down her cheek.

"He didn't come on to you, did he?"

Lexi shook her head uncertainly and wiped her tears. "Talan thought he was."

"Aah, the dungeon sentence makes more sense now," Tiger commented, scratching at his scalp absently. "I'm sorry. Thought it might be better coming from me."

"It is," Lexi sighed, covering her face. "Poor Mona." Dropping her hands she met his gaze. "Is Van the same? I heard..."

Tiger stared down at his boot as he worried some disintegrating grout in the stone floor. "Yeah, I heard that, too."

"Rotten noblemen," Lexi cursed, dashing away the last of her tears angrily.

"Who you going to marry now, Lex?"

"I didn't come here to marry Van; I didn't even know he was here until we stopped at their estate on the way," she explained, her tone defensive. "I came to find someone I loved."

"A *peasant*?" Tiger asked, giving the word mocking emphasis.

"Yes," she retorted, jutting out her chin.

Tiger shook his head. "So you're not going home again, Lex? Just going to give all that up?"

Lexi shrugged stiffly, her eyes drifting away from his face.

"You'll miss it."

"You know I hate being a princess," she declared vehemently.

"I know you think you do."

Lexi stamped her foot. "I do! I'll miss my father, your mom, Raven, and...and you," she admitted, "but not the rest of it!"

Tiger laughed gently as he swept a strand of hair out of her face. "Lex, you're ill-equipped to be an ordinary wife and mother. You don't even know how to do your own hair."

She leapt away from his hand as if he had struck her. "Worst thing you've said to me...ever," she whispered.

"I'm not trying to hurt you, Lex; you're just not being realistic."

Lexi shook her head, trying to stop the tears that threatened, then leapt into flight as they began to fall.

Tiger caught up to her easily. "Lex, land before you crash into something."

She shook her head, refusing to look at him.

Sighing, he flew in front of her and caught her, landing neatly as she struggled. "Promise you won't fly again, and I'll let go."

"No!" she shouted, fighting to get away from him.

"If you were safe alone, I'd let you go, but you're not, so walk with me until we find your guard and then I'll go away. Okay?"

Lexi stopped fighting and sobbed quietly. Tiger looked down at her unhappily and relaxed his hold, but didn't let her go.

"You shouldn't have come," he murmured, distressed. "Couldn't you just have waited for another noble to come into season?"

Furiously, she shoved at his chest, forcing him to free her. "My mother *insisted* I marry Talan," she choked out, angrily wiping away her tears.

"Why?" he demanded irritably.

Lexi glared at him, her breath coming in heaves. "Because I kissed him. Because he was there for my wing birth, and had to tear my dress open. Because he came to my balcony in the middle of the night, and I opened the door. Satisfied?!"

Tiger's frown deepened into a scowl. "Then why didn't you stay and marry him?"

"Because I don't even *like* him, and he's a liar! He was fine with throwing me off that horse when he thought I was you. He wouldn't even let me keep your mom as my lady's maid! He wants to control me, and my whole life with him stretched out before me, robbed of the few things that give me joy, and I was just miserable!"

They stared at each other for a few angry breaths, then Lexi stalked away, fury punctuating her footsteps. She could hear his soft tread just behind her, and it somehow irritated her more. Spinning on her heel, she confronted him. "I *do* know how to do my hair. Your mom taught me."

His mouth pulled into a weak smile. "How is my mom?"

"Fine," she muttered, resuming her walk.

Matching her pace, he walked alongside her. "Did she lose her job, then?"

"I don't think so. I gave her the night off, and didn't tell her what I was doing, so Mother couldn't blame her," Lexi said, her worry for Cercy cooling her anger.

"But she's *your* lady's maid. If you don't go back, she won't have a job."

Lexi frowned. "I'm ashamed to admit I didn't think of that. I'm sure Mother will find another position for her; they're obligated to keep her since your father died working for them."

Tiger shook his head with a frown. "You know your mother doesn't like her...no more than she likes me."

"If it's any consolation, she's not fond of me just now, either," Lexi said, trying to smile.

"This isn't a joke, Lex. My mom's out of a job, and I'm not there to help her."

"It's not a joke to me. I love your mom like she was my own mother. I don't want to see her out of job any more than you do," Lexi said miserably, tears of guilt making her voice catch.

Tiger clutched at a tuft of hair from the back of his head as he stared down at the uneven floor. "You just...shouldn't have come Lex."

"Thank you," she said bitterly. "Now where is that stupid room?"

Tiger glanced around them with a rueful laugh. "We've walked a full circuit of the castle. It's this way," he said, pointing down a different corridor.

They walked the remaining distance in awkward silence.

"Finally!" Beck complained as soon as he saw them. "He's snoring now, but he tried to sneak out twice. He's really upset that you're making him nap."

Tiger snorted. "I take it back, you'll be a great mom."

Lexi's mouth tightened into a firm line as she stepped past Beck, pulled open Cam's door, and marched inside, slamming it heartily behind her.

Cam jerked awake, looking around with a sleepy grin. "Is it dinner time?"

In the dim light of the lantern, Lexi crossed the small room and sat gracefully at his little stool and table, willing herself to calm down. "Go back to sleep," she directed.

"Lex," Tiger called, knocking heavily. "Come out of there."

"No, thank you," Lexi answered in a polite tone.

145

"Is that one of the Cretins?" Cam asked, tossing aside a gray rag of a blanket and sliding out of bed.

"No, that's my best friend, Tiger."

"Lex," Tiger warned.

"I don't think he wants you in here with me," Cam observed as he started for the door.

Lexi caught his wrist and held it. "Don't let him in."

"There's no lock, Lexi. I think he's just going to open it."

The door flew open with a bang as it ricocheted off the wall. "Lex, come out," Tiger directed.

"Why? I'm safe here." Lexi slid her hand from Cam's wrist to his hand and closed hers around it.

"You shouldn't be in any man's room," Tiger chided.

"I was in yours," Lexi countered, her expression a pleasant blank as Cam flinched and looked down at her.

"No fights, guys," Beck warned from behind Tiger.

"Fine, I'll just stand here." Tiger planted his feet and crossed his arms; his entire body radiated obstinance.

"Cam, signal," Lexi commanded, squeezing his hand.

Cam laughed nervously. "I don't think that's a good idea right now."

Lexi gave Cam's arm a little yank. "Signal!" she demanded.

Cam blushed as the smell of stolen cookies infused the room. "Happy?" he asked uncomfortably.

Lexi stood and faced Tiger. "Look at my eyes. They're not dilated, right? He doesn't make me pheromone drunk. So you can go away now."

Tiger peered into her eyes, then let his arms fall to his side. "You still shouldn't be in here."

"We can go somewhere else," Cam suggested.

"No, we'll stay right here. Beck will be just outside the door. I'm safe. You've done your duty, now go away."

Tiger nodded once, his chocolate-brown eyes cold. "Don't make me sorry I trusted you," he warned Cam, poking one finger at his chest.

Cam knocked his finger away with a steely look, and Tiger turned and left. Sucking in a big breath, Cam quietly shut the door. "What just happened?"

Lexi stared at the door a moment before dragging her eyes up to Cam's. "I'll tell you if you lie down and rest."

Cam's full lips tightened into a pucker. "I didn't like that very much."

"I'm sorry, I just needed to get away from him," Lexi explained, leading him back to the bed and forcing him to lie down.

"Why? Did you two have a fight?" he asked, his wings pulled tightly back so he could watch her.

Lexi nodded as she dragged the little stool over to the bed.

"What's pheromone drunk and why is he worried about it?"

Lexi sighed and sat down carefully. "Relax your wings," she directed.

"You don't want to tell me?" he asked, his dark eyes looking black in the dim lantern light.

"Relax your wings and I will," she promised.

He let his wings fall, covering his face, and she told him, coaxing him back down onto the bed when he became too agitated by her story. He was silent for a time when she finished.

"Are you disappointed I don't have that kind of effect on you?" he asked.

"No," she said emphatically. "Now try to sleep."

"Are you going to leave if I fall asleep?"

Lexi shifted in her seat, rearranging her dress. "I promised to tour the castle with my roommate, Clodi, before dinner."

"I'm coming."

Lexi smiled at the stubborn tone of his voice, and ran a finger along the edge of his wing until he shivered. "No, you're not."

"I'll be too worried about what's happening to you to sleep."

"I'll have Beck and Clodi; I'll be fine."

He unfolded an arm from beneath his head and softly touched her ankle, caressing it. "Please stay."

"Just until you sleep," she said, removing his hand from her ankle.

Reluctantly, he folded his arm back under his head. "Tell me everything else I missed."

Sighing, she told him, editing out much of her conversation with Tiger.

"But why did you fight with him?" he asked, his voice sounding drowsily distant.

Lexi changed position, using the delay to sort her thoughts. "He's upset I came here. He thinks I should have stayed home and married a noble because I'm not equipped for anything else," she explained, bitterness seeping into her tone.

Cam lifted one wing to look at her. "Why would he say that?"

Lexi stared down at her manicured hands. "I don't know how to cook, or clean, care for children, sew... I'm not even very good at doing my own hair," she whispered, running her fingers through her tangled tresses.

Cam reached a hand under his bed and pulled out his bag, fumbling through an outer pocket until he drew out a comb. "I'll do it," he offered.

Lexi laughed and covered her face, the sound coming out more akin to a cry.

Cam got out of bed and stood behind her. He gently drew the comb through her long hair, working out the tangles without pulling. "I can cook and clean, too," he added, gathering her hair back from her face with careful hands.

Lexi laughed softly, her scalp tingling pleasantly. "And what will *I* do?"

"Whatever you wish, and I will treat you like a queen."

Lexi's smile faded as Tiger's words echoed in her head: *Lex, you're acting like your mother*. Frowning, she reached up to catch his hand on the comb and remove it from her hair. "You should sleep," she said, standing up to go.

"What did I say?" he asked, following her to the door.

Lexi turned to look at him, lifting a hand to his cheek. "You're very sweet. You remind me of my father."

Cam smiled at her, turning his mouth into her hand to kiss it gently before she pulled away.

"Bye, Cam." She flashed him a parting smile as she slipped out the door and gently pulled it closed.

Lips pursed like a fish, Beck flicked his cheek to make the sound of dripping water. "I'm bored out of my mind. We need to get you a second guard so I have somebody to talk to."

"Which way to my room?" she asked, turning one way and then the other. The gray stone interior of the Old Castle all looked the same to her.

"This way," Beck nodded and began to walk. "You know that friend of yours has made about seven laps past Mr. Crescent's door in the last hour. If he gets stranded here, I'm definitely recommending him for guard duty."

Lexi swallowed back that unpleasant thought without comment.

"He said you got pheromone drunk off the infamous Wes," Beck mentioned, his eyes alight with interest.

Lexi turned away to hide her irritation while she calmed her expression.

149

"I should report that to the Governor," Beck said, lifting one coppery eyebrow as he watched her out of the corner of his eye.

"Please don't," Lexi said.

"Is that an order?" Beck asked, his mouth pulled up in a lopsided smile.

"Would you get in trouble if he found it out from someone else?"

Beck thought for a moment. "Yes."

"Then it's not an order, but I really don't wish to discuss it with him."

Beck waited a moment, then seemed unable to resist the question. "Why's that?"

Lexi stopped outside her door and turned to him. "Is Limen cheating on my sister, Beck?"

Beck's eyes went wide at the question, and his mouth opened and shut. "My orders prevent me from answering," he grumbled, staring down at his haggard shoes.

Lexi took a deep breath, then blew it out slowly before opening the door to her room.

Chapter Eight

Psyche looked up from the table with a catty smile. "Oh good, you're back." Her platinum blonde hair, dark blue eyes, and regular features should have made her a great beauty, but her conniving expression spoiled the effect.

Lexi glanced around the otherwise empty room. "Where's Clodi?"

"I sent her on an errand so we could talk. Have a seat." Psyche pointed to the stool beside her.

Lexi looked at the stool, then back at Psyche's gloating mien with a sense of foreboding. With a nod to Beck, she shut the door and moved to sit beside her.

"I would like to eat life servant meals for the rest of my time here," Psyche announced, running a brush through her smooth, blonde hair as she gazed into the cloudy mirror. "I want them brought to our room, three times a day."

Lexi lifted a single dark brow. "That sounds pleasant."

"And I want to be exempt from the daily morning pregnancy tests."

Lexi allowed her face to show mild surprise. "I wasn't aware there were daily pregnancy tests."

"Oh, yes. At 5:30 every morning a bitter hag bangs on our door and marches us down to the clinic where we spit on a table. If the test comes up positive, we get kicked off the mountain within an hour."

Lexi's mouth fell slightly ajar before she recovered herself. "I can understand why you would want to avoid that."

"You're going to arrange that for me."

"What makes you think I can?"

"Because you outrank the Governor, *Your Highness*," Psyche crowed with a triumphant grin.

Rather than panic, Lexi could feel the tangle of emotions within her galvanizing to an iron core. She smiled as she wondered if this was the same sense of exhilaration her mother felt each time she took command.

"If you wish to alter the terms of your stay here, you will have to speak to the Governor," Lexi countered dispassionately. She took a moment to enjoy the bemused frustration on Psyche's face, then Lexi turned and opened the door. "Beck, Psyche wishes to negotiate with the Governor regarding her food and pregnancy tests. Will you please escort her to him?"

Psyche stood abruptly, knocking over her stool. "There's no need for that," she blurted as Beck entered the room and took her arm.

"And Beck, please be certain she doesn't discuss it with anyone before she's had a *thorough* conversation with the Governor," Lexi requested as Beck led Psyche out of the room.

"You can't stop me from talking. I'll shout your little secret all the way there!"

Lexi suppressed a laugh as she realized how little she cared if Psyche did exactly as she threatened. "That will make it rather difficult for you to bargain the terms of your silence."

Psyche's mouth snapped shut as she glared venomously. Amused, Lexi gave her a sunny smile and shut the door.

Humming to herself, Lexi meandered about the room as she braided her hair. Absently, she glanced up at the ceiling and sniffed; her humming stopping abruptly at the disappointment of not being able to smell Tiger and Wes' room. Shaking her head with a little frown, she searched for something to tie her hair. The unexpected knock at the door made her jump, and Lexi's fingers fumbled to reclaim the hair that was quickly unwinding. Giving up, she moved silently to the door and inhaled. The musty scent of the room's mildewed rugs and wet stone filled her nose. The knock came again and Lexi reached for the handle, but the door was already opening from the outside. Lexi jumped back, then relaxed as Tiger let himself in.

"That door really needs a lock," she commented.

"I agree with you," Tiger said emphatically as he glanced around the room. "You're alone?! You sent your guard away *again*?!" Tiger released an angry laugh as he turned to slam the door behind him. "I can't leave you alone for a minute."

"Have you tried?"

"Funny. What happened to your hair?" He flicked at the unraveling strands with his fingers.

Lexi picked up the unwinding ends and began to rebraid her hair. "You startled me."

"Did you send Beck off to enforce nap time again?"

"No," Lexi snapped. "My roommate tried to blackmail me so I had Beck take her to the Governor."

"Psyche?"

Lexi nodded as she tied off her braid.

Tiger snorted. "We're keeping Beck busy today."

Lexi let out a heavy breath. "Tell me you didn't go talk to Limen about me."

"Are you asking me to lie to you?"

Lexi gritted her teeth. "What did you do?"

Tiger grinned. "Just about now they should be hauling Wes off to the dungeon, and you're about to get another guard."

"Why do I need two guards if Wes is in the dungeon?"

"So that when you send one off on an errand, you'll still have one to guard you," he explained, tugging at the end of her braid. "I take it back, you *can* do your own hair."

Lexi smacked at his hand. "How much are you taking back?"

"All of the hair part," he said, his mouth serious while his dark eyes lit up with amusement.

"But none of the you're-ruining-my-life-by-being-here-and-you're-going-to-make-a-rotten-wife-and-mother part?"

The amusement faded from his face. "I didn't say that."

Lexi shook her head. "It's a fair paraphrase, don't quibble."

"I'm not *quibbling*," he mocked. "I just didn't say that."

"Fine. Then I'll assume that's what you meant. Move, please. I have a dinner date."

Tiger crossed his arms and stood more squarely in front of the door. "You're not going without a guard."

"Don't be ridiculous. You know you're going to follow me anyway."

Tiger laughed, but didn't move.

"I *order* you to move."

"I have special permission from the King to ignore your orders," Tiger reminded her with a grin.

"When we were eight!" Lexi protested.

"You're just as bossy now as you were then, and he has never rescinded it," Tiger said, laughing at the fury on her face."Tiger," Lexi warned through gritted teeth. "Move *now*."

"Or what?" Tiger asked, lifting her chin and shaking it back and forth.

Lexi slapped his hand away with a little smile. "Or I'll tell your girlfriend you wet your bed until you were ten."

"That's low," he said, shaking his head.

Lexi laughed. "So is using your brute strength to keep me locked up in my room. Now move!" She grabbed him around the waist and tugged. "Ugh, you're like a tree trunk," she complained, ignoring his laughter and abruptly switching tactics with a jab to his armpit. Clenching his arm to his side with a surprised laugh, he jerked away from her. Lexi had the door open before he recovered, but he smacked it shut again before she could get through.

"Do you have to practice to be this annoying?" Lexi demanded with an outraged laugh.

"Yes. Up until about a month ago, I practiced every day," Tiger quipped, grinning at his own wit.

"You know, I can be annoying. I whine rather well," Lexi threatened with a mischievous smile.

"Weren't you already doing that?"

"Tiger!" Lexi yelled, stomping. "Let me out!"

Tiger broke into a full laugh, leaning forward with the force of it, while his beautiful yellow and black wings shook.

Lexi darted to the balcony doors, simultaneously pulling out the rug with her foot while she yanked the door open. A cascade of raindrops hit her face as she slipped out onto the balcony and jumped over the rail with a delighted shriek. She flew rapidly over the courtyard, feeling the increasing drag on her wings as the heavy rain pelted and soaked her. She knew it was ridiculous, but a delighted burble of laughter kept escaping, fueled by her freedom and the familiarity of the game. Where flagstones returned to forest, she landed, tucked her drenched wings behind her, and ran down the nearest trail. The path was slick and her water shoes slipped with every step, flinging mud up the back of her long dress.

"Stupid dress," she panted, hitching it up as she ran. She could hear Tiger's rough breathing behind her, gaining, and it spurred her forward with another involuntary giggle.

Tiger's throaty laugh answered. His hand grazed her elbow and she shrieked, increasing her pace. Matching it, he pulled alongside her. "I can't really tackle you. It would break your wings," he panted. "How am I supposed to win this game?"

"You can't!" Lexi laughed. "And I am free from the tyranny of Tiger!"

"*I'm* tyrannical?"

Lexi nodded with a gasp. "As bad as my mother!"

Tiger let out a threatening growl as his arm shot out in front of her, his fingertips curling around her waist and forcing her to slow down. Lexi fought to remove his arm, then resorted to pulling his arm hair until he released her. Her triumphant chortle was cut short when he leapt into her path, catching her up in his arms. He staggered as she crashed into his chest, then regained his balance.

"Take it back," he commanded, his arms tightly folded around her waist as he held her aloft.

"No!" she yelled, then laughed. The tree canopy was open above the trail, affording little protection from the deluge, and it ran down their faces in rivulets. "At least your hair looks better," she giggled, tousling the locks that lay plastered to his head.

"Say I'm not a tyrant!" he insisted, squeezing tighter.

Lexi collapsed against him in helpless giggles, her head laying comfortably on his shoulder. Abruptly, he released her, steadying her at arm's length when she stumbled.

"You're giving up?" she asked, her giggles dying out.

"We should go back. It's cold and you're wet," he said, without meeting her gaze. "Come on." Stepping around her, he began to walk back.

"Does this mean I can call you Tiger the Tyrannical?" she teased, turning to follow him.

"Yeah," he said, staring at the muddy path in front of him.

Lexi frowned and laid a hand on his arm. "What's the matter?"

"We probably shouldn't spend so much time together up here."

Lexi let her hand drop and laughed merrily. "Well, that's hardly *my* fault."

Tiger grimaced, his eyes still tracking the ground ahead of him. "I know that," he said, sulkily. "But you'll have two guards now, Talan and Wes are in the dungeon...you should be fine."

"I never thought I wasn't."

Tiger turned to look at her. "That's the problem."

Lexi laid her hand back on his arm. "Could we not have this argument again? We never fight this much."

Tiger's jaw tightened and he stared back at the sodden ground.

"Guess it's the hormones," she commented, letting her hand fall.

He shot a look at her, but she only shrugged. "What?"

Turning away, he shook his head.

"Maybe my pheromones make you grumpy," she teased, smiling to herself.

"Your smell is...distinctive," he allowed.

"Distinctive," she repeated thoughtfully. "Distinctive like popcorn or distinctive like a skunk?"

Tiger laughed. "Neither."

She punched his arm lightly. "That's not helpful. Talan said I smell like apple blossoms."

"That's nice," he said irritably.

"Well, do I?"

Tiger let out a weak laugh. "It's a very subjective thing, Lex."

"So tell me what I smell like to you."

Tiger shifted his shoulders awkwardly, his mouth opening and closing several times. "No," he finally said.

Lexi laughed, tugging at his arm. "Why not?"

Tiger pulled away from her, increasing his pace so that she had to jog to catch up to him.

Lexi laughed again, hanging on his arm this time until he stopped walking and faced her. "Come on, Tiger, tell me," she coaxed.

"You stink, okay?" he blurted, then abruptly began walking again. "Like nauseating rotten things that force me to breathe through my mouth," he added over his shoulder as he stomped away.

Lexi stood, blinking away the rain that ran through her lashes until Tiger was only a bobbing dark blur against the pale gray stone of the castle.

Glancing back, he stopped and turned around with a heavy sigh. "See? I knew I shouldn't have told you."

Lexi forced herself to start walking again. "You should have told me sooner; I would have stayed downwind."

"Lex, it's not that big of a deal. I'm getting used to it."

"It's good you told me before a meal. Imagine what I would do to your appetite." Lexi could hear the bitterness in her voice, but couldn't seem to stop it.

Tiger's expression was pained as she passed him. "Just forget I said anything, okay? You smell fine."

"Yeah. I'll be sure to do that," she said, hurrying away from him.

"Are you going to have a bath now?" he asked, catching up to her. "You need one," he commented, eyeing the mud splatters that covered her legs and dress.

"No," she said breezily, "I think the mud improves my scent."

"Lex," he protested, helping her open one of the heavy front doors, then pulling it shut behind them. "Don't be like that. It doesn't bother me that much."

Lexi sped ahead of him, waving away his comments with an irritated hand. Each time she caught glimpses of him following her, she felt a surge of irrational irritation. She wiped impatiently at the water on her face, finally realizing that her eyes were replenishing it. Outside her door two uniformed guards waited expectantly, and she steeled herself to receive them.

The two men exchanged a few low words before the yellow-winged guard spoke. "Are you Miss Fritillary?"

Lexi rose to her full height, looking remarkably regal though soaked and muddy. "Yes, I am."

"The Governor has sent us to guard you," he announced, looking deferentially away as he resumed his post.

"Thank you," Lexi answered graciously. "What are your names?"

"I'm Erid," the yellow-winged guard said, and this is Avell." He nodded at the smirking flame-winged guard beside him.

Lexi took the measure of both men. Avell met her gaze brazenly, his wing tips swinging down, grotesquely broken. Erid carefully averted his gaze, blushing when he realized she was looking at him. If Limen hadn't told him who she was, he had at least guessed.

"Erid, I'm in need of a change of clothes. A young man locked up in your dungeon carried some of my clothing here for me. Would you please retrieve them from Talan Admiral?"

"Yes, Miss Fritillary," he answered with a quick bow, and hurried away. Avell stared after him open-mouthed, his dumbfounded gaze only returning to her when she opened the door.

"*I'm* not your errand boy," Avell protested.

"I'll remember that," Lexi said evenly, shutting the door behind her.

Quickly stripping off her sodden clothes, Lexi used them to wipe the mud from her legs, then dropped them into a soggy pile and put on her bathing suit. She sniffed curiously at her hair, and then her arm, smelling only the outdoors. A sulky frown creased her features as she pulled out her bag, her mind running an inventory of all the scents that made her feel nauseated, then wondering which scent was most similar to her own. When she retrieved her dripping clothes from the floor, she held them to her nose first, but wet earth was all she could detect. Sighing, she left her room, holding her wet laundry at arms' length. She was momentarily tempted to fling it at Avell when she saw his tightly folded arms and defiant expression, but she restrained herself and hurried past him. She could hear his reluctant footfalls behind her, but they were oddly comforting; it was unnerving walking around in her bathing suit. Fortunately, the halls were nearly empty, and she only passed two others before reaching the laundry room.

An older woman with charcoal-smudged white wings was just pulling the door shut. She glanced at the muddy clump of clothing that Lexi held gingerly away from her and frowned.

"You'll have to wash it yourself; we're done for the day," the laundry woman said blandly, then nodded to the guard. "Avell."

Lexi stared down at the sodden mass in her hand. "Could I just leave them somewhere, for tomorrow?"

The laundress cackled. "Haven't you washed your own clothes before? Your mother did you a disservice not teaching you. Look at you: helpless as the day you were born. And with Avell following you around, you must be a noblewoman," she surmised, glaring at Avell when he snorted in derision. "Well then, I guess I better make an exception or the Governor will have my hide."

Lexi smiled with relief as the older woman took the filthy clothing. "Thank you."

"What's your name?" The laundress asked as she retreated into the laundry.

"Raven Fritillary."

The laundry woman looked back with a strangled snort. "Sure it is."

Lexi squared her shoulders and turned resolutely towards the pool. She could hear Avell muttering behind her as she walked, but couldn't make out his words. She regretted not flinging her laundry at him.

The pool was nearly empty. A couple was hurrying out as she stepped into the water, and the last remaining occupant stared at her steadily. Lexi flashed him a polite smile, noting that his protruding blue eyes and oversized lips rather reminded her of a frog. His green and gray wings somehow exaggerated the effect rather than diminishing it. He returned her smile enthusiastically, his unblinking stare sending an involuntary little shudder down her back as the stench of summer kitchen refuse caught her nose.

"What's with the guard?" he asked, flicking his uncomfortable gaze up to Avell.

Lexi ran through several plausible explanations as she unwound her braid.

"Governor's new favorite," Avell drawled.

Lexi whirled to glare at him, her wings dragging unpleasantly through the water. "You are mistaken."

"Am I?" Avell shrugged flippantly. "You won't last long; they never do."

Lexi took several slow, deep breaths as she tried to regain her temper.

"So, does that mean you get special dinners in his chambers?" frog man asked, his lips curling back into a sneer.

"No," Lexi said icily.

"You're skipping dinner, you know," frog man continued, his sneer fading into a toothy grin. "Last chance to eat for twelve hours." Without warning, he lurched towards her.

Lexi sped up her already hurried washing, loathing her two companions equally.

"I have food—if you're not the Governor's mate," frog man offered, gliding up next to her.

"Back off," Avell whined irritably.

Frog man moved back grudgingly as Lexi gave her hair a final rinse and bolted from the water. "Nice bruise," he jeered. Avell snickered.

Out in the corridor, Lexi gagged several times; the reek of rotting garbage seemed to follow her. She straightened as soon as Avell joined her, her face hardening into a frozen mask.

"I don't wish for your protection. Leave," she ordered.

Avell sputtered an unpleasant laugh as he glanced up and down the corridor to ensure he had no audience. "I don't want to give you my protection, believe me, but I have orders."

"Where is the Governor now?" Lexi demanded.

Avell glared at her sulkily. "At dinner. Weren't you invited?"

"Yes, I was. Take me there, please," Lexi requested, the *please* more warning than pleasantry.

Avell shrugged, sending his broken wings waving, then sullenly led the way. He stopped before ornate double doors and gave an odd-patterned knock. The door opened a crack, and Avell rolled his eyes as he nodded back at her. Charis quickly swung the door open and ushered them through with a deferential nod to Lexi. Dominating the left side of the room was an enormous bed with an ancient-looking burgundy spread bedecked with golden tassels. Assorted furniture ran along the back wall until it met a poorly-constructed corner room of unpainted pine. Directly in front of the protruding addition, an ornate banquet table ran the length of the room, set with various dishes at only one end. Limen abruptly stood, folding a moth-eaten robe more tightly around him.

"I didn't think you were coming," he apologized, two spots of color dotting his pale cheeks.

"Avell believes me to be your mistress, and is sharing his supposition with others," Lexi announced without preamble.

Limen's pale mien gradually assumed a mottled purple as she spoke. "Avell, you are relieved of duty. Report to Pol, and ask him to lock you in his wettest cell," he commanded, his voice disturbingly calm. "Charis, Apollo, out."

"I don't intend to stay," Lexi said, her tone clipped as she turned to follow the retreating guards.

Limen moved quickly to her side, his arm halting her as the door shut.

"This is inappropriate, Limen," she chided, staring at his arm until he dropped it.

"Psyche said you didn't wish to speak to me, because...because," Limen floundered, his voice sounding young and lost.

Lexi looked up with surprise, further startled at his unusual pallor. "I didn't send her to speak for me."

Limen blinked his confusion, "but she said..."

Lexi released an angry breath. "I sent her to you because she tried to blackmail me, Limen."

"Oh." Limen meandered away from her, rubbing his face with a weak laugh. "She's rather clever. At your fictitious request, I have granted her life servant meals delivered to your room, exemption from pregnancy tests, and snacks from the kitchen at any hour." He turned around to look at her. "Do you want any of those things?"

"I want to go," Lexi answered, crossing to the door.

Limen flew across the room and landed in her path, his face desperate. "I didn't mean to! I was faithful to her for *six months*, and then my season just kept dragging on and on, and I *missed* her!"

Lexi frowned her distaste and stepped around him.

"Please don't tell her! What good can it do?" he begged, blocking her way again.

Lexi met his gaze, eyes blazing. "Maybe she would stop mourning the loss of you! Maybe she would stop talking about you like you're the most perfect man God ever created! Maybe it would be less painful if *I* tell her what you are than it will be the day one of your pregnant mistresses stumbles to her door!"

"That won't happen! I provide for them! I arranged it so Mona never has to know...just don't," he pled, "don't tell her."

Pushing around him, Lexi yanked open the door and stalked furiously away, too angry to hear the undignified squeaking her wet shoes made with each hasty step. Her trembling rage had subsided by the time she reached Cam's door, leaving behind an exhausted melancholy.

"Sorry I'm late," she greeted, slipping past him and falling heavily onto the little stool. She inhaled deeply, the scent of stolen cookies calming her.

"You had another bath?" he asked, glancing out into the hallway before shutting the door.

"I got muddy outside," she began, then let the whole story slip out while she absently picked at the food he had laid out on the table. She hardly noticed when he slipped behind her and began combing out her wet hair. When she stopped speaking, he continued to run the comb through her hair with soothing strokes.

"You've had a bad day." The humor ran through Cam's voice until it erupted in a pleasant, low chuckle. Then he leaned down and inhaled deeply. "You know that smell when a fruit is perfectly ripe, and you've just picked it off the tree, and brought it up to your mouth?"

Lexi looked back at him with a puzzled smile.

163

"*That's* what you smell like."

Lexi's face lit up with a slow smile, and he answered with his dimpled one.

"Come on, I'll take you back to your room."

Lexi shook her head decidedly. "I'd rather stay here. I don't want to see any guards or Psyche or Tiger. And..." She looked down at the food in front of her with sudden realization. "You haven't eaten anything."

"I'm not hungry," he said smiling.

Lexi stood and faced him, her hands firmly on his shoulders, though he was a few inches taller. "There are enough dishonest people in my life. You have to promise to always be truthful."

"Okay," he agreed, tipping his forehead against hers. "I'm starving," he confessed with a low laugh.

Lexi laughed with him a moment, feeling the zing of electricity between them as she looked down at his lips, just inches away. Still he hesitated, and when she looked into his eyes, she saw the question there. Smiling, she gave him the slightest of nods, sliding her hands up his broad arms as he caressed her cheek, the brush of his fingertips on her ear sending a little thrill shooting down her arm. Leaning forward, he found her lips, kissing her so gently and sweetly that it somehow made her want to cry. She swallowed down the lump in her throat as he pulled back, and kept her eyes down so he wouldn't see the tears.

"Now sit down and eat," she ordered, fighting the emotional waver that broke her voice.

"Are you okay?" He ran a soothing hand slowly up and down her bare arm.

She nodded without looking up, and pointed to the stool. "Sit," she commanded, quickly turning away to ensure her eyes were dry.

"How about we get you dressed first?" Cam suggested.

"Can't," she said simply, still facing the wall as a blush rose up her neck. "Nothing is clean."

"I can wash your clothes for you."

Lexi let out an uncomfortable laugh as she turned around to face him. "You're not my lady's maid."

Cam shrugged with an abashed grin. "I don't mind."

"I do," Lexi began, stopping mid-sentence as the door pounded behind her.

"Hey! Is Lexi in there?" Tiger called through the door.

"Can't you tell by the stench?" Lexi hollered back, her anger surprising her. Blushing, she turned to look at Cam.

The door opened, and Lexi caught it halfway, meeting Tiger's unreadable expression with her chin thrust out. Tiger stopped in the doorway, his glance falling to Lexi's swimsuit, then stopping on her bruised arm before finding its way back to her face.

"You didn't come to dinner," Tiger said, his voice calm though his brown eyes stormed. "And your guards don't know where you are."

"How clever of you to find me, then," Lexi said sarcastically.

Tiger shifted his weight from one large foot to the other, then looked between Lexi's wings at Cam. "Could you give us a moment?"

"Are you asking him to leave his own room?" Lexi demanded.

"No," Tiger said, yanking her out into the hall and shutting the door behind her before her startled protest found words.

"Let go of me!" Lexi snarled, her fingers prying at his.

"Hey!" Cam yelled, trying the door and realizing Tiger was holding it shut from the other side.

"Lex," Tiger said. "You don't have any reason to be angry with me. And you've got to stop acting so stupid."

"*Stupidly*," Lexi corrected as she successfully ripped her wrist from his grasp, and glared up at him. "And you think *I'm* being stupid?" The door thumped repeatedly in its frame, each man pulling the opposite direction. "You're holding a man prisoner in his room for no reason!"

A vague blush rose in Tiger's tanned cheeks, and he released the door handle just as Cam yanked it. The door flew open and Cam stumbled backward, crashing into the stool and table. Lexi pushed past Tiger, her wings brushing his face as she hurried into the room.

"Are you okay?" Lexi asked, inspecting Cam's wings for damage.

"Yeah," Cam said darkly, staring at Tiger.

"Sorry," Tiger muttered, scowling as he turned to leave. "I'll send your guards," he called over his shoulder as he flew away.

Lexi slammed the door behind him with an irritated slap. "What is the *matter* with him?"

Cam set his table and chair upright, then began to pick the food off the floor.

"Did he ruin your food?" Lexi asked, bending down to help him.

"Most of it is fine," he assured her, his voice still tight with irritation.

Lexi set the last of the spilled food on the table, then stood next to him, watching a muscle in his jaw jump as he gazed down at the mess. Tentatively, she laid a hand on his arm.

"I'm sorry he keeps showing up yelling," she apologized. "He's really not like that. Normally he only yells when I scare him." Lexi's eyes went wide with sudden understanding. "Oh. I guess I'm scaring him." Her surprise melted into an impish grin. "Once, he had to get something out of this old wooden box in the tack room. He opened it and the entire thing was crisscrossed with spider webs. Tiger's terrified of spiders," she explained, smiling up at Cam and receiving a weak smile in return. "I was standing there teasing him about it, so after searching around for a spider and not finding one, he bravely stuck his hand in. As soon as he was in up to his elbow, I screamed, 'Spider!'" Lexi laughed merrily. "I've never seen him jump so far. Of course he was furiously angry as soon as he noticed I was laughing. He lectured me for half an hour, and made me promise never to scare him again."

Cam gave her a half-hearted grunt of laughter as a polite knock sounded at his door.

"Guards, probably," Lexi guessed and walked over to open it.

Erid smiled with a polite little bow as he handed her a small pile of clothes, then turned to stand guard outside the door. Lexi peered out to see Charis flanking the other side of the door and smiled at him. Turning back to Cam, she examined his face.

"You still look tired," she observed. "And you didn't eat yet." Lexi looked sadly at the pile of food Cam had retrieved from the floor. "Sorry. I'll pay to replace it," she offered.

Cam shook his head dismissively and stepped forward to block her view of the table.

Lexi took his hand and pulled him close, then kissed his cheek. "Goodnight," she whispered, pleased to see his expression soften. "I'll see you in the morning."

"I'm not tired," he assured her. At her look of complete disbelief, he laughed. "Okay, I'm tired," he admitted sheepishly. Cam glanced at the guards in the hallway, then leaned in to kiss her softly without making a sound. "Goodnight."

Lexi grinned with her eyes shut, savoring the feeling of his lips touching hers. "Goodnight," she repeated, retreating to the doorway as she opened her eyes. She could feel a little giggle bubbling up her throat, but she forced it down, drawing herself up into princess posture as she passed the guards. She walked confidently to the laundry room, pleased she was beginning to recognize her surroundings. Erid hurried ahead to open the heavy laundry room door, and she rewarded him with a smile. Inside, a soapy, dank smell prevailed. The room was divided into large vats of water on one side and drying racks on the other. Lexi wandered the room, searching for the muddy dress and blue shirt that the laundry mistress had set aside to wash in the morning. She found them at the back of the room with her name pinned to them. Shifting the pile in her arms, she removed her mother's red dress, then blew out a breath through clenched teeth. The remainder of the clothing in her arms was Talan's, not her own. The unmistakable scent of cloves and hickory wafted from them, and she wondered why she hadn't noticed before.

"Something the matter, Miss Fritillary?" Erid asked.

"Talan has played a trick on us," she fumed, tucking her mother's dress into the laundress' pile, then marching swiftly out of the room.

Erid looked mortified. "I'm sorry, Your Highness," he said jogging alongside her with arms outstretched to take Talan's clothes. "I'll take care of it right away."

"No need," Lexi assured him, thinking of Tiger's old clothes still in Talan's possession. No doubt Talan would insist they were *his* unless she were there. *Which is what he wants*, Lexi thought. *He wants to see me.* Lexi seethed, replaying all the unpleasant things Talan had done to her in the last four days, then weighing it against Tiger's old clothes so lovingly altered by Cercy— whom she might never see again. Swallowing a sudden lump in her throat, she spun to face Erid, who had fallen behind.

"Take me to the dungeon, please," she requested politely.

Erid's objections died on his lips and he gave her a quick bow. "Yes, Miss Fritillary."

As they wound their way down the seemingly endless stairs to the dungeon, Lexi began to rethink her errand, painfully conscious of her bathing suit, her bruises, and the three men incarcerated because of her. The temperature was steadily climbing as they descended, and Lexi was grateful for her cold wet hair cooling her bare back.

A grizzled old guard with brown wings tightened up to attention as she approached and gave her a deep bow. "Your Highness," he greeted.

"Miss Fritillary," Lexi corrected with a polite smile.

The dungeon guard nodded. "Of course, Miss Fritillary. How may I assist you?"

"I need to see Talan Admiral," she said, holding the offending clothes away from her, annoyed by their pleasant scent.

The gate guard looked uncomfortably at Erid and Charis, then turned and unlocked the gate, frowning as they passed him.

The stench of wet sulfur was overpowering as Erid led her back to the cells with Charis hovering nervously beside her. As they rounded the first corner, Avell jumped up to the bars.

"Who is she, Erid?!" Avell demanded in his whiny voice. "And what am I doing in here?!"

"Don't make it worse for yourself," Erid cautioned, with a finger to his lips as he walked by.

"Come on!" Avell whined. "Charis? Somebody tell me!"

"Shut up!" yelled someone further down.

"I heard that! Who was that? I'm still a guard! I'll remember you when I get out!" Avell threatened futilely as a deep laugh echoed from the same direction.

"Mmmm," a male voice said loudly as Lexi passed, and Charis thunked his bars with a swift rap of his club. Startled, Lexi noticed that Erid had his club drawn as well. The prisoners were all lining up at their bars now, their faces alight with curiosity. Lexi carefully avoided their eyes, focusing her gaze on the back of Erid's mousy-brown head.

"Hey, why am I here?" a familiar voice demanded. "I haven't done anything!"

Lexi's legs stopped moving of their own accord, and she turned slowly to look at Wes, only one cell down from where she was standing.

"Hey," he said, his mouth spreading into a smug smile. "You came to visit me."

Lexi was suddenly grateful for the masking stench of sulfur that made Wes' floral musk little more than a suggestion.

"She better not have."

Lexi whirled around to see Talan in the cell opposite, leaning expectantly against the bars. Walking over, she turned the pile of clothes sideways and shoved it through, careful to avoid Talan's hands.

"Give me my clothes, Talan," she quietly ordered.

169

"I see you're in need of them, my love." He grinned appreciatively and momentarily overpowered the sulfur with his own scent.

"She's not yours, little man," Wes said, his fists tightening around the bars.

Talan let out an indignant laugh. "What did you say?"

Lexi fought a smirk as she looked between the two. It was probably the first time anyone had dared address Talan that way.

Wes drew up to his full hulking height, flexing both arms to show the bulk of them. "I said, the girl doesn't belong to you, *little man.*"

Talan's face burned red while he affected a hard laugh. "Moronic peasant, we'll have a chat later, when the *lady* isn't present."

Wes smirked. "Sounds good to me. Now, how about you shut it so I can talk to her?"

Charis gave Wes' bars a warning tap as Talan bristled.

"That's right. Keep him in line, boys," Talan praised with a smug grin, which quickly dissolved as Erid gave his bars a warning tap as well.

Wes laughed loudly, then caught Lexi's eye. "Raven," he coaxed, "come here."

Lexi looked at his outstretched hand, sorely tempted to take it. His musky scent overcame the sulfur for a moment and her knees sagged beneath her, her expression going soft. Erid caught her arm, steadying her while Charis gave Wes' bars a sharp rap.

"No more signaling...either of you," Charis commanded.

A surprised laugh sounded from a couple cells away as Talan stared at Lexi with confusion. "What did you do to her?" he demanded of Wes.

Wes chortled. "She likes me."

"That's enough talking," Charis said, rapping his bars again.

Lexi inhaled the sickening sulfur smell gratefully, shaking herself lightly as her head began to clear. Erid released her, watching her face with concern.

"I'm okay," she assured him softly.

"What just happened?" Talan demanded.

"Never mind, Talan. Just give me my clothes," she snapped, a little too loudly.

"What did he do to you?" Talan persevered.

"Let it go, Talan," Lexi warned, lowering her voice. "I'm ordering you to hand over my clothing now or you will stay in the dungeon as long as I'm here."

Sullenly, Talan took his bag from his bed and opened it.

"Why does he have your clothes?" Wes asked.

Charis rapped the bars of Wes' cell. "You just added another day to your sentence."

"What sentence?" Wes demanded, carefully stepping out of the club's range. "Nobody told me why I'm here in the first place or for how long. I haven't done anything wrong."

Wes' words echoed uncomfortably in Lexi's head as she took her clothing from Talan's hands, annoyed that he handed it to her one piece at a time, always endeavoring to brush her hand as he did so. The tingles that ran up her arm when he succeeded irritated her immensely.

"Raven, will you find out why I'm stuck in here? Nobody will tell me," Wes pleaded, a vulnerable note in his voice that sent a funny thrill through her chest.

Lexi clutched her clothing to her, trying to dampen the sensation as she exchanged a look with Erid. Erid shook his head slightly, but Lexi ignored it. "Release him after I leave," she commanded in a whisper.

"Miss Fritillary," Erid objected.

"Release him," Lexi mouthed the words emphatically.

"Thank you," Talan said, his grin making it clear he had misunderstood.

Leaning closer to Talan's cell, Lexi spoke softly. "Limen put you here; you need to work it out with him."

"Then who are you releasing?" Talan asked, his face tensing as he realized the answer. "*Him*," he huffed. "*You* put him in here? What did he do to you? He had better stay away from you," Talan hissed, his whispers increasingly loud.

Lexi shook her head wearily and walked away, ignoring the calls of both men, then their threats to each other.

"Are you related to the Governor?" Avell demanded as she passed his cell. "I'll find out!"

The graying guard quickly opened the gate as they approached, and Erid stopped to whisper to him in a low tone. The dungeon guard shook his head grimly and looked at Lexi, but handed Erid the keyring.

Charis glanced at her with a deep frown as they climbed the stairs, but Lexi pretended not to see it. She was far from certain she had made the right choice, but it seemed unjust to incarcerate Wes for what he *might* have done. A slight shiver twitched her shoulders at the possibilities. They had just reached the top of the stairs when Wes flew up behind them, a grin lighting his usually hooded eyes.

"I'm free," he announced. "How about another dance?" He eyed Charis disdainfully as the guard moved between them.

Lexi breathed carefully through her mouth, still tasting Wes on the back of her tongue. "No, thank you," she managed, propelling herself forward on her increasingly uncooperative feet.

"What's with the guard?" he asked, tossing his head at Charis, then glancing behind him as Erid's rapid footsteps sounded on the stairs.

Lexi increased her pace, gulping hungrily at the fresher air. She could hear *and smell* Wes following her. Steeling herself, she spun and faced him.

"They know you make me pheromone drunk, and they're waiting for an excuse to drag you back to the dungeon," she blurted, feeling her knees soften.

Wes looked at her steadily, fighting a grin as Erid pushed past him and took her arm. "Then I won't give them one," he said, backing off with both hands raised.

With Erid's assistance, Lexi turned unsteadily and walked into the blissfully multi-scented air. The hallways were quickly filling up as the in-seasons left the dining hall and dispersed.

"I swear that was rat meat," a girl with orange wings insisted as her yellow-winged companion pretended to gag. A red-winged male herded them both forward making rat noises, and Lexi froze. His red wings were black-rimmed with streaks of yellow on his hindwings– an exact match to her mother's. Without thinking, she plunged after him, trying to get a look at his face. His dark hair was the same shade as her own, and when he turned to scowl at someone who had bumped his wing, Lexi gasped. The chilling expression was so like the Queen: the high cheekbones, cool brown eyes, and perfectly straight, thin nose. Lexi was suddenly eager to get away from him. Turning, she struggled against the crowd. Charis and Erid helped to clear a path, but that only made everyone stare, their glances darting back and forth between the guards and Lexi in her bathing suit with a pile of clothes clutched to her chest.

"Caught another dangerous criminal?" someone asked wryly, and several in the crowd laughed.

Lexi's face went carefully blank. She pulled Erid in front of her, and once again changed direction to move with the tide of the crowd.

"Are we returning to your room, Miss Fritillary?" Erid asked over his shoulder.

"Yes," she nodded, her answer changing to a gasp when someone ran a hand up her bare thigh. She peered around her forewing, but the faces of the three men behind her were blank as they moved with the herd, their scents blending unpleasantly. Taking Charis' arm, she pulled him behind her until she was relatively hidden in the protective screen of Erid's beige-streaked yellow wings in front, and Charis' white wings with their bright orange tips flanking her. When they finally reached her door, she could have cried with relief, though her expression never betrayed her.

Beck stood before the door, grinning. "Miss Fritillary," he greeted with a tiny bow.

"I thought your shift was over," Lexi said, reaching around him to open the door.

"Wait," Beck cautioned, putting out his hand. "The Governor had me escort Psyche back to the room, make sure she didn't leave until she apologizes to you, and receives your permission to continue as her roommate."

Lexi wanted very much to laugh and Beck's expectant expression said the same. Taking a deep breath, Lexi allowed herself a smile.

"She has to keep her *information* to herself or the Governor said he'll put her in the lifer section of the dungeon with the murderers and rapists," Beck informed her. "I think she's scared enough to behave, but I'm to wait until you decide for yourself."

This time Lexi did laugh. "Poor Beck; did you even get dinner?"

"No, but one of the cooks likes me; I'll get something."

Lexi patted his shoulder and entered the room. Psyche was lying with her head at the foot of the bed, her expression blank as she rested her pointed chin against her folded arms.

"You win," Psyche began. "I'm sorry for trying to blackmail you, and as big-mouth Beck just told you, I get dungeon time with the lifers if I talk. So," Psyche drawled, pushing herself up to her elbows, "you can accept me as an ally or send me away as an enemy."

Lexi squelched the urge to laugh, and mirrored Psyche's blank expression. "And why would you want to be my ally?"

One corner of Psyche's mouth curved into a smile. "He didn't revoke any of the privileges I negotiated. If I stay here, I'll be well fed and get to sleep through the pregnancy tests. For that, I'd befriend even *Wes*," Psyche said, her smile turning smug, "or *Van*."

"Find a new room, Psyche," Lexi sighed wearily.

Psyche's face hardened as she crawled off the bed. "You're making a mistake."

"Surely you're done threatening me by now?" Lexi made little effort to hide her yawn as she opened the door behind her. "Beck, Psyche needs a new room. Sorry," she added when she heard him groan.

"It's okay; I expected it," he said, glancing in to where Psyche was gathering up her things to a steady stream of muttered profanity. "I only ever saw her get along with two people, and they married each other a couple of days ago."

Lexi let out a sigh. "I'd pity her if she would stop threatening me every two minutes."

Beck's rusty eyebrows rose high in his freckled forehead. "A room in the dungeon, perhaps?"

Lexi waved the idea away. "I think I've incarcerated enough people for one day."

Beck smirked. "Yes, you have."

Erid turned from his post to give Beck a shocked look.

"What? We're old friends. Grew up in the same town," Beck chortled.

Lexi smiled at him, then stiffened as Psyche hoisted her bag and came marching towards her.

"What? Did you change your mind? Get out of my way," Psyche grumbled.

Lexi exchanged a look with Beck and mouthed the words "no pity" as she moved aside.

"I can get my own room," Psyche snapped at Beck. "I don't need you following me."

Giving her a martyred eye-roll, Beck followed her anyway. Lexi offered him a sympathetic smile, then shut the door, looking happily around her empty room. The table was cluttered with three dinner plates: one empty, two covered in cold stew. Lexi prodded a chunk of meat and wondered if it was indeed rat, before she opened the door again and handed Erid and Charis the plates.

"It's gone cold, but maybe you're hungry enough not to care?"

"Thank you," they answered simultaneously, and Lexi smiled as she shut the door.

With a sudden burst of energy, she shoved the three center beds together, creating one nearly the size of her own back home. With a nod of satisfaction, she hung up Tiger's old clothes to wear tomorrow, tossed her black pants and her mother's frilly red shirt under the bed, then slipped into her nightgown. The clinging scent of Talan both pleased and annoyed her as she snuggled into a deflated pillow and drifted off to sleep.

Chapter Nine

"That is *my* room, and you're going to let me in it," Clodi insisted from the hall.

Lexi tried to open her eyes, groaning with the effort.

"Raven! Psyche! They won't let me in!" Clodi hollered amidst a slight scuffle, then Erid murmured something too low to hear.

"Where did she go, then?" Clodi demanded.

Sighing, Lexi kicked her scratchy blanket away and crawled backwards off her large, makeshift bed. "It's all right," she called sleepily, stumbling to the door. By the time she pulled it open, Charis had Clodi restrained and Erid was whispering to her urgently, casting side glances down the hall at a gathering curious crowd.

"It's all right," Lexi repeated, pulling Clodi away from Charis and into the room. "She's my roommate."

The triumph beaming from Clodi's doll-like face was unmistakable. "I told you!" she crowed at the guards before Lexi shut the door behind her.

"They wouldn't let me in," Clodi announced unnecessarily. "And he said Psyche moved out. Did she get married?"

Lexi crawled back onto the giant bed before answering. "We weren't getting along, so she moved to a different room."

"Instead of you? I mean, I'm glad you didn't, but wasn't she here first? And why are there guards out there? Damus—that's Psyche's brother—thought it was best if we waited for them to leave, but they've been out there for hours, and I was too tired to wait any more. Are you in some kind of trouble?" Clodi finally paused for an answer.

Lexi laid her head down on her arms and let her wings cover her face. "Wes makes me pheromone drunk. The guards are trying to protect me from him."

"Oooohh, that makes sense," Clodi nodded, sitting on a delicate stool with a heavy thump. "Wait, is pheromone drunk what it sounds like?"

"Yes," Lexi yawned, distorting the word.

"Wow! So when you smell him, can you even say no?"

"Not really," Lexi answered, letting her voice fade sleepily, hoping Clodi would get the hint.

"No wonder you need guards! Damus told me all about the seducers I need to watch out for, and he says Wes is the very worst." Clodi paused thoughtfully. "Damus is nice but he smells like radishes. He went on the tour with me since Psyche said you were going to be too busy, and then because the guards were out there, he took me to dinner, too. And then the guards were *still* there, so he took me dancing. Damus is nice. He makes me laugh, but I don't like radishes. My mom grows them in the garden, but I don't even like to weed around them, even the greens have a sharp smell that makes my nose tingle." Clodi rubbed at her nose absently. "His brother Everes is nice, too, but he smells too much like him, and he doesn't talk much. They had another brother that got married this morning, and one of their sisters got married and left a couple of days ago. They have a really big family because their dad was a big seducer..." Clodi continued on, but her loud voice weaved itself into Lexi's dream, and she fell fast asleep.

Lexi awoke with a panicked jolt to Clodi's rumbling snores. Rising up on her knees, she wiped perspiration from her forehead, then shook her head, trying to erase the image seared inside. When she shut her eyes, Wes was there choking the life out of Tiger while she watched, unable to move. She blinked repeatedly, then climbed out of bed to pace, vainly hoping to calm herself.

"You should have at least warned him you released Wes," she scolded herself in a whisper. "And after he threatened Tiger, too! What were you thinking?" Lexi slipped a manicured nail between her teeth, then drew it back out again automatically, flicking her nails with sharp little clacks as she continued to pace, distraught. More than once she moved to the door, then drew back again. Finally, she forced her face to a careful blank, and opened the door. A guard with big white wings turned an inquiring face to her.

"Miss Fritillary?"

Lexi glanced quickly at his companion with the shredded brown wings, recognizing neither of them. "Do you know the time?" she asked politely, swallowing down her request to find Tiger and make sure he was okay.

"Just after three in the morning."

"Thank you." Lexi quietly shut the door. The nightmare images kept playing through her mind with startling clarity, snatches of detail returning with each waking moment. She kept straining for any noise from the room above her, but Clodi's loud snores seemed to block out everything else. She couldn't even tell if it was still raining. Thoroughly vexed, she yanked out one of the rugs and swung open a balcony door. The frigid air bit at her skin. Lexi started to shut the door again, then stopped. Despite the puddle at her feet, it was no longer raining, and she peered up at the silent balcony above her, inhaling deeply. The pleasant scent of the wet forest caught her nose, but nothing more. Eyes straining at the cloudy night sky, Lexi tiptoed around the puddle and shut the balcony door behind her.

"Stupid," she condemned herself quietly. Her flowing nightgown flared out in the gentle breeze as she flew the short distance to Tiger's balcony. Landing silently, she leaned in to the wet door and inhaled deeply. The faintest scent of musk tickled her nose and brought an involuntary smile to her face. Her feet began to ache in their icy puddle, and she shifted her weight back and forth to warm them with movement. Rolling her eyes at her own behavior, she started to leave as the nightmare images danced back through her mind, this time with Tiger's room as the background. Grimacing, and promising herself that she would only peek in, she leaned against the heavy door, willing it to move despite the rug tangled beneath it. The door gave slightly with a muffled lurch, and Lexi jumped at the sound. Holding her breath and placing one hand over her thundering heart, she strained to hear inside the room. A measured, even breathing filled the room. Lexi waited impatiently for her eyes to adjust to the darker interior. Peering at the closest bed, she stared at it until she could make out the tangled empty blanket. Lexi released her held breath and pulled in the next thoughtlessly. She gasped as the heady musk made her knees go weak. She stumbled back, sucking in the night air and clearing her head. Tiger had taken Wes' pillow from the bed nearest the balcony, so the sleeper she couldn't see had to be Tiger, she reasoned. He was fine, of course. And now she could go. Pulling in a deep preparatory breath, she held it and moved forward to clutch the icy, wet handle. She checked for the sound of deep, measured breaths one last time, then gently pulled the door to close it. But it didn't move. Doubling her efforts, she gave the door a solid yank, but it still wouldn't give. Bemused, she released the door and it swung further open. Lexi stared at it a moment, then looked down at the rug, doubled over and peeping out beneath it. Poking at it with a numb toe, she tried to pull it flat, but it remained stubbornly stuck beneath the door. Folding her wings tightly, she tried to squat down and tug it with her hands, but she couldn't reach it without bending her wings against the door, the balcony railing, or the puddled stone beneath her feet. Lexi stood up straight with a frustrated sigh, then yanked the door again. This time it moved a fraction of an inch, punctuated by a noise of stifled mirth. Startled, Lexi leapt into the air and flew several feet before realization narrowed her eyes and tightened her mouth.

"Tiger! That was a rotten trick," she hissed, flying back to give the door a hard shove that resulted in a thump and a grunt of pain. "You scared me," she accused, pushing the other door open and stepping through it, expecting to see him behind the suspiciously unmoving door. But the muted light spilling in through the door revealed an empty corner. "Tiger?" Lexi's strained gaze swept the dark room. "This isn't funny." The musky scent made her feel unnaturally calm as she walked over to stare at the three empty beds. An uncomfortable laugh escaped her. "Unless of course I'm really the only one here."

"You're not," Wes replied, dropping down from the ceiling to land next to her in a veritable cloud of musk.

Lexi let out a strangled shriek and leapt for the door, but Wes caught her by the hair and pulled her back.

"You sneak into my room in the middle of the night, hit me with the door, scream, and run out again? I don't think so," he chuckled coldly. Taking her hand, her released her hair and spun her around to face him, his large hands settling heavily on her waist.

Lexi's eyes watered with pain, and she rubbed her tender scalp."Let go of me or you're going back to the dungeon."

"Such a tease," Wes said, looking down at her nightgown. Lexi immediately crossed her arms over her chest. He laughed, then leaned in to whisper just above her ear. "What charge will you bring against me? I haven't done anything."

Lexi fought the urge to tip her head into his and forced her wandering thoughts to make words. "Doesn't matter."

"Really?" he asked, sliding one hand up her side and running the other along her jaw and neck. "Why's that?"

Lexi turned her head towards the balcony, trying to breathe in the fresh air to clear her mind, but Wes only signaled again and drew her face back towards him.

"You didn't answer my question," he reminded her.

"Oh." Lexi's mind was beginning to float along with her body. "What did you ask?"

Wes chuckled softly while he used his rough thumb to play with her bottom lip. "You were telling me why you could have me thrown in the dungeon."

"Oh," Lexi said again, trying to concentrate as he ran a finger down her neck, then wound it in the ribbon on her nightgown. "That's a secret," she finally managed, frowning at her own silly answer.

"Tell me," he coaxed, pulling on the ribbon to draw her closer.

Lexi stared at his beautiful mouth, so like Tiger's, then a jolt ran through her as another fragment of her dream came back. Before Wes strangled Tiger, Wes had been kissing her. The realization sunk to her belly like a stone as the dream sensation of kissing him tingled on her lips.

"Tell me," he repeated, his mouth just inches from hers as he wet his lips in anticipation.

"No," Lexi murmured weakly, cringing. "You'll hurt Tiger."

Wes drew back, his dark brows knit together. "If you tell me your secret, I'll hurt Tiger?"

Lexi shook her head in confusion. "Please just let me go. If he caught you with me, he would fight you. You'll hurt him."

Wes snorted a laugh. "Sounds about right. But you're free to go anytime; the door is open." He nodded at the balcony door with a mocking grin.

"You're...holding me," Lexi said haltingly.

Wes abruptly released her, then caught her again as she began to fall. "I have to hold you; your legs don't seem to be working," he noted with mock concern.

A little flicker of anger burned through her drunken haze for a moment. "Then carry me to the balcony," she said, her voice coming out more complaint than command.

"Yes, Your Majesty," he laughed, not noticing when Lexi started at the title. "Threaten me with the dungeon, boss me around...I'll bet you're an only child." Wes lifted her by the waist and carried her out to the balcony, lifted her wings up over the rail, then carefully sat her atop it, his thumbs pressing into her hips. "This is as good a place as any."

"For what?" Lexi leaned away from him to escape the cloud of scent that surrounded him, her hindwings bending uncomfortably against the rail. As she sucked in the clean night air, alarm began to streak through the fuzzy sensation of pleasure in her mind, and she gasped when she felt his face against her throat.

"Better hold on," Wes advised, trying to wrap her legs around him, "you might fall and break a wing against the railing."

Kicking and pushing away from him, she flew backwards off the rail. "You'll get dungeon time for that." Her voice shook with fury now that her head had cleared.

Wes smirked. "I didn't even kiss you. And if you want to complain about me, you'll have to explain why you came to my bedroom in the middle of the night...in your nightgown."

Lexi could feel the iron core within her as she landed on her own balcony and glared up at him. He was leaning over the rail, laughing. "No need," she retorted, her face a blank mask. "You kidnaped me from my bed and dragged me to your room. It's lucky I escaped."

Wes leapt down from his balcony to hers before she finished speaking. "If you're going to have me punished for *that*," he menaced, clutching her to him roughly. "Then I might as well enjoy myself."

"Clodi!" Lexi screamed and managed to kick her balcony door with a heavy thud that made her numb foot sting.

Wes freed her and flew to his own balcony with a string of expletives as Clodi ripped open the doors.

"What happened? Are you okay?" she demanded just as Wes shut the doors above.

"Wes tried to kidnap me," Lexi asserted, her guilt assuaged by the nasty names he had just called her.

"That was him?" Clodi demanded, pointing up. At Lexi's weary nod, her face galvanized. "I'll get him," she promised, starting to fly just as the guards belatedly entered the room.

"No," Lexi said emphatically, pulling on the bigger girl's wrist to bring her back to the floor.

The two guards halted midway into the room, their clubs drawn and faces tight as they made a quick visual search of the room. The guard with the big white wings flushed. "Did you scream?"

Lexi nodded, beginning to shiver. "Wes Swallowtail jumped down to my balcony and grabbed me. Put him back in the dungeon," Lexi commanded, her hand tightening around Clodi's wrist as she felt the girl move to join them.

"Yes, Miss Fritillary!" Both guards hurried from the room.

Clodi looked at her wide-eyed and bemused. "Why don't you want me to go? And why did he bow to you? And why are they obeying you? What is going on?" Clodi asked, her voice high and childlike.

Lexi released Clodi's wrist with a sigh and walked back into the room, pulling her nightgown, wet from the railing, away from her body.

Without taking her eyes from Lexi, Clodi shut the doors and kicked the rugs back underneath them.

"Raven, are you okay? I'm feeling like a lost piglet here."

"I'm okay," Lexi lied, frowning at the heavy scent of Wes emanating from her nightgown. Fumbling with the ribbons above her wings, she quickly removed her nightgown and kicked it under her bed.

"How come you can order people to the dungeon?" Clodi asked softly, staring at the floor to give Lexi privacy. "Are you going to send *me* to the dungeon if I keep asking you questions?" Clodi played with a button on her shirt, nervously unbuttoning and rebuttoning it in quick succession. "Is that where Psyche went?"

Lexi released a weak laugh as she slipped on Tiger's old clothes, comforted by the feel of them, despite Talan's scent. "No."

"No, you're not going to send me to the dungeon? Or no, Psyche's not there?"

"No to both," Lexi sighed, sinking onto a stool as she met Clodi's troubled gaze.

A heavy thump overhead made them both start, then a tight smile curved Lexi's mouth.

"Sounds like they got him," Clodi tittered, her fingers going back to worrying her button. "You don't have to answer my questions. But do I have to obey you?"

"Are you good with secrets, Clodi?"

"Uh, sort of. My brother stole a bunny once, and I kept the secret for four hours until my mom asked me why my shirt was wet and I blurted out 'bunny pee.'" Clodi looked apologetic. "I never mean to tell."

Lexi stifled a laugh. "I'm friends with the Governor," she explained. "He's worried about me, so he gave me guards and lets me boss them around."

"You must be really good friends."

No! she thought as she nodded in agreement. "I've known him since we were both children." *I met him once when we were both children*, she corrected silently.

"Oh," Clodi said nodding, "that makes sense." Clodi's eyes crinkled at the corners as she grimaced. "Will it be really bad if I accidently tell someone?"

"It will be better if you don't, but if you accidently let it slip, just let me know who you tell."

Clodi gave a great sigh of relief. "Okay, I can do that. Whew! What a wake up! I'm not tired at all now. I'm ready to milk the cows and feed the chickens!" Clodi announced as she clapped her hands together with a big smile. "Too bad the life servants ate the last of them fifty years ago. I learned that on the tour. The guide told us some really interesting stories, too. Did you know the real reason the king from a hundred years ago turned this place into the Mating Mountain?"

"Besides morality and convenience?" Lexi asked, only half listening.

"Tinus —he's the guide— says that's just the lie they tell everybody in school now. The real reason was because the king's only child fell in love with a stable boy and mated with him. The king was so angry that he burned down the stable, disowned his daughter, and abandoned the mountain castle to build the new one. He made this place the Mating Mountain to keep the nobles and the commoners separate, so they wouldn't mate with each other."

Clodi had her full attention now, and it was with difficulty that Lexi kept the shock from her face. "That can't be true," she finally said.

Clodi shrugged. "Tinus says it is. He says he's a descendant of the princess and the stable boy."

Lexi let out a relieved laugh. "Now I'm certain it isn't true."

Clodi looked disappointed for a moment, then her face brightened. "Well, he also said the band only stops for meals and bathroom breaks, and I'm pretty sure that's true. Want to go dancing?"

Lexi nodded as she stood, still eager to find Tiger and put her nightmarish fears to rest.

"Yes!" Clodi said happily, then glanced at Lexi's clothes. "Could I maybe wear the yellow dress now that you're not?"

Lexi frowned apologetically, "I'm sorry Clodi, I got it muddy; but it's yours as soon as it's clean."

"That's okay," Clodi said cheerfully, opening the door. "We look just alike right now anyway. Are those your brother's clothes?"

Lexi smiled as she passed through the door. "They're Tiger's."

Clodi's dark eyebrows rose high, wrinkling the perfect skin of her forehead as she closed the door behind them. "Wes' cousin? How old was he when he wore those? Twelve?"

Lexi laughed as she gave the hallway a quick anxious glance, pleased to find it empty. "Sixteen. Right before a big growth spurt."

"I guess! He and Wes are like giants." A distracted smile flitted across Clodi's mouth as they walked. "I saw another giant on the tour last night. He was cute." Clodi blushed deeply.

Lexi smiled. "What's his name?"

"Tull," she said softly, then her smile faded. "But his wings are broken. He said it was an accident, but I think he was lying. He scratched his eyebrow with his thumbnail and looked at the floor when he said it. My brother pulls his nose and looks at the floor when he lies. My Daddy says men usually do something funny like that when they fib. He says to always watch their eyes when you ask them a question. If they look away, they're probably lying."

Lexi made a polite noise of interest, but looked away uncomfortably and made a mental note to maintain eye contact the next time she lied.

"I don't lie," Clodi announced. "I don't know why everybody else does. Lying is bad. But I don't think Tull is bad. Do you think there are good reasons to lie?"

"I suppose there could be," Lexi said vaguely, relieved to hear the music up ahead. Only a single couple stood outside the doors to the display hall, and the hall itself was only sparsely populated. Lexi scanned the small crowd eagerly, searching for big black and yellow wings, cringing when she saw the man who looked like her mother. He was talking to the same two girls he had been with before, a wide grin on his broad mouth. Lexi looked quickly away when he caught her staring, then pulled Clodi to the opposite end of the room.

"Oh! There's Psyche and Damus! And the other brother...I forgot his name. Do you want to meet them? Oh wait, you said you and Psyche weren't getting along. You probably don't want to talk to her. I'll just pop over there quick and say hi. Will you be okay by yourself?"

Psyche glared at Lexi and her mouth twisted maliciously as she spoke to her brothers. Whatever she said prompted both brothers to turn and stare at Lexi. The brother with the violet-blue wings turned back around quickly, but the one with silvery-blue wings gave her a slow grin and a nod.

"No, I'll talk to her," Lexi said, eager to find out if Psyche was keeping her secret.

"Maybe you two can make up, and she can move back in," Clodi suggested as they weaved through the crowd.

Lexi took a deep breath and blew it back out again without answering.

"Hi, I'm Damus," the brother with the silvery-blue wings said, still grinning.

"Hi again, Damus," Clodi chirped. "And Psyche, and..." Clodi looked at the brother whose name she had forgotten and blushed.

"Everes," the forgotten brother mumbled.

"Oh yes! Sorry, Everes! I'm terrible with names!" Clodi apologized.

"This is *Raven Fritillary*," Psyche said, giving the name sarcastic emphasis.

Lexi's eyes narrowed as she met Psyche's, her expression a clear warning.

Psyche's little pink mouth folded into a tight line. "These are my brothers," she said irritably.

Damus laughed out loud. "Psyche, I think your manners are actually improving." He jumped a little when Psyche elbowed him in the ribs, then continued laughing.

"Everes," Psyche said, a cunning glint in her eyes, "you should dance with Raven."

The man with the violet-blue wings colored and rocked back on his heels before offering his arm. Lexi hesitated almost imperceptibly before taking it and letting him lead her away to a clear spot on the floor. He set one hand gently on her waist, then held out the other, waiting for her to take it.

Lexi examined his thick thatch of dark hair and matching brows that framed his dark blue eyes, a perfect complement to the sky-colored underside of his wings. Lexi took his callus-roughened hand, noting the slight blush that still colored his cheeks. The softest hint of a spicy scent hovered around him, getting stronger as he whirled her about the floor.

"Fly?" he asked, meeting her eyes and making Lexi's stomach do a funny little flip.

Lexi glanced up at the whirling dancers above them and swallowed. "I get dizzy."

Everes nodded and gently drew her closer, sliding his hand around her waist before lifting her off the ground. Despite being the same height, Lexi found it difficult to keep even with him in the air. Her larger wings pulled her higher with each beat, and when she beat them slower, she began to descend. With an amused smile, Everes brought their joined hands to his shoulder, then released her hand to hold her waist with both of his. Lexi awkwardly held his shoulders until a quick, dizzying glance at the other dancers made her realize her hands belonged around his neck. She had clung to Nireus' neck out of necessity during her first dance; she had not realized it was the fashion. With a subtle blush, she slid her fingers under Everes' dark fringe of curls until her hands met behind his neck. Only married couples ever danced at the palace; her mother declared that even *learning* to partner dance before then was unseemly. Lexi had secretly watched a dance before, but the couples had not held each other like this. Wrapping her arms around anyone's neck felt decidedly intimate, and his hands gripping her waist were even more so. Everes flew in slow, lazy circles despite the upbeat song, and when it ended she felt only slightly dizzy.

"You all right?" he asked when they landed, keeping one steadying hand on her waist as they drew apart.

"Yes, thank you." Lexi accepted the hand that slipped from her waist, and let him lead her back.

"My turn!" Damus announced as he came towards them grinning. Taking her hand from his brother, he led her back out before she could protest. "After the silent Everes, I imagine you could use some conversation."

Lexi gave him a polite smile, silently comparing him to his brother. Damus' hair and solid jaw matched his brother's, but his watery blue eyes, broad nose, and larger mouth set him apart.

"And I am very eager to talk to the woman who can best my sister," Damus said, his sweet and spicy scent filling the air as they began to dance.

Lexi lifted a single eyebrow as she met his gaze.

Damus grinned. "From her cryptic comments earlier, I can only assume that she meant to blackmail you. And from her very sour temper and new room assignment, I can only assume she failed. I'm very impressed."

Lexi left her face carefully blank as he spun her up into the air, going round a little too quickly. "You assume quite a bit."

Damus chortled delightedly. "Yes I do, but I don't think I'm wrong." He peered at her curiously with an enormous grin. "I find myself so completely intrigued by you that I can hardly bear it."

"How painful for you," Lexi said, her face still pleasantly blank.

Damus grinned widely. "So tell me about your family and where you grew up."

Lexi straightened her shoulders, her head lolling a bit to one side from her dizziness. "I'm an only child from a horse ranch in Sumpter," she lied, remembering to meet his eyes part way through her sentence.

"What's Sumpter like?"

"Small, dull. Where are you from?"

Damus' blue eyes sparkled to match his delighted grin. "You're very good," he praised.

"My dancing?" Lexi asked innocently, as the song came to an end.

Damus laughed. "That, too. Dance with me again?"

Lexi shook her head. "I'm going to sit this one out."

"Later, then?" Damus pressed as they landed.

"Perhaps." Lexi released his hand and stumbled dizzily to the water table. The life servant there handed her a cup of questionable cleanliness, but she took it anyway, the cool water soothing her stomach as she clutched the table.

"Hi," an unfamiliar voice said, leaning close behind her.

Lexi jumped, spilling her water.

"Sorry," the voice said, chuckling.

Lexi folded her wings and spun around, her mouth dropping open when she saw who it was.

The man with her mother's wings gave her a wide grin. "Long-lost cousin, I presume?"

Lexi closed her mouth quickly, suitable lies flitting across her mind before she forced herself to laugh. "I don't think so."

His eyes narrowed in a familiar way. "Really? Because you look just like my sister, and," he paused, leaning towards her neck and inhaling before she could push him away, "you smell like nothing. So you have to be Aunt Ami's daughter."

"Hey, back off," Damus called, emerging from the crowd to stand protectively in front of Lexi.

"Relax, Damus. No need to mark your territory. She's my cousin."

Damus lifted his dark, unruly brows as he stood aside to look at Lexi. "Is that so?"

Lexi shook her head dismissively. "He's confused me for someone else."

Her cousin shot out his hand and caught Lexi's, brought it up to his nose, and inhaled deeply before she could yank it away. "No scent," he declared with a challenging air.

Lexi's jaw tightened as she leaned toward her cousin and inhaled deeply. "Dirty horse stalls," she lied.

Damus laughed and clapped her cousin's shoulder with an audible smack. "Leave her alone, Ryp."

Ryp's face froze into a chilly mask exactly like her mother's, and Lexi couldn't help but shiver. When Damus took her hand and pulled her away, she followed him gratefully until he stopped next to Psyche.

"That was very interesting," Damus said, a suppressed grin lighting his eyes.

"What was?" Psyche demanded crossly.

"Ryp Leafwing thinks..." Damus began.

"Let's dance again, Damus," Lexi interrupted, dragging him back to the dance floor as he chortled.

"So he *is* your cousin," Damus said, still chuckling as they began to dance.

"Of course he isn't; I can smell him." Despite fluttering panic, Lexi's voice was calm.

Damus threw back his head and laughed.

Lexi bristled. "Did I say something amusing?"

"Yes!" Damus allowed himself another guffaw, then quelled his laughter as they lifted into the air. "Why don't you want to claim your cousin?"

"He isn't. I just don't want to excite Psyche's paranoid suspicions," Lexi explained.

"So if she finds out that Ryp is your cousin, she'll have something new to blackmail you?"

Lexi took a deep breath, then met his eyes. "What do you want, Damus?"

Damus grinned. "I'm not the blackmailing type."

"You just entertain roommates while your sister attempts blackmail?"

"Ouch," Damus complained with a wounded air. "She didn't tell me what she was doing when she asked me to keep Clodi busy."

"But you knew enough to guess?" Lexi prompted.

Damus grimaced. "Okay, maybe. Sorry about that. But I will make it up to you," he assured her.

"How?"

"By keeping all your secrets, *Your Highness*."

Lexi's breath caught in her throat. "Did she tell you before or after she tried to blackmail me?"

Damus gave a little delighted chortle. "Neither. I'm a good guesser. I can't believe I'm dancing with a princess!"

Lexi shushed him with a severe look, glancing around them to make sure he hadn't been overheard.

"Sorry," Damus apologized, still grinning. "I won't tell anyone, and Everes and I can watch out for you when your guards aren't around. He won't ask questions; I think he's smitten."

Lexi blinked back a blush, the ghosting sensation of Everes' hands on her waist distracting her for a moment. "I'm involved with someone."

Damus nodded as if he had expected it. "I'll tell him so you don't break his heart." A slow grin spread across his face as he led her back to the ground. "Wes' cousin is giving us dirty looks. Want me to keep him away from you?"

Lexi followed his gaze to where Tiger stood glaring, but rather than dread the coming argument, a little bubble of joy closed off her throat at seeing him alive. "No," she said, looking down to blink away the sudden tears. "Tiger's my best friend."

"Oh. So *he's* the guy?" Damus asked as they landed.

Lexi shook her head. "No, but I do need to talk to him." Lexi squeezed his hand before releasing it. "Thank you for keeping my secrets, Damus."

Damus grinned and gave her a tiny bow before she hurried away.

"Lex," Tiger growled as she approached.

Ignoring his anger, Lexi threw her arms around his neck as she felt the tears spill over.

"Okay," Tiger said, bringing one hand beneath her wings to clasp her back as she continued her enthusiastic hug.

"I dreamed Wes choked you to death, and it seemed so real," Lexi explained, trying to swallow down the lump in her throat. "I'm glad you're okay."

"Uh, let's get you back to your room. People are staring." He sidestepped awkwardly while gently trying to remove her arms.

"No, I don't want the guards to see me like this," she pled.

"Lex, let go so we can walk."

"Okay," Lexi sniffed, hiding her face in his shoulder as he took her arm and led her out into the hallway.

Stopping, he turned to face her. "Lex, it was just a dream. Calm down."

Lexi shook her head miserably. "I flew up to your balcony to check on you. I thought you were hiding behind the door laughing at me, but it was Wes."

Tiger sucked in a huge breath. "He was in the dungeon! How?"

Lexi stared at the floor. "I let him out."

"You did what?!" Tiger paced back and forth, his fingers laced over his head as he pulled in deep breaths and tried to calm down. "What did he do?"

Lexi began to cry again. "He wouldn't let go of me. I threatened him with the dungeon, but he just laughed and said he hadn't done anything." Lexi stopped and hid her face when Clodi came out into the hall.

"Are you crying?" Clodi asked, her brow bent in concern as she hurried to Lexi and hugged her. "What's the matter?"

"Wes," Lexi choked out, fighting to regain control of her emotions as she hid behind Clodi's big cream-colored wings.

"It's okay," Clodi soothed, patting Lexi's shoulder briskly. "He's in the dungeon now. Do you want to go back to the room?"

Lexi shook her head and started to pull away. "I need to talk to Tiger," she said, wiping the tears from her face in embarrassment.

Clodi released her and they both looked around. Tiger was gone.

"Oh no," Lexi moaned. "Stay here!" she commanded Clodi as she leapt into the air, beating her wings as fast as they would go. She flew towards the dungeon, always expecting to catch Tiger around the next turn in the stairs. When she reached the gate, the guard was holding it open for him to pass through.

"No!" she yelled. "Guard, I command you to stop him!"

A guard she didn't recognize looked up, startled, as Tiger hurried through.

"Stop him!" she repeated as he stood inert. She flew past the dazed guard as Tiger rounded the corner. "Tiger, no!" Lexi cringed as the heavy smell of heated sulphur filled her throat and lungs. Tiger had slowed his pace, his head snapping back and forth as he passed the cells. There wasn't room to fly beside him, so Lexi reached between his wings on the offbeat and grabbed his shirt, giving it a heavy tug. Tiger jerked and landed, turning on her with a look of fury.

"Let me do this," he hissed.

"No! You can't settle anything!" Lexi insisted in a harsh whisper, glancing at the waking inmates in this unfamiliar part of the dungeon. "All you can do is have a very public argument that will expose me to ridicule! Think about it!"

Tiger hesitated, the hard lines of his face softening slightly with uncertainty.

Seeing it, Lexi touched his arm. "You're angry he touched me?" she asked softly. "Fine, I am, too. But letting him sit alone in this hole is the best punishment we can give him. If you try for more, you punish me, and probably yourself as well."

"I'll make it quick," Tiger promised, turning away.

Lexi gripped his arm. "And what do you think he's going to say back to you—loudly, with an audience? You can't fix anything, Tiger! You can only make it worse," Lexi whispered urgently, her face pinched in worry and strain.

"I can't let it go," Tiger hissed through his teeth. "Don't ask me to."

"I know what he's going to say," Lexi admitted, panicked. "I'll tell you what he already said, just please get away from him before you make things worse!"

A little muscle in Tiger's jaw began to jump in time with his pulse. "I'm not promising I won't come right back."

Lexi sighed and pulled on his arm. "You won't. Let's get out of here," she whispered, hurrying him past an older inmate who was standing at his bars with a disturbing smile.

It was a long, sullen walk back, broken only by an argument as to whose room they would talk in. Lexi insisted that her guards not see her until she was more composed, and that Clodi was sure to interrupt them if they went to her room. But standing on the threshold of Tiger's room, her stomach knotted with nausea.

"I don't want to talk here either," she murmured.

Tiger stood in the middle of the room inhaling. "I can imagine. This whole room reeks of you and Wes." He marched angrily to the balcony doors and threw them open.

Lexi's face crumpled. "Please try not to be so angry with me. I'm out of danger. Can't you just try to make me feel better?"

Tiger picked up Wes' pillow and flung it off the balcony. "No! No, I can't! You put yourself in this spot, Lex! I did everything I could to protect you, and you still ended up alone with him! I told you what he was like! Why weren't you more careful?!" Tiger turned away as his eyes filled with tears.

Brushing away her own tears, Lexi stepped into the room and slowly shut the door behind her.

Tiger stood facing the balcony, one hand gripping his forehead with the other clenched in a fist. "Do you think Cam will marry you?"

"What?" Lexi asked, taken aback by the question. "Why do you ask?"

Tiger laughed bitterly as he turned to look at her. "Because Lex, you need to get married quick."

"Why? I just got here."

"Lex, you're probably going to lose your ability to fly soon. You need to get married and down the mountain before you get stuck here," Tiger explained patiently, his eyes on the floor.

Lexi shook her head. "It hasn't been a week yet. I should have a little time."

Tiger's head snapped up with a bemused expression. "Lex, pregnancy ends your season. You know that."

Lexi blinked several times, finally seeing Tiger's reaction in its true light. "Wes didn't rape me."

Tiger's mouth fell open and he turned back around, running one hand slowly through his thick, sandy locks. "Oh."

Lexi fidgeted in the silence. "You thought I got raped, and then went *dancing*?"

"I don't know!" Tiger blurted, turning around, but still avoiding her eyes. "You cried! You said he wouldn't let go of you."

"He wouldn't! I kicked him until he let go!"

Tiger looked at her, a hint of a smile on his strained face before it quickly faded. "Then why are you so afraid of what he's going to say?"

Lexi blushed scarlet. "Because," she sighed, her eyes dropping to the floor, "he thought I was sneaking into your room in the middle of the night, in my nightgown...to...offer myself to you." The last was nearly inaudible, and Tiger stepped closer to hear her.

"What?"

Lexi put her hot face in her hands. "I'm not repeating it," she groaned. "He accused me of teasing him. Even with the pheromones, I was so frightened. He wouldn't let me leave and he wouldn't stop touching me. I nearly told him who I was just to get him to stop. And when I got away from him, he laughed at me and said he hadn't done anything to deserve the dungeon, especially since *I* came to *him*. So I said I would just tell the guards that he had kidnaped me from my room and dragged me to his." Lexi winced at her own words, still unable to face him. "He got mad and caught me again," she whispered. "He said he might as well enjoy himself if he was going to get punished for it."

Tiger placed a comforting hand on Lexi's shoulder, but she startled at the unexpected contact. "I screamed for Clodi, and kicked my balcony door to wake her up. She and the guards came running, and Wes flew away." Lexi turned towards him, wiping a few stray tears. "End of story."

"Sorry I yelled," Tiger apologized, pulling her into a hug. "Promise not to let him out again?"

Lexi let out a weak laugh. "Promise."

"Promise to quit running around without your guards?" he asked, caressing her hair as he held her.

Lexi's face scrunched up in a grimace and she poked Tiger in the ribs.

"Hey!" Tiger protested, jumping away. "It's a reasonable request!"

"No, it isn't! I've spent my whole life confined to a palace with guards watching over me. I want a little freedom!"

Tiger leaned forward until his forehead touched hers. "No. No freedom for you."

Slow grins grew on both their faces before Lexi shoved him away and they both laughed, then stood staring at each other.

"You look terrible," Lexi observed. "Did you stay up all night?"

Tiger drew his lips into a grim smile and sat down on a stool with a groan. "Yep."

"Not because of me?"

"Nope. Thought you were safely sleeping."

Lexi smirked as she shivered in the early morning breeze. "Fooled you."

"Ha. Nice outfit by the way," he said, kicking at her boot.

Lexi grinned. "Mother designed it for me. It's the latest style among the nobility."

"I'll bet. Keep bragging about it and I might take it back."

Lexi snorted. "I'd like to see you fit into these."

"Are you saying I've gotten fat?" Tiger teased, standing.

Lexi pinched his side, finding only lean muscle. "I think you might be too fat to catch me."

Tiger sat back onto the stool with another groan. "Nah, too tired."

Lexi gave him a pitying smile and patted him on the head as she passed by to close the balcony doors. "I'll let you sleep, then. And I will run amok all day with or *without* my guards, as I please," she announced.

Tiger caught her hand and held it tight. "No," he said emphatically.

"Go to sleep, grumpy," she teased, and impulsively kissed the top of his head. Tiger tensed, releasing her hand, and Lexi stepped back.

"Sorry. Forgot about the smell thing. Are you going to barf?" Lexi winced apologetically. "I'll just go," she said, hurrying to the door.

"Straight to your guards," he insisted, wearily getting up from his stool to follow her.

"I'll think about it." Lexi smirked at his scowl. She fairly skipped from the room, impishly leaving the door open. She resisted looking back until she heard it shut.

"You knew I'd follow you," Tiger accused, shuffling after her.

Lexi stopped to wait for him. "Maybe. Wasn't sure how strong your stomach is."

"I'll vomit when I get back to my room," he said easily, laughing as she shoved him.

Walking side by side, she smiled at him sadly. "Sorry I can't turn it off. You men are lucky. I don't even know what you smell like."

"And you're not going to," Tiger said with a maddening grin.

Lexi scrunched up her nose irritably. "Why not? I won't take it as a sign of intent or anything...just satisfy my curiosity."

"So you can gag, and liken my scent to skunk musk?"

Lexi laughed. "I wouldn't do that. Dead skunk *rotting in the heat* maybe."

Tiger made a noise of disgust as he gave her a light shove. "All you women are so vindictive."

"I am not! I'm very forgiving. I even let Wes out of the dungeon," she added, immediately regretting her example as soon as the words had left her mouth.

"Stupidity is not the same as forgiving."

Lexi gave him a heavy shove, but he only laughed at her show of temper. "I knew it was dangerous; I let him out because it wasn't *just*."

"Because he had only taken advantage of you once?" Tiger asked, his tone suddenly exasperated.

Lexi frowned at him and stopped walking. "He's in the dungeon. I won't let him out again. Let's not talk about it anymore."

"You brought it up."

"I know I did," Lexi snapped, "but I didn't mean to; let it go."

Tiger put a finger over the puckered skin between her brows and rubbed. "You're making wrinkles."

"I am too young to have wrinkles," she declared, knocking his hand away.

Tiger released a heavy breath. "We're fighting again."

"This isn't a fight," Lexi argued weakly, looking up at the growing amusement on his face. "You," Lexi hesitated, struggling for the right words, "don't approve of me anymore."

"What?" Tiger protested, his amusement turning to surprise.

Lexi shook her head slightly, and shut her eyes at the inadequacy of her words. "Back home, you called me 'gutsy' for the way I rode Raven, 'clever' for sneaking around my Mother, and a 'good person' for the way I treated the servants. But since I came here, you keep telling me I'm stupid, incapable, and now vindictive. I don't know why, but I don't think you really like me anymore." She dropped her gaze to his chest and tried to swallow back the lump of emotion that strangled her throat.

"I like you," Tiger said solemnly.

Lexi shook her head. "You don't like having me here." She frowned as she looked at the floor. "I thought you would be excited for me: breaking away from my mother, from Talan, having a chance at a normal life; but you just want me to go home, don't you?" Her turquoise eyes were brimming with tears as she fixed them on his.

Tiger grimaced. "It's...harder having you here."

Lexi turned away quickly, her rapid steps changing into flight.

"Lex, your guards are back this way! Where are you going?" he called after her.

She flew faster instead of answering him, knowing he would probably guess where she was going, and she desperately needed a few minutes alone before he caught up to her. She didn't knock at Cam's door when she reached it; she just threw it open, leapt inside, and shut it quickly behind her. The room's lantern was off, the room in inky darkness but for the sliver of hallway light that showed beneath the door.

"Lexi?" Cam asked in a sleep-slurred voice.

"Yes, shhh."

Cam put out a searching hand that bumped against her thigh before finding her hand. "You okay?"

Lexi cursed the involuntary sniffle that betrayed her crying, a much louder one following the first.

"What happened? I thought you were sleeping." Cam drew up to his knees and wrapped his arms around her. "Tell me," he coaxed.

Lexi held her breath, her hands trembling against Cam's bare chest as she waited for Tiger to burst in and demand she come out. But he didn't come, and dizziness forced her to breathe.

Cam began wiping her tears, his pheromone scent heavy in the air with his face close to hers. "Tell me," he coaxed again, and she did. When she told him about Wes, his grip on her tightened, and she laid her head on his shoulder, feeling his sinewy muscles flex in agitation. Respecting her mother's secret, she left out her cousin Ryp, but everything else came tumbling out in a tearful jumble. She sighed as she finished, the skin beneath her eyes pulled tight by her dried tears.

"I must have slept much longer than I thought," Cam joked as he kissed her cheek, then stepped off the bed to turn on the solar lantern. "Are you hungry?"

Lexi nodded numbly as he led her to the stool and set out his remaining food before her. When she began to pick at it, he smiled, then retrieved a shirt and sniffed it before putting it on. Returning to her side, he began to comb out her tangled hair while she ate.

Lexi let out an embarrassed laugh. "You don't have to do that."

"But I like to," he insisted, leaning down between her wings to kiss the top of her head. "Does Cretin number one get out of the dungeon this morning?"

"Probably," Lexi said, enjoying the sensation of his hands in her hair and the gentle tugging of the comb.

"Can I stay with you today, then?"

Lexi tipped back her head to look at his hopeful expression. "You don't have to ask my permission." The words had barely left her lips before she realized they weren't true. She quickly dropped her gaze.

"Good," he said, happily working through a snarl.

"Five thirty, testing time! Ladies report to the infirmary!" A booming voice hollered from the hallway. "What are *you* doing here?"

Lexi stood up as she listened to a murmured response. *Was that Tiger? Her guards?* She threw her shoulders back as she crossed to the door and pulled it open.

"Testing?" Cam asked from behind her.

"Pregnancy tests," a white-winged old woman barked and shook her wizened head in disgust. "Good thing we test you little tramps," she spat, grabbing Lexi's arm between her gnarled fingers and yanking her from the doorway. "Get to the infirmary," she commanded, then bent over in a fit of coughing after releasing Lexi's arm.

Lexi glanced back at the guards outside Cam's door, taking in the mortified expressions on their faces.

"She's not a tramp," Cam countered, stepping up behind Lexi, his eyes dark with anger.

The white-winged woman straightened with a last feeble cough to glare at him. "Is she your wife?"

"No," Cam said, his face reddening.

"Then she's a tramp," she snapped, giving Lexi a shove as she continued down the hall. "Five thirty, testing time!"

"Phidia's not well," the white-winged guard apologized.

Lexi nodded, her face blank as she drew up into princess posture and walked alongside the muttering Phidia.

"The Governor has excused you from the testing," the white-winged guard protested as he followed them.

"What are you talking about?" Phidia snapped. "No one is excused from testing!" She stopped to pound on a door. "Five thirty, testing time!"

Lexi's jaw only tightened as she replied in clipped tones. "My absence will only excite suspicion."

"Miss Fritillary," the white-winged guard implored, his blue eyes squinting in distress. "Standing in line outside the infirmary with two guards will excite suspicion, too."

Lexi nodded. "Then you'll wait outside my room."

"I'll wait there, too," Cam said, his words more of a question.

Lexi turned back to him in surprise. She hadn't realized he had been trailing behind their odd procession. "That's fine," she allowed, her blank expression unaltered.

"Okay, then," Cam said with forced cheerfulness as Lexi walked away.

Chapter Ten

"Oh good!" Clodi called out with relief from the front of the line. "I was so worried about you when you ran after Tiger and didn't come back!" Clodi joined Lexi at the end of the line, smiling at the glaring Phidia as she passed. "Did you find him?"

Lexi nodded coolly, her face still a blank mask as Phidia shook her head and walked away muttering.

"Why did he leave? And where did he go? I didn't even hear him move," Clodi continued.

Lexi hid a flicker of irritation, and turned to Clodi with a polite smile. "He was just around the corner waiting for us to finish talking."

"Oh. Did you tell him about Wes?"

Lexi met the gaze of several girls who had turned around to stare. "We can talk about it later."

Clodi shrugged. "Okay." They shuffled forward in silence for a few minutes. "I think Damus and Everes like you; do you like their radish smell?" Clodi asked, her perfectly-formed nose scrunching up in distaste.

Lexi smiled. "I like radishes."

Clodi grinned. "You do? Which one do you like better?"

Lexi shook her head slightly. "I have a boyfriend."

"Tiger?!" Clodi asked, her excitement plain.

Lexi's eyebrows constricted until she forced her face blank again. "No."

"Just no? You're not going to tell me?" Clodi threw up her hands in exasperation.

Amusement flickered across Lexi's face then faded. "You don't know him."

"So?! Tell me his name! Where's he from? What's his apprenticeship? Are you going to marry him?"

At Clodi's excited tone, the remainder of the line looked back at them. Lexi turned a blank gaze on them until they looked away.

"I don't know," Lexi admitted.

"You don't know his name?!"

Lexi sighed as the same heads turned around. "His name is Cam."

"Cam what?" Clodi asked in a bright tone.

"Crescent," Lexi fairly whispered.

Clodi's forehead wrinkled up in consternation. "A crescent? Don't they tend to be pretty small?"

Lexi suppressed a frown. "He's taller than I am."

"But small wings?" Clodi prodded.

Lexi allowed herself a slight shrug. "Smaller than mine."

"Doesn't that bother you? I hate feeling big. I mean, I *know* I'm big, but I want to be with a guy that makes me feel small. Puny even," Clodi added with a thoughtful grin. "Besides, if something were to go wrong on the flight home, I want a husband with wings big enough to fly me, at least safely to the ground."

Lexi's jaw tightened as they drew to the front of the line where a middle-aged medic greeted them with a lethargic smile. "Name?"

"Raven Fritillary."

"And Clodi Parnassian," Clodi interrupted with a grin. "We're brand new."

"Well then, please go wait right over there until Zelic calls for the next four," the medic instructed, the corners of her mouth pulling up into a more genuine smile as her yellow wings wavered with suppressed amusement.

"Thanks," Clodi said enthusiastically, fairly skipping into the infirmary. She stared down the double row of beds, craning her neck, then lifted into a quick flight to survey the room. She returned to Lexi with a dejected frown.

"Tull isn't here," she pouted. "He is so big and beautiful; I want you to meet him."

Lexi smiled her answer, then stiffened as Van's angry girlfriend joined them with a venomous smile.

"Hello girls. I'm Dina, but then you probably knew that. This is my twin, Ria," she said, waving an arm dismissively at the girl who shuffled up next to her with solemn eyes. The two tall brunettes were identical, but where Dina's face lit with an energetic malice, Ria's self-conscious, shifting glance reminded Lexi of the Queen's browbeaten lady's maid.

"I'm Clodi," she announced, recovering her smile. "This is Raven. We're new."

Dina gave them both a nasty smirk.

"Next four!" a male medic called from behind a curtained operatory.

"Excuse me," Dina said insincerely as she bumped Lexi's shoulder and forced her to move quickly to protect her wings. Dina sashayed behind the curtain without looking back, her sister trailing in her wake.

Clodi's forehead crumpled up. "That was rude. Did you two already meet?"

Lexi merely nodded as they followed the sisters.

Behind the curtain, a medic with curly brown hair waited impatiently, his beautiful yellow and black wings twitching as he flicked a piece of paper against the metal table in front of him. When he caught sight of Lexi, his movement stopped abruptly and his mouth fell slightly open. Lexi noted the change, and folded her wings tightly behind her to interrupt his rapt inspection. Closing his mouth, he looked down at the paper in front of him, then back at Lexi.

"What's your name?" he asked.

"Raven Fritillary."

The medic leaned sideways to squint at her folded wings with a dogged shake of his head. He was about to speak when Dina leaned forward and spat on the table in front of him, her spittle spattering against his dingy white shirt. "Are you going to do the tests or not?" she demanded as her twin blushed.

Clodi's mouth dropped open, and a single nervous guffaw escaped her.

Glaring, the medic wiped Dina's spit from the table with a rag reeking of alcohol. "I have to check your mouth first."

"Sorry," Dina lied, then opened her mouth obediently.

Hesitantly, Clodi and Lexi did the same, pulling back reflexively as the medic leaned in to ensure their mouths were empty.

"Swallow, then spit," the medic directed irritably, his gaze once again falling on Lexi's wings.

Clodi's cheeks burned with color. "We're *supposed* to spit on the table?"

The medic's pale cheeks colored slightly. "We can't spare the cups."

Clodi leaned close down to the table, letting the spit fall and dangle from her mouth before she self-consciously withdrew, licking her lips. "It's bad manners to spit," she muttered.

Dina rolled her eyes, her tanned arms folded tightly against her chest. "Just test it," she demanded irritably as Lexi spit quickly.

The medic clenched his jaw as he tapped a tiny amount of powder into each pile of spittle, waiting as each little puddle changed color.

"You're pregnant," he announced, eyeing Dina.

Dina gave him a smug smile. "I know."

The medic glanced down at the table again. "The rest of you are negative; you can go."

Dina grabbed her sister's arm to prevent her from leaving while Clodi and Lexi exited.

"You have one hour to leave the mountain. You can pick up travel rations at the kitchen with this card," the medic said quietly. The rest of his instructions were inaudible as they walked away.

"I can't believe she was pregnant! And she seemed so pleased about it! What's the matter with her?" Clodi whispered loudly as they slipped through the door.

Lexi merely shook her head.

"I wonder who her mate is? Do you think he'll actually marry her?" Clodi continued.

"Van West," Dina announced loudly as she flew up behind them, "and of course he will. We only waited this long because he wanted to be sure I could produce an heir. See, Van's going to be a Lord some day, just like his daddy." She peered into Lexi's face with a wicked smile. "Oh sweetie, you didn't actually think he was interested in you, did you? He said you smell like rotten apples, and the only reason he was even talking to you was to please his old friend, the Governor." Dina coolly appraised Lexi's blank face. "I'll bet you're one of the Governor's illegitimate sisters, aren't you?" Dina laughed when Lexi didn't respond. "Well, I have to be going now; can't be late to my own wedding. Bye, sweetie," she taunted, patting Lexi's hand, "I'm sure you'll have better luck with someone of your own *class*." Dina drew out the last word heavily, a cruel smile on her face as she turned and flew away.

"What a nasty, little..." Clodi began, then pressed her lips together to prevent her final epithet from escaping her mouth. "If she wasn't pregnant, I'd whack her one."

"Pity her, Clodi," Lexi said, letting out a puff of air.

"Why? She's getting it all her own way, and being rotten about it, too."

Lexi merely shook her head, then stopped short as she saw Talan and Cam arguing outside her door, her guards separating them. Drawing a deep breath, she hurried forward.

"She's practically my wife, you ridiculous peasant," Talan sneered, taking a threatening step forward before the white-winged guard blocked him.

"She doesn't want you! How many times does she have to tell you no before you go away?" Cam shot back.

"Are they fighting over you?" Clodi asked as she hurried to keep pace with Lexi. All four men turned at her question.

Lexi frowned as Talan moved forward to greet her. "I've arranged a private breakfast for us in Limen's room, my love."

"I've already eaten," Lexi said, stepping around him to take Cam's offered arm.

Talan's jaw tightened, his mouth still open. "Then it's true. You've taken to toying with peasants."

"I'm not toying with him," Lexi declared, her face hard.

Talan smirked. "You're going to take *rock boy* here home to the palace and have him sire the next king?"

"What?" Clodi asked.

"Talan, you're an idiot," Lexi sighed, releasing Cam's arm with a regretful little pat. She took Clodi's hand, pulled her into their room, and quickly shut the door.

"I'm not leaving," Talan yelled through the door.

Lexi swept her hair back from her face and looked into Clodi's wide blue eyes.

Clodi sucked in a huge breath, then let it out in a rush. "You live in the palace?"

Lexi shook her head and released Clodi's arm. "You know how you told me it's hard for you to keep secrets?"

Clodi nodded, her mouth open.

"It's important I keep my secrets, so I can't answer your questions."

"But who is 'rock boy,' and why is he going to sire the next king?" Clodi asked, her forehead creased in confusion.

Lexi shook her head and turned away, her face tightening as she listened to Talan and Cam's angry voices.

"She's a *princess*, not some peasant bride!" Talan hissed loudly.

Clodi gasped, her blue eyes frozen in an unblinking stare. "That's why! You're...you're one of the princesses!" Clodi let out a delighted chortle as she clasped her hands together and jumped up and down. "Oh!" Clodi exclaimed, suddenly stopping to bend in a clumsy curtsy. "I'm sorry, Your Highness, my manners are all wrong. Do you want me to go away?"

"No Clodi, please stay here. I think they'll deliver breakfast soon. If you would open the door only wide enough to take the food, and let them think I am in here with you; that would be helpful," Lexi said, moving to the balcony.

"But where are you going...er, Your Highness? Can I ask you questions or is that just bad manners?" Clodi asked, following her.

Lexi gave her a rueful smile. "You're fine, Clodi. I just need a few moments to myself."

Lexi slid out the rugs and opened the balcony doors as quietly as possible. Outside, birds heralded the twilight dawn as the chilly air made her breath visible. The courtyard beneath her was still empty. With a relieved sigh, Lexi flew up the face of the castle to land on the roof jutting out of the mountainside. Taking deep breaths, she forced herself to wait, hoping Clodi would soon go back inside and shut the door. Shivering, she began to pace around the rows of solar lanterns chained together and waiting to be charged. On her third lap, she flitted down to Tiger's balcony and listened. Finally, satisfied by the silence, she slowly pushed the door in and peered inside. A mollified smile flickered across her face at the empty beds and she slipped in and shut the door behind her. Lexi inhaled deeply. The scent instantly dulled the tension, relaxed her muscles, and soothed her even as she blushed in shame. It wasn't Wes she needed or even wanted, she just needed the artificial calm of his scent, and a short reprieve from the tangle of thoughts that were cluttering her mind. Leaning forward, she rested her elbows on her knees, caught her face in her hands, and lost track of time.

When Tiger returned, she lifted her head and smiled hazily. Frowning, he shut the door, walked over, and lifted her chin.

"Your eyes are dilated again. Why are you sitting in here with the doors shut?" Tiger asked, only partially suppressing his irritation.

Lexi blushed and pulled her chin from his grasp. "Just waiting for you," she lied.

"Talan and Cam are fighting outside your room."

Lexi looked up with slight alarm. "The guards are letting them fight?"

Tiger's frown deepened. "They're keeping them apart, mostly."

Lexi let out a soft groan. "You were right, Tiger."

Tiger smirked. "I'm always right. And though I enjoy your drunken praise, I think it's time to open the door."

"No," Lexi insisted, catching his sleeve. "Just a little longer."

Tiger scowled. "You came in here to get pheromone drunk?!"

Lexi pulled herself up by his sleeve, and put a hand over his mouth. "No yelling," she said, one hand gripping his arm. "If I was home, I would sneak away and ride Raven. Here, this is all I have."

Tiger licked the hand covering his mouth, and she pulled it away in disgust.

He grinned. "So go flying, don't sit in here like a lonely drunk." He punctuated his last two words by lightly tapping her nose.

Lexi shook her head dismissively as she swatted at his hand. "You would have yelled if I had gone flying by myself, too."

Tiger grimaced as he considered her words. "Okay, that's probably true," he conceded. He picked up his pillow, then flopped on his bed, making it creak and shudder. He fussily arranged the pillow under his arms at the end of the bed before looking up at her. "So why do you need an escape?"

Lexi sat back down on the stool. "Everyone is finding out, and Talan is going to follow me around until I go mad."

"So put him in the dungeon."

Lexi rolled her eyes. "You're as bad as Limen. I can't go incarcerating everyone who bothers me. Besides, he's only following me because Mother ordered him to."

"See, the problem with you is that you haven't learned to properly abuse your power," Tiger said with feigned gravity.

Lexi laughed softly. "You have all the best ideas, Tiger."

"I know. Problem's all fixed now, right?" he teased, setting his chin on his folded arms and letting his beautiful wings relax.

"Of course. Go to sleep."

Tiger scowled at her. "As long as you realize I'm going to sleep out of sheer exhaustion and not because you ordered me to."

"I know you secretly like me to boss you around."

Tiger growled, but shut his eyes to the sound of her laughing.

Lexi listened to his steady breathing and watched his golden wings shudder with each exhale. "Tiger?"

"What?" he asked sleepily, his lips pressed against his arm and distorting the word.

"Does this room smell like you, too?"

He waited so long to answer that she began to wonder if he had fallen asleep.

"Yes," he finally admitted.

Lexi slumped on her stool with the heavy sensation of icicles sliding down her throat. "You make me pheromone drunk, too?"

"Maybe."

Lexi let out a heavy breath. "Why didn't you tell me?"

Tiger rubbed his forehead along his arms. "Could we not talk about this?"

"Not now or not ever?"

"Ever," he groaned.

Frowning, Lexi dragged the stool over to sit squarely in front of him. "Why?" she asked, leaning forward between his wings.

Tiger lifted his chin on to his arms and met her eyes. "Let it go, Lex."

Lexi pulled back from the nearness of his face, feeling a sudden flush in her cheeks as her heart began to pound. Her gaze dropped from his intent brown eyes to his crooked nose, then lingered on his lips. "Oh," she breathed and leapt off the stool. Beginning to pace, she nibbled on her thumbnail. "But we can still be friends, even though I'm..." she trailed off, embarrassed to tell him how attracted she was.

Letting his head sink back onto his arms, Tiger nodded. "Sure."

Lexi bit the corner off her perfectly manicured nail. "Did I just ruin everything?" she asked, her voice barely audible.

Tiger sighed. "It's fine."

It doesn't feel fine, she thought. "Good," she said aloud. "Well, I'll go so you can sleep."

"I can sleep with you here."

Lexi pulled the balcony door open without answering him, the fresh air feeling like a slap of reality.

"Are you going to fly alone?" Tiger asked, rising up on his elbows and closing his wings to watch her.

Lexi drew herself up into princess posture with her back to him. "No," she lied with a pleasant tone. "I've got a roommate to calm and a fight to break up. Busy day," she explained, leaping from the balcony and flying downward before sailing across the courtyard and up over the trees. She flew hard for two hours, pushing herself until sweat ran into her eyes and mingled with a few humiliated tears. Beneath her, the solid forest opened up into a clear blue lake and she eagerly landed on the shore, stooping to scoop water and dribble it into her mouth. The rustle and thunk behind her startled her into spilling water down the front of her as she spun around.

Tiger shook his head, panting as he shook perspiration from his face. "That water is going to make you sick."

"Don't care," she said, striving to sound lighthearted and failing. She turned her back on him and frowned. "How did you know?"

"You used your princess voice; I always know when you're lying."

"Then why not stop me in the courtyard?"

Tiger shrugged. "You needed to escape."

Lexi laughed bitterly, clenching her jaw to stop the sobs that threatened. She bent to the water and splashed the icy liquid on her face as she listened to Tiger's noisy drinking. "I thought you said the water would make us sick."

Tiger shrugged with a partial grin as water dripped from his chin. "I said the water would make *you* sick. I'm tough."

Lexi snorted, blowing a tangled strand of hair from her face. Self-consciously she attempted to run her fingers through the wild mass, wincing as she yanked the knots.

"Van thinks I smell like rotten things, too," she suddenly blurted, without turning around.

"He told you that?" Tiger asked, his voice incredulous.

"No. He pretended he was attracted to me. His girlfriend told me," Lexi said, hating the sound of self-pity in her voice. "She's pregnant. She thinks he's going to marry her."

"You think he won't?"

Lexi turned to look at him, one hand still tangled in her hair. "His grandmother is going to give his inheritance to his sister unless he marries me."

Tiger's usually hooded eyes grew wide and he let out a surprised laugh. "So why wasn't *he* fighting outside your door?"

"I suspect he's hiding from his girlfriend."

Tiger laughed softly with his mouth closed, the effect almost musical.

Lexi's face softened and a smile tugged at one side of her mouth; she loved that sound. Tiger caught her expression and quickly sobered.

"Uh...speaking of girlfriends, mine will be ticked if I don't show up for lunch," he said, trying to shake the shore's heavy mud from his boots.

Lexi nodded and scooped another drink of water. "I can go back now."

"Feel any better?"

Lexi stood up straighter and forced a smile to her face as she nodded.

"You're lying."

Lexi grimaced. "How can you tell? I didn't even speak!"

Tiger laughed softly. "I'm not telling you. Then you'd be able to lie to me."

"I *need* to be able to lie to you," she protested, then blushed.

Tiger shook his head. "Poor Lex, I've never seen you blush so much."

Lexi pressed her hands to her betraying cheeks. "Let's just go," she groaned.

Tiger nodded and jumped into flight with Lexi trailing him.

"You'll get over it," he assured her as she caught up.

"Yeah, when your season ends," Lexi grumbled.

"You'll get over it before then...just as soon as you remember what a jerk I am," Tiger said, grinning.

Lexi frowned at him. "You're not a jerk."

"Sure I am," Tiger disagreed cheerfully. "I yell at you, try to boss you around, and I took your secret stash of stolen cookies."

Lexi gasped. "I thought my mother had found them! I spent days dreading her lecture and the diet she was sure to force on me! Tiger! You *are* a jerk!"

Tiger laughed gleefully. "I told you."

Lexi flew in front of him and gave him a shove.

"Oh, you'll regret that," he warned, still laughing as he chased after her.

The entire trip back was one long game of got-you-last. As they neared the castle, they could hear the crowd in the courtyard taking advantage of the warmer, overcast day by eating on the patio.

"Wait," Tiger said urgently, pulling Lexi down onto a trail winding through the trees. "Coli said to meet her on the patio."

"That's good; I'd like to meet her."

Tiger grimaced as he ran a hand roughly through his hair. "Uh...not just yet."

"Why?"

Tiger stared into the trees. "She thinks I'm spending too much time with you. Now would not be a good time to prove her right."

Lexi knew she ought to be sympathetic, but somehow all she could do was laugh.

"Yeah, that's great. You laugh," Tiger said sarcastically. "Because it's really, really funny," he said, tickling her.

Lexi let out a shriek and jumped away from him, still laughing. "I think it would be good for you to have to admit you're wrong. I'm not sure I've seen that before," she teased.

"Ha ha," Tiger deadpanned, glancing nervously back at the patio. "Just stay here until I sit down, okay? Then you can fly to your balcony and get cleaned up."

Lexi frowned. "I'll still smell like rotten apples."

"Yeah, but you won't *look* like one," he quipped, grinning as she took a swipe at him. "Just stay here," he pleaded, backing away.

Lexi made a face at him but obeyed, watching curiously as he weaved among the patio tables to greet a yellow-winged girl with fluffy blonde hair, a sloped nose, and a big smile. She stood and embraced him, then quickly pulled away, her freckled nose turned up

217

at the sweat marks on his shirt and perspiration on his forehead. Tiger shrugged, his face turning mischievous as he threatened to hug her again and she squealed. Lexi's smile faded as she watched. They were so *happy*. Carefully blanking her expression, she flew up over the trees and made a wide arc to avoid the patio, then hesitated as she saw her balcony. Cam was standing there, his face creased in worry as he met her eyes.

"Are you all right?" he asked.

Lexi landed on the rail, allowing him to reach up and help her down. "I'm fine," she replied, not meeting his gaze.

"Where did you go? Clodi thought you would only be gone for a few minutes. She panicked when you didn't come back. We've been searching for you all morning."

Lexi could hear the just reproach in his tone and bristled at it. "I needed some time to myself." She met his accusing gaze briefly, then walked into her room.

"You've been out flying alone all this time?" he asked, his reproach turning to exasperation as followed her into the room.

"No. Tiger followed me to make sure I was okay," she said, sitting down to remove her riding boots.

Several emotions streaked across Cam's face as his mouth hung open to speak. "And you couldn't tell someone you were going?"

Lexi let her boot fall with a heavy thunk. "Are you angry with me?" she asked, surprise and warning lacing her tone.

Cam gave a short, mirthless laugh. "Yeah. The last five hours weren't very pleasant, Your Highness."

Lexi's eyes narrowed slightly as she met his angry gaze. She knew she ought to apologize to him, but it felt so wrong and infuriating for Cam to chastise her that she instinctively rose to the challenge. "You wanted me to come break up your fight with Talan so you could both follow me?"

Cam looked startled for a moment. "No, but you should have told Clodi."

"Clodi can't keep secrets, and she would have insisted on coming."

"But you let Tiger go with you," he accused.

"No, I didn't," Lexi snapped. "I flew all the way out to some lake before I realized he had followed me."

"Oh." Cam's shoulders fell beneath her steely gaze. "I'm sorry. I shouldn't have said any of that." He rubbed his forehead and grimaced, making his left dimple show. "Talan kept demanding to speak to you, and Clodi gave him some of the worst excuses I've ever heard." Cam chuckled half-heartedly at the memory. "He pushed his way into your room after she told him you were untangling your ribbons and couldn't be bothered."

A tiny smile quirked the corner of Lexi's mouth. "And did he have a tantrum?"

Cam's face darkened. "He yelled at Clodi until she cried."

Lexi swallowed down guilt as she removed her other boot and fought to keep her face expressionless.

"I don't even want to call him a cretin anymore. It's too nice a word," Cam continued as he picked up her boots and set them neatly beside her bed. "Where's your brush?" he asked, glancing around the room.

Lexi put a self-conscious hand over the worst of her tangles. "I think I'll just wash it."

Cam nodded. "I'll be back in a few minutes to take you down to the pool." He hesitated with his hand on the door, then turned back with an uncertain expression. "Will you wait for me here?"

Lexi fought back a smile. "No. But if you're fast enough, I may still be here."

Cam shook his head, but gave her a dimpled, closed-mouth smile as he slipped through the door and closed it softly behind him.

Lexi frowned. "I *am* turning into my mother," she murmured, getting up and shoving the balcony doors shut with a resounding thud that vibrated up her arms and shook her wings. She changed

219

into her bathing suit at a deliberately slow pace while replaying the entire conversation with Cam in her head. She was still shocked that *he* had apologized. Lexi gathered her dirty laundry strategically in her bruised arm, then looked down at the fading yellow bruises on her knees and debated whether to wait for Cam.

"Your lunch, Miss Fritillary," called an unfamiliar female voice as something thumped against the door.

Lexi opened it to see a blue-winged woman hefting a tray with three plates of steaming food. "Thank you," Lexi said, opening the door wider. "You may set it on the table."

The woman gave her an apologetic grimace as she removed a plate. "I have to take the tray back to the kitchen," she explained.

"That's fine." Lexi's eyes narrowed slightly as she stared at the woman's bright blonde hair; the color reminded her of something. With a short intake of air, it came back to her with a guilty pang: Lord Admiral's stable boy and his sad message. She looked carefully at the woman's wide-set eyes and broad, snubbed nose as she turned to go.

"Miss Blue, is it?" Lexi asked politely.

The woman nodded, a blush deepening the ruddy hue of her skin. "The life servants all go by their first name," she explained. "Marina is fine for me."

"Is your nephew the stable boy on Lord Admiral's estate?"

Marina's thick blonde brows rose as she nodded. "One of them is, yes."

"I was asked to relay a message to you," Lexi said, pulling out a stool. "Would you like to sit down?"

Marina swallowed heavily. "Is it bad news, then? Is my mother all right?" she whispered, clinging to her empty tray with whitened knuckles.

"Your mother is fine," Lexi assured her, gently pressing her down to the stool. "She's gone to live on Lord Admiral's estate with your sister."

"She left him?!" Marina popped up from her stool with an incredulous smile.

Lexi hid her surprise behind a carefully blank face. "No, I'm sorry, but your father is dead," she said gently.

Marina let out a strangled laugh. "Don't be sorry." She laughed again, the sound strangely akin to a cry. "He wasn't my father." She covered her mouth to stop the odd noise that kept slipping out. She shook her head and swiped at a tear with the other hand. "Thank you for your message." She fled through the open door and hurried down the hall.

Lexi stared after her retreating figure a moment, then glanced at the three plates on the table. It looked to be a potato dish with peas and onion. Lexi took an experimental bite after shutting the door. The food was better than she had expected, and she was halfway through a plate of it when the door swung open.

"You *are* here! I *knew* he was lying!" Talan crowed. He tried to slam the door behind him, but Cam caught it and burst into the room.

"You should knock first! What if she had been dressing?" Cam demanded, irritable relief crossing his face when he saw Lexi, her fork frozen in the air as she watched them.

"Then it would be my right to see her! She *is* my fiancée, you pebble peasant," Talan sneered as he sidled up to Lexi and tried to slip a possessive hand up under her wings.

Lexi deftly stepped away from him, setting her fork down with deliberate care.

"You're not her fiancée, and you'll knock next time," Cam ordered, stepping closer with a menacing air.

Lexi took a deep breath, her face blank. "Have either of you eaten lunch?" she asked politely, trying to ignore the dueling pheromone scents that blended to smell oddly akin to a cinnamon roll.

"No. Is this for me?" Talan asked, picking up a plate and scrutinizing the food.

"Have a seat," Lexi offered, pointing to the two empty stools and dropping her load of laundry as she claimed the third.

Talan's eyes widened as her took in her swimming suit, his gaze running down her long legs and up again before the bruise on her arm disturbed his perusal. "I didn't mean to do that," he murmured, trying to pretend Cam was not standing behind him, glaring.

"Yes, you did," Lexi answered expressionlessly. "Sit, Cam."

A muscle in Cam's jaw jumped with an unhappy twitch as he dragged the remaining stool over to the vanity table and slid the remaining plate onto his lap to avoid touching Talan.

"Now," Lexi began, reclaiming her fork, "I realize my mother ordered you to follow me, but I need more privacy than you are allowing me."

"What for?" Talan demanded, giving Cam a dark glance.

Lexi fought the threatening smile, so tempted to tell him precisely what she wanted to do alone with Cam that her lip twitched. "You can voluntarily give me that privacy," she continued smoothly, "or I can have you locked up in the dungeon again."

"You wouldn't," Talan said, his voice unsure.

Cam lifted a forkful of food to his mouth with a smirk.

"I would," Lexi assured him. "The more you interfere, the longer it will take me to find a mate, and the greater the chance that your season will end here, on the mountain."

Talan slammed his fork down with a clatter. "You can't marry him," he said, jerking his head back at Cam. "The Queen will imprison him the moment you return, force the King to void your marriage, and you will *still* end up married to me. You are just delaying the inevitable."

"I do not intend to return home." Lexi laid her fork aside, her appetite gone.

Cam froze mid-bite. "Ever?"

Talan leaned back with a disbelieving laugh. "You're going to give up everything? The palace, your title, your money, even your beloved maid just so you can go frolic around in a dusty quarry with this low-born grunt? Do you think your sons will thank you when you tell them they could have been king?"

A pained expression flickered across Lexi's face before she could hide it.

"You're fooling yourself, Princess. Your only palatable future is with me or Van. Please just choose one of us so I can go back to the palace," Talan said wearily, then resumed eating.

Cam carefully laid his fork aside despite his half-eaten meal. His eyes settled on Lexi with a searching glance.

"Will you excuse us, Talan?" Lexi asked, retrieving her pile of dirty clothes from the floor and her bag from the bed.

"No. You need a chaperone and I'm following the Queen's orders," Talan argued, taking a last bite before abandoning his plate and following them to the door.

Cam barred his way as Lexi continued into the hallway. Talan knocked at his arm, but it didn't budge.

"We can always stop by the dungeon first," Lexi threatened pleasantly.

Talan drew back with a sullen expression. "Fine. I'll meet you at the pool."

Lexi turned her back without replying, listening to Cam's quick steps as he caught up with her and lifted the bag from her hand.

"That was hiding my knee bruises," Lexi protested.

Cam handed her bag back to her without hesitation, and she once again let it swing awkwardly before her. A small silence followed, and then they both began to speak at once.

"You first," Cam demurred.

"You work at a quarry?" Lexi asked again.

Cam nodded, then hesitated, his eyes on the floor. "Will the Queen really imprison your husband?"

"I don't intend to find out."

223

"You're not going to see the King again?" Cam asked, his heavy eyebrows raised.

"I hope to," Lexi said, keeping her voice steady with difficulty.

Cam shook his head, his forehead creased. "I don't like you giving up so much."

"Shall I marry Talan, then?" she teased half-heartedly.

Cam shook his head without smiling. "That's too much to give up, too."

Lexi hid her upset expression by turning into the laundry room, annoyed to discover it was empty for lunch. Her pile of dirty laundry from the night before was no longer there nor could she find her things hanging among the drying clothes. Irritably, she shoved Tiger's old clothes into her bag and hoisted it up to cover the bruise on her arm as she left.

"I can wash them for you," Cam offered.

Lexi held her bag tighter. "No."

Cam frowned, but slid his hand into hers. "It bothered you what he said." Receiving no answer, he took her silence for assent. "It bothered me, too. What if one of your sons wants to be king?"

"And what if I have only daughters? Or no children at all?" Lexi pulled her hand away irritably. "You want me to choose my husband based on the whims of my future offspring?"

Cam stopped and turned to her. "No. I want you to choose me," he said fervently, dropping his intent gaze as she returned it. "I just don't want you to have to suffer for it."

Lexi's eyes swam as she stared at the dimples that were almost hidden in his earnestness. "Are you asking me to marry you?"

Cam grinned and met her gaze. "You know that I am." He caressed her cheek and tucked a strand of hair behind her ear. "Are you saying yes?"

Guilt ricocheted through her as she thought of Tiger. "I'm saying..."

"What are you doing?!" Talan demanded. He flew with rapid strokes and barreled into Cam, knocking both men off balance. "Don't you touch her like that," Talan roared, then backed away under Lexi's cold glare. "You have an audience," he fumed, darting a glance at the two couples who had stopped to stare.

"I'm proposing," Cam said through clenched teeth, retaking Lexi's hand.

Perfect horror froze Talan's face for a second before he blinked, turning to face Lexi. "And what is your answer?"

Lexi drew herself up to her full height, her mouth hardening. "My answer is *yes*."

Cam squeezed her hand and she glanced at him, her expression unchanged. "Go find my guards please, Cam."

"I don't want to leave you alone with him," he pleaded, his dark eyes soft.

"He'll behave himself," Lexi said, her gaze turning back to Talan as she freed her hand from Cam's. "He has *an audience*." Lexi brushed past him, forcing him to move his wing as he spun to follow her.

"You can't be serious," Talan said, his face still incredulous as he caught up with her.

"Why not?" Lexi asked, yanking open the pool door.

"*Why not*?!" Talan repeated, his face reddening as he prepared his arguments.

Rather than stay and hear them, Lexi breezed past him into the well-populated bathing room, then glanced back with a defiant smile.

Talan chewed at his healing bottom lip and winced.

Lexi laughed inwardly and scanned the room. Van's wispy blond hair caught her eye as he bent close to a pouty redhead with orange wings. The girl shoved him playfully, and his large mouth spread into an enthusiastic grin. Lexi stood up straighter, her face a pleasant mask as she waded into the pool and deposited her bag at the edge.

Though she was careful not to look his way, she smelled cabbage before she had even begun to wash.

"I thought you might come here," Van said with a pleasant smile.

"Hello, Van. Did you say goodbye to Dina?" Lexi asked, unable to resist glancing at the abandoned redhead. The girl gave her a sulky glare.

Van shrugged uncomfortably as his face twitched. "Is she gone?"

Talan had finally succeeding in stripping off most of his clothing and joined them in the water. "She just got engaged to some peasant!" he announced to Van.

Van blinked up at him in confusion. "Dina's engaged?"

Talan shook his head emphatically. "No! The *Princess* is," he hissed in a furious undertone.

Van's head whipped back around to Lexi, all traces of his smile gone. "So soon?"

Lexi ignored him and dipped her head in the water, running her fingers through her knotted hair. When she brought her head back up, both men were in the water next to her.

Van reached out to brush the water from her forehead, then pulled back under Talan's steely gaze. "Your Highness," he said, careful not to be overheard, "is the Queen likely to accept your choice?"

Lexi tapped shampoo into her hand before meeting his gaze. "Do you enjoy the scent of rotting apples, Van?"

Van blushed, making his wispy blonde hair seem lighter. "They have a sweet scent," he faltered.

Talan laughed loudly. "Right. And that's why you gagged like a girl during our last rotten apple war in the orchard."

Van's wide mouth twitched with a false smile. "You hit me in the cheek, and it splattered into my mouth." He shuddered subtly at the memory.

Talan's intelligent eyes darted back and forth between Lexi's smug smile and Van's embarrassed grimace. "Wait. Is that what she smells like to you? You're not a pheromone match?"

Van shifted his shoulders and jaw as he and Talan appeared to have a mute conversation. Lexi tightened her mouth to hide her amusement.

"She has to produce an heir," Talan blurted. "And Anna won't take all the old lady's money. She'll let you have some. Lady Nessa might even forget what she said."

Van's face lost all trace of his usual good humor. "Anna will remind her," he predicted glumly.

Talan pressed his lips into a grim line to hide the smile evident in his voice. "Probably."

"You owe me an inheritance," Van said sourly, punching Talan's arm.

Talan laughed in open glee. "I do not."

Van inclined his head in a solemn bow. "Your Highness," he said, then glided back to the pouty redhead.

Talan watched him go with a delighted grin, a soft chuckle making his shoulders and wings shake. When he turned back to Lexi, his eyes were still bright with amusement, sending a thrill through her that she shook off irritably.

As if sensing her reaction, Talan bit his lip and caught her hip under the water with a little squeeze. "You're all mine now," he said happily.

"I'm engaged to Cam," Lexi reminded him as she pushed his hand away.

His blue eyes lit with a perceptive glint. "Only out of spite. It was stupid of me to interrupt. You weren't going to say yes."

Her aggravation too intense to stifle, Lexi dunked her head under to rinse her hair. His laughter sounded garbled through the water, increasing her ire. Finally, the need for oxygen drove her back to the surface.

"You look beautiful wet."

Lexi let her arm fall heavily into the water to splash his face.

Talan chortled. "Very unladylike; what would your mother say?"

Lexi turned away from him, her wet wings blocking her face as she strove to contain the fury that lit up her eyes. With jerky, stiff movements, she continued washing.

Talan came up behind her, his voice soft. "I can behave myself. I just don't want to." Talan chuckled as she lurched away from him. "But I'll try."

Lexi exited the water abruptly, wincing at the heavy cascade of water falling from her wings. "I doubt that."

He hefted her bag before she could lift it and stepped out to follow her. "You know, you've really seen all my worst behavior. You've nothing left to discover but my charms."

Lexi allowed herself a tiny scowl at his wide grin, and snatched fruitlessly at her bag.

"Allow me," Talan insisted, holding it out of her reach.

Lexi glanced down at the large bruise on her arm, then around the room. Van was completely distracted by his redhead, but one or two others glanced away as she met their eyes.

Talan slid his hand into place over the bruise. "I'm so sorry," he said, all hint of playfulness gone.

Lexi removed his hand carefully, his repentant eyes catching hers for a moment before she hurried from the room. He followed her out into the hallway, both of them trailing water like small storm clouds.

"I'm sorry I lied," Talan blurted as the door shut behind him. "I knew my season wasn't ending. I was trying to trick you into mating with me."

Lexi jerked to a stop, then spun around, her heavy wings flinging spray. "Why are you telling me this?"

He came to a stop next to her. "I wanted to tell you so maybe you would believe me when I say I'm not going to lie to you anymore."

Lexi frowned. "I already knew you lied about that."

Talan nodded. "I figured. So ask me something else."

"What did you say to get that marriage certificate?"

Talan blushed under his light dusting of freckles. "I embellished a little."

"*What* did you say?"

Talan let out a little laugh that died when he met her gaze. "I said you let me into your room."

Lexi gasped, her hand itching to slap his face. "They think we mated?"

Talan dropped his gaze guiltily. "Your mother does."

Lexi trembled at the overpowering rage that swept through her. "You've made it so I can't go home again."

Talan met her furious gaze, his expression rueful. "Not without me. Sorry."

"Sorry?" Lexi demanded incredulously. "You're not sorry. You've cheerfully destroyed my life."

"I know." He hung his head in remorse. "Do you hate me now?"

"Yes," she assured him, ripping her bag from his hand to march down the hall. Angry tears skewed her vision, but she increased her pace, wincing with each bounce of her sodden wings. She could hear his steady tread behind her, and the maddening sound drove her faster. Halfway there she realized she was headed for Tiger's room. She just needed to inhale the scent and calm down. When she reached the door, she raised her hand to knock and caught a glimpse of Talan's contrite face in her peripheral vision. She couldn't bear to look at him or speak to him. Instead of knocking, she impetuously opened the door and dodged inside, quickly slamming it behind her. The room was blissfully empty, and her shoulders sagged with relief.

"You were right," she whispered. "Part of me *did* want to go home." She inhaled deeply, then frowned at the fresh breeze wafting in from the balcony. Dropping her bag, she hastily shut the balcony doors and inhaled again.

"Whose room is this?" Talan asked after a soft knock.

"An empty one," Lexi called out irritably, her deep breaths failing to calm her. Her eyes fell on Wes' blanket, then back to the door.

"Can I come in?" Talan asked.

"Of course not," Lexi snapped, snatching up the blanket and holding it to her nose. The threadbare, gray fabric was heavy with scent and made her legs feel weak. She sat heavily on the stool and inhaled again, her mind beginning to drift. Absently, she reached up to scratch at her cheek, wondering at the drying moisture there before she realized she had been crying. She stared at her wet fingertips while her other hand clasped the blanket over the lower half of her face.

"I'm sorry. I was just trying to make sure you would marry me," Talan called through the door, his tone defeated.

Rather than answer, Lexi dropped the blanket to her lap and inhaled the fresher air. She stood slowly, grabbed her bag, and walked unsteadily to the balcony doors. Straining for silence, she wedged one open and slipped out to the balcony. Fanning her still-dripping wings behind her, she tossed her bag and the blanket down to her own balcony before climbing awkwardly down. She prepared answers for Clodi's inevitable questions during her descent, but was delighted to see she wouldn't need them as her inquiring roommate wasn't there. Someone had removed the lunch plates and tidied up the room. Clodi? Or had someone else been there? Lexi lifted the blanket to her nose to quell that minor irritation, then quickly shut the doors behind her. She stripped off her wet suit, then glanced around the room; she had nothing clean to wear. Inhaling the heady scent again, she wrapped the blanket around her, and climbed onto her bed. The four hours of sleep and the vigorous flight to the lake were catching up to her. Pulling the end of the blanket up to her nose, she fell fast asleep.

Chapter Eleven

Lexi woke with a delicious sense of well-being. She stretched her sore muscles, readjusted Wes' blanket, and dozed. She was vaguely aware of a knock, followed by a rattling dinner tray and a soft-spoken life servant, but it all passed in a dreamlike haze. Unperturbed, she slept on. It was Cam's voice that finally roused her.

"Raven?" Cam asked, repeating the soft knock she hadn't heard. "You've been asleep for a long time. Are you all right?"

"Hmm?" Lexi forced her eyes open to see a blurry view of her own hand still clutching the blanket. *Wes'* blanket. Wes' very *fragrant* blanket. "Um, yes, I'm fine," she called, leaping up and ripping the blanket off of her. She yanked her bag out from under the bed, flung Tiger's old clothes across the floor and stuffed Wes' blanket inside her bag. Grabbing one of her own blankets, she wrapped it around herself as she kicked her bag back under the bed.

"May I come in?"

"No!" Lexi leapt to the door, scooping up Tiger's clothes as she went. She sniffed her bare arms, then opened the door just wide enough to push the clothing through. "Could you drop those off at the laundry for me and pick up my clean clothes? I don't have anything to wear," she added as she quickly shut the door.

"Uh, the laundry is closed, but I'll try."

"What? What time is it?"

"It's about midnight."

Lexi's mouth fell open, and she glanced at the blanket's hiding place, but didn't answer. She listened to Cam walk away with her heart pounding. At least Tiger didn't know. She bit her lip as she thought of the missing blanket and wondered if Tiger would notice. She would have to replace it with one of her own...just as soon as she found some clothes. Agitated, she paced the room, debating whether or not to get out Wes' blanket again. Fear of Cam smelling it in her room stopped her. *This is stupid*, she thought, quietly resolving to put the blanket back, but knowing she probably wouldn't. She shifted her own blanket around her until it bunched uncomfortably under her wings, then jumped when the door flew open.

"You finally woke up!" Clodi exclaimed, her face brightening as she swung the door shut and hurried over to hug Lexi.

Lexi gave her a stiff smile and a half-hearted pat while clinging to her blanket.

Clodi pulled away with a pinched expression. "Is it okay to hug a princess?"

"It's fine."

"And you want me to treat you the same?"

"Yes," Lexi said emphatically.

"Okay," Clodi said, nodding solemnly. "Where did you go this morning? I thought you were coming right back, and I tried to lie for you, but that Talan got so mad at me. I don't like him; he's not nice."

Lexi gave her an apologetic grimace. "I'm sorry he was unkind to you. I didn't intend to be gone so long."

Clodi flashed her a forgiving smile. "That's okay. Were you alone?"

Lexi shook her head. "I thought I was alone, but Tiger followed me."

Clodi tipped her head sideways. "Does he like you?"

"Just as a friend. He says I smell like rotten things." Lexi forced a careless smile.

Clodi's forehead wrinkled in a slight scowl. "He shouldn't have told you that."

Turning away, Lexi made a dismissive gesture with her hand.

"If somebody told me I smelled like rotten things, I think I might punch him."

Lexi laughed lightly, racking her brain for a change of topic. "Have you been to see the guy with the broken wings? Tull, was it?"

Clodi's face lit up like sunshine on dandelions as she nodded. "He's a plumber. He's got all these great plans for fixing up this place."

"He doesn't plan to leave?"

Clodi's glow dimmed as she sat down. "He thinks his wings won't heal in time, but I think they will," she added defiantly. "And I think he's going to fall in love with me, and marry me, too." She laughed at Lexi's look of surprise. "He might not, but I have a feeling. I'm not giving up on him."

"You're not interested in anyone else?"

Clodi shook her head. "Nobody else smells very good. Tull smells like this dessert my mom used to make on special occasions. She'd get down her biggest bowl and break six eggs into it, and then she'd add the cream..."

Clodi continued with a detailed recipe, but Lexi was no longer listening, just making eye contact and nodding at polite intervals. She kept redraping her blanket in a vain attempt to sit on one of the stools with a modicum of modesty. Finally, she gave up and stood. Clodi had stopped speaking and was looking at her expectantly. Lexi gave her a mm-hmm, hoping that was an appropriate answer.

"Oh good," Clodi said, slumping in relief. "I thought maybe I was weird." Clodi's tan skin suffused with color.

Lexi was suddenly sorry she hadn't been listening.

"Talan says he's kissed you," Clodi continued, speaking faster as she saw Lexi's frown. "If he has, does he taste like he smells?" Clodi put a hand at either side of her head like a horse with blinders. "I can't believe I just asked a princess that."

Lexi shook her head slightly, trying to divide her irritation with Talan from her answer. "I suppose he does, a little."

Clodi folded her hands into fists that she pressed into widely-smiling cheeks as she leaned forward onto her elbows. "I hope I get to kiss Tull."

Lexi gave her shoulder a soft pat, then resumed her pacing around the portion of the room Clodi's broad wings didn't close off.

"Talan says you're engaged to *him*. Cam says you're not. I think they might have torn each other's wings off if the guards hadn't been here."

Lexi stopped her pacing, facing the wall. "I was engaged to Talan, but I came here to get away from him." The words *now I'm engaged to Cam* hung on her tongue, but she closed her mouth. Turning, she faced Clodi. "It's very important that you not tell anyone who I am."

"Because then they would *all* want to marry you?"

Lexi thought of her mother's secret and her cousin Ryp as she simply nodded. Raised voices outside their door caught her attention.

"You will let me into my fiancée's room!" Talan shouted imperiously.

Lexi clutched her blanket tighter as the door began to open only to be pulled shut again.

"She isn't sleeping any more; I heard her voice. Now, stand aside this instant!"

Low voices followed Talan's furious speech, and then silence.

The quiet knock from the balcony door made Lexi jump.

"Lex," Tiger called through the door. "We need to talk."

"Is that Tiger?" Clodi asked, pointing to the balcony.

"Lex, I'm coming in."

Clodi scowled. "We need guards on the balcony, too." She shoved both balcony doors closed just as Tiger began to open them. "She isn't dressed!"

"Then she needs to get dressed, because I need to talk to her *now*," Tiger insisted.

"She's a princess; you can't boss her around."

"Hasn't stopped me yet."

"Bossy bossy bossy," Clodi said, spinning around with a couple beats of her creamy black-streaked wings. "What?" she asked, catching the flicker of fear before Lexi's face went blank.

"Until Cam gets back from the laundry, I don't have any clothes."

Clodi frowned. "My spare clothes are dirty or I'd let you borrow them."

"Thank you anyway. I'll just wait for Cam."

"They're sure quiet out there," Clodi commented, walking over to the hall door and leaning her ear against it. After listening, she opened it a few inches and peered out. "Where did everybody go?"

Lexi retreated behind the door where she couldn't be seen from the hallway. "Probably took Talan to the dungeon."

"Hooray for that! That man has the temper of a smacked hornet." Clodi stuck her head back into the hallway. "Cam's coming. Hi, Cam," she greeted, taking a stack of clothes from him. "Ooo! My dress!" Clodi grinned at the yellow fabric atop the pile as she absently shut the door in Cam's face.

Lexi quickly dressed in her black riding pants and a blue top while Clodi cooed over the yellow dress and tried it on. Pulling on her riding boots, Lexi hopped to the hall door and pulled it open.

Cam gave her a smile that didn't reach his eyes or his dimples. "I tried to send your guards to you after your bath, but we couldn't find you."

There was an implicit question in his statement, but Lexi ignored it. Instead, she leaned out and kissed him, smiling when he relaxed and kissed her back.

"Your hair," Cam said, his fingers caught in the dark tangle.

Lexi pulled back and smoothed her hair self-consciously. "I forgot to comb it out."

"I'll do it," he volunteered, stepping forward.

Lexi put one hand to his chest with an apologetic smile. "Tiger is waiting on the balcony to talk to me."

"Can't he wait a little longer?" Cam asked, his expression wistful as he gave one of her tangled tresses a soft tug.

Lexi shook her head. "I'll come to your room when I'm done." She watched his smile fade, then leaned in to give him another kiss before pushing him back into the hallway.

"Does *he* taste like he smells?" Clodi chortled, her face red.

Lexi licked her lips and smiled. "Like cookies," she affirmed as she yanked her bag out and hurried to the balcony.

Tiger scowled down at her when she flung open the doors, his glance dropping to her bag. "Is my blanket in there?"

Lexi's face flamed red as she pulled the doors shut behind her, forcing them close together in the small space. "I didn't take *yours*," she whispered, trying to read his expression in the moonlight.

Tiger reached down and took her bag, pulling the scent-laden blanket from it. "Mine has holes," he announced as he stuck his fingers through two sizable holes and wiggled his fingers in front of her face.

Lexi swallowed, drawing calm from the scent of it before she responded. "It was on Wes' bed."

"I know. I switched them this morning when the holes were bugging me. Why did you take this?" he demanded, noticing too late the effect it was having on her. Swearing softly, he wadded it and tossed it up onto the balcony above them.

Lexi looked after it a moment, then slowly brought her eyes back to his. "I hoped you wouldn't notice."

"Lex, you're acting like an addict."

"Maybe I am," she whispered.

Tiger grabbed her chin and forced her to look at him. "Stop this! Just stop!" He released her chin and groaned. "I can't even imagine how this could be worse. Talan had a fit when I came back to my room this afternoon. He thought you were still inside and tried to stop me from going in. We had a bit of a fight." Tiger laughed mirthlessly. "I'll probably get the cell next to Wes. And Coli saw you fly to your balcony, so she knows I was with you all morning."

"I'm sorry," Lexi murmured. "If it makes you feel better, I think my guards hauled Talan off to the dungeon."

"You're without your guards again?"

Lexi looked up at him wearily.

"Fine, I'll let that go. But Lex, you stay out of my room and away from Wes."

"And what about you?" she asked, immediately kicking herself for the words she had let escape.

"Can you smell me?"

Lexi leaned in gingerly and sniffed at his shirt, trying to hide her smile when she caught a faint whiff of his scent. "No," she lied, squaring her shoulders and forcing herself to make eye contact.

Tiger shut his eyes and let out a pained sigh. "Then you have to stay away from me, too."

"I said no!"

"You lied."

Lexi let out a frustrated cry, and clutched at his shirt to hold him there. "Don't do this. Talan told Mother I mated with him. I can't go home unless I marry him," Lexi blurted, tears in her voice. "Up here is the last bit of time I have with you."

"But you didn't mate with him," he said, a question in his voice.

"Of course I didn't! But Mother is so convinced I did that she forced Father to sign a marriage certificate and ordered Talan to follow me. She probably told the court we're already married. Mother would never let me come home with another husband now."

Tiger put his big hands awkwardly on her shoulders, giving her a consoling squeeze as he gently pushed her away despite her tightening grip on his shirt. "I'm sorry. I'll hit him harder next time."

A sob choked out of Lexi's throat. "You usually don't smell. Maybe you just need a bath. Please. I'll stay out of your room."

Tiger shook his head. "I'll still look out for you while you're here, but I'm not part of your future, Lex. Let me go."

"No," she cried, embarrassed at the emotional warble in her voice. She dropped her forehead against her extended arms, still clinging to his shirt as another sob shook her.

"Ah, Lex," he said, fingering the knotted disaster that was her hair. "You shouldn't have come."

Lexi pulled away angrily. "Stop saying that! I did come. Quit condemning me and help me fix it!"

Tiger shook his head again. "I can't fix it, Lex." He pulled his wings back in the tight space and stepped onto the sturdy railing. "Can you?"

He jumped off the railing and flew back to his own balcony before Lexi could think of an answer. She stared up at the dark rectangle of his balcony until she heard the door behind her move.

Clodi cleared her throat. "I was trying not to listen, but you sounded pretty upset." Clodi cleared her throat again when Lexi didn't immediately answer and patted her roughly between her wings. "Are you okay?"

Lexi wiped her cheeks surreptitiously then forced her expression into its customary blank as she turned around. "I'm fine. I think I'll fly a little before I meet Cam."

"Lex," Tiger warned from above.

Lexi started at his voice, then sucked in a breath of fury as she flew up to confront him. Tiger stood stalwart on his balcony, backlit from the lantern in his room. Grinding her teeth, she flew high above him, forcing him to lean out and search for her against the starry sky as she rounded the balcony above, then slipped in behind him through the open doors.

"Lexi!" he called angrily, whirling around to follow her into his room.

"You order me around just like my mother! Even when you don't want me around, you still want to control my life! What for? I can't be a princess without marrying Talan. So now I'm nobody! A farm girl from nowhere! My future is somebody's ordinary wife, and I shouldn't have guards and I should be able to go anywhere I want *alone*."

"You haven't enough common sense for that! You're so sheltered, you've fallen prey to one man after another, and constantly need rescuing," he shouted angrily.

"I've rescued myself! From Talan, Wes, a rotten guard, and even the frog man at the pool!" She shouted back, feeling her muscles relax at the soft, musky scent emanating from the beds.

"What? *I* saved you from Wes," Tiger argued with an indignant snort.

"Only the first time," she reminded him. "And I would have come up with something if you hadn't been there."

"Like what?" Tiger scoffed.

"Like 'I'm Princess Lexi, and the royal flying guard will hunt you down and execute you if you don't let me go.'"

Tiger started to speak, then stopped with a tight grimace as he scratched his head. "That might actually have worked," he conceded.

"I know!" Some of Lexi's vehemence died out at the unexpected agreement, and she stared at him with bemusement. "Tiger, what is happening to you? You taught me to gallop bareback, steal treats from the kitchen, and climb the palace walls. You never considered me helpless before; why are you treating me as if I am now?"

Tiger squinted his eyes shut as if in pain. "Because this is different."

"Why?"

Tiger turned away from her, his wings fanning slowly. "Too many of them want to hurt you, Lex. And even the few who don't mean to hurt you probably still will."

Lexi wrinkled up her long, straight nose. "Just because I'm in season?"

"And because they are."

Lexi let out a heavy sigh. "If that's true, then all the girls need guards."

Tiger nodded. "Maybe they do."

"So does Coli have guards?"

Tiger turned back towards her with a grin. "Coli has *brothers*." He rubbed the left side of his jaw absently. "They take care of her."

"So you've appointed yourself my brother?"

Tiger's warm brown eyes looked startled a moment before he blinked it away. "Yep," he nodded.

"Then you have no business telling me I have to stay away from you," Lexi snapped, some of her ire returning.

Tiger laughed with his lips closed, the soft musical sound calming her. "Fine," he said, lifting both hands in defeat. "But no stealing my blankets or sneaking up here with the balcony doors closed."

Lexi blushed deeply, her gaze falling on the blanket wadded atop Wes' bed.

"You promise?"

Lexi bit her lip. "It's so soothing," she whispered, half-hoping he wouldn't hear. "It makes me feel like everything will be okay."

"It's just a cleverly camouflaged lure, Lex. It's an illusion."

Lexi looked up at him, her eyes searching his until he dropped his glance. "Maybe for Wes."

Tiger's mouth was open, but he said nothing as she slipped by him and stepped out onto the balcony. When she flew, he finally spoke. "You didn't promise yet."

Lexi landed on her balcony with a smile. "I know."

Clodi stood just inside the open balcony doors, repetitively smoothing down the yellow dress that was too tightly fitted to need smoothing. "Is everything okay? Did you two make up?"

"Everything is fine," Lexi assured her, her smile broadening as she realized part of her sentiment was probably pheromone-induced. She picked up her discarded bag and flung it under the bed, feeling satisfied when it slid neatly out of sight. "Now I'm off to soothe Cam," she announced, walking swiftly to the door.

Clodi winced. "Would you like me to help you with your hair first?"

Lexi tried to run her fingers through her hair, but they caught in the tangled mass. Frowning, she smoothed it away from her face. "Cam will fix it," she said, and tried to slip out the door before Clodi could comment.

"Your boyfriend does your hair?"

"Fiancé."

Clodi's eyes grew large. "You're getting married?! When? Am I invited?"

Lexi smiled at her enthusiasm and opened the door. "You're invited," she confirmed as she slipped out into the empty corridor.

"But when?" Clodi asked as Lexi shut the door.

Not wanting to answer that question, Lexi flew down the hallway, then all the way to Cam's room. She grinned broadly when he opened the door, then wrapped her arms around his neck, pushing him back into the room.

"Whoa, you're in a better mood."

"Am I?"

"What did Tiger want to talk about?" Cam asked, disentangling her arms from his neck and leading her to a stool before retrieving a comb.

Lexi suppressed a blush and carefully blanked her expression. "He just wanted me to be more careful."

Cam snorted as he began to carefully work through her tangles. "Is that why you're here without your guards?"

Lexi's shoulders twitched. "I don't obey him. Besides, the guards had to take Talan to the dungeon again."

Cam's hand stilled mid-tangle. "What did he do this time?"

Lexi frowned, her stomach suddenly upset. "He was just fighting with the guards trying to get in my room."

"Why did he do that?"

"Angry, I guess," Lexi said vaguely, then tried to change the subject. "Talan says my mother believes I mated with him. That's why she made my father sign the marriage certificate."

Cam took the comb from her hair and clenched his fists at his sides, the teeth of the comb biting into his hand. "Do you think he's telling the truth?"

Lexi turned to look at him, startled by the anger in his face. "You think he's lying?"

"I think it's interesting he didn't tell you that until you got engaged to me."

Lexi dropped her gaze and turned back around. "Oh. Maybe he waited because he knew I would hate him when he told me."

"You didn't before?"

"No."

Cam let out a long sigh and went back to combing her hair. "So you can't go home again."

Lexi shook her head dully.

"Did you want to?"

Lexi turned to give him a rueful smile. "I would have liked to visit."

"We could drag Talan back with us and make him admit he lied."

Lexi shook her head slowly. "I don't think he would do that. He has too much to lose."

"So he'll go back to the palace after we get married, report, and receive his reward?"

Lexi frowned down at her hands. "Hopefully my father won't let her reward him."

"If the Cretin tells your mother where you are, won't she send someone after you?"

Her stomach lurched as the color slowly drained from her face. "Wallowa is pretty far from the Royal City."

"But your mother wants a grandchild on the throne?"

"Not if his father is a commoner," Lexi admitted with a blush.

Laying a gentle hand on her shoulder, Cam stepped around to face her. "Lexi, your mother believes you mated with Talan. She'll think our children are his."

Lexi swallowed back a gagging sensation. "Then we'll just have to wait to get married. If I'm here for more than a week, everyone will realize I'm not...pregnant," she finished softly, her face scarlet.

Cam patted her shoulder and kissed her forehead. "I think so, too...especially if Talan spends the week in the dungeon."

Lexi jerked around to look at him, and he stepped back to avoid her wing.

"If he's not in the dungeon, he could claim to have mated with you here on the mountain as well," Cam explained, picking up another tangled strand and working the comb through it.

Lexi slowly turned back around, staring down at her clenched hands. "You're right."

"Will you do it?"

Lexi sighed before nodding her head. "I don't see a way around it."

"You shouldn't pity him. He lied himself into this situation."

"I know. I'm angry with him, but being a life servant looks so miserable; I can't wish it on him."

"You're not. It's just a week," Cam soothed.

"But he said his family has a history of short seasons."

Cam frowned. "Did he tell you that when he was pretending his season was over to get you to mate with him?"

Lexi grimaced and nodded.

"It was probably all part of the lie. I could ask him for you, but I doubt he'd tell me the truth."

"Van would know," Lexi said, cringing slightly as Cam pulled at a tangle.

"I'm more concerned about you. Your family's long history of quick arranged marriages could be hiding some pretty short seasons. I don't suppose you know how long your father's season was?"

Lexi shook her head. "He never mentioned it." *But the Old Castle's records would show how long they were here.* Her mother had been careful never to mention her maiden name, but those identical red wings had to mean Ryp's father was the Queen's brother. Queen Ami Monarch must have once been Ami *Leafwing*. Lexi once again tried to imagine her mother as the farmer's daughter in her homemade, ruffled shirt. *Impossible*, she thought.

Cam let out a long breath. "Then prolonging your stay is too big a risk."

"What other choice do we have?"

Cam's brows knit together in thought. "Maybe Tiger or the Governor would know how long your father's season was."

Not likely, Lexi thought. Before her father told her, she had never even heard the false story of him traveling to a distant nobleman's house to marry his daughter. The Queen always masterfully changed the subject whenever Lexi or her sisters wondered aloud about their mother's family. As the subject change usually involved chastisement or the imposing of an unpleasant task, they had stopped asking. Lexi shook her head lightly as if to dislodge the unpleasant memories, and stood.

"That's a good idea," she lied.

244

"You're going now?"

"Why wait?"

Cam laughed. "Umm, because it's the middle of the night? Because you haven't had dinner? Aren't you starving?"

Lexi's stomach growled at the suggestion, but she smiled and hoped he hadn't heard it. "I had dinner in my room."

"Then I'll go with you."

"Thank you, but no. It's better I take care of this myself."

Cam rubbed at his neck unhappily as he watched her slip through the door. "Okay then, guess I'll just wait here."

Lexi flashed him a grateful smile, then hurried down the hallway debating whether to talk to Tiger or Ryp first. The jittery nerves that bounced in her stomach decided her; she needed to calm down. *Pheromones first*, she thought with a quickly-hidden grin.

Her knock was tentative, but quickly followed by an exasperated noise. "What do you want, Lex?"

Startled, Lexi let herself into the dark room, using the light from the corridor to find the solar lantern and switch it on. Sprawled across his bed, Tiger groaned as he covered his eyes.

"You're supposed to wait until I say 'come in.'"

Lexi grinned and shut the door. "How did you know it was me?"

"I can smell you."

"Through a door?" Lexi asked, running her eyes over the blanket he had carelessly tossed over his legs until she located the familiar holes ventilating his feet.

"Yep."

"Maybe it's the blanket," Lexi said, sticking her fingers through the holes to tickle his feet.

Tiger lurched onto all fours. "Don't do that!"

Lexi laughed merrily and reached under his wing to poke his ribs before he could get away from her.

Tiger flew off the bed, wadding up the blanket as he landed. "I'm trying to sleep here," he grumped.

"Are you really so afraid I'll take it again?" she asked, nodding at the blanket.

Tiger stared at the balled-up blanket, then tossed it on the bed. "Leave it there," he warned.

Lexi stuck out her tongue at him, then stared at the blanket. "Why are you using it again?"

"What?"

"Why are you using your old blanket? You said the holes bothered you."

Tiger shrugged. "The other one reminds me of Wes."

"But that one," Lexi said, pointing to the blanket on his bed, "should be covered in *my scent.*"

"No, I aired it out."

Lexi's eyes narrowed slightly as she walked over to stand next to him. "You didn't have time," she accused.

Tiger pressed his lips together and scratched at his head, avoiding her gaze.

"Tiger!"

"What?" He finally met her gaze, then quickly looked away.

"You said I smell like rotten things!"

"So?"

"You normally curl up to sleep with rotten things?" she challenged.

He shrugged defensively as he picked up the blanket and inhaled. "It doesn't smell like you."

"I slept all day wrapped up in it," she asserted, then blushed furiously, "*without* my clothes."

Tiger made a sound like he was trying to clear his throat and failed. She risked a quick glance at him and caught sight of his stubbled cheek, ruddy with embarrassment, as he gripped the blanket in both hands.

"Aren't you going to say anything?" she demanded. "You lied to me."

"You lie to me, too."

"I never get away with it!"

Tiger chuckled. "No, you don't," he agreed, tossing the blanket across his bed.

Lexi shoved at his chest. "Why did you do that?! I was miserable thinking I disgusted you!"

"And is it so much better now?"

Lexi swallowed her answer as the air filled with the rich scent of musk, less floral than Wes' and twice as soothing. Lexi clutched at his shirt as her legs weakened.

Tiger laughed without amusement. "You can't even stand when you smell me." He cradled her face in one large, calloused hand while the other covered hers. "Couldn't let it go, could you?"

Lexi drew an uneven breath and shook her head.

He smiled sadly. "I should have known. You want to hear that I'm attracted to you? I am. But what good can come of that?"

Rather than answer, Lexi leaned forward and kissed the hand covering hers.

"No." Tiger pulled both hands back as she clutched his shirt more tightly. "Come on, let's get you some air," he urged, gently towing her over to the balcony doors. He kicked the rugs aside and pulled both doors open. Still clinging to his shirt, Lexi stumbled with his movement, and he steadied her. "Big breaths," he directed as they stood in the moonlight.

Lexi released his shirt, flushing, and cast a quick glance down into the courtyard to assure herself no one was watching. Catching sight of a couple strolling, she drew herself up taller, and squared her shoulders.

"Hello, *Your Highness*," Tiger teased.

Lexi shook her head. "Don't do that, Tiger," she warned, and stepped back into his room where they couldn't be seen.

Tiger caught her arm. "That's not a good idea, Lex."

"Perhaps you should have considered that before you signaled me."

Tiger released her arm with an irritated breath. "I wasn't *signaling* you, I was just *showing* you."

"Thank you for the demonstration," Lexi said coldly.

"I don't blame you for kissing me. I don't think you could help it."

Lexi's face froze into a frigid smile as her hair blew around her face. "How generous."

"I'm not trying to offend you. I'm trying to salvage our friendship."

Lexi gave him a slight nod. "I appreciate that," she said, her voice expressionless.

"Do you, *My Queen*?" Tiger mocked.

Lexi drew in a long breath before answering. "Harsh."

Tiger winced and ran a hand through his disheveled hair. "Now you can see why I had to lie," he muttered.

"No. No, I don't understand that at all."

Tiger stared at her incredulously for a moment. "My mother is your servant. *I* am your servant for that matter. If I try to marry you, the Queen will probably have me executed and imprison my mother. If we try to hide, my mother bears the brunt of the Queen's fury. Not to mention, we have no way to live because I can't transfer my apprenticeship without them knowing. I really don't even think the Governor will agree to marry us. So where does that leave us? Unmarried, hiding, with my mom in a dungeon. We have no future! Now do you see? Wasn't it nicer when we weren't having this miserable conversation? Wasn't it better when I was the only one trying to figure out any possible way for a happy ending?"

Lexi stood wide-eyed at his harangue, flinching slightly each time he raised his voice, until he stood directly in front of her waiting for an answer. A foolish corner of her brain was fluttering with happiness despite the heavy wash of acidic reality that surrounded it. Ridiculously, that same corner seemed to have control of her eyes. Rather than meet his and give him an answer, they traveled the length of his mouth, finding the exact place where the stubbled skin softened to lips. Almost involuntarily, she moved forward to meet them, a hesitant hand touching his chest, then clutching his shirt as he grabbed her shoulders and kissed her hard. The brown stubble was rough to her lips, but the kiss was so heady that she didn't feel the discomfort of it until he pulled back.

"Now it's worse," he said, wiping his mouth as if to erase what he had done. "Sorry."

Lexi slowly released her grip on his shirt and opened her eyes. "I'm engaged to Cam."

"Well, good. You can hide somewhere with your obedient little servant boy, and I'll see you back at the palace in about two months."

Lexi shook her head. "I'm—we're— not going to the palace."

"Not by choice, but that is where the royal guard will take you once they track you down."

"You're being unfair to her; she wouldn't do that," Lexi asserted, her jaw tightening.

"She sent Talan, two guards, and a marriage certificate after you the first time."

Lexi shook her head. "But I'll be pregnant by then; she won't try to move me. And then she won't try to move the babies. I should have at least two years for her to calm down."

"Better hurry, then. I expect more of the royal guard is already on its way."

Lexi fought down panic. "Why do you say that?"

249

"She thought Talan would bring you back before now. I expect phase two of the *Bring Lexi Home* project is well under way."

Lexi leaned a hand against the wall and tried to steady her breathing.

Tiger smirked and threw her the blanket.

Lexi caught it, then nonchalantly folded it over her arms, trying to hide the comfort she drew from the scent. "We can't leave yet. She might think I'm carrying Talan's children."

Tiger's bushy eyebrows drew together in a scowl of thought. "When did he tell you that?"

Lexi shrugged. "An hour or two ago."

"*After* you told him you were engaged to Cam?"

Lexi frowned. "Talan was there when we got engaged. And yes, he told me afterwards."

Tiger shook his head. "Talan's trying to keep you here. I'm sure he knows your mother will send more guards after you. It's possible he's lying about your mother believing you mated with him."

Lexi drew the blanket up to her chin in agitation. "So what now? Run with Cam?"

"They'll still find you. And even if they don't want to risk moving you or your children, they'll have no trouble imprisoning Cam."

Lexi covered her face with the blanket. "This seemed like such a good idea when my father suggested it."

"No offense, Lex, but the King has never been good at anticipating the Queen's behavior. If he was, he never would have married her."

Lexi dropped the blanket from her face abruptly. "He *loves* her. He thinks she's a good Queen."

"Well, good. That probably makes her abuse a lot easier to take."

"She isn't *abusive*, she just goes too far to get what she wants."

Tiger laughed. "Fine. Do you want my advice?"

Lexi folded the blanket back under her chin with a scowling forehead and pouting mouth. "Yes," she admitted.

"Forget your obedient fiancé, and when the royal guard shows up, go home with them. Convince your mother you haven't mated with anyone, then wait for a decent nobleman to come into season."

"She won't let me wait," Lexi said, her voice weary. "She'll make me marry Talan."

"Lex, she can't *make* you do anything. Your choices may be lousy, but you always have them." Setting his hands on her shoulders, he waited for her to meet his eyes before he continued. "She can't force you to seal yourself to Talan. Do you really not get that?"

"But it's not just me. If I defy her, she'll make everyone around me suffer for it, too."

Tiger snorted. "And you don't think she's abusive." Seeing her scowl, he quickly changed the topic. "And that's why you shouldn't get married yet. Any commoner you marry will become a convenient target for the Queen's wrath."

Lexi sighed deeply, her mouth twitching into a smile from the pheromones she had just inhaled.

"Yeah, okay," Tiger said, taking the blanket and stepping away from her. "You've had enough."

Lexi yanked the blanket back. "You shouldn't have it, either."

Tiger scowled and reached for it. "I'll have it laundered."

Lexi held it behind her back. "No, I will."

"Fine. I'll go with you," Tiger said, pulling on a boot.

Lexi smirked, then her lips broke apart as a full laugh bubbled up her throat. "This is stupid. We're escorting a blanket to be washed."

"I'm escorting an addict to dispose of her stash."

Lexi slugged him in the arm, throwing him off balance as he tried to put on his second boot. Giggling, she made it to the door before he stomped on the trailing blanket, pulling it from her grasp.

Still laughing, she ran back to fetch it just as Tiger gathered it up. She tried to wrest it from him, but he held it over her head. Lexi immediately flew up, took it from his hands, and fluttered towards the balcony doors.

"That worked better when you couldn't fly," he chuckled, grabbing her ankle as she tried to escape. Lexi shrieked and turned to kick at him, but he deftly caught the other leg and pulled her down. Bracing himself, he caught her by the waist as she fell against his chest, and she grabbed his shoulders to steady herself. Laughing, she looked up at him, but his proximity quieted their humor.

"Last time," he promised, letting his scent cloud her mind into a delicious haze of security and warmth. His lips were gentle on hers as her hands slid up to twine around his neck, the blanket forgotten at their feet.

They both froze when the knock sounded, then reluctantly pulled apart.

"Yes?" Tiger called without moving to open the door.

"Have you seen Miss Fritillary?" Beck's cheerful voice called through the door. "The Governor would like to speak with her, and she seems to have escaped her guards again."

Lexi blushed at Tiger's scowl, then touched his fingers lightly with hers, smiling as he clutched her hand.

"I have company just now, Beck. But I'll come help you look as soon as she leaves."

Beck chortled delightedly. "Before your company flies off the balcony, would you tell her that the Governor is going to release Mr. Admiral again if she doesn't come talk him out of it?"

Tiger and Lexi exchanged a startled glance, then released each other's hands as Lexi turned and opened the door.

"How did you know?" Lexi asked, glancing back as Tiger tossed the blanket on his bed.

The top of Beck's balding head turned red with his rowdy guffaw. "I may be out of season, but I still have a nose. You were both pumping out enough pheromones to fill the hallway."

252

Lexi passed Beck and took a few steps down the hallway to regain her composure. Tiger stepped out face aflame and shut the door behind him.

"Don't tell anyone, please, Beck," Lexi requested, turning to face him with a calm visage.

"Especially not Mr. Crescent, eh?" Beck asked, starting down the hallway with another chortle. "Or Mr. Admiral?" Beck slapped his thigh with another fit of laughter.

"I'll be happy to order you if it makes it easier," Lexi warned as she walked a step ahead of him.

Beck continued his raucous laughter, but shut his mouth to do it, making a series of splutters and snorts.

"That's enough," Tiger warned, looming over Beck with a soft-spoken menace.

Beck turned to look at him, choked out a final chortle, then let it drop.

"I wasn't aware out-of-seasons could still smell female pheromones," Lexi said, eager to divert Beck's attention.

"Can't usually," Beck said, shrugging. "There are only a few of us that still can. But it's not like when I was in season...all the exhilaration is gone. Now they're just scents...some nice, some nasty. Yours is just fine—kind of like apples. But Mr. Swallowtail here..." Beck laughed nervously as Tiger looked down his crooked nose at him. "Never mind," he finished with a wide grin.

"Is Talan still in the dungeon?" Lexi asked, stepping between them.

Beck shook his head in disgust. "No, Mr. Fancy Pants already talked his way up to the Governor's office. He's under guard, but he got the Governor all worked up that you're about to marry Mr. Crescent," Beck flashed a knowing grin before Tiger's frown squelched it. "And he says you and Mr. West aren't a pheromone match, so Mr. Admiral is demanding that the Governor marry you and he *immediately*." Beck perfectly imitated Talan's imperious tone.

Lexi stopped walking and turned to face Beck. "Is this an ambush wedding?"

"No," Beck said emphatically, then looked a little guilty. "Maybe. The Governor wasn't convinced when he told me to fetch you. Maybe Mr. Fancy Pants has talked himself into a hole, or rather a cell, by now."

Lexi sighed and looked at Tiger, who shrugged. "Just put on the princess, and get it over with."

Lexi gave him a playful glare. "Did you— the very paragon of sincerity and truth—just advise me to be false?"

Tiger smirked as he took her arm. "Wouldn't they be confused if you gave them anything else?"

Lexi pulled away from him as they began walking again. "No. I'm not always *the princess* with them."

Tiger began his musical closed-mouth laugh as Lexi's wings twitched. "I let other people see the true me," she argued, elbowing him.

"Do you? Has Beck here seen one of your tantrums?" Tiger asked, turning to nod at the stocky guard.

Lexi colored, then forced her face to its usual pale. "I don't have tantrums," she announced airily, ignoring Tiger's loud guffaw of laughter and Beck's snicker. Only a slight protruding of her bottom lip betrayed her petulance as she hastened her graceful steps down the remainder of the corridor. Outside Limen's office, she hesitated, her shoulders drooping. She flinched at the soft touch on her arm, then gave Tiger a weak smile.

"Your mother isn't here," Tiger whispered. "And even if she were, she can't *force* you to marry him. No one can. You outrank everyone on this mountain," he continued, his lips tickling her ear, "except me."

Lexi laughed and pushed him away.

"What? I'm serious," Tiger said aloud, keeping an admirably straight face.

Lexi smiled at him as she smoothed down her hair and threw back her shoulders.

"Oh sure, fix yourself up for *them*," Tiger teased.

Beck tittered until Tiger's dark look shut him up. Leaning forward, Beck gave a patterned knock, then grinned at Erid when he opened the door. "I brought the bride," he said, his grin widening as Lexi and Tiger glared at him. "Only kidding," he added, waving a hand dismissively as a tight-lipped Erid let them in.

Feeling Tiger close behind her, Lexi whirled on him in the doorway. "Wait here," she commanded.

"No," Tiger said, laughing. "I can't believe you're still trying to boss me around," he added in a whisper.

"You'll only work Talan into an irrational rage," Lexi whispered, sparing a glance for Erid, who emanated deferential disapproval.

Tiger grinned. "Exactly, and then the Governor will have to put him back in the dungeon."

"Oh."

Tiger's grin widened. "Let's go."

"Miss Fritillary to see you," Beck announced with wry formality as Lexi slipped around the guard curtain firmly grasping Tiger's arm. Talan and Limen both stood near the throne, jaws set and arms folded in twin resolve.

"You brought your pet stable boy?" Talan asked, his smug smile changing to one of suppressed fury.

"Don't be hateful, Talan," Lexi said calmly, her eyes traveling over Limen's guilt-ridden face.

"Your Highness," Limen said, with a short bow.

"Brother," Lexi greeted coldly, watching with satisfaction as Limen's cheeks burned two bright spots of color.

"This is a private conversation between your betters, boy," Talan said haughtily, his hickory and clove scent rising with his ire. "You had best leave."

Lexi felt the muscles in Tiger's arm tense, and patted it soothingly. "Don't threaten him before the Governor," she whispered softly.

"I'm not an idiot," Tiger whispered back as he stared coldly at Talan.

"Tiger is here as my friend and advisor," Lexi said, digging her thumbnail into Tiger's arm when he snorted softly at the word *advisor*. "What did you wish to discuss?"

Talan looked expectantly at Limen, and the latter cleared his throat uncomfortably. "I understand that Van was not...uh...a match," Limen stumbled verbally, raising his eyes briefly for Lexi's confirmation.

"Van was unsuitable in several ways," Lexi agreed.

"Then," Limen paused hesitantly, seeming to writhe in his own skin. "You're going to have to marry Talan."

Lexi allowed her merry laugh to ring across the room, startling Talan out of his arm-folding solidarity. "I have other options."

"Breathe through your mouth," Tiger whispered. Lexi barely had a chance to obey before a heavy dose of his musky scent hit the air, tasting vaguely of delicious memory, and making her tongue curl as her mouth watered.

"How dare you?" Talan fairly shrieked, closing the distance between them in a single wing beat.

Tiger swiftly slipped her hands from his arm and stepped away to brace for Talan's attack. Lexi tried to edge back in between them, but Tiger gave her a gentle shove just before Talan smashed into his chest, knocking him backwards into erratic flight.

"Stop it!" Lexi commanded, fighting the soothing buzz that eked into her senses despite breathing through her mouth.

"Guards," Limen called out wearily as he watched Tiger's aerial avoidance as Talan continued to come at him, muttering outrage.

Beck, Erid, and another guard watched the chase above them, moving in quickly as Tiger zipped between them, delivering Talan to their waiting grasp.

"He attacked me!" Talan accused, straining against their grip.

"No, he didn't," Limen said, his disapproving glance falling on both Talan and Tiger.

"He hit me earlier today," Talan asserted. "Just ask him!"

Limen's frown deepened as he waited for Tiger's response.

"Talan was waiting for me outside my room and attacked me when I tried to enter."

"You hit me!" Talan sputtered. "He hit me," he reiterated to Limen.

"Enough. Talan, go home or go back to the dungeon," Limen commanded.

"She was in his room! And now he's signaling her! He's probably controlling her like his cousin did!"

As everyone turned to stare at her, Lexi took a short breath through her nose, immediately regretting it as Tiger's scent soothed her senses, relaxing her posture and softening her expression. "Don't be ridiculous," Lexi managed.

Brows knit, Limen gave her a hard look before turning back to Talan. "Dungeon or leave the mountain."

"You know I can't leave her. The Queen wants us married; why isn't that enough? Just marry us, Limen. She has no other choices," Talan argued as he struggled futilely under Beck's iron grip.

Limen winced faintly and looked at Lexi. "I can't marry you to anyone else."

Tiger had been slowly working his way back near Lexi, and now gave her a furtive prod in the small of her back. Rousing herself, Lexi took a deep breath through her mouth and spoke.

"Beck, Erid, put Talan back in the dungeon."

Limen's head shot up, his eyebrows high. Talan sputtered in protest as Beck and Erid dragged him to the door.

"If my season ends down there, Princess, I doubt you'll ever forgive yourself," Talan warned spitefully, his words echoing in her head until the heavy door closed behind him.

"You can have him released a day after you leave with the flying guard," Tiger whispered. "He's only trying to manipulate you."

Lexi squared her shoulders at Tiger's words. "Was there anything else you wished to discuss?" she asked Limen, her tone cold.

Limen staggered back a step as his hazel eyes searched hers. "No," he finally said, his gaze falling to the floor.

"Good," Lexi said. "Let me know when my royal flying guard escort arrives."

Limen shook his head in confusion. "Are you going home, then?"

"You said it yourself; I've no choices here," Lexi countered, her tone more challenge than explanation.

"But I thought..." Limen began, nodding at Tiger.

Lexi's blank mask hardened. "Don't release Talan again without my approval," she said haughtily, then turned slowly and left the room with Tiger in her wake.

As the heavy door closed behind them, Tiger gave an exaggerated shiver. "You sounded just like the Queen at the end there."

Lexi made a face and elbowed him. "You're lucky I could talk at all."

"I told you to breathe through your mouth," Tiger said defensively.

"I did! Mostly."

Tiger laughed, then looked at her carefully as they walked. "Are you okay? Or can you still smell me?"

Lexi's face split into a grin she tried to hide by turning away.

258

He stepped in front of her to see her face.

"I can still smell you," she admitted, "but that doesn't mean I'm not okay."

Tiger scowled and took her arm. "You just fall down and lose the ability to think and speak."

"I don't either. I'm speaking and walking...both require thought."

"You were breathing mostly through your mouth," he reminded her.

"Well, try it again and see how I cope," she suggested, her smile hidden behind a dark panel of hair.

"We already tried that, remember?"

When Lexi didn't answer, Tiger's scowl increased with the silence. "Why did you come to my room, anyway?" he finally blurted.

"Oh." Her entire conversation with Cam seemed a very long time ago. "Do you happen to know how long my father's season was?"

Tiger's eyebrows rose high with a half laugh. "He didn't tell you?"

Lexi shook her head. "I assume it wasn't too short since he encouraged me to go."

Tiger shook his head apologetically. "I have no idea. I don't think we're even allowed to discuss the royals' seasons."

Lexi frowned and looked away.

"I'm sure you'll have enough time to get home and find some suitable noble."

Lexi turned back to him with a false smile, removed his hand from her arm, and walked towards her waiting guards. "Get some sleep," she said over her shoulder. "You look tired."

"Thanks, *Your Highness*," Tiger muttered, watching until the door shut behind her.

Chapter Twelve

Clodi's steady snoring helped cover the sound of the balcony door. After pulling out a mildew-scented rug, Lexi opened the door at a glacial pace, stopping frequently to listen for Tiger above, the guards outside, and any disruption in her roommate's cacophonous breathing. When the space was wide enough, she slipped out and slowly pulled the door shut. Grinning, she turned and ran right into Tiger.

"Going somewhere?" he asked.

Lexi let out a tiny shriek and slapped Tiger's chest with a loud thwack. Clodi's next snore ended abruptly, and Lexi turned to stare at the balcony door until she heard Clodi's next labored intake.

Relieved, she turned back to Tiger. "You scared me!"

"And you are scaring me. Why are you sneaking away from your guards in the middle of the night?"

Lexi squared her shoulders and looked him in the eye.

"No, don't lie," Tiger chided before she could speak.

"I wasn't..."

"Yes, you were. Now where were you going?" Tiger insisted.

Lexi frowned. She had meant to find the castle archives and discover how long her parents had been on the mountain before their marriage, but she couldn't tell Tiger that without betraying her father's confidence.

"I can't tell you that."

"What? Why not?" Bemused and irritated, Tiger spoke a little too loudly and Clodi's snores suddenly stopped.

Alarmed, Lexi took Tiger's arm and pointed up to his balcony. Begrudgingly, he flew up with her just as the door to the queen's suite began to open.

"Who's there?" Clodi asked with a yawn.

Landing soundlessly, Lexi pushed Tiger into his room, shushing his whispered objections. Then they waited quietly until they heard Clodi go back inside. Lexi let out a breath, then inhaled deeply. Even with the balcony doors open, the scent of the room was soothing, and her tense muscles began to relax.

"Why can't you tell me?"

Lexi turned her head and took deep breaths of the cold night air while she tried to construct an answer.

"You're trying to figure out a way to lie to me that I won't be able to tell," Tiger guessed.

Turning back, she glared at him, but the room was too dark for him to read her features.

"Were you coming *here*?" Tiger asked, a chiding note in his tone.

"No."

"Were you going to Cam's room?"

"No!"

"Were you going home?!"

"Shh! Of course not! Stop guessing. You'll never figure it out." Lexi pushed him further into the room and shut the door behind her with a shiver. The sudden and complete blackness felt oddly intimate, and Lexi removed her hand from his chest and backed up until her wings brushed against the balcony doors.

"Open the doors."

"We're being too loud and it's too cold," Lexi explained, her tone already softer, her words slower.

Tiger let out an exasperated sigh as he walked across the room, first to switch on the lantern, and then to open the hallway door. Marching back to Lexi, he took her hand and led her to the open door. "You stand there," he directed, releasing her hand to fold his arms across his chest. "Now, what's this big secret?"

Lexi merely shook her head and walked out into the hallway with Tiger close on her heels.

"You're not going to tell me, *and* you're going to go wandering without your guards again?!"

"I'm not wandering," Lexi shrugged, a little smile tugging at her lips.

Tiger flew quickly over her head and landed, blocking her path. "You're right," he challenged, grinning. "You're *not* wandering."

Lexi shook her head with mock gravity, "Tiger the Tyrannical has returned," she announced. "I haven't missed you."

Tiger took a step forward, his grin widening. Lexi feinted left, then flew right, shrieking as he caught her legs. Laughing, Lexi pulled his hair until he let go, then flew down the hall with him close behind.

"You'll regret that," he teased.

"I regret nothing!" she called, rounding the stairwell.

As she turned, Tiger grasped her arm and pulled her to him as they both stumbled into a landing, clinging to each other. Lexi laughed, resting her head against his shoulder. As Tiger's laughter died down, he slid his arms around her, and they stood at the top of the stairwell, swaying slightly in their embrace.

"Tiger?" she asked, reaching up to smooth one of the unruly curls over his ear.

"What?" he asked, surreptitiously pressing a kiss into her hair.

"Did we ruin our friendship?"

Their swaying stopped as Tiger knit his brows and pressed his lips together. Lexi looked up at him and poked the puckered skin between his brows.

"You're making wrinkles."

Tiger gave her a small smile. "I'm too young to have wrinkles."

Sighing, Lexi pulled away from him. "You were right."

"I'm always right."

Lexi swatted his arm half-heartedly.

"What was I right about this time?"

Lexi looked up at him, then felt a betraying blush rising in her cheeks.

"Oh. That. Can't resist me now?"

Lexi swatted his arm harder this time, and Tiger let out musical closed-mouth laugh.

"Don't tease me," she complained.

"You mean like this?" Tiger gathered her back into his arms and bent down as if to kiss her.

"Tiger!" she grumbled, trying to wiggle away. When he laughed and held tighter, she grabbed his head and forced a rough kiss before shoving his forehead back.

Tiger froze for a moment in surprise, then a mischievous grin lit his face that had Lexi looking nervously around them for witnesses. His ensuing attack of kisses were planted all over her face in rapid succession while she laughed and tucked her chin until he could only reach her forehead.

"Stop!" she giggled, finally reaching up to cover his mouth.

He kissed the hand that covered his lips until she drew it back, then he resumed kissing her face. This time she didn't fight him, and kissed back when he finally reached her lips. The faint musky scent that she had been catching on his clothes was now overwhelmed by a fresh signal, and her arms slid around his neck as her knees weakened with the delightful smell. They were too caught in the moment to notice the first throat clearing, but the second was accompanied by a false coughing fit that ended in a choking noise. Tiger and Lexi pulled apart, concern tempering their embarrassment. Lexi's guards stood at the foot of the stairs, Charis bent over in feigned distress as Erid half-heartedly patted his back between his wings.

"Miss Parnassian came out into the hallway to search for the 'yelling man' who woke her up. She asked us why we were there when you weren't. So we went searching for you, and..." Erid trailed off sheepishly, his face suffused with color.

Charis stood, but turned away in another faux coughing fit. Faces aflame, Tiger and Lexi exchanged a glance and took a step further apart.

"We didn't mean..." Erid held out a hand, his gesture taking the place of the rest of his sentence.

"It's fine," Lexi assured them, squaring her shoulders as she willed her blushing cheeks to return to their natural color. She started down the steps, then looked back at Tiger.

Still embarrassed, he gave Lexi a tight smile and waved goodnight as he headed back to his room. She watched him go for a moment, then joined her guards at the bottom of the staircase. Charis still had a hand over his mouth, as if he anticipated the need for further coughing.

"Where are the records kept?" she asked abruptly.

"Uh, back room of the library," Erid blurted.

"Please take me there."

"Um, it's locked." Erid looked at her curiously. "The library, too."

"And you don't have a key?"

"No." Erid shook his head, dropping his eyes when she met his gaze.

"Who does?"

"The Governor, Erynnis, the librarian, and Eros," Charis answered, his voice still hoarse from his coughing.

Lexi nodded, considering. Though she hadn't met the librarian, Eros seemed most likely to hand over his keys without informing Limen. "Will you show me where the library is?"

"Even though it's locked?" Erid reminded her.

"Yes."

Erid walked in front of her while Charis brought up the rear all the way to the library. Their stilted formation made Lexi uncomfortable, especially when they passed others who eyed them speculatively, then exchanged whispers with their companions. The carved wooden library doors were nearly as grand as those leading into the throne room and echoed the hunting scenes of the stoned-carved frieze that adorned the outside of the castle.

Erid rattled the handle, then gave Lexi a confirming nod. "Locked."

Lexi wanted to try the handle for herself, but she resisted with a stately nod. She didn't really doubt Erid, but it was frustrating to know that the information she wanted was just out of her reach. Surely her father wouldn't have encouraged her to come if her parents' seasons had been short. Lexi shook off her thoughts with an almost imperceptible shake of her head. Both guards were looking at her expectantly, and the remainder of the night suddenly seemed like an annoying thing to fill. She regretted sleeping through the day, squandering time she might have spent with Tiger— only Tiger had probably spent it with his girlfriend. Lexi turned away from the guards so she could scowl as she walked. *Coli seems perfectly nice, and if she makes Tiger happy*...Lexi couldn't even finish that thought. She needed a distraction *now*. Her steps sped of their own accord, turning into an angry march instead of the stately gait of a princess. She hadn't even realized where her storm of jealousy was taking her until she stood in front of Cam's door. Her conscience smote her, and she reached up to touch her lips. She had been kissing Tiger; would Cam know? Lifting a lock of her hair, she held it under her nose. She recognized the faint scent of Tiger. She sniffed her collar, then carefully backed away from Cam's door, stepping lightly. Grateful for her guards' lack of commentary, she hurried back to her room and slipped inside. She quickly changed to the symphony of Clodi's snores, fetched her bag, then walked down to the bathing pool, bruises exposed to the empty halls and the deferential guards who followed in her wake. At the door, she peered inside.

"Raven!" Damus called, motioning her over just as Psyche slapped his arm. They stood in the far corner of the lightly populated pool, Damus lounging while Psyche began to rush through her bathing.

"The Royal City is awfully far away from Wallowa. Are there quarries nearby so I could transfer my internship? Or would you want to live at the palace again?"

The knock was a welcome interruption, and Lexi hid her sigh of relief by getting up to answer the door. A female life servant held out a small tray with two dishes of hot oatmeal. She examined Lexi curiously, her eyes lingering on her wings.

"Thank you," Lexi said, grasping the hot dishes and quickly closing the door to end the inspection. She set them on the table, her hands smarting from the searing metal bowls. She looked down at them a moment, then reopened the door. The same servant was holding out two spoons, an amused expression on her face. Lexi repeated her thanks and quickly shut the door again, handing a spoon to Cam.

"I was wondering how we were going to eat it," Cam chuckled.

Lexi gave him a brief smile, then focused on her oatmeal. It scalded her tongue and throat, but was a welcome reprieve from conversation. They ate in silence for several minutes until Cam laughed.

"You know, this is *really* hot. It's burning my mouth, it has to be burning yours, and yet we just keep eating. Maybe we should just talk about what's bothering us." Cam took a big breath and blew it out. "Did we make a mistake? Maybe we shouldn't be engaged yet." Cam frowned down at his remaining breakfast bracing for her agreement.

Lexi thought of Tiger and Coli, and bitterness overcame the pleasantly bland taste of the oatmeal. "Why do you say that?" she asked, taking another spoonful and willing her envy away.

"Maybe I should meet your parents first; isn't that the way the nobles do it? I could ask for the King's approval, and then he could marry us."

Lexi stared down at her now-empty bowl. "That might work with my father."

"But not the Queen?"

"You know she wants me to marry Talan."

Cam blew out a great gust of air. "Surely she wants you to be happy with your husband. Can't you just tell her you don't like Cretin number one, but you *do* like me?"

Lexi leaned forward and patted his hand. "I should go before the pregnancy tests. I don't want a repeat of yesterday." She stood and bent down to kiss his forehead. "Perhaps I'll see you at lunch."

Cam let out a surprised little grunt at his dismissal and crossed his arms while his brows tightened into a slight scowl. "We should talk."

"Isn't that what we've been doing?"

"Sure." His sardonic tone was unmistakable.

Lexi hid her displeasure behind a tight smile and quickly left the room, the guards following at a close pace. She silently berated herself for being irritated with Cam. It wasn't his fault. She felt guilty and frustrated with her circumstances; he just forced her to think about them. The last expression on his face was now plaguing her conscience. He was unhappy. It was her fault. Her walk slowed as she considered returning to his room to try to make it right. But what would she say? That her mother would never allow their marriage? That she was in love with Tiger? Lexi stopped dead at the thought, her guards leaping to either side to avoid collision with her wings. *I'm in love with Tiger?!* Lexi forced herself to continue walking, though she was no longer aware of where she was going. She listened to the footfalls of the guards behind her resentfully. It was impossible to truly wander with an entourage. Angry banging at doors and shouts about pregnancy tests woke her from her reverie. Phidia was working her way down the hallway with a rheumy march that would inspire sympathy were she not so unpleasant. That woman really needed a different job. *If I were governor*, Lexi thought, then smirked. *What a ridiculous idea.* Laughing inwardly, she hurried down the nearest corridor that led away from Phidia's wrath. Erynnis' office was nearby and she turned toward it decisively. She had no idea of the hours he kept, but tried the door optimistically: locked.

Stepping around her, Charis gave the door a rhythmic knock, then waited patiently. Within a minute, Erynnis opened the door. His sour expression melting into his approximation of charm.

"Good morning, Erynnis," Lexi greeted. "Might I have a word with you?"

"Of course!" Erynnis threw open the door to his office and gave her a deep bow.

"Privately," Lexi added to the guards as they tried to follow her. She gave them an apologetic smile and shut the door behind her.

Recovering from his deep bow, Erynnis pulled out a stool for her and remained standing until she sat.

"What did you wish to discuss, Your Highness?" His lined face was lit with an earnest enthusiasm that belied his years.

"A couple of things. First, I'm very interested in the Castle's records. Would it be possible for me to look at them today?"

After an abortive noise, Erynnis smiled. "Certainly."

"I understand that the records room in the library is locked; may I have the keys?" Lexi held out her hand expectantly.

Erynnis stared at her hand. "Oh. Well, I could certainly escort you..."

"There is no need, and I wouldn't want to interrupt your responsibilities here." Lexi gave him a pleasant smile and further extended her hand.

Erynnis blushed and bobbed a little nod as he retrieved a ring of keys and removed two of them. "This one is for the library, which doesn't open for another three hours." He dropped an ornate iron key in her palm, then held up another that was half the size of the first. "This is for the records room; it is always kept locked." Erynnis hesitated, a slight grimace crossing his face as he placed the final key in her palm.

Lexi slipped both keys into her pocket before he could change his mind. "I will take very good care of them, and return them to you when I am done."

Erynnis nodded unhappily, unconsciously clutching the remaining keys to his chest. "What was the other thing you wanted to discuss?"

"Oh, it's more of a procedural question, really." Lexi bestowed another charming smile. "Does Limen have to approve all the marriages? Or is that within your discretion?"

Erynnis slowly dropped the keys down to his lap. "I can *perform* them, but the Governor must *authorize* them."

Lexi smiled as if she were pleased to receive this interesting tidbit of information. "Thank you for clearing that up."

She stood, and Erynnis immediately leapt to his feet, sending the keys clanging against the stone floor. He bowed deeply, retrieving the keys as he did so.

"Thank you. I'll return the keys shortly," Lexi assured him, slipping out of the room before he was fully upright. She forced herself to keep an even pace down the halls as sleepy girls obediently filed out of their rooms for their morning pregnancy test. At the library door, she waited until the hallway was empty, then unlocked it. The dark room smelled ominously of mildewed paper. Locating a lantern near the door, Lexi switched it on and removed it from its sconce. Her guards followed her inside, closed the door, and took up position next to it. The library was shabby, its shelves only spottily filled, and the few books that remained were well-worn. One table sat in the middle of the room, its uneven leg propped up by a broken chair back. Lexi held the lantern higher, casting eerie shadows on the shelves that lined each wall. The room was much smaller than the library at home, and Lexi felt a momentary pang of homesickness. Shaking it off, she walked the length of the library, her search rewarded when she found a recessed door partially hidden behind the shelves. Pulling out the smaller key, she unlocked it and turned the handle, but the door didn't budge.

"It sticks," Charis explained from across the room. "Do you want help?"

Lexi closed her wings and threw her weight into the door, the hinges creaking cacophonously as it swung open. "No, thank you," she called.

The room smelled of dust and wood, the latter coming from the shelves lining the walls and the wooden boxes neatly arranged along them. Lexi found the box with her birth year and pulled it off a high

274

shelf. Inside was an ornate leather-bound book that recorded all the marriages and a stack of paper. Each loose page held the record of an in-season that had arrived at the Old Castle that year. Lexi slid the box onto a lower shelf and began to peruse the names. Halfway through February's arrivals, she found her mother: Ami Leafwing of Wagontire. Lexi laughed out loud, then self-consciously closed the door, berating herself for not doing so sooner. No wonder her mother so carefully hid her past. Wagontire was a tiny farming community out east, best known for its onions, which were said to outnumber the people 10,000 to 1. Lexi allowed herself another giggle as she thought of her stately mother pulling up onions, then read on. "Father's name: Lamin Leafwing." Lexi swallowed back a sudden lump in her throat. She finally knew her grandfather's name. "Mother's name: Menapia White." Her grandmother was a white? Lexi indulged another giggle at her mother's expense. There was such a stigma associated with being a white; their hormonal surges during their season essentially made them mentally ill; it was extremely difficult for a white to find a mate. And this was her mother's heritage! This was *her own* heritage. Lexi smiled and ran a finger over her grandparents' names. Belatedly, she remembered her purpose and scanned to the bottom. "Married March 13." Her mother had been on the mountain a single month. Lexi blew out a slow breath that made the dust bunnies stir on the neighboring box. Only a month. Hopefully her father's season had been longer. Lexi set her mother's record aside and returned to the pile looking for Chip Viceroy, the name her father had used on the mountain. But it wasn't there. She searched the pile again, then pulled down the record box for the previous year. After checking the individual records twice, she huffed out a breath of frustration. It simply wasn't here. Maybe it had never been made. Lexi referred back to her mother's record. Though someone had filled out the "Married" date, the "To" had been left blank. Lexi returned to the first box and pulled out the ornate leather book. There was a marriage on March 12th and three on March 14th, but nothing for the 13th. Lexi ran her finger along the inside seam of the book and felt tiny jagged pieces of paper. A page had been torn out. Lexi let out a small groan, then replaced the book and boxes. Untucking her shirt, she slipped her mother's record up underneath it, then carefully tucked it back in. She patted her stomach and the paper crinkled. Standing up taller, she repositioned the paper slightly, then left the room and locked the door. Both guards' faces were openly curious, but she ignored them as she replaced the lantern and locked the library door. All the way back to her room the paper rustled softly, the sound alarmingly loud to Lexi. She was relieved to find her room empty, though the balcony doors were thrown wide to let in the bright mid-morning sunshine. Lexi quickly closed them and removed her mother's record. She read her grandparents' names over again, committing them to memory, then took out her bag and ripped the inside lining an inch. Rolling up her mother's record until it resembled a straw, she slid it inside the hole, then pushed it over until it was no longer visible. Sliding her bag back under the bed, she sat down on a stool and stared at it. She wasn't certain why she had removed her mother's record. She told herself it was to protect her mother's secret, but some part of her wanted to brandish it before the Queen and demand to be released from her engagement to Talan. Lexi guiltily banished the thought, shifting uncomfortably as the keys poked into her from her pocket. Reluctantly, she stood to return them. Rather than taking the direct route to the officiant's office, she purposely meandered, liking the feel of the keys in her pocket. She could hear the guards trailing behind her, but it did not hurry her gait. Wearing a pleasantly blank mask, she strolled through the castle people-watching. She passed three couples holding hands, one openly kissing, and another waiting excitedly outside the throne room to be married. Lexi felt her mask slipping as she knocked on Erynnis' door.

"I think he's in with the Governor," Charis said, squelching a yawn.

Lexi looked back at her guards, noticing their droopy, bloodshot eyes. "When are you to be relieved?"

Erid shrugged. "Should have been dawn, but our relief probably couldn't find us."

Her mouth tightened into a tiny frown. "You're relieved."

Both guards merely shifted their weight and exchanged glances.

"I will ensure that you are not docked a meal or locked in the dungeon. Go get some rest."

Erid started to move, but stopped when Charis kept his ground with a pained expression.

"This is silly. You're both exhausted. I will stay here." Lexi tried the door, but it was locked. She frowned her chagrin, then squared her shoulders and turned to face her guards. "Go find your replacements."

Erid nodded, then weaved through the waiting wedding party to give an odd knock at the throne room door. It opened a moment later for a quick whispered conversation before Beck stepped out and sauntered over with a grin on his face.

Lexi couldn't help but return the smile. "Good. Now Charis and Erid can go."

Erid's shoulders sagged gratefully as he hurried away, but once again Charis stood his ground. His face colored as Lexi looked askance and Beck chortled.

"Best obey her; you know she's the real boss," Beck advised.

Charis' mouth fell open, then closed with a resigned sigh. "Make sure you get another guard, Beck," he admonished, then shook his head unhappily as he walked away.

Beck clapped his hands and rubbed them together. "There. All the dour fun-suckers are gone; how shall we entertain ourselves this morning, Miss Fritillary?"

Lexi found herself returning his grin. "What do you recommend?"

"I myself like a good game of poker on my mornings off, but I imagine you'd prefer some activity that involves Mr. Swallowtail."

Lexi colored and began walking away while she battled her blushes.

"Oh-ho! I guessed right! Now catch me up. Are you still engaged to Mr. Crescent?"

A guilty grimace flickered across Lexi's face before she could hide it.

Beck gave a low whistle. "Poor guy; does he know?"

"No. Shh!" Lexi hissed. The halls were far from empty and Beck's loud conversation was attracting attention. Beck merely chortled as if she had told a funny joke.

"Are you going to tell him?"

Lexi gave him a little glare rather than answer.

"I could tell him," Beck offered, grinning. He clasped his hands beneath his chin and batted his eyelashes. "Oh, Mr. Crescent…" he began in falsetto.

Lexi elbowed him, but he just dissolved into laughter. She attempted a disapproving glance, but her smile gave her away. *This is what it must be like to have a brother.* She grinned at Beck until she remembered she *did* have a brother—a cheating *brother-in-law*. Her hands tightened to fists at her sides and she slid them into her pockets until she could school them back into relaxation. Her right fist bumped up against the keys and she was reminded of her errand.

"I have to go back, Beck," she said, stopping in the middle of the hall.

"To the palace?" he asked in an undertone.

"No, I need to return Erynnis' keys."

Beck's rusty eyebrows shot up his balding forehead. "*Erynnis* gave up his keys?"

Lexi merely nodded.

"He never gives up his keys…to anyone. He even gets put out when the Governor uses his. And he would never ever *ever* lend them. What did you do to him?"

"I asked for them."

"You didn't order it?"

"No."

"Were you torturing him at the time?" Beck asked, miraculously maintaining a straight face despite his teasing.

"No."

"Perhaps you didn't realize you were torturing him; were you chewing loudly?"

Lexi laughed. "No, but I'll try to remember that if we ever share a meal."

Beck looked at her quizzically. "What did you need them for?"

Lexi resumed her pleasant mask. "I wanted to see the library and it was locked."

"It's open now. You couldn't wait?"

Lexi smiled blandly. "Apparently not."

"Hmm, probably better that way. In-seasons aren't allowed to use the library."

"Why is that?" Lexi asked, turning back towards the officiant's office.

"Governor says it distracts them from mating," Beck explained, following. "Same with the plays—he put a stop to those. And bathing...he said it was too much time apart having separate pools for men and women, so the men had to give up their pool to the in-seasons," Beck complained. "Did you know it even has a sauna? It's so great, especially in the winter after you've had outdoor duty...just sitting in there until you can' t hardly breathe anymore because the air is so hot." He let out a great sigh. "I miss it. The stupid women's pool doesn't have one. Who cares if it's 'cleaner and has pathways so you don't cut your feet?'" Beck spoke in falsetto, waving his arms about in effeminate affectation.

Lexi laugh openly. "Who were you imitating just now?"

Beck grimaced. "Lady who runs the kitchen. Bit of a terror, but a decent cook. She has 'tender toes!'" he mocked in the same falsetto.

Lexi smiled at his antics, her expression falling back into neutral as they returned to Erynnis' door. The wedding party had disappeared, but the officiant's door was still locked.

"Another wedding," Beck explained, nodding at the Governor's office. His expression took on a suddenly impish mien as he held out his hand. "I could take care of Erynnis' keys for you."

279

Lexi smirked. "And why would I let you torture the poor man like that?"

"Aw, let me!" Beck whined good-naturedly. "He puts on airs like you wouldn't believe. Having lowly me in possession of his keys would be good for him."

"I doubt very much that he would agree."

"Well of course he wouldn't! That's how you know it'd be good for him."

Lexi squelched a laugh and took up her post to wait patiently.

"And then we could be having fun right now instead of just standing here waiting."

"Oh, yes. I'm still waiting for your entertainment ideas," Lexi reminded him.

Beck thought for a moment, scratching at his bald spot absently. "All that's left—aside from in-season drama—is poker and pranks."

"And who do you prank?"

Beck's face lit up with a wicked smile. "Avell, mostly. Takes him forever to catch on, and then he gets so mad!"

"And now that Avell's in the dungeon?" Lexi reminded him.

"Oh yeah, forgot about that. He still hasn't figured out who you are...nobody will tell him," Beck chortled.

Lexi gave him a tight smile as the Governor's double doors burst open and the boisterous wedding party spilled out into the hallway.

"He'll be in there now if you want to return the keys," Beck advised.

Lexi eyed the wedding party still clustered outside the door and merely shook her head. "I can wait."

"Sometimes they have ridiculously loooong conferences about the dumbest topics," he warned. "He could be in there with the Governor for hours."

A click sounded at the knob beside her and Lexi grinned as she opened it. Erynnis was still walking away from the door and looked startled as she handed him back the keys.

"Thank you, Erynnis."

"Oh? Oh!" Erynnis trilled an awkward little laugh as his cheeks heated. "No, thank *you*."

Seeing his discomfort, Lexi merely smiled and closed the door behind her.

Beck waited until they were ten steps away before he burst into loud guffaws. "He *thanked* you for taking the keys? That man has a serious case of royal-worship. He must think you can set him free."

Lexi looked momentarily startled. She hadn't considered life servants as lacking their freedom before. "I don't think I can. The life servant law is a king's decree."

"Figured. Besides, if you could free anyone, it'd be me, right?"

Lexi laughed. "Of course, Beck."

Chapter Thirteen

Back in her room, three meals were once again laid out on the table. Lexi handed one to Beck, picked at another, and left the third for Clodi. Her odd sleeping schedule had begun to catch up with her, and she impatiently squelched a yawn as she slid out the balcony rugs and threw open the doors. Though few of the in-seasons had been served any food, the pleasant weather ensured that all the outdoor tables were filled. Lexi surveyed the riot of color created by clothing and wings until she found Tiger's broad shoulders framed by gold and black wings. He was facing the front of the castle, his lower face swallowed by the large hand that held it up. Occasionally, he drew his shaggy brows together and nodded. Across the table from him, Lexi recognized Coli's yellow wings edged in black. Her blonde curls cascaded down her back and across her wings in artful layers that shifted with their owner's expressive head. Lexi tried not to watch them, but her gaze kept drifting back. She replayed her stolen kisses and wished she had a good reason to interrupt their lunch. Two yellow-winged men were joining them now, and Tiger sat upright with badly-disguised annoyance. Coli's head and wings stilled as the two men became animated. One of them slapped his hand against the rusting metal table, making the others jump. Coli was shaking her head now, her wings twitching as she faced one newcomer and then the other as their conversation quickly devolved into a shouting match. Tiger grimaced, then stood. As he stepped away, the remaining three argued with vigor as the lunch crowd unconsciously leaned away from them. Tiger walked among the tables, scanning for a spot before he gave up and flew to his balcony, his eyes meeting Lexi's as he flew by. Without invitation, she joined him.

"They'll see you," Tiger warned, pulling her into the fragrant room.

"Coli?" Lexi asked, trying to inhale deeply without making a sound.

"And her brothers."

"Ah. Why were they yelling? You didn't tell them about..." Lexi hesitated how to finish that sentence while her face lit with a warm glow.

"What? That I've been kissing you?" He leaned in and perfunctorily kissed her on the mouth. "No, I didn't tell them."

Lexi's head felt momentarily jumbled and it took her a second to remember what she had been saying. "Then why?"

"Oh, you're not her favorite person. And her brothers think I'm cheating on her with you."

Lexi shifted uncomfortably. "I guess they're right."

Tiger nodded. "Yep."

They fell in to an awkward silence of shared guilt.

"Are you going to marry her?" she finally asked, her voice sounding unnaturally high.

Tiger shrugged. "I thought I was going to."

Lexi swallowed, wetting her lips before she could get the words out. "And now?"

Tiger let out a deep sigh. "I don't know. I'm figuring it out."

Lexi nodded, letting the conversation peter out until Tiger's stomach growled loudly, and they both laughed.

"There's lunch in my room," Lexi offered, walking towards the balcony.

Tiger caught her arm and pulled her back. "You must *really* want to get me in trouble."

Lexi shook her head innocently. "No, but if I go by hallway, then Beck will know I flew off without him."

"Ahh, Beck again. I can see why you wouldn't want that annoyance. Fine. You go your way, and I'll go mine. Just try to avoid being seen." He eyed her magnificent wings and grimaced. "Or something."

Lexi grinned back at him, then flew off the balcony and back to her own. She avoided making eye contact with anyone in the courtyard, hoping that would somehow help. She sat down at her little table, rearranging her plate so it was no longer obvious that she had picked at it. Then she waited happily as giddy bubbles of emotion made it near impossible to sit still. She could hear Beck talking to someone in the hallway, followed by a sharp rap on her door.

"Come in," she called.

Tiger entered, rolling his eyes, and quickly shut the door on Beck's eager face. "That was annoying," he grumbled, taking a seat at the small table.

"Why? What did he say?"

"To remember that I'm visiting an *engaged* woman and to behave myself."

Lexi's grin quickly turned into a snigger.

"Keep laughing and I *will* behave myself," he warned.

Lexi immediately stopped, though her lips betrayed an irrepressible smile.

Tiger shook his head and looked down at his plate. "Of course your food is better."

Lexi looked down at the potato and pea dish. "What is everyone else eating?"

"Some kind of watery soup," he said, then bowed his head in silent prayer.

She held still, watching him. Lexi had seen him pray before—Cercy always insisted he do so—but she was pleasantly surprised to see him make the choice away from home. It reminded her of her father and his quiet faith.

Tiger finished and quickly tore into his food. "I'm going to be full for the first time in a month," he announced happily.

Lexi watched him eat with growing unease. Looking closely at Tiger's clothing, she noticed it was looser than it had been when he left the palace; he had lost weight over the past month. Lexi frowned and slid her plate over to him.

"Don't you want it?" Tiger asked. "It's good."

Lexi shook her head. "I'm not hungry just now."

"I would warn you to eat while you can, but I guess the same rules don't apply to you." Tiger finished his plate and started on hers.

Lexi colored slightly, her frown deepening. "Everyone should be getting enough to eat."

"Well, they're not."

"I'll talk to Limen."

"I thought you were avoiding him," he reminded her between bites.

"I am, but there need to be some changes before I leave."

Tiger let out his musical closed-mouth laugh between bites.

"What? Surely you don't disagree?"

Tiger shrugged his shoulders while he chewed his last bite. "He's not going to like you telling him how to do his job. Can't you just wait until you get home and have the King tell him to change?"

Lexi turned away, hiding the mischievous look on her face. "Maybe, but consider how scrawny you could get before that happened."

"Scrawny?"

Lexi stood with a ponderous air, then nodded with mock solemnity. "Pitifully so."

Tiger moved so fast, she barely got a shriek out before he caught her.

"Say I'm not scrawny," he insisted.

Lexi laughed hysterically while she writhed in his arms. "But you don't like it when I lie," she protested between peels of laughter.

Two sharp raps sounded at the door making them both stiffen. "Everything okay in there?" Beck asked.

"Yes, Beck," Lexi called through the door. When she turned back to Tiger, he kissed her. Lexi giggled into the kiss, getting her teeth and nose kissed as well. Tiger's soothing scent filled the air, and she leaned forward with a little sigh. Snuggling into him, she let the stubble of his jaw graze her forehead. She smiled into his shirt, then reached up to scratch at his burgeoning beard.

"You need a shave."

Tiger ran a hand over his stubbly jaw. "I know."

"I could pluck them out," she offered, catching a whisker between her nails.

"No," he laughed, swatting her hand away.

"Just one," she coaxed, reaching for another.

Tiger bit at her fingers, prompting another round of laughter that dissolved into more kissing. A soft breeze was blowing in from the balcony, lifting Lexi's long tresses to tickle her wings, but the sweetness of the kiss obliterated all annoyances, even knocking.

Beck's insistent raps continued despite the lack of response. "I can smell that!" he chastised.

Tiger and Lexi finally pulled apart, their self-conscious grins unrepentant.

"I'm beginning to understand why you escape your guards so often."

"Does that mean you approve?"

"No." Tiger shook his head. "You definitely shouldn't do it."

Lexi laced her hands around his neck, entangling her fingers in his sandy hair. "Then you'll just have to listen to Beck yell at you all afternoon."

Tiger chuckled and gently removed her hands. "I'd better go." He leaned down to kiss her now frowning lips. "You have a governor to boss around, and I..." Tiger left his sentence unfinished and rubbed his chin as he stared at the floor.

"Have to go smooth things over with Coli?" she guessed.

Tiger gave her a slow nod, then puts his hands on her shoulders, rolling them back. "Princess posture now," he teased. "So you can properly tell the Governor how to do his job."

Lexi smacked his hands away. "Is that how you always know when I'm lying?"

Tiger grinned at her. "Maybe."

Lexi pushed him out of her way as she marched to the door.

"Wait!" Tiger insisted, grabbing her hand, and pulling her back towards him. He ran his thumb around her mouth, then self-consciously scrubbed at his stubbled face. "You're a little red around your mouth," he explained, coloring. "Might want to wait or put something on it? I don't know." Tiger's blush deepened. "Sorry. I'll shave next time."

"There's going to be a next time?"

Tiger grinned and kissed her lightly. "No."

"Never again?"

Tiger kissed her forehead. "Never."

"In that case…" Lexi clutched his shirt and pulled him to her, indulging in a long kiss.

"Hey, now!" Beck called, once again knocking at the door.

With a happy smile, Tiger pulled away, then waited until she released his shirt. "Later," he promised, then opened the door.

"Finally!" Beck complained. "I thought we established some ground rules before you went in." Beck's scolding petered out at the quelling look Tiger gave him as he passed.

Lexi quickly shut the door before Beck could direct his lecture at her, then flew to the cloudy mirror. The chaffing around her mouth was visible despite her obscured reflection. She rubbed the reddened skin lightly to no effect. Frowning, she laid down on her bed, staring out at the bright, sunny sky, and promptly fell asleep.

Chapter Fourteen

Lexi woke feeling chilled in the waning daylight. Intertwining conversations carried up from the courtyard in a pleasant cacophony. She stood and made her way over to the mirror. The rosy chaffing was gone, and Lexi smiled at her reflection as she relived Tiger's kisses. Then she remembered his loose clothing and the conversation she needed to have with Limen. Squaring her shoulders, she smoothed her hair and clothing, then headed for the door.

"New arrivals!" A small male with brown and white checkered wings shouted as he sailed past her open balcony doors.

Mildly curious, Lexi stepped out on her balcony, the evening breeze making her shiver as she surveyed the crowd below.

"You vile little man!" The sharp crack of a slap carried up to Lexi's balcony and her eyes irresistibly followed the sound.

"Ow!" the small male with checkered wings complained, rubbing his cheek.

"How dare you touch me!" huffed a blonde with orange and black wings.

"Excuse me, *Miss High and Mighty*," the small male mocked with an exaggerated bow.

Before the blonde could respond, a brown-winged male stepped between them, his words too low for Lexi to hear. The blonde tossed her golden tresses with an outraged laugh at something he said, and Lexi gasped. Leaping off her balcony, she flew down to the courtyard just as the brown-winged male ushered the blonde through the front doors. Lexi followed, brushing by the small male who was still rubbing his cheek. The brown-winged male spoke in a deferential undertone as he guided the blonde into the clerk's office. Lexi caught the door before he could close it, then stopped dead in the doorway.

"Anna?" Lexi blinked, wondering if she was still napping and this was only a terribly odd dream.

Slightly bedraggled, the lovely blonde looked up with relief and a quick curtsy. "Grandmother insisted I come fetch you and Van," she said apologetically. As she spoke, the brown-winged man slipped behind her, his hands clasped and head respectfully bowed, but she ignored him.

"Aah, the fiery beauty has a lovely friend," the small male with checkered wings wriggled past Lexi, waggling his eyebrows with a knowing smirk.

Lexi looked down at the small male, her blank expression slowly draining the leer from his face.

"Get out, Mr. Skipper," the clerk commanded from behind his desk.

"You can't order me around, old man" the small male groused, then held up an impatient hand before Eros could speak again. "And don't tell me you'll make me share a room, I've heard that one before."

Rather than respond, Eros lifted a whistle to his lips, sending the little man skittering through the door before he could blow it. Eros settled back into his seat with a grim smile. "Perhaps you had better shut the door, Mr. Duskywing."

The quiet man who stood behind Anna nodded and shut the door as Lexi moved into the room.

"Grandmother had one of her fits," Anna explained, ignoring the clerk just as she was ignoring the servant behind her. "She's convinced she's dying, and she wants Van home *now*. She was sending Tris," Anna indicated her servant with a graceful hand, "but then I came into season, and she insisted *I* go with him." The suppressed outrage was still evident in her voice, even as her lower lip trembled. "But I wouldn't want to deny her a dying wish," she insisted, a little too brightly. "So please, let's get Van and Talan, and leave this nasty-smelling place before anyone finds out I was here."

Lexi let out a sigh and turned to Eros. "She'll share my room this evening. Please find a room for Mr. Duskywing."

Eros nodded, but no one noticed. Mr. Duskywing held the door open for Lexi and Anna, then hung back for his room assignment.

"Aren't there enough rooms for everyone?" Anna protested, looking back at Eros. "Not that I wouldn't be honored to share a room with you, Your Highness."

Lexi suppressed a grimace as she slid her arm through Anna's and pulled her along. "There are a great many people here, and my room is already guarded."

Anna's blue eyes grew wider still. "Do the commoners behave criminally up here?" She darted a paranoid glance around her. "Are we in danger? Surely, they wouldn't dare harm a noble."

"They don't know who I am, and I would like to keep it that way," Lexi whispered, grateful they were moving against the crowds so no one heard more than small bits of their conversation.

Anna laughed, then stopped abruptly when she saw Lexi's serious expression. "Why?"

"Perhaps this discussion can wait until we are alone."

"Of course, Your Highness, I apologize."

Lexi's mouth tightened at the title as she stopped in front of the guards posted at her door. "You must have relieved Beck."

Both men looked chagrined. "We thought you were inside."

"I was." Lexi turned to the more familiar looking guard with spotted white wings. "I need you to find Van West and bring him here."

"Yes, Miss Fritillary," he said with a slight bow, then hurried away.

"Fritillary?" Anna mouthed, but Lexi ignored her and stepped past a gray-winged guard who held the door open for them. Anna stood numbly in the doorway, looking around at the sparse furnishings and wrinkling up her nose at the lingering smell of mildew from the neatly-folded balcony rugs.

"This is *your* room?"

Lexi smiled blandly. "This is the queen's suite."

"Nasty old castle," Anna complained under her breath as she unstrapped the neat little pack around her middle and set it on the bed Lexi indicated. "Where is the bathing chamber? I'd like to freshen up before dinner." She fluffed her golden locks, then wrinkled up her nose again. "I can still smell that horrid little man that had the audacity to touch my hair."

Lexi hid her smile by smoothing the blankets on her own bed. "There is a public bathing chamber."

Anna looked startled. "You don't want me to use yours?"

Lexi's smile broadened before it fell away into a blank mask as she faced Anna. "I use the public chamber. Would you like to borrow my swimsuit?"

"I need a swimsuit?"

"The pool is for men and women both," Lexi explained, feeling guilty that she was taking delight in Anna's discomfiture. "However, the Governor would probably allow you to use his private chamber."

Anna's wings sagged with relief. "Oh yes, that would be better."

Lexi opened the door and looked out at the gray-winged guard.

"Is the Governor likely to be in his bath, right now?" Lexi asked politely.

"No. He usually bathes later."

"Good. Would you please escort this young lady down to the Governor's bath, and then bring her back again?" Lexi asked.

The guard looked down the hallway where his fellow guard had departed moments before.

Lexi fought the temptation to order his obedience. "Yes I know you're not supposed to leave me unguarded, but the other guard will be back soon. This young lady is Van West's sister; the Governor would want her protected as well."

The guard nodded his assent, and Lexi turned to look back at Anna. "The guard will take you."

"Thank you Your Highness," Anna said with a smiling half curtsy as she took up her bag and walked quickly out the door.

Lexi sighed as she shut the door behind them. Now it would be a virtual parade returning home. Somehow the mountain had become as confining and restrictive as the palace, though a lot less comfortable. Lexi eyed the sagging beds with their threadbare blankets and recalled the dismay on Anna's face with a returning smile. Leaning forward, she smoothed down her bed cover, her eyes involuntarily straying to the ceiling. A devious grin lit her face as she darted to the balcony. In the courtyard below, Tiger's distinctive yellow and black wings spread lazily out behind his stool while Coli's twitched irritably across from him, her arms tightly folded over her chest while she let her gaze wander. Lexi swallowed a little pang of guilt, then flew up to the balcony above and darted inside with a triumphant smile. The smile froze on her lips as she gazed at the beds. All three had been stripped bare of their bedding, including the pillows.

She let out an irritated puff of breath and went back to the balcony. Tiger looked up at her with an enormous grin, then quickly turned his attention back to Coli. A waving hand caught Lexi's eye framed by tan-spotted underwings and familiar auburn hair. Lexi sucked in her breath, visibly sinking as a boulder of guilt settled in her stomach. She had forgotten about Cam.

He appeared to be visibly counting the floors as he flew, a little confusion showing on his face when he realized Lexi was standing on someone else's balcony.

"You didn't ask Tiger yet?" he asked, glancing into the empty room as he landed on the rail.

"No, I did." Lexi turned away from his greeting to hide the deep blush that refused to be quelled. "He didn't know."

Cam followed her into Tiger's room with confusion. "Something wrong with your room?"

Lexi trained her face to a pleasant smile as she turned to face him. "Just giving my new roommate a little privacy."

"You have a new roommate?"

"Van's sister came to fetch him," Lexi said, taking a step back as the scent of stolen cookies overwhelmed the last traces of Tiger's calming scent.

Cam let out a short bark of laughter. "So Cretin number two is going home?"

Lexi took a deep breath and gave him an apologetic smile. "Cam, I might be going home, too."

Cam's heavy brows knit together and he gave a light snort as his jaw tightened. "You mean, without me?"

Lexi nodded somberly.

"You're not going to marry me?" he asked, a rumble of anger hiding his hurt.

Lexi laid a hand on his arm to soften her words. "Tiger thinks the royal flying guard is already on its way to escort me home. I don't think we're going to have a week."

Relief softened Cam's features as he laid a calloused hand over her own. "Then we'll have the officiant marry us now. We can hide somewhere."

Lexi shook her head slowly. "Erynnis can't marry anyone without Limen's permission. I asked."

Cam gripped her hand tightly as he let out a long, frustrated sigh. "Would your father marry us?"

"I don't know. I'm certain he would like you, but he's never married anyone without my mother's approval."

Cam gave a hard laugh, and released her hand to scratch the back of his head. "So you're telling me that after all this effort to get away from the Cretin, you're still going to marry him?"

Lexi let her hand fall away as the muscles went taut underneath her fingertips. "I hope not. But if you follow me to the palace, there's a fair chance you'll be imprisoned."

Cam pressed his palms into his eyes, then dropped them abruptly. "Just leave with me. We'll hide somewhere. We'll…" Cam's shoulders sagged as he trailed off.

"You said yourself, my mother will think our children are Talan's; she won't give up searching for us. She would..." Lexi paused as she searched for the right word. "She would bother your family."

"Bother?"

"When she feels really strongly that something is right, she will say or do almost anything to make it happen." Lexi caught the mixture of disgust and alarm on Cam's face, and shook her head. "I'm making her sound like a monster."

"What would she do to my family?" Cam asked, his dark eyes stormy.

"I don't know, Cam. Imprison them? Close the quarry? Something."

Cam's mouth shut in a firm line as he nodded once. "So we're done, then?" he asked, the anger returning to his tone.

"I'm sorry."

"Don't be sorry. You're nothing more than a puppet in this," Cam said, his voice seething with suppressed anger.

Lexi drew back as if she had been slapped, then her startled expression smoothed into a blank one as she threw her shoulders back. "I'm hardly a puppet."

"You act like one," Cam shot back.

A little shudder of anger broke Lexi's smooth facade. "If you believe me a puppet, you should save your ire for the puppet master."

"Excellent idea! Let's head to the palace tonight so I can do just that," Cam suggested with acrid irony as he threw his arms in the air.

A single lifted brow betrayed her emotion, her voice eerily calm. "You need to go." Lexi nodded coolly towards the open balcony.

"This is *Tiger's* room; shouldn't *he* be the one to kick me out of it?"

Lexi opened her mouth to command him, to remind him of her rank, but her imperious words fizzled at the pain in his eyes. Without a word, she opened the hallway door and closed it behind her. Her anger propelled her down the corridor, but she slowed when she didn't hear the door open nor his expected footsteps coming after her. She imagined his apology, the soft words he would use to urge her to change her mind, but the door didn't open. He didn't follow her. He didn't take it back. Lexi's dismay returned to anger before she reached her own door. Van was fidgeting in the hallway while the guard with spotted white wings stood stiffly beside him. Both looked up with relief as she approached.

"You sent for me?" Van asked, wearing an uncomfortable smile.

"Your sister is here. She'll meet us for dinner shortly," Lexi said in a flat tone, breezing into her room with a perfectly blank expression masking her face. Lexi nodded satisfactorily at the three covered meals set on her vanity table.

"What? Anna came *here*? Is she at the pool?" Van asked, his uneasy charm giving way to veiled panic.

Lexi sat down without looking at him. "She's using Limen's bath, and she has a guard."

"But why did she come *here*? She shouldn't be here," Van muttered, pushing back the wispy blonde hair that cascaded across his forehead. "She *can't* be here," he said with more force, meeting Lexi's eyes.

One corner of Lexi's mouth twitched with amusement. "She *is* here. I'll allow her to explain why."

Van leaned out of the doorway to peer down the hall. "She takes forever to wash," he complained. "She only has one guard with her?" He began to pace jauntily back and forth from the room out into the hallway.

Lexi's twitch became a half smile, but she willed it away with thoughts of her unpleasant conversation with Cam.

"Limen usually bathes after dinner," Van announced, and abruptly stopped pacing while several emotions flickered across his face. Turning to her, her gave her a short bow. "Please excuse me, Your Highness. I will return shortly with my sister." Van disappeared out the door, then briefly reappeared. "Please don't spoil your dinner waiting for us," he added, and then was gone.

Lexi laughed silently as she uncovered her dish and peered at the odd array of greens dotted with carrots and flanked by some sort of grilled meat.

"Shall I close the door, Miss Fritillary?" the guard asked.

"Yes, thank you," Lexi answered, intending to laugh out loud once the door shut, but when it was, she found her mirth had left her. Instead, a frown puckered her brow as she ran through her conversation with Cam. *You betrayed him with Tiger*, an inner voice accused. Lexi only shook her head and picked listlessly at her food. The loud conversation and laughter drifting up from the courtyard below further irritated her until her appetite was gone. She covered her food with a heavy clang, then wandered out to the balcony with a listless gait.

Tiger was sitting alone now, picking at an ash-colored stew with thoughtful abstraction. Coli was across the courtyard speaking with her brothers, who were casting furtive glances at Tiger. Coli clutched their arms, but one broke free and flew across the courtyard to stand in front of Tiger. Tiger got up slowly, his expression grim as he faced Coli's brother.

Lexi leaned forward, squeezing the balcony rail until her fingers began to ache.

Coli landed beside her brother and Tiger, pushing them apart. "You promised!" she reminded her brother a little too loudly, hushing the conversation around them.

Coli's brother leaned around her to smell Tiger. "He's been cheating on you, Coli," he announced. "He reeks of some female."

Lexi drew back involuntarily, a heavy blush on her cheeks as Coli's head whipped around to face Tiger. Lexi sniffed her own hair and groaned as she detected Tiger's scent. Had Cam noticed?

Coli said something in a low voice to Tiger, whose face was as red as Lexi's. Then she cast a single livid glance up at Lexi's balcony before disappearing into the crowd. A few people followed Coli's gaze, but Lexi had withdrawn too far back into her room to be seen.

"I warned you," Coli's brother said.

Lexi flinched at the alarming smack of knuckles against flesh, and leapt back onto the balcony. Tiger straightened, his hand on his jaw as Coli's brother struck again. This time, the shrill of a whistle masked the sound of it. The boisterous crowd tensed at the sound and glanced around for a guard before they turned their attention back to the conflict. Tiger was straightening slower this time. Lexi had landed beside him before she realized what she was doing.

"Go away, Lex," Tiger groaned, pushing her away from him as she tried to examine his face.

"Ah, the source of the stench finally shows her face," Coli's brother drawled.

"Walk away, Talis," Tiger warned, his hands hardening into fists. "That's all I'm taking."

"Oh, you're going to fight back now, are you? That should make this more fun," Talis goaded as Tiger dodged his jab.

"Though I think you have the advantage with that rancid tramp at your side. Her scent is actually making my eyes water," Talis quipped, blinking for effect until Tiger smashed his nose. Talis stumbled back a few steps, the crowd helping him right himself as he returned to the fight with blood dripping from both nostrils.

"You'll regret that, horsey-boy," Talis taunted, lunging at Tiger.

"Stop it," Lexi commanded through clenched teeth, shoving Talis sideways with all her strength.

Talis stumbled over a stool, then fell against a table as the crowd gasped. A couple of men helped him to his feet, then drew back with open mouths as he stood. Talis' left forewing hung down unnaturally at the level of his head. Talis stared at it agape, then tried to straighten it gingerly. He winced as it fell back down.

"You broke my wing!" he accused Lexi, his voice seeming to echo back from the gray stone of the castle.

Lexi shifted closer to Tiger as the crowd began to part for a tall, gray-haired man with brown wings. "What's going on?" he demanded irritably.

"She broke my wing, Pol!" Talis complained loudly, smearing the blood from his nose across his cheek.

"No, I did it," Tiger announced, stepping in front of Lexi with his wings spread wide. "We were fighting and I pushed him into the table."

Lexi clenched the back of Tiger's shirt in her fist and leaned into the back of his neck. "No," she hissed.

"Quiet, Lex," Tiger warned.

"No," Talis said doggedly. "She did it," he insisted, taking a few steps sideways to point where Lexi stood behind Tiger.

Pol met Lexi's eyes, and his face went slack with recognition. Lexi tried to step around Tiger, but he blocked her.

"You and your tramp are both going to the dungeon," Talis said vindictively, as his brother held his broken wing upright.

"Shut your mouth, Mr. Sulfur," Pol warned with a gravelly voice. "Who started the fight?"

Talis chewed the inside of his lip angrily before speaking. "I did," he admitted.

"All right," Pol said, nodding sagely as he looked at Tiger. "Mr. Swallowtail, is it?"

Tiger nodded grimly.

"You'll come with me," Pol directed, and then turned to look at the guard that had remained hidden behind him. "Lance, you take Mr. Sulfur to the infirmary. He can spend the first day of his sentence guarded there."

"Wait," Talis protested. "That reeking tramp broke my wing, and you're not even going to punish her?"

"I broke it," Tiger growled, stepping towards him menacingly. "And I'll happily break another."

"That's enough," Pol said, taking Tiger's arm.

"This isn't justice!" Talis yelled before Lance clapped a heavy hand over his mouth.

Lexi followed along behind Tiger, ignoring the stares. The murmurs of the crowd were a palpable thing, weighing her down in their disapproval even as the crowd parted before their single-file procession. As soon as they entered the castle, she drew alongside Pol, keeping pace.

"You can't lock him up," she whispered.

"He was *fighting*, Your Highness," Pol answered in a soft tone.

"Tiger let that man hit him twice without defending himself. I doubt Tiger would have hit him at all if he hadn't said such vile things about me."

"Lex, stop," Tiger commanded.

"No," Lexi snapped at Tiger, then turned back to Pol. "And then he leapt at Tiger, and I shoved him away. He stumbled over a stool, and then fell into a table. You can't punish Tiger for it."

Pol's grip shifted uneasily on Tiger's arm. "Is that a command?"

"Yes," Lexi said at the same moment that Tiger said, "No!"

Pol stopped their march to the dungeon and released Tiger's arm.

"Ignore her," Tiger insisted, offering his arm. "Take me to the dungeon."

"No," Lexi said, trying to press his arm back to his side.

"Lex, you can't have it both ways. You can either be Raven Fritillary the farm girl or you can be the princess. You can't take the perks without the responsibilities."

"What's that supposed to mean?" Lexi demanded.

"Do you want to run the Mating Mountain?" Tiger asked.

"No."

"Then you should stop interfering with the way your brother-in-law runs it," Tiger argued.

Pol cleared his throat. "I'll just go report to your brother-in-law now, if Your Highness has no objections."

Lexi focused a particularly blank expression on him. "I will accompany you," she said regally.

Tiger sighed and rubbed his stubbled cheeks as they changed directions and ascended several staircases. "How can you think you don't want to be a princess?" Tiger whispered from behind her. "You live to boss people around."

"I do not!" Lexi swatted at him without looking and missed entirely. "Why did you break up with Coli?"

"I don't know. Why did you break up with Cam?"

Lexi turned to frown at him around her wing, and he gave her a little shove in the middle of her back.

"How did you know?" she demanded, stopping and turning to stare at him defiantly.

"How did *you* know I broke up with Coli?"

Lexi blushed and turned away as she mumbled, "I was watching you."

"Well, maybe I was watching you, too," Tiger answered, his grin evident in his voice.

Lexi sneaked a look at him, blushed when he caught her, and resumed climbing the steps. At the top, Beck stood guard beside a partially-opened door.

"Great! Are we doing this again? Should I go get Talan from the dungeon so it's more fun?" Beck asked with a wry grin.

"No, thank you, Beck. Mr. Admiral is best enjoyed from a distance," Lexi quipped while giving Beck a shrewd examination. "Shouldn't you be sleeping?"

Some of the amusement faded from Beck's face as he shook his head. "Somebody had to pick up Avell's shifts."

"Sorry," Lexi said, patting his arm as she passed into the Governor's room.

Limen stood when they entered, a table covered with a dozen different dishes strewn in front of him. His cheeks flushed their two spots of color when he noticed her gaze resting on his elaborate meal.

"Your Highness," he said with a strained smile. "Please join me."

"No, thank you, Limen." Lexi politely waved away his invitation as she looked askance at Pol. "Has Pol informed you of our little problem?"

The Governor's tight smile grew more strained still. "Which one?"

Lexi's shoulders squared as her smile become more pleasant, but less genuine. "The fight in the courtyard."

"Ah yes, you don't want Mr. Swallowtail here punished," Limen said, acknowledging Tiger for the first time.

"He doesn't deserve it, Limen. He didn't begin the fight, and he allowed the man to hit him twice without defending himself or retaliating. No guards were present to stop the fight, so I attempted it. The other man verbally assaulted me, and kept trying to hit Tiger, so Tiger hit him once. When the man came at him again, I told him to stop, and pushed him away from Tiger. The man stumbled over a stool, then fell into a table, breaking his wing. The man insisted *I* broke his wing and must go to the dungeon."

Tiger rolled his eyes, one of which was rapidly swelling shut. "I'll take the punishment for the broken wing. Just lock me up and get this over with."

"No," Lexi said emphatically, but calmly. "That isn't right."

Limen held his breath and stared at the table, his lips pressed together. "What was the fight about?" he finally asked, directing his question to Tiger.

Tiger blushed slightly and cleared his throat. "He felt I had mistreated his sister."

"Ah," Limen said, returning his gaze to the table with a grim smile.

"It's not what you think, Limen," Lexi said.

"Hmm," Limen answered. "One night in the dungeon for fighting, then," he ordered, nodding his command to Pol, who hesitantly walked over to take Tiger's arm. "The punishment for wing breaking, however, is a month in the dungeon. Are you certain you want to take that punishment?"

"Yes," Tiger affirmed.

"I won't allow it," Lexi said simply, her face blank.

Limen grimaced, again studying the meal before him. "Pol, take Mr. Swallowtail to the dungeon while the Her Highness and I discuss the length of his stay."

Pol nodded and left with Tiger, while Lexi watched them with a tightening jaw.

"Beck, Tryp, out," Limen commanded with a curt nod to his guards.

Lexi shifted uneasily. "I don't think it's appropriate for me to be alone with you."

Limen waited until the door shut behind his guards, then shot her an exasperated glance. "I will stay right here and hopefully this won't take long. Your Highness, you're creating chaos. My guards are all second-guessing my orders, I'm fielding constant questions as to your identity, negotiating bribes for silence, and now the most basic rules of the mountain have to be flouted for your sake. I can't order you to go, but I'm asking you to, *please.*"

Lexi met his request with a stony silence.

"Now even Anna West is here. She wants a lady's maid, a private bath, and a private dining room."

"Anna is here because of *Van*," Lexi objected.

"Do you really think Lady Nessa would have sent her if you hadn't been here?"

Lexi folded her lips together in begrudging agreement.

"There are good reasons nobles don't come here. It just doesn't work," he finished, emphasizing each word.

"You would have me leave before my escort arrives?" Lexi asked calmly, a single dark eyebrow raised.

Limen blew out a long breath and laid his hands on the table. "Are you certain they are coming? Have you sent for them?" At her lack of answer, Limen shook his head. "What if they don't arrive for a week? Or they never come at all?" he asked as he walked around the table.

Lexi stiffened at his approach, and he stopped, frowning. "Van, Anna, her servant, and Talan are a sufficient escort," he said, retreating back to his stool.

Lexi stretched taller still and eyed him as he turned. "I disagree with you."

"Of course you do," Limen mumbled, pinching his lips together as he stared down at his unfinished meal. After a full minute of silence, he met her eyes again. "I don't understand why you're still here."

"I told you why I came," she answered steadily, her voice almost monotone.

"I won't marry you to a peasant," he snapped, then dropped his eyes self-consciously. "You've rejected your choices here. Back at the palace, there's sure to be another in-season nobleman…eventually."

Lexi stared at the top of his dark head, the unruly curls indifferently cut. Sensing her gaze, he slowly raised his head, two spots of color burning in each cheek.

"Do you intend to blackmail me into marrying you?" he asked quietly.

"Would it work?"

Limen shook his head obdurately. "I don't believe you'd do that. You love your sister too much. You'll tell her or not as you think best. You wouldn't genuinely bargain to keep my secret."

Lexi smiled faintly before her mouth faded back into its blank mask. "Then we are at an impasse."

"There's nothing to be gained by staying here!" he blurted, then added in a softer tone, "and much to be lost."

"I'm sorry you feel that way," she said blandly. "Now, let's discuss Mr. Swallowtail."

"Fine," Limen agreed, nodding tightly. "Someone needs to be punished for the broken wing."

"It was an accident. There should be no punishment."

"Without punishment, they would all be carelessly breaking each other's wings and the number of life servants would quickly become unsustainable; it's barely sustainable now!" Quieted by her steely gaze, he continued in an undertone. "With such a public fight, even the transfer of the punishment will afford me endless complaints and insubordination. The punishment must be quick and severe."

"Then punish the man who began the fight," she said, her posture rigid.

"Did he break his own wing?" Limen demanded irritably. "There's no justice in that."

Lexi trembled a little as she fought to control herself. "You will not punish him."

"Are you ordering me?" he challenged, stepping towards her again.

"I am."

"Then we have a new governor," he declared sarcastically, returning to his seat. "Congratulations. I suppose I can go home now."

Several emotions flickered across Lexi's face as the silence dragged on. "Would you go if I sent you?"

Limen turned a startled gaze on her, his mouth hung slack, his body shocked to rigid attention. "You can't...it isn't...I hold this position for the duration of my life."

"I was at the ceremony, Limen. He said, 'unless relieved by a higher authority.'"

Limen's breath came rapidly and his eyes darted around the table before returning to Lexi's face. "I don't remember that."

"Mona joked that she was going to follow you and relieve you of your duties. She might have done it if she hadn't been pregnant."

"They would have let me stay longer if she hadn't been," Limen said absently, his gaze falling back to the table. "Why would you? Why do you even suggest it? Are you tormenting me?"

Lexi shook her head with the slightest movement. "If I go home, Mother will find a way to make me marry Talan. If I try to hide with my...fiancé, she will find me and bring me home."

Limen blew out a heavy breath like a cork leaving a bottle. "In such disgrace, perhaps she would let you go."

Lexi's eyes narrowed as she shook her head. "The marriage certificate Talan mentioned; do you know the lie he told to obtain it?"

Limen's attention was riveted to her face as he shook his head.

"He claimed we had already mated," Lexi intoned, her voice cold.

Limen's jaw tightened as a mottled red began to suffuse his skin. "You should have told me. I never would have let him out of the dungeon."

Momentarily pacified, Lexi's face softened. "I know, Limen. He only told me yesterday."

Limen's nostrils flared as he shook his head. "That's unforgivable. If you leave, I will keep him here."

Lexi smiled slightly. "Where would I go? She is going to assume I am carrying a noble heir to the throne. Even if you did agree to marry me to someone else, she would only force my father to annul it."

"The royal flying guard will come. I'm actually surprised they're not here yet," Limen mumbled to himself as he returned to his scattered peas.

"I think she hoped Talan and I would work it out quietly, and no one would be the wiser."

Limen shook his head with new determination. "I still can't marry you. And she'll only make me come right back if I return to Mona."

"How long have you been in season, Limen?"

"Eleven months, two weeks," he responded without hesitation.

"You'll be lucky to make it down the mountain before your season ends."

Limen laughed: heavy, startled guffaws that made his diaphragm bounce beneath his robe. "You're not serious? You can't be serious."

"Limen Viceroy, I hereby relieve you of your position as governor, and command you to return to my sister, immediately," Lexi said loudly, a smile playing about her lips. "And beg her forgiveness, so I won't have to keep wondering whether I ought to tell her or not."

Limen abruptly sobered, his laugh dying in his throat. "She won't forgive me."

Lexi nodded. "She might not, but she'll never forgive you for staying after I relieved you. Go. Tonight."

"But you can't run the mountain. You don't know the first thing. You can't perform the marriages, and you'll have to tell everyone who you are in order to rule."

"Fine. Call an assembly in one hour. I will publicly relieve you. As to the marriages, Erynnis can perform them."

"Yes," Limen said excitedly. "I had forgotten. He was grandfather's officiant, too. He performed all the marriages after grandfather died and before I arrived."

"You can give an officiant the authority to perform marriages?"

"Yes, but Erynnis..."

"Is old. Appoint a second officiant before you leave," Lexi commanded easily, her forehead wrinkled in thought.

"You can't really be doing this."

"I am. You will leave the mountain directly after the assembly. An escort will take you as far as Scio."

"Who will agree...?"

"I'll pay them," Lexi said, cutting him off. "Now get ready; you don't have much time."

Lexi barreled out the door, ignoring Beck's exclamation as he jumped aside. "The Governor has orders for you, Beck. Go talk to him," she called over her shoulder as she flew down the hallway, dodging the returning dinner crowd. She could hear the whispers, and even see a few pointed fingers, as she made her way to the clerk's office and flew through the door.

A young man with horribly tattered white wings looked up at her with a relaxed smile. "In a hurry, Miss *Fritillary*?"

"Ryp Leafwing's room number, please," she requested, her face pleasantly blank.

He looked at her curiously, one eye wrinkling up as he examined her.

"Quickly, please," Lexi added.

His smile tightened as his gaze dropped to the pages before him. "He's in 211."

"Thank you," Lexi said, already out the door. She flew slower this time, watching the crowd beneath her for vivid red wings. In the hallway outside his room, he stood joking with a fuzzy-haired girl with an annoying laugh.

"Ah, the girl who has no scent," Ryp greeted her as she landed beside them. "What can I do for you?"

"I need to speak with you privately," Lexi said, trying not to bristle at the annoying titter of the girl beside her.

"He's a little busy just now," she drawled out, her eyes narrowing as her gaze swept over Lexi.

"Thank you for sparing him," Lexi said pleasantly as she took her cousin's arm and dragged him into his room.

"Hey!" the girl yelled when Lexi shut the door in her face.

"Relax," Ryp yelled back. "She's my cousin."

Lexi spun to look at him, her wings grazing the door as she turned. "Yes, I am your cousin," she whispered.

"Then why the big denial show?"

Lexi swallowed, her blank mask failing her as the consequences of her rash decision fell upon her. "My father asked me to keep my mother's secret. She didn't marry the Governor's illegitimate son, she married the heir to the throne. My father is the king. Your Aunt Ami is the Queen."

Ryp smirked. "Is this a joke?"

"No, it's not. Look at my wings. I'm a Monarch. Princess Lexi Monarch."

Ryp chuckled. "You almost had me. I do believe you're not a Viceroy, because the Governor's illegitimate brother can smell you. He's interested, by the way."

"How many people have you told we're related?" Lexi demanded, her irritation bringing back the smooth, blank mask.

Ryp shrugged. "Why do you care? Are you ashamed of me?"

"No, but my mother is. She would lose power if people knew she wasn't of noble blood."

Ryp chuckled. "Power with your father? The neighbors? This is absurd." He shook his head as he stood to go.

Lexi held up one hand to stop him. "The Governor will announce my identity in front of everyone in less than an hour. Then I will relieve him of duty, and become the new governor."

"What? You're insane." Ryp no longer looked amused as he tried to pass by her.

"I need your help," Lexi said, stepping in front of him.

"With what?" he asked irritably, looking around her at the door.

309

"Tell everyone you made a mistake. That you can smell me; it's just faint."

"Why would I do that?" he demanded, once again meeting her eyes.

"Because I'll pay you." Lexi evaluated his perturbed frown, her shoulders slumping as she released her breath. "Because my very kind father asked me to keep this secret, and he would be so upset if it got out," she pleaded, allowing her emotions to show on her face.

"That's a better reason, but still a lousy one."

"The assembly is in less than an hour. Then you'll know I am who I say I am. We can talk again afterwards," Lexi said, regaining her reserve.

"When you're the first female governor?" Ryp snickered.

"Yes," Lexi said, wishing she had waited to confront him.

"Sounds good to me. Can I go now, *Your Highness*?"

Lexi fought a cringe at the title and wondered again what she was doing. "Of course," she said coldly, opening the door herself. She was relieved to see the girl with the unpleasant laugh had disappeared, but the conversation weighed on her. As he stepped out behind her, she turned to face him.

"I require your silence," she said stonily.

Ryp snorted. "I think I liked it better when you were pretending I smelled like manure."

With a carefully blank expression, Lexi walked away.

Chapter Fifteen

Both guards were outside her room, greeting her with discreet nods as she caught a tidbit of the heated argument within. Squaring her shoulders, she pushed open the door.

"Your Highness," Anna said, jumping to her feet to bob a little curtsy. "Please help me reason with Van; he's being *completely* obstinate," she accused, dropping back to her stool with a vindictive pout.

Van unfolded himself from the little stool with an uncomfortable laugh, gave Lexi a slow bow, and offered her his hand. Lexi dismissed it with a polite shake of her head and remained standing in the doorway.

"Don't embarrass yourself, Anna," Van replied, still standing and smiling awkwardly. "This is a family matter. We'll take our discussion elsewhere so we don't bother you, Your Highness."

"I've hardly eaten," Anna protested, gesturing at her full plate. Van quickly swallowed his perturbed expression and let out another uncomfortable laugh.

"Please, remain and finish your meal," Lexi soothed. "Limen will be leaving the mountain this evening if you're up to traveling with him. If not, I am certain, Anna, that your brother will fulfill his family obligation and escort you to the palace in your father's absence."

"*Limen* is leaving? The Governor is leaving?" Anna clarified as Van stared, his large mouth agape.

"Yes. I've relieved him of his post and will remain here in his place." Lexi wanted to laugh at their expressions, she had never seen either one of them so stripped of the social varnish they usually wore.

"You *relieved* him," Anna repeated, waiting for Lexi's nod before continuing. "And you're not marrying Van, and you're ordering him to take me to the palace?" A gleam of jubilation lit Anna's eyes as she spoke.

"Surely I needn't order your brother to accompany you. A male relative always accompanies an in-season noble to the palace. Your father is still away, is he not?"

Anna nodded, her triumphant grin enveloping her face.

"Then the duty falls to Van," Lexi concluded with a superficial smile.

Van let out another uncomfortable laugh as he scrubbed his forehead with the palm of his hand. Absently, he rubbed his brows vigorously, his face increasingly serious. "We should travel with Limen," he finally asserted, brows wild as he dared his sister to defy him.

She gave him a little sniff of assent that poorly disguised her delight. "And Talan will remain here with you?" Anna asked, a hint of regret in her voice.

Lexi's hesitation was slight as she chose her words carefully. "I will encourage him to leave as well."

"Then you'll release him?" Anna confirmed happily.

Another slight pause accompanied her response. "If he agrees to leave."

"But wasn't it Limen who locked him up?"

"Yes," Lexi answered, her lips tight in her courteous smile.

Furrowing her brow, Anna glanced questioningly at her dazed brother. "I think I have been misinformed. What is the charge against Talan?"

Lexi glanced at Van's guilty expression, then squared her shoulders. "Fighting."

Lady's Anna's brows rose in evident surprise. "With Limen?"

Lexi stood taller as her words flowed in an authoritative stream. "I will release Talan now so he may accompany you or bid you farewell." She nodded and turned away, then realized how much she must look and sound like her mother. Inwardly groaning, she turned back to give them a brief smile before she stepped back into the hallway. Both guards glanced at her, awaiting orders.

"Remain with Anna," she directed the guard with spotted white wings.

The gray-winged guard lifted his eyebrows in question and she nodded, pleased that he fell into step behind her without her having to ask. She had considered ordering him down to the dungeon to fetch Talan, but she desperately needed to speak to Tiger as well, and she doubted he would leave his cell at her command. When she approached the steps down to the dungeon, the guard's heavy footfalls stopped, and Lexi turned to look at his hesitant face.

"Yes, I must," she said, answering his unspoken question. Without a word, he once more fell into step behind her.

At the gate, Pol stood and gave her an awkward bow, his hands fidgeting with the keys. "What prisoner can I bring to you?" he asked politely.

"One that won't come," she answered simply, pointing to the gate's lock.

Pol fingered the proper key and spoke in an undertone. "Word of the fight has already spread." He shook his head uncomfortably. "It's not safe."

Lexi swallowed. "Then tell Tiger Swallowtail that you're moving him to a different cell for his own safety, then bring him to the gate."

Pol shrugged, absently scratching the back of his neck. "Well, *he's* not in any danger. Do you want me to drag him out?"

"Tell him he has two minutes to come out or I'm going in," Lexi said, her voice betraying irritation.

Poll nodded and unlocked the gate, slipped through quickly, and carefully locked it behind him. "Policy," he explained with an uncomfortable grin, then hurried away.

Lexi held her breath, listening to the cacophony of disgruntled inmates as she waited.

Tiger scowled as he turned the corner, Pol tailing behind him. "I'm not leaving," he announced, his swelling eye now pitifully swollen shut.

Lexi felt ridiculous tears well up in her eyes at the sight of him. She blinked rapidly and turned to face her guard. "Wait for me on the stairs, please." As she turned back to Pol, she prayed the tears were gone. "Pol, we'll need a moment."

The old graying guard nodded and retreated back into the dungeon, jingling the ring of keys against his thigh.

As soon as she met Tiger's irritable gaze, her eyes began to swim again, and she quickly looked away.

"What did you do, Lex?" Tiger asked, his voice soft with dread.

"I sent Limen away. I'm the governor," she announced, laughing weakly as she dashed away her tears with an impatient hand.

"Oh, Lex," he said quietly, unconsciously stepping closer to the bars. "Why?"

"He was unhappy. Mona's unhappy. I can't go home."

"But you haven't announced it yet?" Tiger asked, gripping the bars.

"No," she said, glancing at him quickly, then looking away. "But it's done."

"Tell Limen you made a crazy mistake. Tell him you were kidding. Just take it back," Tiger urged, his grip on the bars tightening.

"No! It was the right thing to do," she declared, her tears suddenly drying up. "It was the *only* thing to do."

Tiger let his head thunk against the bars. "Of all the moth-brained declarations..."

"What would you have me do, Tiger?" she demanded, glaring at him until he met her gaze.

"Well, I think I just told you."

She balled her hands into fists, her nails digging into her palms. "Marry me," she commanded.

Tiger stumbled backwards with a surprised guffaw. "Are you kidding?"

"No. Marry me right now."

Tiger dropped his gaze, his jaw shifting sideways as he smiled. "You really—"

"No joking, please," Lexi interrupted.

"How did you know I was going to?"

"You have a tell. Now," Lexi took a big breath that hurt her lungs. "Will you marry me or not?"

Tiger let out a deflated sigh. "Lex, I can't just abandon my mother to be punished for my actions."

Lexi bobbed a nod. "That's a good point," she conceded, avoiding his gaze. "So you won't?"

"I can't."

Lexi nodded again, then looked past him. "Pol!"

Tiger fell back another step at this sudden dismissal. "Lex..."

"Pol, release Talan," she commanded, her shoulders squared and her face carefully blank.

"What?!" Tiger demanded, returning to the bars in agitation.

"And return Mr. Swallowtail to his cell, please," Lexi commanded, still not meeting Tiger's gaze.

"Lex, this is stupid. Don't release him. Don't do any of it. Lex, you can't!" Tiger pleaded angrily.

Lexi turned steely eyes on him, her voice emotionless. "Yes, *I can*." Turning, she walked briskly to the stairs where her guard waited.

"Lex don't do this! Lex!" Tiger called, his face still pressed against the bars despite Pol's dutiful grasp on his arm.

Lexi stiffly ascended the stairs, not looking back. At the top, she waited, watching the crowds exit the ballroom for the assembly. The inevitable hickory and cloves hit her senses before she saw him.

"You changed your mind," Talan grinned, possessively reaching for her arm.

315

Lexi stepped away and put her guard between them. "I haven't changed my mind. I am releasing you so that you can say goodbye to Van and Anna or, preferably, join them. They're leaving tonight with Limen."

"*Anna* is here? And Limen is *leaving*?" He shook his head incredulously. "Why is Limen leaving? Did the King send a new governor?"

"*I* am the new governor," Lexi answered coolly, nodding when her guard looked aghast. "Limen will announce it in a few minutes. I suggest you find Van and Anna."

Talan laughed incredulously, searched her face, then laughed again before suddenly sobering. "You're *staying*? *Here*?"

"Yes."

Talan shook his head. "What about my estate? I can't stay here." He frowned at the wall before making eye contact again. "Are you getting married?"

"No," she answered, her voice faltering slightly.

Talan gave a little snort of mirth. "Then why are you doing this?" He shook his head. "You're ruining my life."

"The feeling is mutual," Lexi answered in an undertone as she moved away.

"Just marry me and leave," Talan pleaded, following her. "I'll let you have your maid. You'll be comfortable on my estate. You can see your father. You can be around horses. You'll have your own room. Don't send Limen home. It will take forever to get another governor here, and my season might not last that long. Princess, please." At his last words, he grasped her hand, but she pulled it away and turned to face him.

"I am very sorry things have not turned out well for you, but much of that was your own doing. I have to go."

Lexi numbly followed her guard into a huge amphitheater that was already three-quarters full with more people streaming in at every moment. She noticed several perturbed glares on the faces of strangers, and drew herself taller, her weary expression tightening into a careful smile. The irony felt thick enough to choke on. She had left home to avoid her position, and now she would willingly assume another. Mentally she calculated how long it would be before her parents found out what she had done, appointed a new governor (assuming Limen's season ended before they could make him return), and sent the replacement with flying guardsmen to force her home. No more than a month, she decided. She could bear that. No point in staying longer if she couldn't have Tiger. Ridiculous how it all came down to that, she thought, mentally chiding herself. Limen was at her side now, his face fraught with excitement and insecurity.

"Are you sure you want to do this?" Limen asked. "It's not too late to change your mind."

"Make the announcement," Lexi commanded, her throat thick with the words. She stood in the wings of the stage and watched Limen walk out to the center, raising his hands for attention. The deafening sound of the crowd slowly dropped to a murmur.

"I, Limen Viceroy, have served as your governor for nearly a year." Limen began, his sonorous voice carrying well. "But this evening I have been relieved of my duties. My sister-in-law, the Princess Lexi Monarch, now assumes my position. Please welcome your new governor. Your Highness?" Limen held out one hand, waiting for Lexi to join him on stage.

With palpable dread, she forced herself forward, gracefully taking his hand and smiling out to the crowd, then releasing it as she turned to face them. For a moment, the shocked silence was complete.

"I have hidden my identity since I arrived here. Thus, some of you may know me as Raven Fritillary." Lexi scanned the audience for familiar faces, but the solar lanterns at her feet obscured the murmuring audience. "But I am the third-born of the triplet princesses. My sister, Princess Mona, greatly misses her husband, your governor. So tonight, I send him home to her. I shall remain in his place with two officiants who are authorized to perform marriages." Lexi hesitated only a second, unsure if she should say more. "Please join me in thanking Limen Viceroy for his service," she finished smoothly, beginning the applause.

Limen nodded acknowledgment of the perfunctory clapping, but his lips thinned into a tight line as the lackluster applause began to peter out.

"Time to go, Limen," Lexi prodded in an undertone, still clapping with a warm smile plastered to her face.

Limen nodded and exited the stage with Lexi close on his heels, the applause quickly giving way to an uproar of shocked conversation.

"Niiice speeches," Beck drawled, opening a backstage door for them to exit.

"I should brief you," Limen said without attempting to look back and see her. His enormous yellow and black wings so filled the narrow corridor that it would have been nearly impossible to make eye contact.

"Your officiants can do so. Anna and Van will be departing with you. Have you chosen your escorts?" Lexi responded to Limen's wings.

"Yes. I promised to pay them when I reached home."

"Surely they needn't travel so far with you. I'll pay them to take you to Scio, and you can gather agents of the crown to take you the rest of the way." Lexi waited for his answer, watching his wings twitch with irritation.

"I would prefer to fly with my escort as long as possible," Limen finally responded, the sound coming through gritted teeth.

"And if their seasons end in your service?" Lexi let the question hang in the air before continuing. "Once you make it down the mountain, delay is in your favor. If you're still in season when you reach home, Mother will send you right back."

"Then I won't go directly home."

Lexi caught the guilty tone in his voice. "Where is it you want to go, Limen?"

Limen had reached the top of the stairs and stepped out into the corridor, murmuring something to his guards that caused them to

318

back away. He turned to face her, glaring at Beck until he retreated back down the stairs behind her. When Limen felt he had sufficient privacy, he leaned forward confidentially. "It's best if I communicate with the...*others* in person."

"Oh no, it isn't. You will go right home to my sister and beg her forgiveness," Lexi commanded in clipped tones reminiscent of her mother.

"And if they hear I'm home, and show up on our doorstep?" Limen demanded, too loudly. He glanced at Beck, who turned away whistling. "I have to make sure they will stay away."

Lexi turned her face away to hide the expression of perfect loathing that adorned it. After a deep breath, she turned back expressionless. "When you are begging my sister's forgiveness, wouldn't it be simpler if you didn't also have to confess where you stopped on the way home?"

"Mona needn't know..." he began.

"I'll tell her. That, I *will* tell her," Lexi promised as she marched past him.

Limen's expression turned sullen, making him look like a spoiled child as he followed her. He opened his mouth to speak, then thought better of it, and simply nodded. "We should hurry," he said resignedly, "before we're overrun by the masses."

"Too late," Beck said cheerfully as the crowds began to press at the guards behind them.

"Hey, Viceroy!" someone shouted angrily.

Limen paled, then renewed his hurried pace down the corridor. "Erid!" he called urgently, flying the last few paces to the cluster of guards before him. "Shut the doors and guard the balconies. No one else leaves tonight," he commanded. Erid ran to execute his commands while the other guards hurried alongside Limen just ahead of the crowds.

Beck snorted at Lexi's side as they followed closely behind. "He better run."

Lexi gave him a questioning glance, wondering if she ought to fear the crowds as well.

"The man has a lot of enemies, and no title to protect him," Beck explained, quickening his pace as the rear guard caught up with them and the crowds merged from the two hallways.

"They can't think I won't punish them if they try to hurt Limen," Lexi argued.

Beck glanced back at the teeming crowd. "You'd best make some quick examples so they know."

Lexi followed his gaze, noting the angry determination on the faces of several. She stopped abruptly and turned to face the growing mob. The rear guardsmen nearly collided with her before spinning to face the crowd, batons drawn.

Lexi drew herself up and put on her most regal expression. "Gentlemen," she called loudly. The crowd came to a sudden, stumbling stop, the tumultuous noise dissolving into murmurs. "You seem eager for an audience with your new governor. How may I assist you?" Lexi could feel her legs trembling beneath her, and finally saw the wisdom of her mother's full-length gowns.

Recovering from his shock, Beck laughed nervously at her side. "I didn't mean *now*," he whispered.

The few men that had seemed to be chasing them looked at each other in awkward silence as the crowd filled in behind them.

One large man near the front glanced sheepishly at the others before meeting her gaze. "Our business is not with you, Your Highness," he said deferentially.

"You cannot have business with my brother-in-law without it also being mine." Lexi informed him, minutely observing the crowd as she did so. The mob mentality seemed to be giving way to chagrin as the men shifted their weight uneasily and exchanged glances. A few moved further back into the crowd as one or two pushed their way forward.

Lexi's careful mask fell away for a moment as she recognized Cam in the crowd. His eyes were still equal parts anger and hurt, but there was hope in his questioning glance. Lexi swallowed down her emotions, her face resuming its blank authority. Cam stared at her a moment longer, waiting for some sign, his face falling when it didn't come. Slowly, he turned back.

"I will be happy to meet with each of you and address your concerns," Lexi said, watching as Cam's tightly-closed wings were enveloped by the crowd. "Shall we reconvene in the throne room?" She received a few nods of grudging assent, then turned slowly and led the crowd to the throne room at a stately pace.

Chapter Sixteen

She had meant to say goodbye, but giving Limen a safe departure was more important. He may have deserved some of the vigilante justice that she was diffusing, but for Mona's sake and her sweet little nieces, she would protect him. She had led her angry procession into the throne room an hour ago. At first they had been reluctant to speak, but after she requested their feedback on meals, the floodgates had broken. There were only eight women in the group of roughly thirty, but they proved the most outspoken, complaining of the tests, roommates, the shared bathing pool, and the food. Then the men complained of the harsh prison sentences, boredom, and once again the food. Finally, the man who had spoken in the hallway stepped forward, a pleasant smirk on his dusky face, though his dark eyes were still alight with anger.

"Will the old governor be returning to his post?" he asked, pushing dark, unruly waves off his forehead.

Lexi shifted slightly on the cushioned stool that had been Limen's throne. It had been second nature listening to their grievances, expressing concern over the issues raised, and assuring the complainer that she would look into it. She had watched her mother do it a million times while her father looked on and nodded. A third of her childhood had been spent in the throne room receiving petitioners. However, this was a question she could not answer.

"Limen Viceroy has left the castle," she answered, side-stepping his question. "I expect he will be off the mountain entirely by midnight."

A few disappointed grumbles moved through the group, but no one appeared surprised.

"Then your position is permanent?"

Lexi shifted subtly, the upholstered wooden throne making the slightest creaking in the suddenly quiet room. She thought of her sweet, dominated father, Cercy with her good-natured scolding, Raven's rough mane between her fingers, and silently bid them goodbye.

"I intend it to be so, yes," she answered, feeling pleased when a collective sigh of relief seemed to emanate from the crowd.

"Then I have no further complaint," he said with a charming smile on his full lips. "But one request…"

Lexi gave him a slight nod to continue.

"Will you marry me?" he asked, beginning to chuckle as the crowd erupted into loud guffaws around him. Several of the men congratulated him, and a few others added their own proposals.

Lexi stood, smiling serenely despite her discomfort. "That is a matter best discussed in a *private* conference." A fresh round of laughter met her response, along with a few whistles.

"That's not a no," the petitioner said, grinning as he bowed, then allowing himself to be ushered out with the rest of the crowd. Their boisterous amusement could still be heard even after the throne room doors were shut and locked.

Lexi let out an audible sigh and sunk back to her throne.

"Nicely done!" Beck hollered from behind the curtain covering the main throne room doors.

Lexi smiled. "Does that curtain open? Disembodied voices congratulating me are a little disconcerting."

Beck flung the mossy green curtain open. "Finally! I hate that thing. It smells like mouse cheese."

"Mouse cheese?"

"You know, you put it in the trap to catch the mouse, then it gets all stale and hard and nasty: mouse cheese." Beck explained with a broad gesture, then greedily sucked in air. "Ahh, so much better."

Lexi smiled, then stood as Erynnis approached with a stack of paper and a ring of keys.

"Your Highness, if you're not too tired, I have prepared a brief orientation." He bowed until the heavy keyring slipped off his stack of papers and landed with a resounding metallic clang on the stone floor. "Oh, oopsie," he said, coloring.

Lexi held back a giggle. The dignified functionary certainly didn't seem like the "oopsie" type. His flush grew until even the top of his balding head appeared sunburnt and his mottled brown wings twitched. "My mother used to say it," he mumbled, collecting the keys.

Though Lexi would have preferred to sit in his little office behind the curtain, Erynnis insisted on standing before her as he gave his report on the number of life servants (seventy-one), the number of in-season residents (one hundred fifty-seven), the number of prisoners (seventeen), the amount of food available (too little), the meager supplies delivered weekly by crown agents, all the needed repairs, various conflicts between life servants, an accounting of what each key unlocked, and even the number of books in the library (three hundred nineteen).

"And now, Your Highness may wish to retire to the governor's room," Erynnis finished with a little bow. "This key," he reminded her, reverently holding up a single key before handing her the entire ring. "Oh, I forgot!" His cheeks lit up with another profuse blush and he stared down at his shabby, but very clean, boots. "Should Your Highness wish," he continued in a whisper, "to *bathe*, it's the key next to it with three prongs."

"Thank you," Lexi replied with proper gravity, her amusement entirely hidden.

"The marriages," he continued, recovering his voice, "are conducted at all hours, day or night, upon request. Traditionally the governor is present, but I or Howarth, the new assistant officiant, are authorized to perform marriages in your absence as well."

"Oh," Lexi replied, momentarily startled out of her reserve. "The marriages are not scheduled, then?"

"Rarely, and even then with very little notice. There is an urgency to get couples off the mountain as soon as possible to ensure they are still *able* to get down the mountain. Also, some individuals do not choose to marry until they sense their season is about to end; there is a measure of panic in such cases that necessitates a speedy ceremony. They must prove they can still fly, of course, but then the marriage is sealed with all due haste." Erynnis paused to wipe sweat from his brow with a stained handkerchief. "Does Your Highness prefer to be present at all the ceremonies?"

Lexi suppressed a little sigh. "Yes Erynnis, I think it's best for now."

"Very good, Your Highness," he replied, with a double bow that brought another blush to his wrinkled cheeks. "Does Your Highness prefer to keep set hours in the throne room for complaints and marriages?"

Must I? Swallowing her flippant answer, Lexi scanned the spacious room with its cavernous ceiling, relatively clean tapestries, and resounding emptiness. The back wall had several narrow floor-to-ceiling windows decorated with wrought iron vines. Something that looked like dark clay patched spots where cracks snaked the old glass. Only slightly moth-eaten curtains hung limply beside them. The wall opposite the officiant's office had heavy wooden doors leading out to the balcony. Unlike the other rooms' balcony doors, an enormous sliding iron bolt locked them in place. Lexi stared at it a moment, wondering if the queen's suite had ever had one, then let her gaze travel on to Beck, still standing guard before the heavy door that opened onto the second floor of the castle. With a grin, Beck lifted his hands to his mouth and shouted "hello" in a mock whisper. The sound echoed around the room while Lexi fought a smile.

Erynnis cleared his throat. "Um, the schedule, Your Highness?"

"Oh yes, sorry." Lexi gave him a polite smile and forced her wandering mind back to the issue at hand. "If I'm to always be on call, would a couple of hours a day be sufficient for complaints?"

Erynnis wrestled with his suppressed opinions for a moment, then nodded deferentially.

"Very well," she said, hearing her mother's phrase in her own voice and cringing inwardly. "I will hear complaints and attend scheduled marriages from one to three every afternoon."

Erynnis' eyebrows drew up into his forehead. He shifted weight from one foot to the other while his wings began to twitch again.

"Is there something else?" Lexi asked, standing and trying to stretch surreptitiously. Again, she could see the wisdom of those long ball gowns as she tried to awaken her numb legs.

"There are departures and sometimes marriages nearly every morning after the..." Erynnis hummed uncomfortably over the word *pregnancy* "...tests. Do you wish to be present?"

Lexi frowned briefly before returning to a neutral expression. "Only for the marriages." She paused, a slight puckering of her brow the only sign of her displeasure. "I didn't realize there was any fanfare associated with the other departures."

Erynnis' twitching escalated as he opened his mouth to speak, then shut it again, and dropped his gaze.

"Then I shall retire. We can address everything else in the morning. Like the food," she added in afterthought. "The in-seasons need decent meals."

Erynnis' face turned defensive, his mouth twitching with unsaid words.

"But we can address that in the morning," she soothed, suppressing a yawn. With a stately gait she swept past the balding officiant, retaining her composure until Beck caught her eye and made a face at her. "Beck, surely your shift is over," she managed with only a faint smile.

"I couldn't abandon you to the wolves." he protested as she passed him.

"The wolves left an hour ago," she said, passing through the heavy door into the hallway.

"Are you kidding? Erynnis is the worst one!" Beck said with a broad smile as he fell in with her guard detail.

Lexi smirked. "Erynnis is a puppy."

"Only to you, *Your Highness*," he said with a flourishing double bow.

"Be nice, Beck," Lexi admonished quietly, glancing at the officiant's door as they passed it.

"I'm always nice. I am charm incarnate. I am charisma..."

"Yes, yes, Beck. You are a social wonder," Lexi chuckled, then schooled her face for a stately nod to a few in-seasons loitering in the hall.

Beck chortled. "Nice nod, Your Majesty, very regal."

Lexi elbowed him when no one was looking, and Beck guffawed loudly.

The guards stopped and took up position in front of Limen's room. Lexi stood before the door, fumbling with the large key ring.

"Other one," Beck said, pointing when she chose the wrong key.

It felt wrong and vaguely tacky entering Limen's room. His citrus scent still emanated from the neatly-made canopy bed. Lexi hesitated and then turned back to Beck. "I don't think I want to sleep here. Maybe an airing? New bedding? I don't suppose there is any to spare. Perhaps just a thorough washing." Lexi colored as she realized she was thinking aloud. She took a deep breath and squared her shoulders. "I will sleep in the queen's suite tonight."

The guards exchanged looks and shifted uncomfortably.

Beck cleared his throat. "Uh, the balcony doors don't lock. It's an uncomfortable post outside them all night and too tight a space for more than one guard. And we can't guard from *inside* the room, because..." Beck waved a thick hand in the air to pantomime his sense of impropriety.

Lexi turned her irritation into a deep breath, which she blew out quickly with its thick scent of Limen. "Have someone remove and wash the bedding, and put his clothing somewhere else," she said, catching sight of his moth-bitten robe.

"Give it away?" Beck asked.

"Not yet. Make sure he gets down the mountain first," *and that Mother doesn't force him to return*, she added mentally. For the fiftieth time since coming to the Old Castle, she calculated how long it would take her mother to send the flying guardsmen with a decree that would force her home. Surely she couldn't have wheedled her father into signing anything yet, but then she thought of her marriage certificate and reconsidered.

After sending one of the guards to carry out her instructions, Beck cleared his throat. "So are we just going to stand here in the doorway all night?"

Lexi squared her shoulders. "No. I will sleep in the queen's suite."

"And the guards?" Beck reminded her.

"Tiger Swallowtail can serve his sentence as my flying guard." Lexi struggled to keep the triumphant smile from her face at her own clever solution.

Beck snorted laughter.

"Fetch him from the dungeon," Lexi commanded, marching back to her own room.

"And if he refuses?" Beck called down the hallway from the governor's door.

"Explain the situation." Now that only four guards trailed in her wake, she allowed the suppressed grin to emerge. She felt giddy with freedom and something else. It took her a moment to realize that it was the *power* she was enjoying. She frowned, then forced her face blank. Her pleasantly bland expression slipped when she saw who waited outside her door.

"I knew you would come back here!" Talan fairly crowed, eyeing the guards behind her uncomfortably.

"I hoped you had left." Lexi smiled pleasantly to belie her rudeness.

Anger flashed briefly across Talan's face, then diffused with another glance at her guards. "I did," he announced. "I went part-way down the mountain with them and I very much wanted to continue."

"Then why didn't you?"

"You *know* why," Talan muttered angrily. "It was a mistake to choose you."

Though she knew she ought to be pleased, his words stung. With an odd pang, she realized he had not bothered to signal her either. With a carefully blank expression, she turned back to her guards. "Escort Mr. Admiral back to the dungeon, please."

"Very nice. I obey the Queen and end up in the dungeon," Talan complained, jumping away from the guards and flying around them. "I'll escort myself," he called back, bitterly.

The guards glanced to her for approval, awaiting her slight nod before letting him go.

One of her guards preceded her into her room, checking beneath the beds and opening the balcony doors before stepping out and closing them behind him. The night breeze felt icy and her room felt strange. Someone had changed out the rugs for a pair that hardly smelled, there was a bouquet of wild flowers in a pewter cup on the vanity table, and her bed was neatly made with fresh linens that looked almost new. Clodi's bed was neatly made with her same old blanket, and a small note sat in the middle of the bed. Stepping into the room, Lexi lifted the note.

"Dear Princess Lexi (that's so exciting! I'm writing to a princess),

"Some of the nice ladies that work here helped me make our room prettier in case you still want to sleep here. I won't sleep here unless you want me to. They think you need a lady's maid. I don't know how to do that, but I can learn. I will stay in the dance hall until you decide."

Clodi

Clodi signed her name with a messy cloud dotting the I. Lexi's smile was involuntary as she returned to the door. "Would you fetch Clodi Parnassian from the dance hall?" The guards glanced at each other before one of them shrugged and walked away. Lexi was tempted to go herself, but angry murmurs of the crowd after Talis had broken his wing still echoed in her head, and the nervous energy that had kept all her muscles tensed over the past five hours was now dissipating into total exhaustion. Slipping into her nightgown, she crawled into bed. When she heard Clodi's happy bustle as she moved about the room a short time later, she was too tired to even open her eyes. Clodi responded by softening her usual cheerful bellow to a hushed shout, but her excited chatter still lasted well past Lexi's last sleepy *mm-hmm*.

An insistent tapping woke her four hours later.

"Umm, Your Highness? There's a marriage taking place in a few minutes. Did you still want to be present?"

Lexi groaned as she clutched at her pillow, momentarily considering sleeping through it before she dragged herself from bed.

"Whaat?" Clodi asked sleepily.

"Nothing, Clodi. Go back to sleep."

"Okay," she answered dreamily, her even breaths evolving into deep snores within minutes.

Lexi dressed herself clumsily, then opened the balcony door. The shivering guard turned with a hopeful expression and Lexi nodded. "Wedding," she said simply.

The guard grinned, teeth chattering as he leaned back out. "Mr. Swallowtail, we're on the move."

Tiger swooped in a moment later with a sullen expression. His swollen eye had deflated to an angry bruise. Lexi wanted to fuss over him, but limited herself to a sympathetic smile. Tiger merely shook his head and fell into step with the other guards as they walked to the throne room. She couldn't resist looking back at him, but he wouldn't meet her gaze. Forcing him to be her guard suddenly seemed far less clever than she had originally thought. Fighting the urge to bite her nails, she drew her fingers into tight fists and marched with posture that would have pleased her mother.

The throne room was populated by an excited knot of wedding guests who surrounded the bride and groom. The tangle of scents made her eyes water and her sinuses burn. A group of fritillary brothers seemed determined to light the air afire with their spicy

331

scents. Lexi took a breath in through her mouth to spare her nose and set off a coughing fit.

Erynnis was nearly apoplectic with rage. "Stop signaling this instant!" For a moment he struggled with the locking bolt on the balcony door before motioning a guard to help him. They threw the doors open wide letting in a blast of chilly pre-dawn air. Erynnis waved a large, leather book in a vain attempt to speed the airing of the room. As Lexi continued to cough, his waving became more frantic. "You are disturbing the Princess!"

Lexi felt fortunate that the coughing hid her laughter; neither was dignified, but her mother's chastisement: "Ill-timed humor does not become a lady" rang in her ears. She attempted to apologize and congratulate the couple before withdrawing to the less-offensive air of the officiant's office, but her words were difficult to discern between coughs. Tiger and three other guards followed her and secured both of the office doors. It wasn't until she was able to stop coughing that she could hear Tiger's musical laugh. She wiped at the tears streaming down her cheeks with a yellowed handkerchief one of the guards had handed her and allowed herself a smile.

"Well, that went well," she said, and bit back a laugh as she heard Erynnis' irritable lecture on the other side of the door. Tiger's closed-mouth laughter continued, but the other three guards were silent. She held out the damp handkerchief, relieved when one of two identical white winged guards took it from her hand. "Thank you..." she paused, waiting for the guard to supply his name.

"Morph, Your Highness," he answered in a gruff voice as he tucked the used handkerchief back into his pocket.

"Thank you, Morph," she said, another little coughing fit escaping her. The scent seemed to have soaked into her clothing and hair. "Maybe we should go further away," she suggested.

"You'll have to wash it out," the other white-winged guard blurted. Morph gave his brother a slight scowl before nodding his assent.

Lexi suppressed a groan. It seemed like all she did was bathe. "It won't go away?" She looked back and forth between the two brothers, who appeared to be having a silent discussion of scowls and pursed lips.

"It's like when a cat marks his territory; it will reek a day or two unless a competing scent covers it or it's washed away," the second brother explained.

Morph groaned and covered his eyes.

"What? It's a good way to explain it," his brother argued.

Tiger, who had never stopped laughing, now opened his mouth for a full guffaw, earning scowls from the three other guards.

"Have I been marked, then?" Lexi asked, her hands tightening back into fists.

"No. Well, probably not on purpose. Two of the Fritillary brothers have been fighting over the bride; the unsuccessful brother was trying to mark *her*," Morph's brother explained.

Lexi's mouth twisted in involuntary disgust before she schooled her expression. "Is that typical wedding behavior?"

Morph's brother laughed. "Definitely not. Very rude."

"And it's different from signaling?"

Morph's brother blushed. "Uh, you need to touch them."

Morph rolled his eyes. "Phemus, he didn't touch the Princess. You don't know what you're talking about." He turned deferentially back to Lexi. "He didn't have to touch you. He just had to get close and signal a bunch of times in a row."

"So I can cover the smell by having someone else mark me?" Lexi asked as Tiger mouthed the word "no."

Morph blushed.

"It's like declaring yourself mated," Phemus continued, blushing until the tips of his ears were bright red. "Or anyway, it smells like you have."

"Phemus, don't talk anymore," Morph pleaded, his own blush matching his brother's.

The third guard snorted a laugh and tried to cover it by clearing his throat.

"Then I had better wash. Where is the Governor's private bath?"

"This way, Your Highness."

Limen's private bath wasn't at all what she had imagined. When Morph opened the door, sulphur-scented steam rolled out, and Lexi had to fight the urge to gag at the stench. A rotting wooden deck ran from the doorway and surrounded the small blue pool, from which more steam was rising. Empty pegs lined one side of the room, with a pile of wet towels on the deck beneath. The other side of the room was lined with three shelves; the lower was rusted metal and held the largest collection of soaps Lexi had ever seen, in every conceivable shape, color, and scent, all in various stages of use.

"The Governor liked soap," Phemus commented unnecessarily.

Tiger's musical closed-mouth laugh sounded behind her, but Lexi resisted the desire to join him. It felt a little like violating Limen's privacy, stumbling upon his penchant for soaps. Hiding a smile, she took in the remaining shelves with their shampoos and colognes, then stepped onto the rotting deck. It creaked ominously beneath her, but held. Crouching, she stuck her fingers into the water and withdrew them immediately with a little yelp. The lovely blue water was scalding.

"It's so hot," Lexi murmured.

Phemus nodded knowingly. "It's the geyser."

Morph cleared his throat. "There's a little geyser in the back there that shoots up *really* hot water around midnight. The Governor always bathed after dinner so the water had plenty of time to cool."

"Did he use the life servant pool the rest of the time?"

Phemus shook his head. "The last governor could just signal. His grandfather used those," Phemus explained, pointing to the top shelf of cologne bottles.

Lexi took one down and sniffed a masculine, earthy musk, and replaced it. The next three smelled like alcohol, and the fourth just smelled rancid. "I think I'm going to have to bathe in one of the other pools," she decided, unconsciously rubbing her still-smarting fingers.

Phemus cleared his throat, "It's the men's hours at the life servant pool; but we can clear it out."

"Oh no, don't do that. I'll just use the in-season pool," she said as she turned back to her room for her bathing suit. She felt uncomfortably ostentatious parading through the halls with her four guards and searing stench. Every time her hair moved she caught the scent afresh, and her eyes were watering by the time she was able to shed her marked clothing and pull her hair back. There were only a few people in the pool, and they clustered in tight knots of conversation while they stared at her. Her streaming eyes made a blank expression impossible, so she simply ignored them and hurried through her bathing. She caught Tiger watching her once, but he simply returned to scanning the room looking taut and guard-like. Lexi hid a frown and finished washing, irritably pulling at the tangles in her hair. They only reminded her of Cam, then Cercy. The wet march back to her room with squeaky shoes was somehow worse. She needed a robe. She thought of Limen's moth-eaten one in his bedroom and suppressed a cringe.

Exasperated, she glanced at Tiger, then spoke to Phemus in an undertone. "I need a lady's maid."

Tiger's snort grated on her, but she resisted looking at him.

"Is there someone who wouldn't mind?" Though Clodi's offer had been sweet, Lexi didn't want to distract her from finding a mate.

Phemus shrugged. "The clerk would know."

The clerk gave me Psyche as a roommate, she thought, but managed a tight smile as they reached her room. Despite Clodi's snoring form, Tiger and Morph checked for intruders before heading out to the balcony. Lexi watched Tiger's lovely yellow and black wings glide into the early twilight before collapsing onto her bed.

Chapter Seventeen

Lexi awoke to a loud thunk at the balcony followed by a stream of profanity. Lexi and Clodi jumped out of bed, then stood looking at each other with startled, sleep-befuddled expressions.

"Are you okay in there?" Phemus called through the door before tentatively opening it.

There was another thud at the balcony door and Phemus crossed the room and threw the balcony doors open. Morph was leaning out and watching the courtyard below, several fist-sized rocks at his feet.

Morph turned to face the room, blood dripping down his face from a gash on his forehead. "It's fine now. Mr. Swallowtail got him."

"Got who?" Phemus asked, ignoring Clodi and Lexi's gasps. He yanked a gray handkerchief from his pocket and pressed it against his brother's forehead.

"The brother of the guy that got his wing broken yesterday," he answered, taking the handkerchief and glancing at Lexi.

"He threw rocks at you?" Lexi clarified.

Morph nodded, pulling the handkerchief away to see how much blood it had collected.

"Here," Clodi said, pressing white fabric against the wound. "I can take you to the infirmary."

"Yes, do. Thank you, Clodi," Lexi said, letting them pass before walking towards the balcony.

Phemus was out on the balcony, shutting the doors behind him.

"Wait," Lexi called.

Phemus opened the doors again and looked at her expectantly.

"Is Tiger injured?"

Phemus shrugged, "Didn't look it. He took the attacker inside the castle."

Lexi nodded her assent and Phemus closed the balcony doors. She dressed in a flurry, her tangled hair catching on buttons. She glanced at the cloudy mirror and shook her head. She looked unkempt, but couldn't spare the time to fix it. When she opened the door, the remaining guard briefly glanced at her face, then stared at her hair. Lexi groaned inwardly, but set a quick pace down the hall, winding her hair up the way she used to when she rode. She was partway to the dungeon before she realized she had nothing to secure her hair, so she let it unwind back into a snarled mess, and began to fly. The halls were sparsely populated, and most people stepped aside when they noticed her speed and expansive wings. Outside the display hall, she was forced to dodge the distracted conversationalists that spilled out, still shouting to be heard over the music. At the top of the dungeon stairs, a girl with vivid yellow and orange wings refused to make way, blocking the stairwell with her diminutive frame. Lexi landed in front of her. The honey blonde narrowed her green eyes and planted her feet.

"Please move," Lexi commanded, the polite words belied by her tone.

The girl's hands fisted and her lips trembled before a single word escaped. "Wing-breaker," she hissed, her high-pitched voice and short stature making her accusation almost comical.

Lexi eyed her white-knuckled fists and folded her wings tightly behind her. She considered retreat, but her need to make sure Tiger wasn't hurt overrode her caution. Drawing to her full height she leaned over the girl. "Get out of my way," she warned, imitating her mother's iciest tone and expression.

The girl's slitted eyes widened in surprise, and she stepped aside with a faltering step, her wings falling open. Lexi eyed her coldly as she walked around, her expression only slipping when she saw the white backside of the girl's wings. *Was she a white?* Lexi fought a little shiver, then flew down the dungeon steps just as Tiger started up them.

"Whoa," he said, catching her by the shoulders and stepping backwards before he set her down. "That's a little too fast," he chided, then walked around her to look up the staircase. "And where are your guards?"

"Oh," Lexi murmured, just as her winded guards jogged down the last set of steps. "I forgot," she admitted absently, looking him over for injuries.

Tiger drew his brows together until they nearly touched. "I'm fine," he growled. "Ora didn't even see me coming. He was too focused on pelting Morph."

"Ora is Coli's other brother?" Lexi clarified.

Tiger gave her a quick nod. "He's furious no one is imprisoned for his brother's broken wing."

Lexi frowned, then smoothed out her features as Pol walked up to the locked gate.

"What's Mr. Sulphur's punishment, Your Highness?" he asked.

This new responsibility fell heavily on her shoulders and she braced them involuntarily. "What is customary?"

Pol scratched his whiskered chin with a yellowed thumbnail. "Well now, that depends. Ambushed a guard with a weapon...is Morph hurt?"

"Bloody head wound, but he seemed okay," Phemus said, his fury sufficiently palpable that Lexi turned to look at him.

"Would you go check his condition, Phemus?" Lexi asked.

Phemus gave a jerky nod, spun on his heel, and fairly leapt up the dungeon steps.

"Hmm..." Pol continued. "Any violence against the guards has met with heavy sentences under the past two governors, but if you make it too long, then we have to deal with him as a life servant. It'd be different if he were a white, but Mr. Sulphur's anger problems aren't likely to change."

"How long has Ora been here?" Lexi asked.

Tiger twitched his tense shoulders in what passed for a shrug. "Couple of months, I think."

"Was he trying to get into the Princess' room or just hurt Morph?" Pol asked.

Tiger pressed his lips together until they began to turn white. "He threatened Lexi all the way down here."

Pol's grizzled frown deepened. "You could banish him from the castle."

Lexi's eyes widened. "Send him home without a mate?"

"Well, the last one we punished that way didn't go home. He hid out in the woods for a week, then attacked a poor girl before she even made it to the castle. He's in the lifer section now," Pol said nodding back over his left shoulder.

Lexi shuddered. "How many months in the dungeon do you recommend, then?"

Pol rubbed a hand over his balding head and sighed. "Six, but he's going to make a lousy life servant."

Tiger's wings twitched in agitation. "Coli's family tends to have three- to four-month seasons."

"Lousy life servant," Pol repeated, shaking his head, then looked at Lexi expectantly.

"Doesn't the governor usually hold a hearing for the longer sentences?" Lexi asked.

"Nope. Just passed sentences on a whim," the fourth guard spoke up, his face angry.

"Let it go, Heck," Pol chided. "You were so hot-headed, you didn't have a chance of getting a mate. Be happy you get to be a guard instead of a sewage sweeper."

Heck folded his gray-checked white wings behind him and glowered. "I'd kill myself before I did that," he mumbled.

Fighting to keep her face blank, Lexi drew up to her full height, taller than both Pol and Heck. "I will inform you when I've made my decision." She wanted to sweep dramatically from the room, but she lacked both the broad skirts and the space. She had to wait for Heck to move out of her way and the delayed exit felt all wrong, especially when she heard Tiger murmur, "Yes, my Queen," under his breath.

"You shouldn't return to that room," Tiger said out loud as he followed her up the stairs, Heck sullenly trudging behind him.

"Why? Does Coli have another brother?"

"You have too few guards to defend it adequately."

Lexi wanted to wave away his concerns, but the attack had frightened her, and she desperately needed to sleep. "Fine. Limen's room, then," she conceded.

There were two guards waiting outside Limen's room, which pleased Lexi until she recognized their uniform: the royal flying guard. She stopped so short that Tiger pressed a hand against her back to keep from colliding with her wings.

"Princess Lexi," one of them addressed her and came forward pulling an official-looking parchment from an inner pocket. "I have a message for you."

She ought to have said something, stepped forward, taken the message from his hands, anything, but she couldn't. It was Tiger that stepped forward and transferred the document from the guardsman's hands into hers. As his hand touched hers, he signaled subtly, the soothing scent softened the paroxysm of fear and failure into something more bearable.

"Thank you," she managed, and resumed her steps to the governor's room.

"Your Highness, the Governor is being attended by medics at the moment and can't be disturbed," the same guardsman informed her, blocking her entrance.

"The Governor? Has Limen returned?" Lexi could hear the shock in her voice, but couldn't contain it.

"He was attacked and badly beaten."

Lexi's mouth fell open, and she involuntarily took a step back before she recovered herself. "And you brought him back *here*?" she clarified, trying not to sound incredulous.

"I returned him to his post." There was something tight and almost chiding in his tone.

Lexi's nostrils flared at his subtle insolence and her spine elongated involuntarily. "I *relieved* him of his post," she retorted as she lifted her chin and stared down at him.

The guardsman blinked several times, started to speak, then slowly closed his mouth. His gaze drifted to the guardsman beside him in a mute cry for help.

"We found him alone and unconscious, Your Highness," the second guardsman explained.

"Alone?" Lexi whirled to Heck. "Find out who Limen was paying to escort him down the mountain and bring them to me." Turning back, she again addressed both guardsmen. "You didn't see Anna or Van West?"

They both shook their heads.

"They were traveling with the former Governor," she informed them. "Are there more of you? Someone must be sent immediately to locate them and ensure they are safe."

"There are eight of us, Your Highness," the first guardsman responded. "The other six are searching the castle for you."

"Send four of them after Anna and Van."

"Your Highness, we have orders to..."

"Send four of them after Anna and Van," she repeated, her clipped tone alarming both guardsmen. "*Now*," she added.

The second guard hurried away with a "Yes, Your Highness."

"Tiger, Limen needs more guards. Please see to it."

"I'm not leaving you alone," Tiger announced.

"I won't be alone. I'm going to stand right here until you return with more guards."

Tiger scowled. "Yes, my *Queen*," he whispered, turning away.

The first guardsman watched Tiger's retreat. "Is he in season?"

Lexi turned piercing turquoise eyes on him until he took a small step backwards. "I needed a flying guard," she explained icily.

The guardsman swallowed and bobbed his head in a nod.

Lexi looked down at the parchment in her hand and broke the royal seal with a rising sense of dread.

> *Daughter,*
>
> *It is not necessary for me to tell you the distress your actions have caused your Parents. You have been raised to know the duties of your Position. When you shirk them, the Kingdom suffers. I must insist that you now return home* immediately *with your Husband (after your conduct, I can regard Talan as nothing less). You need have no concerns about your probable pregnancy. The guardsmen have brought a cot to carry you down the mountain if you are already flightless. I expect you to leave within the hour.*
>
> *Queen Ami Monarch*

Lexi swallowed repeatedly, forcing the burning bile back to her stomach. She read it again and again, her horror finally softening to calm. "Must insist," though close, was not an order. She read it again. *This was not an order.* It was clear her mother very much wanted to give her one, and had meant for the letter to appear to be so, but the word "order" or "command" was missing. A smile encroached briefly on the corners of her mouth, and she wanted to hug her father. He had been very brave; nothing else could explain it. Tears of gratitude pricking her eyes, she folded the parchment carefully and slipped it into her pocket.

She caught the remaining guardsman looking at her expectantly and stared him down until he dropped his eyes. His submission made her cringe inwardly; she really needed to stop acting like her mother before it became a habit. Shaking off the persona, she tried to slump, but drew up immediately as three flying guardsmen marched towards her. One looked vaguely familiar, but the other two were strangers.

"Good," she nodded, turning towards the remaining guardsman. "You four will remain at the castle. The *former* Governor will need at least four guards outside his door at all times. Please coordinate with Pol when your men need to be relieved." She wanted to laugh at the remaining guardsman's piqued expression, but schooled her face into its usual blank.

"Y-y-your Highness," he stuttered. "The Queen said we would be returning with you immediately."

Lexi gave him her blandest smile. "You may return tomorrow, but *I* will remain here."

"But the letter…" he began until quelled with Lexi's coldest stare.

"Surely you do not imply that you are privy to its contents?"

His eyes widened in horror. Mail tampering was usually punished with incarceration. Tampering with the royal family's mail had once been punished by death when her great grandfather was king. "N-n-no," he stuttered, shaking his head vigorously.

"Good," she answered simply, looking up as Tiger approached with Pol and Charis.

Tiger shook his shaggy head at her, his obvious disapproval hitting Lexi like a slap. Her cheeks colored and she turned to walk away. She could hear Tiger's heavy step fall in line behind her and allowed herself a little sigh of relief.

"Your Highness?" A deferential voice called from behind her.

"Yes?" She turned to see the guardsman who had looked vaguely familiar. Flying guards were necessarily an ever-changing group, but occasionally an apprentice palace guard joined their ranks for the latter end of his season. She was certain she had seen this guardsman around the palace. Lexi's eyes squinted slightly as she struggled to recall his name.

Rather than introduce himself, he cleared his throat and held out a small envelope. Taking it from him, she glanced at the name scrawled across the front. It said "Raven" in her father's handwriting. Lexi's lower lip trembled and tears momentarily blurred her vision. The guardsman was already retreating back to his post, so she thanked him and quickly spun on her heel. She tucked the note in with her mother's hostile missive and resumed her brisk pace. Her exhaustion was making it harder to keep her emotions in check, and she blinked rapidly to prevent the betraying tears that begged to fall. As she opened the door of the queen's suite, a single tear slid down her face in open mutiny before she could dash it away. Clodi was not inside, and a breakfast tray was at the table. Lexi waited impatiently as Tiger swept the room with abrupt, irritable movements that betrayed his mood. His disapproval had morphed into a palpable anger that seemed to trail in his wake. When he attempted to slam the balcony doors, they bounced back open, caught on the rugs beneath them. Tiger muttered under his breath as he flung them out of the way. On another day it would be funny; today his anger coaxed Lexi into her own animosity.

"Did you have something you wanted to say?" she demanded, her abrupt ire evaporating her tears.

He opened his mouth, closed it, and released one note of a bitter musical laugh. "Yeah, I do. This is stupid and miserable. The Governor is back. Quit."

"I can't just quit."

Tiger rolled his eyes. "Yes, you can. Limen's wings are broken. The talk is all over the castle. He isn't going anywhere."

"But they hauled him halfway up the mountain..." she began.

"No, they didn't. They found him in a field half a mile from the castle."

"But Talan said..."

"He lied to you. *Again.*" Tiger shook his head angrily, then returned to his post on the balcony and shut the doors.

It was a full minute before Lexi could close her mouth. Why did Talan's lies still catch her by surprise? She grit her teeth and tore open her father's message.

Dearest Daughter,

I laughed for a full minute when I heard you're calling yourself Raven. I'm sure Raven would laugh, too, if I could make her understand. But I must warn you, Talan is spying on you, writing your mother regular letters of all that you do. Your mother is so infuriated that you're spending time with Tiger that Cercy is now restricted to her room, and a guard kept at her door to ensure she doesn't leave. I tried to talk your mother out of it, but she has convinced herself that Cercy is to blame for you leaving, and that it was she that aided you. She knows it was I, but she prefers Cercy be the scapegoat. She wanted to put her in the dungeon, but I refused. And I will not order you home. You deserve the same chance I had. If your mother says otherwise, disregard it. I will not waver on that point. But please dear, hurry a bit if you can. Your mother is so enraged at the situation that the servants are hiding from her, and even Juno is too frightened to come out of her guest room.

I love you!

Dad

Lexi was halfway to the balcony before she had finished reading. Yanking open the door, she thrust the letter at Tiger, and watched his smirk at the first two lines devolve into fury. He reread it once, then tossed the letter to her.

"I'm going back," he announced.

"How will that make it better?"

Tiger's expression vacillated between determination and indecision. "Lex, I need to make her..." he stopped and took a deep breath. When he spoke again, his eyes were on the heap of rug he had hastily flung aside. "There's a rumor going around that Ryp Leafwing is related to you. And his wings *do* look just like your mother's. Is he...is he your cousin?" He lifted his eyes to hers and held them.

Lexi swallowed, but didn't answer.

Tiger blew out a long breath that turned into a laugh. "I'm going to blackmail the Queen."

"Tiger..." She wanted to argue, chide, defend, but all her words died on her lips.

"What, Lex? There isn't another solution and you know it. Unless you're going to marry Talan, this is how it has to be."

"But she'll..."

"What? What can she do? Aren't Ryp's family *farmers*?" Tiger let out a hard laugh. "Is the Queen a farmer's daughter?"

When Lexi didn't answer, he broke into a guffaw.

"I can't imagine anything the Queen would hate more than people knowing that particular fact. Can you?"

Lexi pictured her elegant mother working a farmer's field and shook her head wearily.

"So I'm going home to blackmail the Queen. Want to come?"

Lexi gave him the weakest of smiles.

"I'm going to tell her we're engaged, so you should probably be there."

"What?" Lexi blushed hotly, her mouth hanging open as she took a ragged breath.

"You asked. I'm saying yes."

"But you..."

"I couldn't figure out how to make it work then," Tiger shrugged, then gave her a quick kiss. "Congratulations. You're engaged."

The tears were back. And the silly things began to stream down her face while she choked on a combination of sobs and laughter.

"Hmm...you need some sleep." Tiger kissed her forehead, then turned her towards her bed. "And when you wake up, you can tell everyone you were just kidding about being governor, and then we'll go home."

"I wasn't kidding," she protested, her voice thick with tears as she climbed onto her bed.

"Fine. You were ridiculously noble and foolish and controlling, but now there's no need for it."

Lexi frowned up at him. "This is how you talk to your fiancée?"

"Yep." He bent down and kissed her tenderly, his rough thumb brushing away her remaining tears.

Chapter Eighteen

Lexi woke with a smile on her face, though her skin felt tight from crying. She jumped up and flew across the room to fling open the balcony doors. Silvery blue wings spun around with the face of a flying guardsman she didn't recognize.

"Good afternoon, Your Highness," he said, bowing as deeply as the balcony railing would allow.

Hiding her disappointment, Lexi gave him a stately nod and slowly closed the doors. When she opened the door into the hallway, Beck turned to grin at her.

"Well, look who finally woke up!"

The two flying guardsmen standing beside him looked at Beck in horror.

"What? I always talk to her like this," Beck assured them, then turned back to address her. "Tiger is asleep. The *ex*-Governor would like to talk to you *in his room*." Beck wagged his eyebrows suggestively before breaking into laughter. "I'm teasing. He does want to talk, but his ribs are broken, so he can't get out of bed. But I'll still chaperone if it makes you uncomfortable."

"Thank you, Beck," Lexi answered, her blank expression never faltering.

"Aw, man, being governor is making you no fun," Beck grumbled in a too-loud undertone as Lexi shut the door.

She took a moment to smooth the clothes she had slept in, then took a comb to her disastrous hair. Halfway through, she opened the neglected breakfast tray and ate all the fruit, then went back to her tangles. When she finally finished combing, her scalp felt raw, but her hair fell to her waist in a shiny cascade. She marched out the door with a stately stride.

Beck kept pace beside her. "Your hair looks better. Do you still want a lady's maid? Phemus said you wanted one."

"I don't think I'll be staying long enough to require one."

"Then you *are* quitting! I wondered if you would with the old Governor back and the flying guardsmen here to collect you."

Lexi frowned momentarily, but kept her gaze straight ahead. "I have business at home that requires my attention."

"And will Mr. Swallowtail be escorting you as well?" Beck's eyes twinkled with the grin that had already claimed his mouth.

Lexi gave him a momentary glance and a furtive smile. "Yes."

"I knew it!" Beck crowed. "First time I saw you together, I knew it!"

Lexi gave him a silencing look with a head tilt to indicate the flying guardsmen trailing them.

"Oh, right," Beck said conspiratorially, his grin impossibly wider as he nodded at the guards outside Limen's room.

Charis turned and gave the door a complicated knock, then another guard opened it from the inside and waved her in. Despite the fresh bedding, the room reeked of antiseptic and despair. Limen lay face down on his bed, obscured by the wooden frames that held his broken wings in place. A medic stood up as she approached and offered her his stool. Limen gave him a low command that was little more than a moan, and the medic scurried from the room. Lexi sat, then bent forward to find the miserable patient beneath the expansive wing frame. His face was heavily bruised and bandaged; a single hazel eye squinted at her, the other swollen shut.

"Oh, Limen," she murmured. "What happened? Why didn't Van and Talan protect you?"

He grimaced and shut his eye for a moment. "They weren't with me." His voice sounded gravelly through his split lips.

"Why not?"

"We weren't traveling in the same direction," he answered evasively.

Lexi shook her head in confusion. "You were all going to the palace."

Limen opened his eye and gave her a beseeching look. "I had to go see them first," he whispered. "To make sure they wouldn't be a problem."

All of Lexi's sympathy hardened into contempt, the metal legs of the stool screeching against the flagstones as she moved away.

"You mean your harem. You were going to visit them," Lexi accused.

"Some of them would have followed me when they found out," he whined.

Lexi stood, shaking with temper. "You don't deserve the sacrifice I made for you. I'm taking it back. You deserve to be here. And you certainly don't deserve my sister or her love." She clenched her fists, wanting to hurt him, but realizing someone already had. She gazed at his battered body and slowly relaxed her hands, letting the acrimony drain out of her. The wing frames were vibrating with jerky movements that puzzled her until she heard the choked cry.

"You're right," Limen lamented.

Now the pity had hold of her again. "I'm sorry. I shouldn't have said that."

"Why? It's true." Limen's voice was distorted with the sobs he no longer tried to hide.

"But it wasn't kind." Lexi frowned at herself, grateful they were alone. "I don't think I have the authority to reinstate you, but I need to go home. I'll call another assembly." She shook her head. "What a mess."

"I don't want to stay here," Limen wailed as she walked to the door.

"I can't help you with that. Not anymore. Goodbye, Limen."

Putting the pleasant mask back on her face was more difficult than usual. She couldn't stop replaying her sister's agony at losing her husband and dreading Mona's suffering when she found out what he had become. She hoped for a fleeting second to keep the knowledge from her, but the fact that she was about to leave the Mating Mountain without an officially appointed governor, coupled with Talan's letters to her mother, made it seem impossible. Lexi allowed herself one last grimace, then opened the door. She nodded at the medic, who hurried back inside with a guard on his heels.

Beck looked uncharacteristically somber. "Did he tell you, then?"

Lexi waited until they were several steps away from the knot of guards before chastising him. "Why didn't *you* tell me?"

Beck shrugged. "Forbidden."

"He's *not* the governor; he can't order you."

Beck twisted up his mouth and one shoulder. "He kind of is. I mean, you'll leave soon, and I'll probably be taking his orders the rest of my life. So a little rebellion today? Probably not worth it in the long run."

Lexi gave him a little scowl before schooling her face once more. "So are the men who attacked him in the dungeon?"

Beck shook his balding head. "Nope. They were sneaky."

"What do you mean?"

"His escort; they're pretty honorable guys. When they realized where he wanted them to take him, they refused. And he couldn't order them, because you had relieved him of his position. So they returned to the castle."

"They left him alone?"

"The *ex*-Governor was all put out. He didn't want to fly back and have you find out what he was up to, but he didn't want to fly alone, either. So he demanded they go find him a new escort—confidentially, of course—and send them out to him. So they got back, started asking around, only no one they asked would agree. They insist they didn't give up his location. And the Governor never even saw his attackers—sorry, *ex*-Governor." Beck gave her a conciliatory smile. It was dark still, and they knocked him silly with the first hit."

Lexi swallowed back the compassion that made her want to weep for Limen, and returned to practical matters. "And you're certain it wasn't the escort?"

Beck looked thoughtful for a moment. "Their hands show no signs of fighting, and they don't seem the type, but I think they know something and aren't saying."

"Was Limen robbed as well?"

Beck nodded solemnly. "They took his money and his food."

"So the attackers have the money?"

Beck nodded. "But there's no place to spend it here, so they're unlikely to give themselves away. We searched the escorts' rooms and locked them up."

"What? On whose authority?" Lexi winced at her own imperious tone, and made a conscious effort to relax the rigid posture she had assumed.

Beck shrunk back a little and gave her an apologetic smile. "The *ex*-Governor's."

And the fury returned. It was irrational. She was about to give Limen back whatever authority she could restore and leave the mountain. Why did it matter if he had already taken it? Lexi sucked in a long breath and blew it out slowly.

"Fine. Call an assembly. Let's end this."

Lexi took her anger out on her clothes, tossing them about the room and shoving them roughly into her bag. Except for Tiger's old shirt, which was lovingly packed as she ran a finger down Cercy's careful stitches. It was odd going on a mission to rescue one mother from the other; Lexi took out the Queen's angry note and ripped it in half. She was about to tear it again when she heard Clodi greeting the guards outside her door. Releasing a sigh, Lexi folded the torn pieces together and put them back in her pocket just as Clodi walked in.

"Morph's okay," she announced. "He just left the infirmary, and he's not even dizzy anymore. But boy, is Phemus ornery! He kept ranting about in-seasons and their violent ways until Morph reminded him that he'd been just as violent when he was in season. Then they argued about which of them had been more violent until the medic made them stop on account of Morph not sitting still enough for his stitches. The medic said unless he wanted a zigzag scar on his face he'd better stop. So Morph stopped and Phemus went back to bellyaching." Clodi finally took a breath and noticed the packed bag that Lexi was just closing.

"That's a lot of clothes to take to the laundry," she commented.

Lexi stifled a grimace and turned to face her. "I'm leaving, Clodi."

"Right now? Are you getting married?" Clodi's cornflower-blue eyes lit up with joy as she clasped her hands together.

"No, not just yet."

"Then why are you leaving? Are your parents making you go back to the palace?"

"I suppose you could say that," Lexi conceded.

"Oh no! Does that mean you have to marry that horrible Talan? I don't think you should. He just isn't nice."

"I don't think I should either. I don't plan to."

"What are you going to do?"

Clodi looked so terribly concerned that Lexi patted her arm. "Tiger has a plan," she confided.

"Oh! Then you're going to marry Tiger?!" Clodi did a little jumping dance and gave her a fierce hug.

"Hopefully," Lexi mumbled into her shoulder, trying to gently extract herself.

Clodi immediately let go with an embarrassed laugh. "Sorry! I'm a hugger; can't help myself." Her tanned cheeks glowed a healthy red and she bobbed an awkward curtsy. "I know you don't want me to do that, either." She waved her hands in front of her tearing eyes. "Sorry, I'm a crier, too."

Lexi hefted her bag, then patted Clodi's arm again and smiled. "It was lovely having you as a roommate, Clodi. Good luck with Tull; I hope his wings heal quickly."

Clodi nodded as tears ran down her cheeks. "Bye," she managed, her voice breaking.

Lexi closed the door feeling guilty and sad, but she pushed it away and hefted her bag. Charis and two flying guardsmen looked at her expectantly. Giving them a nod, she marched down the hallway, the guards falling into her wake. At the stairwell she hesitated before a mischievous smile lifted one corner of her mouth. Instead of continuing on to the kitchens and then to Erynnis, she flew to Tiger's room. Heck's bored presence outside the door told her all she needed to know.

"I need to confer with the prisoner," she announced, opening the door.

Heck merely shrugged, then nodded at the flying guardsman who trailed her, and Charis, who jogged behind them. The door was closed again before they caught up.

Lexi stood just inside the room and inhaled deeply. Tiger's soft snores coupled with his soothing scent calmed all her senses and melted away her agitation. A silly grin flitted across her face at the thought of enjoying this every day for the rest of her life. She dropped her bag with a soft whump, and his big yellow wings that had been vibrating with every snore suddenly stilled. Lexi tiptoed across the room, edged around the top of his wings with her own tightly closed, and leaned in to kiss his stubbled cheek.

"Are we leaving now?" he asked sleepily.

"Soon," she whispered, carefully avoiding his blackened eye by kissing his ear.

He let out a single note of his musical laugh and covered his ear. "Tickles."

She kissed his hand, then stood back as he pulled himself up, stretching with cheerful groans. His sleep-mussed hair stood out at odd angles, and when she reached up to smooth it down, he caught her hands and placed them behind his neck.

"There," he murmured, kissing her gently.

Lexi sighed audibly and snuggled into his chest as he pressed a kiss into her hair.

The sharp rap at the door, followed by a loud and repeated throat clearing, broke them apart. When she opened the door, Charis looked apologetic and the flying guardsmen looked shocked.

Lexi gave them her coldest smile. "What is it?" The unscented air of the hallway brought back all her cares, tightening her muscles into a stately rigidity.

"The assembly," Charis reminded her.

Giving him a queenly nod, she turned to wait for Tiger.

"I'm not going," Tiger said, yanking on his boot. "I have something else I need to take care of."

Lexi frowned, worried he meant saying goodbye to his ex-girlfriend.

Seeing her expression, Tiger laughed. "It's not what you think."

Having her face turned back into the room was already having its effect. Relenting, she gave him a small smile. "Meet you in the throne room, then."

"Yep," he agreed.

Lexi took one last deep inhale, then closed the door behind her.

"Charis, do I have enough time before the assembly to get food and water for the journey?"

Charis shook his head and held out his hand. "I can do it for you, Your Highness."

"Thank you, Charis," she smiled, handing him her bag.

As he walked away, her two remaining guards drew closer. The crowds were all funneling towards the main entrance of the auditorium, but Lexi led them down to the stage door that Limen used. Outside the door, her remaining two flying guardsmen were waiting: the irritating leader and the guard who had brought her father's note. She smiled at the latter as he opened the door and preceded her onto the stage. Though the dark curtain walled off the sight of the audience, it did little to quell their sound. Their loud conversations bled through like the irritated buzz of a bee caught in clothing. When the two guards returned from sweeping the stage, they led her around the curtain to the wings. Curious, she peeked out at the audience. No one was sitting. Rumors were flying and twitching wings betrayed the general agitation. For a moment, she wished Limen were there to once again introduce her, but the thought dissolved into disgust as she remembered his behavior. At least he wouldn't be well enough to seduce anyone else before his season ended.

Beck and Pol sauntered up and down the aisles, quelling aggression by their mere presence. Beck caught her eye and grinned. He mounted the stage's side steps with a jaunty jog and joined her. "Want me to go warm them up with a few jokes?"

Lexi's mouth twitched in what Beck took to be a smile.

"See? I'm hilarious. Send me back out there."

Lexi allowed Beck a small smile, then walked out on the narrow lip of stage in front of the curtain. It had to be done. No sense delaying. She would have liked to have Tiger with her, but he was off on his mysterious errand, which had better not be Coli. A hush fell over the crowd, and most sat down as she stood serenely in the center of the stage.

"Hello again. I know it has only been one day since our last assembly, but circumstances have changed. Limen Viceroy has injured his wings, and is no longer able to travel down the mountain. Thus, I am restoring him to his position as governor. While he is recovering, his officiants will handle marriages and any other issues. Thank you." With the exception of a few harsh guffaws after Lexi mentioned Limen's broken wings, the audience had remained silent

357

until the end. Now the uproar of sound felt like a wave crashing into her. With a pleasant smile frozen on her face, she walked off the stage in a slow, stately pace that sped up the moment she was behind the curtain.

Beck clapped loudly. "Nicely done! Always leave them wanting more, I say."

The four guardsmen's eyes widened at his brash enthusiasm, but they remained silent, dutifully falling into position as Lexi exited the auditorium.

Lexi allowed herself a small sigh. "Fetch Talan," she commanded Beck.

"Must I? You could just leave him here to keep the Governor company."

"That would only be doing Limen an unkindness."

"True. Pretty unkind to me as well. Never mind, I'll happily fetch him if you promise to take him away."

"Quickly, please."

"Right! Keep forgetting you're leaving now…" Beck sprinted off towards the dungeon, letting his words trail behind him until his monologue was no longer discernable.

Lexi smiled after him, then hurried to the throne room with the guardsmen fore and aft. As before, they intersected the crowds before reaching the throne room, but the prevailing mood seemed curiosity rather than violence.

"Is it true somebody beat the Governor up?"

"Is he going to die?"

"Are you staying?"

Rather than address their questions, Lexi increased her pace, feeling the guards draw closer as the crowd pressed in. It was a relief to escape into the throne room and lock the doors behind them. A few people knocked, but the Old Castle guards only advised them to make an appointment at the officiants' office. Lexi shoved the curtain aside that hid the door; someone must have drawn it again in anticipation of Limen's reinstatement. Lexi looked around for Tiger and stopped dead at the vivid red wings that occupied the center of the room. Lexi gasped, her hand reflexively touching the pocket that held her mother's torn note. The owner of the wings executed a slow turn, and Lexi began breathing again.

"Mr. Leafwing, why are you here?"

"He's coming with us," Tiger announced, stepping out from behind the officiants' curtain.

"Why?"

"Your cousin is in season. Naturally he's going to the palace to find a mate befitting his station."

Lexi's eyes widened in pleading horror as she looked from Tiger to Ryp, then took in all the listening guards. Swallowing, she forced her face back into a neutral expression and drew herself up. "Of course. I welcome the company, cousin."

Ryp smirked at her. "Yes, my little *dalliance* here is over. It's time to be serious."

Lexi could feel her eyes widening again. She had never had so much difficulty remaining outwardly calm. Her father would be so hurt that she had betrayed her mother's secret.

The officiants' curtain trembled, then seemed to cough.

"Erynnis?" Lexi guessed, managing a strangled smile for the elderly man when he stepped out and gave her a deep bow.

"Your Highness had some...er...personal belongings in the safe," he said, skittering forward to hand her a small cloth bag, then backing away with his head bowed.

Lexi glanced into the bag, finding her father's ripped signature atop the wad of cash he had given her. "Thank you, Erynnis. I need to return my keys to you, but Charis has them."

Erynnis looked scandalized for a moment, then recovered himself with another deep bow. "Very good, Your Highness."

There was an awkward moment of silence where Lexi could hear the slight wheeze in Erynnis' breathing, and Heck cracking his knuckles behind the partial cover of the open curtain. Lexi's eyes drifted to Ryp's wings, then Tiger's face as he tightened the straps of his bag around his shrinking waistline. Lexi remembered the in-seasons' food issue with a guilty sigh. She glanced at Erynnis and considered bringing it up again, but it was Limen that must be swayed. She gave her head a barely perceptible shake and determined to address the issue with her father...when he finally forgave her for betraying her mother's secret. Lexi glanced furtively at her cousin's unperturbed expression, then Tiger's false bravado. That was the expression he wore when breaking a new horse to the saddle: all determination and suppressed fear. She swallowed on a suddenly dry throat and fisted her hands around the top of the cloth bag.

When an odd knock sounded, she released the breath she hadn't realized she had been holding. Charis entered and wordlessly returned her pack that was now much heavier. She tucked the cloth bag inside, then removed the keys and handed them to Erynnis with a forced smile.

"Thank you, Your Highness." He looked at her with sharp, watery eyes—unsaid words filling out his hollow cheeks. His lips twitched, but he bowed a third time rather than speak.

There was yet another odd knock at the door and Talan irritably pushed through the guards when it opened.

"*Now* you can leave," Beck quipped, trailing Talan with his arms spread wide.

Talan whirled around to menace the smaller man with his height. "You know, if you were one of *my* servants, you would quickly learn to keep your mouth shut."

"Doubtful," Beck laughed merrily, allowing flecks of saliva to spatter Talan's face.

Threats and curses mingled together and erupted from Talan's mouth as he shoved Beck backwards, bringing Charis and Heck surging forward.

"Talan," Lexi warned. "I could always leave you behind."

"That could be fun," Beck joked.

Talan looked momentarily startled before regaining his equanimity. He backed away from the guards, then held out his bag to one of the flying guardsmen. "Carry this for me."

Tiger and Beck snorted their disgust and Lexi took a deep breath. The guardsman who had brought her father's note took the bag and began puzzling how to strap it over his own. Lexi gently took it from his hands and gave it back to Talan.

"You will carry your own bag," Lexi announced, nodding at Charis to open the balcony doors.

"Princess," Talan protested. "These are servants and should be treated as such."

"They are here to protect me, Talan, not to be pack mules," she chided, wondering for the first time if Talan had carried his own belongings before they reached Lady West's estate.

Rather than strap on his bag, Talan glanced around the room and caught Tiger's deep scowl. "You're bringing the stable boy?"

"Talan..." Lexi cautioned.

Rather than heed her warning tone, Talan smugly held out his bag to Ryp.

"That's the Queen's nephew," Tiger said, knocking Talan's bag away. "He's not your servant."

Talan dropped his bag, his mouth opening and closing as he eyed Ryp, then looked to Lexi for confirmation. Knowing she couldn't erase her emotional turmoil from her expression, Lexi avoided Talan's gaze by fiddling with her strap.

Beck chortled, sensing a joke. When no punch line followed, his amusement faltered. "Wait. What?"

Talan cleared his throat awkwardly, then stooped to recover his bag. "I didn't even know the Queen *had* a nephew and suddenly he's *here*? That's odd."

"Unlike Van, I felt it best to keep my identity a secret," Ryp explained as he sauntered towards the balcony, giving Talan a good look at his wings.

Whatever Talan had been about to say died on his lips, and he abruptly pressed them together.

"You're a noble?!" Beck blurted.

Before Beck could say anything else, Lexi interrupted him with a brief hug. "Thank you, Beck. I'm going to miss you."

"Your cousin was here the whole time? Was he secretly protecting you?" Beck continued, nonplussed.

"You did such an excellent job, Beck, that there really wasn't anything for him to do," Lexi assured him.

Two of the flying guardsmen and Ryp had already flown from the balcony and Lexi joined them, Tiger beside her. Talan sulkily strapped on his bag, demanding that the last two guardsmen not leave before him.

Lexi allowed herself a little groan. "It's going to be a long trip," she whispered to Tiger.

He frowned back at Talan and merely nodded.

"And we need to talk," she added in an undertone, looking at Ryp's scarlet wings waving like warning flags in the twilight.

"We need him," Tiger assured her, "or this won't work."

"But you *told*," Lexi protested, her face betraying her hurt and anxiety.

"Yes, that he's a *noble*."

Lexi schooled her face as she mulled that, then Talan flew into her personal space and interrupted all thought with a cloud of his hickory and clove scent.

"Despite the presence of the stable boy, I assume our return means you're going to acknowledge our marriage?" Talan took her hand and attempted to kiss it before she yanked it away.

"You lied to me again, Talan," Lexi hissed. "And you've been reporting everything I do to my mother."

Talan paled, then swallowed. "But the Queen demanded regular reports. I couldn't help that."

"You might have told me. And you lied after you swore you would be honest from now on."

"What..." Talan began, swallowing again.

Tiger snorted. "He doesn't even know *which* lie you're talking about."

Talan glared at Tiger, but didn't speak.

"Get away from me, Talan," Lexi ordered quietly.

"I haven't *lied*," he attempted.

"You didn't fly halfway down the mountain with Limen," she accused.

"That wasn't my secret to tell. A gentleman covers for another gentleman's indiscretions."

Lexi spoke through clenched teeth. "Neither of you are gentlemen."

"I doubt we share the same definition of the word." Talan glanced at Tiger as his face lit up with spite. "You know she'll never let you marry this filthy *servant*. She'll lock him up in the dungeon the moment you get back, and you'll still have to marry *me*."

Talan's wrath had attracted the group's attention, and everyone's flight slowed as they watched him.

Lexi gave the group a pleasant smile and addressed the flying guardsmen in the same tone she might use to offer dessert. "Mr. Admiral has expressed the desire to fly separately. Would one of you please volunteer to escort him?"

"You can't make me leave this group," he hissed. "I'm essentially your husband. Where you go, I go."

Her pleasant facade slipped. "You are *not* my husband and you *never* will be. Leave. Now."

Tiger and Ryp crowded Talan, forcing him to move away for adequate wing space.

"I'm not *allowed* to leave you!" he yelled. "The Queen commanded me to stay with you."

"Then you will show my cousin the respect she deserves," Ryp asserted, his frigid tone and glacial expression disturbingly similar to the Queen's.

Talan paled, slowing his pace until he flew behind the group.

Tiger snorted out a laugh. "I think he's afraid of you, Ryp."

Ryp smirked, then flew up next to Lexi. "Did you actually agree to marry him?"

She frowned. "He was the only noble in season."

Ryp shook his head. "And will my choices be similarly limited and distasteful?"

"I couldn't say."

"Hmm," Ryp answered, his expression unreadable.

Puzzled, she turned to Tiger. "Why is he doing it?" she mouthed.

"Tell you later," Tiger mouthed back.

Lexi grimaced and bit at a manicured nail. Every conversation she wanted to have was impossible just now. The encroaching darkness frustrated further lip reading, and the group flew too closely for even whispers to remain private. She began to torture herself by imagining the conversation she would have with her father. Every version ended horribly. Scowling into the chilly night, she nibbled another nail.

Chapter Nineteen

The quaint little town of Scio was well-lit despite the early morning hour. Though its population was small, it had two inns to cater to the needs of in-season migrators. Few vacancies and Talan's insistence on his own room forced the group to split between them. Lexi was too afraid to object, as her cousin would be Talan's obvious choice of roommate if forced to share. She had yet to learn Ryp's reasons or his concocted backstory, but she was too exhausted to contrive a private meeting. She followed an overly-eager proprietress into an adequate room and collapsed onto a musty bed. The owner was still thanking her obsequiously when she drifted off into a dreamless sleep.

Lexi awoke to the same voice cataloguing the dishes. A heavy clatter followed. Lexi rose up to protesting muscles and clothing that had dried stiff with her perspiration. Her mouth was parched and her stomach whined. Lexi rubbed her eyes, hoping the stimulation would make them more amenable to opening. Finally, she swallowed a yawn and turned her attention to the waiting proprietress. The woman beamed at her and bounced on her toes making her speckled wings tremble.

"We made everything we could think of, because we didn't know what a member of the royal family would eat, because you're the first one to ever visit!" Her sentence ended in a squeak and she slapped a hand over her mouth and giggled, belying her middle-age.

Lexi managed a gracious thank you before it was interrupted by another yawn.

"The yellow-winged gentleman with the black eye sent me to wake you because everyone is ready, and he's impatient."

Lexi wanted to laugh at this description of Tiger until she remembered *why* he was so anxious to get going. "What time is it?"

"Lunch time," the proprietress said, nodding at the enormous tray.

Lexi groaned inwardly; she hadn't meant to sleep so long.

"May I assist you with dressing? My mother was once a maid to Lady Nessa."

"No, thank you. Please inform the yellow-winged gentleman that I will be ready soon."

The woman bounced on her toes and launched herself into a wing-shuddering run across the room. At the door, she looked back to bob a sideways curtsy, then spent a full minute gently opening and closing the door so as not to make any noise.

A genuine smile lit Lexi's face before further movement erased it in a groan of pain. She had flown far too long yesterday. The few paltry breaks had allowed for little recovery and no private conversations. The punctilious flying guardsmen accompanied her everywhere with little allowance for personal space.

Peeling off her sweat-petrified clothing from the day before, she quickly washed and dressed. She had just finished braiding her hair when someone knocked.

"Cousin, might I speak with you a moment?" Ryp asked from the other side of the door.

Lexi let him in, noting that all four guardsmen stood at attention in the hallway. She gave them a pleasant nod and closed the door.

"I'm sorry I didn't believe you before," he began. "I meant to come talk to you after the first assembly, but I didn't know what to say. I still don't."

"Why are you going to the palace?" Lexi blurted, her heart giving an anguished thump in her chest as she pictured her father's disappointed eyes.

"Isn't that the plan? To blackmail my aunt so you can marry Tiger?"

Lexi covered her face with both hands, feeling the pull on her sore back muscles. "I don't want it to be."

"Hmm...well, that actually makes me feel better. I don't really want to be an object of blackmail nor meet my aunt, *the Queen*, in a manner that is likely to enrage her."

Lexi dropped her hands. "You think the Queen is given to rages?"

Ryp shrugged. "My father always called Ami his personality twin; the stories of their hot-headed battles are my favorites. I assume she hasn't changed that much?"

Lexi gave him a small, non-committal smile. "I'd like to hear those stories. She never talked about her family."

Ryp frowned. "She's *really* not going to enjoy meeting me."

"Then why are you doing this?"

Ryp glanced at the elaborate lunch tray and pointed. "May I?"

"You haven't eaten?"

"I have, but I've never even seen most of this food before. Would it be horribly rude if I tasted everything?"

Lexi laughed and motioned him to the table. He sat eagerly and began pulling various dishes towards him.

Ryp spooned some sort of pudding into his mouth and shut his eyes for a moment. "Mmm...now *this*," he said, indicating the dishes in front of him, "is just one of the many reasons I want to go."

"You're going to the palace for the food?" Lexi's lips twitched as she held back a laugh.

"Partly," he admitted, tasting something else. "See, at home, we have boiled oats for breakfast, fruit and cheese for lunch, and soup for dinner. Every. Day. It's not my mother's preference, it's just what we can afford. We're poor." He shrugged as he scooped some sort of vegetable puree into his mouth. "And my dad is all prideful about it. He insists that I take over the family farm, even though I hate farming," he complained, waving a spoon at her. "And then I'll be just as poor as he is, shouting furiously at the weather the rest of my life."

Lured in by his obvious enjoyment of the food, Lexi took the stool across from him and began sampling a fruit pastry without interrupting his narrative.

"And the Mating Mountain wasn't turning out like I expected, either. Terrible food. And not one pheromone match in two months." He stopped to thoughtfully chew a piece of meat. "The Leafwings usually have two- to three-month seasons, in case you didn't already know, so I was getting seriously worried that I was going to end up being a life servant— one of the few professions that is actually worse than being a farmer. So when Tiger came to talk to me, it seemed like a pretty good solution to my problems." He shrugged and popped a dumpling in his mouth.

"So you're going to jump into an arranged marriage and pretend to be a noble the rest of your life?"

He shrugged. "My aunt is the Queen. How am I not a noble? I may have to gloss over some details of my youth, but honestly, I do that anyway. As to the marriage, Tiger said I could arrange that for myself. Was he lying?" Ryp looked slightly perturbed as he gnawed off the end of a sourdough baguette.

"*If* mother acknowledges you as her nephew, she will likely insist on arranging your marriage."

"But I would get *some* say in the matter, wouldn't I?"

Lexi shrugged and hid a grimace from the pain of the movement."Depends on the selection."

Ryp stopped eating and folded his arms. "So what are my choices?"

"I've been gone for a week," she reminded him as she tore some sticky bread and nibbled on it.

"What were my choices when you left?"

"Juno Buckeye and Delpha Sister."

He rolled his eyes. "Their names mean nothing to me. Tell me about them."

"Juno is beautiful, and Delpha is sweet."

"So Juno *isn't* sweet and Delpha *isn't* beautiful?"

Lexi covered her frown with another bite.

"Hmm. Well, still isn't worse than being a life servant." Ryp unfolded his arms and leaned forward. "If we're going to pull this off, it would help if I looked the part."

Lexi eyed his clothes and rough hands. "You'll need a suitable hobby to explain your calluses."

"Do mending fences and plowing count as hobbies?"

She smiled. "No. But woodworking and gardening are fairly acceptable; let's call it that. As to your clothes..." Lexi retrieved her bag and extracted the wad of money her father had given her. "You'd need a tailor to really look the part, but take this," she said, giving him half the money, "and buy whatever makes you look more like Limen, Van, and Talan."

He nodded and took the money. "I'll return whatever I don't spend."

"No, don't. It's best if Talan and the guards see that you have money. And if things go badly, it will make your journey back to the Old Castle more pleasant."

"And what would you say are the odds of this going badly?"

She wanted to give him a serene smile and assure him that everything would be fine, but it felt terribly dishonest when his risk was so high. It was not impossible that her mother would lock him away in a dark corner of the dungeon or even have him put to death for being part of Tiger's blackmail scheme. Panic seized her as she thought of what her mother might do to Tiger and Cercy.

Ryp stood, still looking expectantly at her for an answer.

Hiding her panic, she gave him a blank expression and shook her head. "I don't know."

"Hmm. Fly on without me," he said, grabbing a frosted pastry and walking to the door. Opening it, he looked back. "I'll make some purchases and catch up."

As the door closed behind him, Lexi wondered if she had seen the last of her cousin. Though she found him oddly pleasant, she hoped she had. She couldn't bear the thought of her father's disappointment when he realized she hadn't kept her mother's secret.

"Where is your cousin?" Talan demanded.

"Making some purchases. He'll catch up to us later," Lexi informed the group.

Talan looked up and down Scio's main street with a critical eye. "Here? He's shopping *here*?"

"We all have to make do with less than ideal circumstances," Lexi remarked, letting her icy gaze rest on Talan.

Talan frowned, then jumped into the air. Lexi could see Tiger shaking his head in her peripheral vision, but ignored him. She followed Talan into the air, gasping at the pain of using her sore muscles.

"Isn't that exactly what the Queen said when she took away your riding privileges?" Tiger asked, outpacing her with rapid wingstrokes.

Lexi frowned and called after him. "You know it is; you *heard* her."

He suddenly turned around, forcing her to slow or collide with him. "And yet, you're repeating it."

"He needs to be put in his place," she hissed, wary of the guards now flying around her.

"I agree, but can't you do it without morphing into the Queen?"

"Apparently not," Lexi snapped, then felt immediately contrite. Flying closer, she touched his fingers, her wide wings brushing his. "Sorry."

Tiger gave her a forgiving smile, his bruised eye wreathed in putrid greens and yellows. The sight of it threw Lexi back to the Old

Castle courtyard and the fight with Coli's brother. She shivered as she remembered the sickening sound of the punches, and then Talis' broken wing. She pressed her lips together. She *would not* feel guilty about that. Lexi's hands unconsciously tightened into fists. Tiger took her hand, forcing her fingers to unclench, and giving them a little squeeze. Alarmed, Lexi glanced around at the guards, then Talan. Her wings brushed Tiger's again, this time uncomfortably, and Lexi tightened her strokes to rapid flutters, her hand limp in Tiger's grasp.

"It's not much of a secret," Tiger assured her. "Not after Talan's tantrum yesterday. And I can't figure any advantage to hiding our engagement. Can you?"

"But the display laws..."

"You're surrounded by uniformed flying guardsmen; what crown agent in his right mind would object?"

"And Talan..."

"Has made you miserable enough. Stop giving him that kind of power. Ignore him."

"But he'll come after you," Lexi objected, grateful that Talan was still leading the party and hadn't turned around.

"Let me worry about that."

"I...can't," Lexi apologized, pulling her hand away. She stretched her wings out into broad strokes, breathing deeply to calm herself.

"Fine," he said, his face stony as he fell behind the group.

Lexi groaned inwardly. It wasn't that she didn't believe Tiger could defend himself if Talan attacked him, it was just that wings were so fragile. And if blackmailing her mother didn't go as planned, she hoped Tiger would be able to fly back to the Old Castle, find a mate, and live a happy life. Tears sprang to her eyes as she realized she was preparing for failure. Blinking rapidly, she willed the tears away and increased her speed until she passed Talan.

Ryp caught up to the group just before nightfall, resplendent in new clothes and a fine leather bag. Lexi looked over his clothing with a critical eye; it was almost right. The cut of the shirt and pants were fashionable, but the fabric was poorer quality, and the fit wasn't ideal. But Ryp seemed so pleased with his purchases that Lexi merely gave him a nod and a smile when he looked to her for approval.

Tiger's steady scowl lifted at Ryp's arrival, and they traveled the next few hours in pleasant conversation until Talan could stand it no longer.

"Why are you conversing with this stable serf?" Talan groused, somehow managing to sound both demanding and obsequious.

Ryp raised a single eyebrow and looked askance, letting the silence become awkward until Talan finally flew back to the front of the group.

Tiger erupted into his closed-mouth, musical laughter. "You look just like your aunt when you make that face." Tiger tried to imitate it, raising both eyebrows rather than one and provoking Ryp's laughter.

Talan glared back at them, then quickly looked away when Ryp caught his gaze. Tiger guffawed and Ryp joined him. Their boisterous laughter slowed their flight and both men lost altitude before they regained control of themselves. Lexi watched them with wistful eyes until she noticed the guardsmen had all slowed down to match *her* distracted pace. Giving them a bland smile, she sped up again.

When darkness fell, they stopped in a scenic hamlet appropriately named Edgewood. The forest it bordered was dotted with towering redwoods and crowned with a glacier-topped inactive volcano. The mountain reminded Lexi of the Old Castle, and she felt a momentary longing to return until she remembered Cercy's plight. She glanced at Tiger surreptitiously: his sandy locks were a mess and his lovely wings shook with laughter at something Ryp had said. Glancing away, she noticed Talan watching them as well, his face pinched in sanctimonious disapproval and envy. Lexi resisted a scowl and followed a fawning hotel manager to her room for the night. The place was rather lovely, and her room was only slightly less grand than her own at the palace. She bathed off her grime in a small private pool, then sank into the welcoming mattress. Despite her exhaustion, sleep was slow in coming and peppered with nightmares when it did. In one, her mother turned into a dragon that burned off Lexi's wings with her fiery breath. In another, Lexi *was* the dragon and Tiger slayed her. Troubled, she abandoned sleep before dawn and paced her room, whispering speeches intended for her mother while she stretched her aching back muscles. By first light, she came to the exasperating conclusion that she had no idea what to say. Thoroughly vexed, she abandoned the pursuit and went looking for food. Two sleepy flying guardsmen straightened to attention when she opened the door.

"Do you need something, Your Highness?" the guard that had carried her father's note asked.

"Breakfast," she said briskly, marching down the hallway with enough speed to blow her wings back. She could hear the guards' heavy footfalls behind her, one struggling to keep up until he took to the air. As she walked, she chided herself for not learning their names and for behaving so imperiously. When she reached the dining room, she invited them to sit with her, belatedly noticing that Tiger sat by himself at a corner table. Apologizing, she excused herself and joined him.

"Good morning," she said warily.

Tiger gave her a half smile. "You couldn't sleep, either?"

Lexi shook her head. "Too many dragon dreams."

Tiger let out a one-note laugh. "Why dragons?"

Lexi shrugged. "Because they're scary and destroy lives."

"In their imaginary world?"

"And mine," she nodded.

Tiger took her hand, his large palm enveloping hers. "There are no dragons in your world."

Lexi gave him a tight smile. "Sorry about yesterday."

Tiger waved his other hand dismissively in the air to let her know it was forgotten.

"I'm not myself lately," she admitted, watching Tiger's lips spread wide in a suppressed smile.

"Being a ruler doesn't suit you."

Lexi's mouth dropped open, and she slipped her hand out of his to smack him on the shoulder, making him erupt into a surprised guffaw that petered out into musical laughter.

"What? It doesn't," he said, flinching away from a second smack and eyeing the flying guardsmen, who were fast approaching their table.

Lexi followed his gaze and turned to look at them. "I'm fine," she assured them, waving dismissively. Turning back to Tiger, she let out a groan. "I don't want to live like this. At home, I would be sneaking out to the stables to torment you and ride Raven. But here and *there*," she nodded in the direction of the Old Castle, "I'm all out of escapes." She slipped a fingernail into her mouth and bit it absently.

"You wouldn't need the escapes so desperately if you were doing something you enjoyed. I didn't need them. They were fun, but I didn't *need* them."

"Not even after an afternoon of helping spoiled rich boys with imperious manners?"

"Only when they broke my nose."

Lexi laughed, then immediately sobered. "I'm afraid of what's going to happen when we get to the palace."

Tiger nodded. "I can see why you might be concerned."

"The important thing is that we get your mother free."

Tiger looked at her through half-lidded eyes. "That's *one* of the important things. You have that same look on your face when you told the cook *you* had knocked over the cake."

"It was *my* fault. I threw the ball too near it. We shouldn't have been playing in the reception hall anyway."

"It was raining," he argued, scrutinizing her face until she looked away. "Don't even think of sacrificing yourself because you feel guilty."

Lexi's cheeks heated and she stared down at her bitten nails.

"Lex," he said, covering her hands with one of his. "Everything is going to be okay."

Lexi shook her head. "You shouldn't say that; you can't know that."

Lifting her chin, he forced her to look at him. "It's going to be okay. I know it."

"How?" There was so much anguish and fear in that one word that Lexi flinched at the sound of it.

Now Tiger's cheeks lit with a ruddy blush and he lowered his voice. "Uh, because I, um, I prayed about it. And I...I feel all calm and peaceful when I think about it." He shifted on his stool, making it creak loudly.

"I didn't know you prayed. My father asked me to pray before I agreed to marry anyone."

"Did you?"

Lexi shook her head. "I forgot."

"You could always do it now."

"But you're watching me."

"So?"

Lexi folded, then unfolded her arms. "I can't. I'll do it later."

Tiger's protest was interrupted by their breakfast as a fair-haired girl slid plates from a large tray, wobbling them down until they clattered on the table with her apologies.

When they finished eating the decadent food, Lexi didn't feel like flying at all; even walking away from the table seemed a terrible exertion and her back ached every time she moved her wings. She looked around the dining room, hoping the others were still sleeping. But Ryp and Talan were just finishing their meal in stony silence, and the two remaining guardsmen had joined the others and were furiously stuffing food into their mouths. Lexi brushed her hand against Tiger's, smiling when he grinned at her. Then the guardsmen crowded behind them and the moment was over.

Back in her room, Lexi repacked the few belongings she had used overnight, and attached her bag. Then she examined herself in the mirror. The untailored clothing she had purchased was going to infuriate her mother. She fingered the collar of her navy button-down shirt that was plain enough to belong to a man. This was not the right way to begin the most difficult negotiation of her life. Unstrapping her bag, she dug to the bottom and retrieved her mother's red dress.

Chapter Twenty

The scenery beneath her was becoming familiar, and Lexi's heart beat faster with each recognized landmark. Talan had argued that they should stop and rest at his family's estate, but was met with obstinate silence each time he suggested it. Finally, he had stopped speaking altogether, and was clearly sulking. It amazed Lexi that she had ever found him attractive, that a pheromone scent could have overridden years of observing his character. He had stopped signaling her— likely a combination of resignation and fear his violation of display laws would be reported to her mother. Lexi allowed herself a grim smile; he was the same spoiled, mean-spirited snob he had always been. She wiped her mouth wishing she could erase the kisses he had placed there. Mistaking her action, one of the flying guardsmen held out his canteen. Lexi waved it away and forced herself to fly faster.

Though their journey was an urgent one, this final day of travel had inspired such reticence that she continually caught herself flying at half speed. Partly because she had yet to do as her father had asked and Tiger had recommended: pray about her choice. She had started in her room after her conversation with Tiger, but she felt silly. When Ryp knocked to tell her the group was ready to leave, she was relieved. And none of their breaks since then had afforded her sufficient time and privacy to continue. Lexi squelched the frown she wanted to indulge, a slight narrowing of her eyes the only sign of it. She thought of her father and his silent prayers. She could do that, but closing her eyes would be foolish, if not dangerous. Well, she would just have to do it with her eyes open and hope it worked. She definitely didn't want to face her father under these circumstances *and* tell him that she had ignored his advice.

Squinting, she tried to clear her mind of all the panicky thoughts that beset her. With those gone, she was aware of an underlying sense of guilt for her domineering behavior the past few days. She *still* didn't know the names of the guards. Pasting on a cheerful smile, she turned to the guard who had offered his canteen. It was the bossy guard that she had argued with when he first arrived.

"I must apologize; I still don't know your name."

He looked startled, and a pouty Talan looked back to glare at both of them.

"It's Ebis," he said hoarsely, then cleared his throat. "Your Highness."

"And where are you from Ebis?"

"Uh, Trout Lake."

"Are you a fisherman?"

"Uh, no. There isn't actually a lake; I don't know why we call it that."

Ebis appeared somewhat demoralized by this admission, so Lexi turned to the next nearest guard. "How about you?" she asked the blue-winged guard that had been guarding her balcony in Tiger's place.

"I fish," he answered, smiling.

"So do I," the third guard chimed in to the accompaniment of Talan's exasperated grunt.

"I don't," the fourth guard added, and Lexi turned to smile at him. This was the gray-winged guard that had carried her father's note.

"Were you part of the castle guard before your season?" she asked.

He nodded happily. "I was, and I'll return to it after my season."

"Have we met, then?" Lexi examined his good-natured face and pale gray eyes that matched his wings.

"Oh," he blushed, "yes, but you might not want to remember."

"Why is that?"

"Uh," his blush deepened, making his eyes more remarkable. "The Queen sent the guard to fetch you."

Now she remembered, and it wasn't a pleasant memory. Her sister Dana had just given birth to triplet girls, and her mother had not hid her disappointment well. She lectured Lexi about the importance of producing an heir, taking no risks in her activities, and the level of decorum that befits the mother of a king. She strongly recommended that Lexi stop riding Raven in favor of a smaller, gentler horse, and then only at a slow walk. Lexi had endured the lecture and nodded at appropriate times, then snuck off to ride Raven at a breakneck speed as soon as she was able. Discovering her absence, her mother had sent members of the apprentice guard out on horseback to bring her home. *This* flying guardsman had been part of the group that had found her. She relived that perfectly aggravating and absurdly slow procession back to the palace surrounded by the pupa guards. After that, the Queen had only allowed her to ride once a week with a groomsman on a lead rope. With effort, she suppressed her frown.

"Sorry."

Lexi waved a hand at him. "You were only fulfilling your duty."

He nodded, but the group fell back into silence.

Her guilt partially alleviated, Lexi tried to pray again. She told God that she had decided to marry Tiger, and met with silence. A little discouraged, she began to enumerate the reasons she had chosen Tiger: he was her best friend, he helped her find the humor and fun in life instead of focusing on the worry, and he was a good kisser. That last one had her laughing to herself, then running through each of their kisses, one by one, with a rather dazed smile on her face. When she finally remembered that she was praying and returned to the task, she kept it simple: *God in Heaven, I love Tiger. I want to marry him. Any objections?* This time Lexi felt a humor in her mind that was not her own, like a kind chuckle that warmed her heart. Suddenly tears were streaming down her face, despite the intense joy that had overcome her. She felt loved, she felt heard, and she knew God was just fine with her marrying Tiger, even if her mother wasn't. She looked over at Tiger, trying to catch his eye, but his grim expression and intense focus didn't waver. Following his gaze, she saw the palace gate in the distance. Swallowing back her emotions, Lexi quickly dried her tears and steeled herself for the unpleasantness ahead.

As they approached the walls, the palace guards let out a shout that was quickly answered by Ebis. The guards waved them on and they flew directly over the massive gate. As they passed over the palace grounds, Lexi recognized her riding paths through the royal forest. It was odd seeing them from this perspective and without Raven. A genuine smile twitched the corner of her mouth at the thought of seeing her horse again. She wanted to clasp Tiger's hand and squeeze it, but she settled on a furtive grin instead. This time Tiger noticed and gave her a half smile before his features hardened back into stern concentration. Lexi watched him a moment longer. His lips were moving slightly, his eyebrows occasionally going up while his hands flicked out in partially-suppressed gestures. She smiled, but he missed it, too busy rehearsing what he was about to say. Lexi knew she ought to be solemn and focused, but irrepressible elation leaked out of her like sunshine. She had missed her home. She had missed her father. Though she wasn't always happy here, it felt wonderful to come home. Her emotion surprised her; she hadn't realized she was homesick.

They landed in the main courtyard to shouts of welcome. Familiar servants crowded round, greeting Tiger warmly with handshakes and hugs, and deferential smiles and bows for Lexi. One of the maids tried to take her bag, but she held tight with a pleasant shake of her head. She didn't know how long she would be staying or if she would even be welcome. Her happiness at returning home faltered a bit, but Tiger's hand at her elbow reassured her. Talan had irritably handed off his bag to the first servant that came near him, and was now marching towards the throne room. Lexi and Tiger exchanged a glance, then quickly followed after him, Ryp and the guards at their heels. There was a short line outside the throne room of individuals awaiting an audience with the King. Talan blew past them, shoving an elderly man aside who was first at the door.

"Your Majesties, I have returned with the Princess, my wife," Talan announced loudly before he was even fully inside.

Tiger swore under his breath, and Lexi flew to the front of the line, the small group moving back to let her through.

Inside, the throne room was empty, and Talan was looking around as if he might find the King and Queen hiding behind a tapestry.

Raulis, her father's officiant, stepped forward to address Talan. "They are still at luncheon, but will be here shortly to hear grievances." Though his voice was polite, his bright orange wings twitched with irritation until his glance fell on Lexi. "Lovely to see you again, Your Highness." A genuine smile brightened his face, and he gave Lexi a deep bow. "Do you wish to join the King and Queen in the dining hall?" The end of his question faltered as Ryp and Tiger joined her.

"No thank you, Raulis, we can wait here," Lexi said, just as Talan gave the opposite answer. "We are happy to wait," she reiterated, and Raulis nodded absently, his eyes caught by Ryp's wings.

The grand throne room was designed with intimidation and discomfort for its petitioners in mind. The thrones were up on a dais with no other seats in the room. Even Raulis was required to stand until all petitioners were heard. Lexi's father had protested this arrangement many times, but her mother insisted that it helped keep the petitioning period short. At the moment, it just seemed terribly awkward. Talan eyed the thrones, but even he wouldn't dare take a seat. The acoustics of the room made whispers carry, so Lexi resisted speaking. Ryp looked about in open admiration. Through intricate stained-glass windows, multi-colored light bathed the room. Prisms embedded into the windows' metalwork cast rainbows on the marble floor. The heavy brocaded drapes shone with threads of gold, and the walls were empaneled in white alder stained to a warm hue. Lexi sucked in a breath that smelled vaguely of dust despite the cleanliness of the room. Tiger's lips were moving again, his face tight with concentration as he stared at the floor. She patted his shoulder to comfort him, and he gave her a wan smile.

Noticing her touch, Talan glared at Tiger, his hands fisting as he closed the distance between them to shove in next to Lexi. "Keep a respectful distance, peasant," he spat, glancing up at Raulis as if expecting some sort of approval.

381

Lexi opened her mouth to protest, but Ryp was already speaking.

"Your conduct towards my cousin is unbecoming a gentleman; I'll be certain to mention it to my aunt."

Talan visibly paled and swallowed as Lexi, Tiger, and Ryp moved away from him. He glanced up at Raulis again, but the officiant was watching Ryp. Talan ground his teeth and began to pace a small circuit away from the others.

Ignoring him, Lexi closed her eyes and tried to reclaim the joyous feeling that had come with her prayer. That certainty and peace was exactly what she needed to get through this. She took a deep breath and clutched Tiger's hand. When he pressed hers in response, she surreptitiously kissed his shoulder. Tiger's bushy brows lifted in surprise, his rehearsed speech forgotten. He shook his head slightly, then gently extricated his hand from hers as Raulis opened a side door hidden behind a tapestry. The guards entered first, silently taking their posts, and Lexi unconsciously held her breath. "His Majesty, the King," Raulis announced as her father stepped through.

Jubilant relief hit Lexi when her mother didn't follow. Ignoring decorum, she flew to her father and embraced him. "I missed you," she whispered, cringing as she heard the sound carry.

Her father briefly returned her hug, then stepped back. "We only have a few minutes before your mother gets here. Did you choose a mate, then?" he asked, looking expectantly at Ryp.

Seeing his mistake, Lexi blurted out, "I want to marry Tiger."

Talan let out a snort of disdain.

"Tiger? Oh, hello there, Tiger." The King gave him a half-hearted wave, then muttered to himself, "Well, he *is* better than the other one." The King scowled at Talan before turning back to Lexi. "You're not married yet?"

Lexi shook her head. "I wasn't sure how Mother would react."

"Ah, yes. That is a problem." He glanced quickly at the side door, then drew Lexi in for another hug and whispered in her ear. "She thinks you're carrying Talan's children."

Lexi fought the blush rising in her cheeks as her father released her, then spoke through twitching lips. "Perfectly impossible."

Her father nodded in relief, making his gilded crown slip. "I thought so." He stepped around her to glare at Talan. "You have lied to the Queen and slandered a princess. I hereby strip you of your nobility. You may not inherit your father's land or property, and if you want to marry, you'll have to do it at the Old Castle."

Talan sucked a breath through his teeth and reeled backwards as if the words had physically assaulted him. "But..." he began.

"You are forthwith banned from the palace and grounds. Guards, escort him out."

Two guards immediately stepped forward to obey the King's order. They latched onto Talan's arms and dragged him out, impervious to his panicked protests.

"What is happening?" the Queen demanded.

The cacophony of Talan's exit had masked the sound of her entrance, and they all started at the sound of her voice. Her father cringed, then stepped forward to take his wife's hand and escort her grandly to her throne.

"Her Majesty, the Queen," Raulis announced belatedly.

"Lexi, where is your husband?" the Queen asked as she scanned the room from her throne. Her eyes returned to Ryp, and a little wrinkle creased her forehead.

"I am not married, Mother," Lexi spoke succinctly as she approached to place a perfunctory kiss on the Queen's cheek.

"Perhaps not officially," the Queen conceded, accepting the kiss. "We shall remedy that today." Now her eyes fell to Lexi's attire and widened. She shot an accusatory glare at her husband who crossed and uncrossed his arms before sitting down dutifully on his throne. The Queen turned her piercing gaze back on Lexi. "After you are properly attired and refreshed, of course." She waved a bejeweled hand dismissively at her daughter. "Bring me Talan Admiral."

All the guards seemed to collectively inhale and hold it, their eyes darting around the room to see if anyone would carry out her order.

"They can't do that, my dear," the King explained, with a weak laugh.

"And why is that?" Her mother's most frigid tone, the one that could inflict emotional frostbite, chilled the entire room. Everyone stood frozen in place while Ryp grinned.

"He lied to you. And he slandered our daughter," the King faltered.

"What have you done?" The Queen spaced each word as if it were its own sentence.

"I stripped him of his nobility and banned him from the palace," the King mumbled, staring at his hands.

"Undo it!" she hissed at him.

The King shook his head stubbornly and dared to look at his wife. "No. He deserved it."

"And his *children*?" the Queen demanded, nodding at Lexi.

"He *lied*. She flew here."

To prove her father's point, Lexi leapt into the air and flew to Tiger's side.

The Queen glared at Tiger. "Clearly, there was *some* truth to his reports."

Tiger stirred at Lexi's side, but she grabbed his arm to forestall him.

"Do you *presume* to court a *princess*?" the Queen shrilled.

Tiger glanced at Lexi, and she gave him a tiny nod.

"Your Majesty," Tiger began with a deep bow. "Your daughter proposed to me, and I have accepted."

Livid scorn briefly lit the Queen's features. "That was foolish."

"Maybe," he conceded. "But after I met your *nephew*, Ryp Leafwing, I thought it just might work out."

The King jumped to his feet and the Queen let out a soft gasp as Ryp stepped forward and gave a deep bow. "Aunt Ami," he said smoothly, "my father sends his love."

The Queen made a choking noise, and the King turned his back on them, blocking the Queen from view with his broad orange and black wings. "Are you all right, my dear?" he asked solicitously.

There was a long pause and a furious exchange of whispers from the dais. Lexi gripped Tiger's hand, and even sniffed at his shoulder after she caught the word "dungeon." Ryp's bravado faded a bit, and he stepped back to stand beside them.

Finally, the King stepped aside and the Queen stood. "Ryp, it is wonderful to finally meet you. What an incredibly long journey you must have endured." Her voice was steady and gracious, as was the elegant hand she extended to her nephew. "Come with me. We must discuss your options."

If Ryp felt any trepidation, he didn't show it. "Thank you, my Queen. It is an honor to meet you," he replied, bowing again before offering his arm. With a neutral smile, she took it, and they exited through the same door that she and the King had entered.

The King frowned at Lexi and Tiger, begrudgingly motioning them closer. "That wasn't very nice," he muttered when they stood near. "Your mother wants no part of this," he said, motioning between the two of them. "You'll be on your own, and you'll need to take Cercy with you. Now, let's get this marriage over with."

Lexi began to laugh, tears running down her cheeks while Tiger only grinned.

The King turned to Raulis and nodded. The officiant reached behind the King's throne and drew out a large, square book with gilt lettering and edges. He set it on a little ledge worked into the intricate design of the throne frame and opening it, began to write.

With a little sigh, the King began. "Do you, Tiger, of your own free will and choice seal this woman to you for life, and if it be God's will, for eternity? Of course you do," he added irritably.

Unfazed, Tiger only grinned wider. "I do."

"And do you, my Lexi, of your own free will and choice seal this man to you for life, and if it be God's will, for eternity?" His words were sad. He already knew the answer.

"I do."

"Then by the authority given me by my father, King Danaus III, before God and man, I pronounce you sealed together as husband and wife for life, and God willing, for eternity." Rather than look at their faces, he stared down at their joined hands sadly, only breaking his gaze to add his signature beneath theirs on the marriage certificate.

Lexi hugged her father and kissed his cheek. "It'll be okay, Dad," she assured him. "I prayed about it."

The King smiled, his eyes suddenly wet with emotion. He swallowed once, then nodded. "Take Raven and three other horses from the stables as your wedding present. You can start your own ranch somewhere."

"Thank you!" Lexi hugged him again.

"And when your mother calms down, maybe you could come for a visit. But just now, you should go while your mother is busy deciding whether your cousin is going to marry Delpha or Anna."

"Not Juno?" Lexi asked curiously as she curled her arms around Tiger's bicep.

"Married Van this morning."

Lexi fought the laugh that gurgled up her throat, instead turning her face into Tiger's shoulder.

"Enough of that," her father fussed. "Take Cercy and the horses and go. *Now*, before she changes her mind."

Epilogue

"Good morning, Raven," Lexi called cheerfully, rewarding her horse's whinny with a red apple. Smiling at Raven's enthusiastic chewing, she ran a hand over the barely noticeable swell of the horse's belly, and the horse gave an answering nudge to Lexi's protruding stomach. "Yes," Lexi laughed, "you and I are in the same condition." Smiling, she gazed out at the frosted landscape, the frozen dew making everything sparkle in the early morning sun.

Tiger's and Cercy's savings had been just enough to buy this ramshackle ranch in the little mountain town of Horse Creek. It was a full day's journey by wing from the palace, but the King still managed to send supplies and letters every month. The Queen, in contrast, pretended that she only had two daughters and had resigned herself to her Monarch nephew being the next King. Ryp had married Anna and seemed to be adjusting well to aristocratic life; he thought Lady Nessa was hilarious, and the grumpy old dowager had promised to leave him and Anna all her money.

Lexi gave Raven one last pat, then let her out of her stall to graze in the frost-tipped pasture. The stall gate creaked loudly, then the rusty catch refused to fasten. Lexi fiddled with it unsuccessfully until she heard a musical chuckle behind her.

"Best leave that for the servants," Tiger joked, giving his startled wife a lingering kiss.

"Haha," Lexi said drily, returning to the catch. She lifted the bottom of the gate with her scuffed riding boot until the metal aligned. "There," she said, fastening the gate with a satisfied smile.

"My wife is amazing."

"Yes, I am," Lexi agreed and turned to kiss him again.

"Breakfast is ready!" Cercy hollered from the sloping porch of their humble ranch house. "Quit kissing or it's gonna be cold!"

Tiger and Lexi broke apart, laughing.

"Just coming, Mom," Tiger hollered back, then kissed Lexi again.

When they finally emerged from the horse barn, Cercy shook her head good-naturedly. "It's cold."

"Sorry, Mom."

"Don't be sorry for me. I ate mine hot." Removing her apron, she headed for her room. "Don't forget to clean up after yourselves."

"We will," Lexi assured her. "Thank you. It looks delicious."

"It looks cold," Cercy said, shutting her door.

"Deliciously cold!" Lexi called after her.

"Well, if it's already cold..."

Lexi laughed and pushed him away. "Later. The babies are starving."

Pulling up two humble stools, they sat at their crooked table and grinned at each other, completely oblivious to the temperature of the food.

T H E   E N D

www.ingramcontent.com/pod-product-compliance
Lightning Source LLC
Chambersburg PA
CBHW071644260626
47170CB00001B/223